KATE'S STORY

SEABURY SERIES COLLECTION: BOOKS 1-3

BETH RAIN

Copyright © 2021 by Beth Rain

Welcome to Seabury (Seabury: Part 1)

First Publication: 30th July, 2021

All rights reserved.

Copyright © 2021 by Beth Rain

Trouble in Seabury (Seabury: Part 2)

First Publication: 30th September, 2021

All rights reserved.

Copyright © 2021 by Beth Rain

Christmas in Seabury (Seabury: Part 3)

First Publication: 17th December, 2021

All rights reserved.

No part of this book may be reproduced in any form or by any electronic or mechanical means, including information storage and retrieval systems. Except for use in any review, the reproduction or utilization of this work, in whole or in part, in any form by any electronic, mechanical or other means now known or hereafter invented, is forbidden without the written permission of the publisher.

Published by Beth Rain. The author may be contacted by email on bethrainauthor@gmail.com

WELCOME TO SEABURY

SEABURY - PART 1

CHAPTER 1

Kate Hardy let her eyes rest on the horizon as the sound of the waves washed over her. She knew she really should get up from her grassy perch next to the old lighthouse and get back to the café, but she couldn't resist a couple more minutes in her favourite place in the entire world.

Drawing her knees up to her chin, she wrapped her arms around her legs and let out a contented sigh – a sound that was promptly echoed by a very hot, snuffling breath in her left ear.

'Oi you!' she chuckled, turning away from the sea only to find herself staring directly into Stanley's melting brown eyes.

Stanley sighed, wiggling his expressive eyebrows, and started to pant. Kate grinned and threw an arm around her best friend as the massive bear of a Bernese Mountain Dog leant his whole weight against her and rested his chin on her shoulder.

Kate planted a kiss on Stanley's nose. 'We'll go in just a sec, I promise,' she said, hugging him.

Kate knew that Stanley would be looking forward to getting back to her tiny little café, The Sardine. Not that he disliked coming on her sandwich rounds with her. In fact, he loved nothing better than riding around in the trailer she hitched to the back of Trixie, her delivery tricycle. Of course, there was always the added bonus that he got fussed to within an inch of his life at every stop they made. But this morning, Kate had left Ethel in charge back at The Sardine, and Stanley wasn't stupid – he knew that his old friend kept a stash of his favourite treats in her apron pocket at all times.

'Home looks so beautiful from here, don't you think?' said Kate, her eyes travelling back inland towards Seabury. From out here on the point where the lighthouse stood, she could almost see the entirety of the little coastal town as it hugged the shoreline and nestled into the arms of the cove.

West Beach was gleaming in the morning sun. Today it was covered with golden sand, but it changed with the tides - sometimes rocky, sometimes sandy - the state of the beach was a daily source of conversation for the locals.

If Kate squinted, she could just about make out The Sardine's striped awning right on the tiny seafront road that overlooked the sandy shore. She wondered if there were customers there right now, enjoying a morning coffee at the little tables she'd set up outside before she'd set off. She knew she was biased, but there wasn't a better place in the whole world to enjoy your morning coffee than sitting outside The Sardine, staring out across West Beach.

Seabury had two beaches that were separated by The Kings Nose - a grassy, rocky outcrop that stuck out into the sea. By some weird geographical hiccup, North Beach was actually west of West Beach and was covered by large, smooth grey pebbles. No one could figure out quite how this was the case because there was no sign of any similar rock for miles around.

The locals just took the weird naming anomaly in their stride, but visitors found it amusing and confusing in equal measures. Several years ago, one incomer had launched a campaign to change the names of the beaches to something more "factually accurate". The campaign didn't last very long. Funnily enough, neither did the newbie.

They didn't really get many visitors in Seabury - something most of the locals were quite happy about. The single coast road that passed through the town was narrow and winding, and Seabury wasn't signposted from the main road at all. This tended to keep out the majority of tourists, who found their way to the larger resort towns further along the coast instead.

Of course, there was always talk about *improvements.* Making Seabury *better.* Plans to bring in more visitors. More business. A few people wanted the town opened up . . . developed. Kate shuddered. Change of any kind wasn't something she was very good at dealing with. She loved the place just as it was - just as it had always been. Thankfully, most of the locals were of the same mind. It seemed to be an ongoing battle - but it was one worth fighting.

Luckily, a recent plan to develop the surrounding area and widen the access road had been put paid to by the discovery of some particularly rare wildlife - endangered moths or something like that. Kate wasn't really sure if they were real or not - she'd yet to meet anyone who'd actually *seen* one of these mythical beasts. Still, fictitious or not, they'd been the perfect excuse to kick the developer's plans into the long grass. Now all she had to put up with was the strange dietary requirements of the visiting ecologists who turned up to study the moths - but that was a small price to pay to keep Seabury just the way it should be.

Kate took another deep lung-full of sea air and closed her eyes for a moment, listening to the gulls as they swooped overhead. She'd lived in Seabury all her life. Well – *almost* all her life. There had been that three-month blip where she'd moved to London to be with Tom – but the less time she spent thinking about him the better! They'd been together for less than a year, but he'd now managed to be a thorn in her side for *way* longer than that.

London *definitely* hadn't been for her – neither had marriage, come to that. Three months in and Kate had given it up for a bad job and returned to Seabury – the only place that she ever wanted to call home again. She'd dropped straight back into her life here, took the boarding down from the café windows, fired up her cranky old Italian coffee machine, and did her best to pretend that the interruption had never happened.

Whatever. Today was shaping up to be a perfectly lovely day and she wasn't going to ruin it by thinking about all that crap . . . and Tom . . . and everything she'd almost given up for him. Nope. Nuh-uh.

She couldn't believe she'd even considered leaving everything she had here. If Seabury was home then the locals were her family - the only family she had left these days other than Stanley. She hadn't been back long before he'd appeared in her life, looking for love and a new home. Suddenly she had the best friend a girl could ever ask for. A best friend that, right now, was nudging her in the ribs with his nose.

'All right. Let's get back to work,' she chuckled, hauling herself to her feet. Stanley followed suit, wafting his feathery tail back and forth, ready to follow her wherever she went next.

Kate turned and laid a palm against the stone wall of the old lighthouse for a brief moment. 'See you soon,' she whispered.

The lighthouse was derelict having been decommissioned years ago. As far as she knew, no one else ever bothered to come out here, but in Kate's eyes, it was the most beautiful, magical place in the entire world. It held some of her most precious memories. Her dad used to bring her up here to play when she was little, and she'd spent many an hour as a teenager with her back propped against the wall, a book abandoned in her lap as she stared out to sea.

It belonged to the town council now, and Kate lived with a kind of constant, low-lying dread that they'd do something ridiculous like tear it down or sell it to some developer. But, for now, it sat here on the point - mostly forgotten - standing sentry over Seabury.

Kate jumped as a wet nose nudged at her free hand, and she looked down at Stanley, who was staring at her with his eyebrows raised. He really did have the best eyebrows in the world - and they tended to go into overdrive when he was hungry.

'Okay boy, you're right,' she laughed. 'We'd better go and make sure Ethel hasn't been overrun - race you!'

She patted her thigh then hurtled back over

towards Trixie. Turning to look for Stanley, she let out a laugh. He was ambling towards her, taking his own sweet time. Before he'd come to live with her, Stanley had been the companion of an elderly gent, and he still moved at a pace to suit a frail eighty-something-year-old, even though the vet had assured her that he was still a relatively young dog, and in perfect health.

There wasn't any need for Kate to coax Stanley up into the trailer though – he hopped up and settled in happily, just as he had done on the first day he'd joined her on her delivery round.

Kate had bought Trixie's trailer to carry extra stock and to make it easier for her to collect produce from the allotments - not as a taxi for a great big hairy passenger - but she didn't mind in the slightest. There was plenty of room for her orders as well as Stanley's pillow. Besides, there would be an outcry from her customers if she didn't bring him with her.

Stanley was universally adored, and that was just the way he liked it. He'd become the unofficial therapy dog for the entire town - welcomed into farms and offices alike - and greeted with just as much enthusiasm as Kate's delicious deliveries - if not more!

They'd finished their rounds for today and as usual, Stanley had been well and truly loved on. Now it was time to take Trixie back to her little yard next to The Sardine and then let Ethel off the hook. Kate couldn't be more grateful to her old friend for stepping in and covering the café - but she *was* somewhere in her seventies (Kate would never dream of asking her exact age!) and she didn't want to leave her on her own for too long.

'All right lad, here we go,' she called over her shoulder as she hopped up onto the saddle and pedalled out onto the narrow road that wound downhill all the way back into the centre of Seabury.

This was the bit of the trip Kate liked best – with her deliveries done, the hard pedalling work was complete, and she could now freewheel back down towards the sea.

She let out a great whoop of delight as they sped past a couple of the outlying cottages, Trixie just a pink and red blur reflected in the windows as they pelted past. There was an echoing woof from Stanley in the back and Kate giggled.

She hadn't realised how much she'd needed a little break this morning - just a few minutes out of her busy day to remind herself that she was exactly where she wanted to be, doing exactly what she wanted to do, surrounded by the people she loved.

As much as she tried to push it to the back of her mind, this whole divorce malarkey had been a bit tough to take at times. Kate hated change. She hated confrontation. She hated fuss. Unfortunately, getting a divorce from a complete nincompoop came with a massive dollop of all three. Still – it was all pretty much done and dusted now. Almost. Kinda.

Anyway - thank heavens for Ethel. She'd spotted Kate heading for a mini meltdown when the post had arrived that morning bearing yet another manilla envelope from Tom's solicitor. Her old friend had whipped it out of her hands, ushered her out of the café to do her rounds, and insisted that Kate should take a breather before she came back. When Kate had tried to make a grab for the envelope, Ethel had just folded it in half and stuffed it into the pocket of her voluminous apron.

'You know there's nothing in there that can't wait,' she'd stated, making Kate laugh despite herself. Of course, as usual, Ethel was right - whatever Tom wanted, it could wait until *she* was ready for a change.

Kate slowed to pedal at a more sedate speed through the heart of Seabury, passing North Beach with the Post Office, *Nana's* Ice Cream parlour, and the cavernous, empty surf shop with its *For Sale* sign. It was such a shame that the place was still empty - but there was a ridiculous price on it, and who needed such a vast space in the middle of a sleepy town?

'Morning Stanley!' cried an upright gent as they trundled past The Pebble Street Hotel that stood on the boundary of The King's Nose. 'Morning Kate!'

'Hi Lionel! Painting today?' she called back.

Lionel nodded. 'Yep – as soon as I've had my morning exercise, followed by my Sardine fix!' he grinned. 'You *are* open today, I assume?'

'Of course!' Kate nodded. 'Ethel's been manning the fort, but I'm heading back now.'

'Thank heavens for that. Veronica's got us on even shorter rations than usual this week!'

'See you in a bit then!' said Kate as she pulled away from him.

Lionel touched his hand to his straw hat and then waved goodbye to Stanley.

Kate tutted and shook her head. Veronica Hughes was a piece of work. To say that she wasn't very generous would be putting it mildly - she was about as mean spirited as a person could get. Kate prided herself on her ability to see the best in people, but even *she* struggled when it came to Veronica.

Lionel Barclay, however, was a sweetheart. He lived in a suite on the very top floor of The Pebble Street Hotel. He'd been there for what felt like forever - certainly since before Veronica had purchased the place.

The old hotel was a beautiful building that, in its heyday, had welcomed visitors who were looking for a spot of luxury. Veronica now ran it as a budget bed and breakfast - not that the "budget" part was reflected in her prices.

It was Veronica's dearest wish to chuck Lionel out, but he wasn't going anywhere. He had the only copy of the key to his rooms, and Veronica wasn't even allowed through the door. Lionel being allowed to remain in his suite for as long as he wanted to had been one of the conditions of the sale of the hotel – a condition that he was going to make Veronica stick to, no matter how much she hated it.

Kate grinned to herself. She was pretty sure Lionel rather liked being the thorn in Veronica's side. He paid his rent and kept himself to himself. The fact that his rooms boasted the best views in the entire place was Veronica's tough luck.

Lionel himself was a bit of an enigma. He was a retired something or other – no one was quite sure what... admiral? Banker? Historian? There were plenty of stories floating around, but none of them had been confirmed.

Always impeccably dressed, he had been one of her earliest regulars when she'd first opened The Sardine. He'd been heartbroken when she'd shut up shop to move to London and was the first back when she'd reopened. She still swore that he'd had a tear in his eye that day, but Lionel was having none of it.

'Right, Stanley lad,' said Kate, as they rounded the curve in the road that brought them in sight of West Beach and The Sardine, 'here we are, nearly home.'

Kate held out her hand to indicate that she was pulling Trixie into the yard - and then promptly applied the brakes, dropped her arm and swore loudly. Stanley let out a low bark of disgust in agreement.

'I know!' muttered Kate. 'Inconsiderate a-holes!'

There, parked right across the entrance to Trixie's yard, was a massive, expensive-looking estate car.

CHAPTER 2

'Wow - my plan didn't work then?' said Ethel, her eyebrows raised as Kate stormed into The Sardine.

'Huh?' she muttered distractedly, watching as Stanley rounded the counter to sit on Ethel's toes, leaning his head against her as he stared up at her adoringly.

'Hello, you beautiful boy, at least you're in a good mood!' chuckled Ethel, rummaging in her apron pocket for one of Stanley's biscuits - which disappeared with much eyebrow wiggling. 'So - what happened?' she demanded, turning her attention back to Kate.

'Oh nothing,' Kate sighed, heading to the sink to wash her hands. 'Just some plonker's gone and parked right across the yard again so I can't put Trixie away.'

'Ah!' said Ethel nodding. 'That explains the face then.'

'Face?' said Kate, drying her hands on a checked tea towel, then lifting the lid on one of the cake stands and half-inching a piece of her favourite Victoria sponge.

'Yes - your face!' exclaimed Ethel. 'You're lucky there aren't any customers in here - you'd have terrified them with that face!'

Kate shook her head and sighed. 'Sorry.'

Ethel shrugged. 'No need to apologise to me, it's your café! Just like that's your own stock you're stealing,' she smirked as Kate stuffed half the slice of cream and jam-filled heaven into her gob.

Kate rolled her eyes in delight as the sponge melted in her mouth. She let out a groan. Ethel made all the cakes for The Sardine and there was no getting away from it - they were the best in the county. In fact, they were so good that Ethel had been banned from entering any of the local shows because it "just wasn't fair to the other entrants." Ethel didn't seem to mind too much - in fact, she wore it as a badge of honour.

Kate swallowed, the rush of sugar knocking the edge off her anger. 'It's just so bloody inconsiderate though,' she said, taking another bite.

'I know, love.'

'I mean - there's a sign and everything. Can't these people read?!'

'Maybe not . . .' said Ethel, feeding Stanley another biscuit, 'but I expect it's just a visitor who doesn't realise how things work around here, that's all.'

'Bloomin' visitors,' muttered Kate.

'Now don't be like that,' said Ethel, taking a cloth and going over to wipe the already clean tables. 'You know you need them to survive.'

Kate shook her head. 'I'm here for the locals.'

'Yes, I know. But it's good for everyone if there's a little bit more money coming into the town. Locals have to have something to live on other than the beauty of Seabury, you know.'

Kate nodded. 'I know.'

'Otherwise, we'll end up with more empty shops like the surf shop - and nowhere for the youngsters to work.'

Kate nodded again. 'I know.' She loved Ethel dearly, having known her all her life - but her old friend could make her feel like a naughty schoolgirl when she was in one of her moods.

'Actually,' said Kate, finishing up the cake and doing her best not to eyeball a second slice, 'that's reminded me - I need to get on and advertise for a replacement for Claire.'

Ethel nodded. 'No rush. You know I'll help out as long as you need me to.'

Kate smiled at her gratefully. Claire had been with her for what felt like forever. She'd been her only member of staff other than when Ethel popped in to help out during the busy summer months. But Claire had left Seabury three weeks ago to live with her boyfriend in one of the larger towns just along the coast. The problem was, Claire had always just . . . fitted in. Kate dreaded trying to find the perfect replacement. She wasn't even sure if such a thing existed.

That was the thing with The Sardine – just as the name suggested, it was tiny. Small but perfectly formed or, as one of the locals had dubbed it, *The Smallest Café in the World.*

There was just about enough space inside for a couple of chairs and tables, the counter and the kitchen. The open plan meant that everything was piled in together. The effect was cosy and eclectic.

In the summer, the tables outside on the pavement under the awning doubled Kate's seating space, but in the winter, when she stashed the awning indoors to stop the wind ripping it to pieces, everyone piled inside, and things got even more intimate. Right next to her oven there was an old, wood-fired stove that was incredibly handy when there was a power cut - which happened fairly regularly.

A bit like with a ship's galley, everything in The Sardine had its place - it was the only way to make such a small space work. That's why it was important to have the right people working there. Or – the right person, she should say. It was, after all, Kate's home as well as her workplace. She lived on the two levels above the café, and it took a lot for her to trust people to treat The Sardine with as much love as she did.

Luckily, for now, she had Ethel.

'Thanks so much for this morning by the way,' said Kate gratefully, smiling at her friend and making an effort to shrug off the funk that had landed on her.

'You know it's my pleasure, Kate!' said Ethel. 'It was quite a busy morning actually - not that it looks like it now.'

'Not too much for you, I hope?' she said.

'Of course not - just the usual suspects wanting their toasted teacakes and gallons of coffee!'

'Speaking of usual suspects, I saw Lionel - he's on his way over,' said Kate, turning to her cantankerous old coffee machine - dubbed the Italian Stallion by Claire. There were very few people who could get a decent cup of java out of it. You had to talk to the machine nicely - that was the key.

Kate loaded up the puck and inhaled. Hm - maybe that's what she needed to set her back on course for the day - a good hit of rich, aromatic coffee.

'Bless Lionel,' said Ethel, replenishing the pile of teacakes under the glass dome on the counter, 'he's probably coming in for a top-up on his breakfast - I reckon Veronica's new plan is to starve him out of the hotel.'

Kate shook her head. 'Not on my watch!'

'Indeed. Well, you've still got a good few pots of my marmalade left, so he'll be alright.'

Veronica was notoriously mean, and Kate had heard plenty of horror stories from Lionel over the years - old eggs, single rashers of watery bacon, and cereal that was measured out using an eggcup.

Lionel always had the same thing when he came to The Sardine – a strong, milky coffee and two slices of well-done toast spread thinly with home-made marmalade. He preferred Ethel's if he could get it, but as long as Kate never tried to fob him off with any of the "supermarket gloop" Veronica gave her guests, he was happy.

'Actually,' said Ethel, you mentioning Veronica's just reminded me - I ran into her on my walk last night.'

Kate turned and handed her a latte, just the way she liked it.

'Thanks lovely,' she said, taking it over to one of the tables and perching on a chair. 'Yes - you'll never guess what she told me.'

Kate shrugged. Knowing Veronica, it wouldn't be anything nice - though, owing to her propensity for sticking her nose into all kinds of business, she did tend to be a pretty accurate source for all kinds of juicy gossip.

'Apparently, the old surf shop has sold at last.'

'You're joking?!' said Kate, leaning against the counter and raising her eyebrows. 'I was thinking about that when we went past just now. Do we know anything about who's taken it on?' she asked with interest.

She couldn't deny that having such a big, vacant space filled at long last would be good for Seabury - if only so that the pretty stretch overlooking North Beach wasn't marred by the gaping hole that was the boarded-up shop.

'Well . . .' said Ethel, 'I'm not sure you're going to like this.'

Kate's attention was instantly caught by the concern on her old friend's face.

'Why? How bad's it going to be?' she said with a laugh. 'Unless of course, you're about to tell me Tom's decided to move to Seabury just to make my life a living hell?'

Ethel went to say something and then paused, looking anxious.

'Okay - now you're scaring me!' said Kate. 'He's not, is he?'

'Tom?' said Ethel. 'No of course not.'

'Well then?!' said Kate, starting to get impatient.

'Well . . . Veronica told me it's going to be another café. One of those big, posh New York Froth affairs,' said Ethel, not taking her eyes off Kate - clearly waiting for her reaction. 'Of course, you know Veronica - she could just be stirring!'

'Oh - she's definitely stirring,' sighed Kate, 'but yes, I do know Veronica - so do you - and you *know* her gossip tends to be spot on. She's probably got it directly from the estate agents or the council.'

Ethel nodded. 'Sounds like Veronica.'

'Well . . .' said Kate, blowing out a breath. 'It's not the best news I've had today - but I'm not worried.'

'You're not?' asked Ethel, raising her eyebrows.

'Nope,' said Kate with a determined smile and a shake of the head. 'I've been here a long time. I've got my regulars and my sandwich round on Trixie. I know everyone and everyone knows me. I'm sure there's more than enough business to go around . . . these new guys will just have to cater to all these visitors people keep trying to bring into Seabury.'

Ethel grinned at her. 'Good for you, love!' she said, pride shining in her eyes. 'There's the girl your dad was proud of.'

The words brought an instant lump to Kate's throat, but she beamed with pride nonetheless. Her dad had been gone several years now - but it was amazing how much she still missed him.

'Thanks Ethel.'

'Hello ladies!' The cheery call came from the doorway, and they both swung around to greet Lionel as he strode in, rosy-cheeked from his walk in the sunshine.

'Hello deary! Your usual?' asked Ethel, getting to her feet and indicating for Lionel to take the table.

'Of course. Nothing better. Hello again, Stanley old boy!' he said, reaching down to ruffle the big bear's ears as he wandered over to greet the newcomer. 'Now then, how would you like a bit of toast when it arrives?'

'Don't go spoiling my dog,' laughed Kate as she got busy and fired up the Italian Stallion again.

'Why ever not? He loves it!' chuckled Lionel.

'Because my poor little legs won't be able to pedal Trixie up that hill if he puts on any more puppy-fat!' she laughed.

In all fairness to Stanley, he was exactly the same size he'd always been - huge - and she wouldn't have him any other way. But it *was* a miracle that he didn't explode, given the number of titbits he was slipped each day in the café by his adoring fans.

Kate delivered Lionel's coffee and set the table for him while Ethel piled up his toast and brought it over with a dish of marmalade.

'Thank you!' he sighed, grabbing a knife and slathering a good dollop of the golden preserve onto his toast. He took a massive bite and sighed with bliss. 'Heaven,' he said as soon as he'd swallowed his mouthful. 'Ethel, you really are a wonder!'

'Oh, get on with you!' she laughed.

'I'm serious, it's no wonder Charlie's smitten.'

Kate watched with interest as Ethel turned a rather fetching shade of pink and bustled back to the kitchen without saying a word.

'Something I said?' asked Lionel under his breath, quirking an eyebrow at Kate.

'Erm . . . yes, I think so!' she replied quietly.

Everyone knew that old Charlie Endicott was head over heels in love with Ethel. Charlie was Lionel's best friend, and they made a rather unlikely pair - the dapper artist and the salt-of-the-earth gardener.

Charlie spent most of his waking life at the allotments, tending to his prize-winning veg. In fact, he grew most of the veggies for The Sardine. Kate loved nothing better than when a customer dared to ask about "food miles". She'd lead them outside and point to the hill on the far side of Seabury where the allotments lay, with their patchwork of plots, dotted with colourful little sheds.

Charlie was a good, kind soul - but rather lacking in the words department. He was someone who tended to show you how he felt, rather than tell you. Somehow, though, she doubted the regular batches of luscious strawberries, raspberries, rhubarb and gooseberries he sent to Ethel had *quite* managed to convey the extent of his true feelings.

Kate was pretty certain that Ethel knew Charlie felt *something* for her - after all, most of the locals had ribbed her about it at some point. But she'd never once seen her friend react with anything other than a cheerful "get away with you" when anyone mentioned it. This rather more teenaged reaction was new. Kate made a mental note to ask her what was going on when they were in private.

'So,' said Lionel. 'Have you heard the old surf shop's being turned into a café?'

His clumsy attempt at a change of subject made him wince as it quickly dawned on him that he'd jumped from the frying pan into the fire when it came to controversial topics of conversation. Kate decided to let the poor guy off the hook.

'Yep - great news that there'll be something in there after all this time, isn't it?' she said cheerfully.

'I like your attitude, young lady,' said Lionel warmly, taking another bite of his toast.

Kate just smiled at him and decided to grab the lull in conversation caused by much chewing as an excuse to quickly duck outside for a moment. She was just about the head through the door when a man barged into the café and she bumped straight into him.

'Ooff!' grunted Kate as she bounced off his front, the surprise of the collision knocking the breath out of her. She steadied herself and straightened up, only to find the man brushing down the front of his very expensive-looking suit.

'I'm so sorry,' she said, forcing a polite smile onto her face. 'I didn't see you coming.'

'Clearly,' he harrumphed.

Kate felt her spine stiffen and she stared at him. He wasn't a local. She'd definitely remember if she'd seen his face around before. Sharp cheekbones. Cold grey eyes peering out from under a dark, swept-back mop of hair. Stern. Stroppy. Maybe he'd be quite attractive if he smiled, but it didn't look like that was something he did very often. Or- *at all.* She thought he was probably in his late thirties - or maybe a little bit older. It was hard to tell with all the glowering he was doing.

'Can I get you a coffee?' she asked. 'On the house, of course!' she added. After all, she *had* just managed to body-check him on his way in.

'No. But you can tell me who the *hell* owns that monstrosity that's blocking me in?!' he demanded, glaring at the three of them in turn.

Kate felt something shift behind her, and the next thing she knew Stanley had ambled over from crumb-duty under Lionel's table and plonked himself down between her and the guy. He didn't growl - but he did fix his eyes on the man's face, his tail unusually still.

'Get away from me,' muttered the man, taking a step back.

Kate raised her eyebrows in surprise. Stanley was the least threatening dog she'd ever met. He was basically an oversized teddy bear who loved nothing more than a good cuddle, but this stranger was staring at him like he was some kind of crazed attack-dog.

'He's friendly,' said Kate, gently laying her hand on Stanley's huge head, fighting down the urge to add *"unlike you"*.

'He shouldn't be in a public place.'

Kate bristled. She'd already had enough of this idiot. Messing with her was one thing, but *no one* messed with her dog.

'He's not in a *public place* - he's in my café. His home. If you've got a problem with that, you're more than welcome to leave.'

'Trust me - there's nothing that would give me more pleasure - but you've blocked me in with your . . . your . . . pile of scrap metal.'

Kate fought the urge to growl at him herself. 'I parked Trixie next to your car because you've blocked the access to my yard - where she belongs,' she said. She didn't like her voice like this - all hard and angry. The sooner she got rid of this git, the better.

'Trixie?!' he said incredulously. 'You've given that pile of rust a name?'

Kate's hands bunched into fists, and she fought the urge to push this idiot backwards and physically remove him from the café.

'Just don't park there again.'

'It's not double-yellowed.'

'There's a sign.'

'It's hand-painted - hardly legal!'

'You're blocking access to my private property. You're lucky I didn't have you towed!' growled Kate, causing Stanley to stand up.

The guy's reaction was instant. He backed up a couple more paces looking petrified.

Good. The further away he was from her, the less likely it was that she'd "accidentally" punch him on the nose for being a prick.

'Okay, okay. Just get out of my way and I'll move the car,' he muttered.

'Honestly,' said Kate. 'Tourists!'

'*Excuse* me!' he said. 'I'm not a tourist. I live here.'

'Rubbish,' said Kate firmly.

'These say otherwise,' he said, taking a bunch of keys out of his pocket and rattling them at her.

'Goodness.' Ethel's voice behind her made Kate jump. She'd forgotten for a moment there was anyone else here.

'Huh. Great. Well,' said Kate, feeling wrong-footed. 'Welcome to Seabury,' she huffed.

'Thanks!' the guy smirked. 'I'm Mike Pendle by the way. I own New York Froth.'

CHAPTER 3

Kate was still fuming by the time she'd finished tucking Trixie up in the yard. She paused for a moment and patted the handlebars, trying to suck up some of the joy the tricycle's bright pink paint job and jaunty red handlebars usually brought her . . . but right now, it just wasn't working.

Trixie lived out here in the yard all year round. Sure, Kate threw an old tarp over her when the weather was bad - well weighted down to stop the mad, swirling gusts of wind off the sea from stealing it away. But still, the salty air meant that every year, Kate cleaned Trixie down and gave her a new paint job. She was particularly fond of this year's colour combo - though she had to admit, the six-year-old inside her still missed the orange and green polka dots from the previous year.

Anyway - no matter what that . . . that . . . *blow-in* said, Trixie was definitely not a "pile of scrap metal!"

'Don't listen to that git,' Kate whispered, patting Trixie again. '*I* love you.'

'First sign of madness you know!'

Kate whirled around to find her friend Paula peering at her with a grin on her face.

'First sign? You know I'm way past that!' laughed Kate, opening her arms and pulling her friend into a hug. 'Swimming today?' she asked, linking arms with Paula and heading back out of the yard.

Paula shook her head. 'Nah - tomorrow. We're back to our usual Wednesday morning. We only shifted last week around because I had that appointment. Anyway - that's why I was popping in - wondered if we could change in The Sardine again?'

'Of course!' said Kate. 'You know you never need to ask!'

Paula was a founding member and trouble-maker-in-chief of the Chilly Dippers, Seabury's wild swimming club. She often joked that it sounded a lot more daring than it actually was. Skinny dipping was frowned upon, but not entirely outlawed, and their members were mostly made up of a group of what might be described as "older and wiser" local women. It wasn't that men were excluded . . . it was just the way things had worked out.

The group boasted a wide variety of splashing and swimming styles and you only had to go in as far as your ankles to be considered a proper "Dipper" - and that was just about a far as many of them ever went. Kate, however, was full of admiration for them. They were a tight-knit group, and they went in the sea come rain or shine - all year around.

Sometimes Stanley liked to join them for a swim, and the group always loved having him. Kate had cottoned on pretty quickly to the fact that it was a good idea to attach a float to him so that they could keep an eye on his whereabouts. No matter how much he hated having a bath, Stanley loved to swim - and liked nothing better than heading straight out to sea in search of some friendly seals to play with. Kate had had to get someone to go out in a boat to collect him from these impromptu playdates more than once.

When the weather was particularly bad, with the rain lashing horizontally across the beach, Kate would open the café early so that the Chilly Dippers could come in to change in the dry. Wednesday mornings were always a rowdy time in the café because the Dippers would invariably pile in after their swim, steaming up the windows and warming up with bowls of Kate's hearty, homemade soup that she made specially for them in the winter, or with hot drinks, pastries and plenty of cake in the summer.

'Coming in for a coffee, then?' Kate asked, glancing at Paula and noticing, not for the first time over the past few weeks, that her friend looked pale and rather tired.

Paula nodded. 'Yes please. And the biggest piece of cake you can find . . . if you haven't eaten all of it yet?'

'I *might* have left you a slice,' laughed Kate.

'Perfect. Then you can tell me why you were declaring your undying love to your tricycle and muttering about a "git".'

Kate snorted. 'Okay, deal. And you can tell me how your appointment went last week,' she said, holding the café door open for her friend.

Paula shot her a look and shrugged. 'Nothing to tell. A few blood tests, no biggie!' she said lightly. 'Morning Ethel, hi ya Lionel!' she said cheerily, striding over to the counter to investigate the cake stands.

Kate watched her closely. She knew Paula's answer should put her mind at ease, but she couldn't help the nagging sensation that her friend wasn't telling her everything. Ah well, all in good time.

'Rhubarb streusel cake!' Paula sighed in delight. 'Ethel, you're a marvel!'

Ethel smiled and cut her a mammoth slice.

'Made with Charlie's prize rhubarb too,' added Kate, watching Ethel's face closely. There it was again - that fetching pink blush spreading across the older woman's cheeks. Curiouser and curiouser!

'Right Kate lovely - I'd better go,' said Ethel,

bustling around behind the counter and keeping her back to them while she grabbed her handbag and bits and bobs.

'Of course!' said Kate, glancing at her watch. 'Sugar, I'm so sorry - I hadn't realised it was that time already!'

'It's no problem dear. That man's got you all of a dither!' said Ethel, going over to give Stanley a final pat and another sneaky bit of biscuit, which he wolfed down.

'Man?' demanded Paula. 'Kate Hardy, you've been withholding important information. Is it that French bloke? Has he finally decided to settle down a bit?'

'Chance would be a fine thing,' muttered Ethel.

'You two!' said Kate. 'No - it has absolutely nothing to do with Pierre. And just for your information, I don't want him to "settle down", I like things exactly how they are, thank you very much.'

'But you never know when you're going to see him next,' said Paula indignantly. 'He just . . . shows up!'

'He does text sometimes,' she laughed, 'and anyway, what's so wrong with that? A little bit of spontaneous romance never hurt anyone!'

'Neither does a bit of commitment,' said Ethel.

'Tried that, didn't like it,' grumbled Kate as the image of Tom flashed in front of her eyes.

'Only because you tried it with an idiot,' said Paula.

'Exactly,' agreed Ethel.

'Rubbish,' said Kate. 'Anyway - I a*m* committed - to this place, and Stanley, and Seabury, and my friends...'

'None of which are going to keep you warm at night!' said Paula, raising her eyebrows.

Kate was about to argue that actually, having Stanley weighing down the duvet was like sleeping next to a furnace some nights, but she thought better of it.

'Paula's right, Kate. I know you're practically married to this place and to Seabury, but don't let it get in the way of you finding true love. It's a rare thing, and when it happens...'

Kate frowned as an unusually sober look passed across Ethel's face. 'Okay,' she said, forcing a laugh and trying to lighten the mood. 'If Pierre tries to whisk me away to France with him, I'll give it some serious thought!'

'You're hopeless!' said Ethel, kissing her on the cheek and heading for the door. 'See you tomorrow?'

'I'll be here if I'm not already in France!'

Ethel snorted and disappeared through the door.

'So - if it wasn't your French shag-buddy you were muttering about just now, who was it?' asked Paula, sipping her coffee and watching as Kate busied herself in the kitchen.

'Urgh - just this absolute knob head who blocked

the yard this morning so I couldn't get Trixie back in there.'

'Nothing unusual about that,' chuckled Paula. It happened at least once a week during the summer months - hence Kate's decision to put up some signs.

'No - but most of them are apologetic when they realise what they've done. This guy burst in here, was rude about Trixie and then announced that he's the new owner of the old surf shop.'

'Mike Pendle?'

'You *know* him?!' demanded Kate.

'Nope - but I know *of* him. He built New York Froth up from scratch - had a whole bunch of them along the coast. You must have heard his name before - I mean, he was in all the magazines - won all the business awards as South West's very own fancy-pants coffee chain.'

'Eewww gross!' whined Kate. 'How on *earth* did he get permission to come to Seabury?! I mean - that's not what the town needs, is it?! A horrible chain moving in?!'

'Not a chain anymore,' said Paula, draining the dregs from her cup and leaning back in her chair. 'Apparently, his wife got everything in the divorce . . . all apart from the company name! So he's got to start from scratch again - without his flagship café.'

'Oh no, my heart breaks for him,' Kate dead-panned, bending to pop a couple of savoury pies in the oven.

'I thought you'd be a bit more sympathetic!' said Paula, clearly surprised that her usually kind and caring friend was being so uncharacteristically cold. 'I mean - imagine if Tom had taken this place from you in the divorce.'

Kate straightened up, a horrible swooping sensation going through her.

'Yeah . . . well . . .' she said, suddenly realising that she still hadn't opened the manilla envelope from Tom's solicitor. It was probably still tucked away in Ethel's discarded apron. 'You didn't see how obnoxious this *Mike Pendle* was earlier.'

'He *is* quite handsome though, don't you think?' said Paula with a sly grin. 'I've seen his picture. Dark hair, kind of dashing in a brooding way . . .'

Kate shook her head. 'A person who is that stroppy is *not* handsome. He looked like he spent most of his time chewing wasps. And he called Trixie a monstrosity, *plus* he didn't look like he knew how to smile if his life depended on it.'

'Methinks you protesteth too much,' laughed Paula.

Kate shook her head decidedly. 'Nope - if anything I protesteth too little. I mean - he didn't like Stanley!' she said as if this was the end of the matter.

'How could anyone not like Stanley?' said Paula, looking surprised, and glancing with affection at the massive black, white and tan mound of fur snoozing in the corner.

'Exactly,' said Kate.

'So . . .'

'What?'

'What are you going to do?' she said, a note of worry creeping into her voice. 'I mean, about New York Froth coming to town?'

'Absolutely nothing,' said Kate with a big smile that was decidedly braver than she was feeling. 'Sounds like the deal is done, so there's no point in me whining about it, is there? Besides, the old surf shop's in a state - it'll take him a good few months to get ready to open. I'll just keep doing what I'm doing, make the most of the summer, look after my customers, deliver my sandwiches and keep serving the best coffee in Seabury.'

'And when he *does* open up?'

'Well . . . I'm sure there are plenty of coffee addicts in this town for the both of us. And besides, a little bit of friendly competition never hurt anyone!'

CHAPTER 4

*I*t was one of those days when Kate thanked her lucky stars that her commute was so short. She'd kept a warm smile plastered on her face all day, greeting customers, making toasties and serving coffees, bantering, laughing and reassuring every single one of them that *no she wasn't at all worried about New York Froth opening* and *yes, it would be brilliant for the town.*

She'd managed to keep a lid on the low-level anxiety that had been bubbling away in her gut ever since she'd got back from her delivery round. But now, as she walked the ten paces from The Sardine's door to her flat door just around the corner, she couldn't wait to be safely back in her own space. She needed the freedom to examine how she was feeling, without the fear of those feelings showing on her face.

'Here you go Stanley boy,' she murmured, pushing the door open for him. Just as he did every day, Stanley ambled up the steep wooden stairs in front of her, heading up to her flat that sat snugly above the café.

In her head, Kate still called it a flat, but in reality, it was a maisonette - narrow and tall - with a cosy living room and galley kitchen on the first floor and her bathroom and bedroom at the top.

By the time she'd reached the first floor, Kate peered into the living room to find Stanley already sitting in his giant bed in front of the wood burner - just as she'd expected. The fire wasn't lit - but that never put him off. This had been Stanley's routine ever since he'd come to live with her - at the end of a busy day in the café, he'd retreat to his bed for a nap - bonus points if the fire was lit!

Kate knelt down next to him and stroked his silky ears for a moment, trying to let the calm of her sanctuary wash over her. She took in a deep breath and let it out as a laugh when Stanley matched her sigh and flopped sideways, tongue lolling.

'I know what you mean!' she said, gazing at him adoringly. This was why Stanley was her best friend - no matter how she was feeling, he always made her day better just by being himself.

Stanley wasn't *really* her dog, although these days, he was never far from her side. He'd come into her life not long after she'd returned to Seabury from her ill-fated attempt at London life.

He'd originally belonged to an old man called Harold, who'd lived in one of the cottages on the outskirts of Seabury. Shortly after Harold had passed away, his family descended on the cottage, emptied the place of all his belongings and put it on the market - all within a week. Of course, it had promptly been snapped up as a holiday home.

Their work done and the money pocketed, the family left Seabury just as suddenly as they'd arrived - leaving Stanley behind to fend for himself.

People had reported seeing him wandering around the town, but it had taken a while for them all to realise what had happened. Then, on a particularly wet, blustery evening, Kate had opened her door to find him sitting there, looking sad but hopeful. She'd let him in - of course she had - and Stanley had made his way slowly up the stairs, found a place for himself in front of the wood burner, and curled up to sleep.

It still made Kate's heart squeeze when she thought of how sad and lonely he must have been after losing his owner like that - only to be turfed out of his house and abandoned. *How* anyone could be so cruel as to just leave him behind was beyond her. She bent low and kissed his soft, snoozing head.

'Right boy, I'll be back in a bit, okay?' she whispered.

Stanley didn't even open an eye, which made Kate

crack a genuine smile. He wouldn't budge for a good hour now that he'd crashed out.

She stood up and stretched, looking around her living room. It was light and bright and full of shells and driftwood from her wanderings along the beaches. The walls were covered in little paintings by Lionel - scenes from around the town, the Chilly Dippers, the sun rising, the sun setting, the ebb and flow of life in a seaside town. Even here in her home, she surrounded herself with her one true love - Seabury.

But the magic of her little sanctuary wasn't working on her this evening. The knot of unspoken worry was still there, sitting low in her stomach. Well - there was only one cure as far as she knew!

～

Kate twiddled with the bath tap until the water was gushing at full pelt into the tub. If ever there was a day for a bubble bath that was full to within an inch of the top of the tub, it was today.

As she swished the water with one hand, watching the bubbles mounting into white, fluffy peaks, she reached out and took a sip of wine before placing the glass carefully back on the corner of the bath.

Now then, was she ready to finally take a proper, logical look at what was worrying her? Wine?

Check. Bubble bath? Almost ready. Okay. It was time.

She'd been putting a brave face on the New York Froth news all day - assuring locals that it wouldn't be a problem for The Sardine, that nothing would change, and she was *happy* that a new business was opening and filling the sad, empty space that used to be the surf shop - but how much of that did she actually believe? After all - it *was* more change.

She reached for the bottle of lavender oil she kept on the mantlepiece and splashed a few drops into the already bubble-laden water. Why not? She needed all the additional relaxation vibes she could muster.

It wasn't as though she was worried that The Sardine would struggle with this new competition . . . of course it wouldn't. Would it?

Kate took another deep, steadying breath. She needed to look at the facts. She had a thriving delivery round that was just about as full as she could manage if she was going to continue to deliver on Trixie. It was local - and that was the whole point of it - the way she liked it. She couldn't cycle any further than she already did every day, and she didn't want to start delivering by car.

On top of that, the café was pretty much always busy - she certainly never had any cake left at the end of the day! Plus it was relatively cheap to run because it was so small, the most she needed was one member of staff - plus Ethel.

There was the rub, though - the thing that had been quietly bugging her. Her business was full to capacity. It survived and it supported her - but there was no room to grow. And if she *did* lose any custom because of New York Froth, she might well run into problems.

But she didn't need to worry about that, did she? Her customers were loyal. Mike Pendle wouldn't be able to open for a good month or two, and besides, he'd be catering to a very different set of customers anyway. She'd keep her locals, and he could deal with the visitors and second home owners. Hell - she'd even throw in the blasted ecologists who came to study the mythical moths if he wanted them - it would save her a fortune on buying the fancy-pants alternative milks they always seemed so keen on.

Yep - she would put New York Froth to the back of her mind and stop worrying about it. Straight away. Yes she would.

Yes she would, yes she would, yes she would.

Balls.

It wasn't working. Her mind was spiralling, and she could feel her logical, sensible side giving in to mounting, irrational fear.

She turned off the tap and stared at the bath. It was time for drastic action. The bath and the wine weren't going to cut it on their own. It was time to pull out the big guns.

Not for the first, Kate sent up a little prayer of

thanks that she had a bathroom with a working fireplace. She adored her whole flat, but this was probably her favourite room. In the depths of winter, there was nothing better than sinking into a deep bath - candles lit, wine or hot chocolate on hand - and the fire crackling away in the grate as she stared up at the stars through the skylight overhead.

Unfortunately, right now, it was the middle of the summer and the room was rather warm, but she wasn't going to let that put her off. A fire would be therapeutic and just what she needed to help her relax.

It didn't take her long before she was submerged in bubbles and a merry little fire was crackling in the grate. She'd opened the skylight as wide as it would go to let some much-needed fresh air into the room - just so she didn't roast. She'd also lit about a dozen candles. Now, this was more like it!

Kate let out a long breath, took another sip of her wine and then rested her head back to watch a couple of fluffy clouds scud across the patch of blue sky visible through the skylight. Yep - this was better. At long last, the tight knots that she'd been carrying around in her shoulders all day started to loosen.

She was okay really, wasn't she? The Sardine wasn't in any trouble, and she'd been going long enough that she could face a little bit of friendly competition. Besides, maybe it really *would* be a good thing for the town. She'd been saying it to customers all day just to prove how *fine* she was with everything, but it was probably true. It *had* to be better that there wasn't a great big empty space like that marring their lovely seafront.

As for Paula's take on Mike Pendle being hot . . . not so much. She'd stick with her original assessment when it came to that. Sure, he had all the pieces of that particular puzzle - the dark hair, chiselled jaw - and there was no denying that he could wear a suit well. But he was just so . . . so . . . arsey - *that* was the word. There was no way she'd ever be attracted to someone that grumpy.

That's why she'd fallen for Pierre. Okay - maybe *fallen for* was the wrong way of putting it. She wasn't in love with Pierre. That was something she'd be very careful about avoiding for the foreseeable. She'd thought what she'd found with Tom was love . . . but it just turned out to be a failed attempt at escaping the well of sadness inside her.

No - she wasn't in love with Pierre - but they had a wonderful time when he did come to town. He was easy-going and fun. Dark-haired, dark-eyed and quick to laugh. He'd rock up bearing a gift of lobsters from his boat, or some other thoughtful parcel he'd brought her from Brittany. He never stayed more than a night or two and then he was off again. But for Kate, that was the joy of it. No matter what Paula and Ethel thought, she loved the romance of his short visits. They gave her exactly what she needed. She was too busy for a full-time relationship. And besides, Stanley would never forgive her - he liked to keep her to himself as much as possible.

Kate picked up her wine again and swirled it around thoughtfully. There was still something nagging at the back of her mind - that *what if* feeling - but then, that was part and parcel of hating change. Because changes came, no matter what she did, and there was nothing she could do about that. She had her man - or *enough* of her man to keep her happy. She had her business - and things were fine just the way they were. All she needed to do now was find someone to replace Claire. What else was there to worry about?

CHAPTER 5

Sod it!

Kate tumbled out of bed and disentangled herself from her duvet cover for what felt like the hundredth time. She gave up. Sleep was just not going to happen, was it?

She hadn't been up this early in a *very* long time. It was light outside – but the kind of light that made it feel like the sun hadn't had its first cup of coffee yet.

One of the joys of living above the café was the fact that Kate could literally fall out of bed and be at work in under a minute – and because Ethel did most of the baking, there was never much of a rush for her to get started on the day. But it did mean that she'd become fairly lax about actually getting herself out of bed at a sensible hour.

Not this morning though. After spending the

night tossing and turning, winding herself up in the duvet so badly that she'd had to get out of the bed in the middle of the night to straighten everything out - Kate was desperate to get outside and shake the uncomfortable, scrunched up feeling out of her limbs. She badly needed to fill her lungs with the salty sea air. Maybe that would help dispel the gnawing, anxious feeling that had haunted her all night.

Even poor old Stanley had given her a disgusted look when she'd kicked him off his spot on the duvet so that she could remake the bed sometime around midnight. He'd ended up decamping back downstairs to his own bed, sick of her constant wriggling.

Kate pulled on a scruffy pair of jeans and a warm jumper. It might be July, but she knew it would be chilly down on the beach this early in the morning. She nipped into the bathroom, splashed her face with some cold water in an attempt to wake herself up, then made her way down to the living room.

'Fancy a walk?'

Stanley lifted his head off his paws, blinking in confusion, before letting out a huge sigh and dropping his head back down with a *flump*.

'Seriously?' laughed Kate. 'You're going to sulk?'

She grabbed his lead from where she'd dumped it on the sofa the night before and rattled it at him. That did the trick. This time Stanley sat up, wiggling his eyebrows at her as if to say *Really? Not a trick like that time you took me to the V.E.T.?*

Kate patted her thigh. 'Walkies!' she said, then laughed as he just blinked at her. 'Fine. If you're too tired, I'll just head down to the beach on my own. Bye.'

She took two steps out of the living room, and suddenly, there at her feet was a large bundle of fur, excitedly wagging his tail.

'Thought so!' she laughed.

～

The moment Stanley's paws hit the golden sand of West Beach, she knew he'd forgiven her for turfing him out of bed early. She snuggled down into her thick jumper and laughed as she watched him haring back and forth between her and the gentle, early morning waves as they lapped at the shore. It was the one place where he seemed to shrug off his slowcoach persona and turn into an absolute loon - a side of him she loved to see.

Considering how much Stanley hated having a bath - so much so that he never voluntarily entered the bathroom - it never ceased to amaze her how much he loved the sea. Watching as he pranced around in the shallows, leaping the little waves, she wondered whether Paula would be happy for him to join the Chilly Dippers for today's swim.

It had been a while since she'd taken him in for a proper dip and she didn't dare let him get into his stride right now without there being someone in the water with him ready to reign him in. Stanley had a habit of heading straight out into the open water, and she could really do without the added excitement of finding someone with a boat to go and fetch him this morning.

'Stanley!' she called sharply as he got in a bit deeper.

Stanley sloshed back out onto the beach, headed straight for her and promptly had a good shake.

'Gah! Thanks, you idiot!' she laughed, bending down to scruff his head as he bounded around, sending sand flying everywhere.

Kate straightened up, grinning. She'd been right about one thing - a good blast of early morning beach air was just what the doctor ordered. She'd managed to get herself in such a tizzy overnight but now, with the sky boasting that beautiful hazy glow that promised a scorching day ahead, and the fresh, salty breeze blowing through her hair, she felt braver, more sure of herself – and like she could take on any challenge.

'Come on Stanley, I've got an idea,' she muttered, turning her steps so that they were heading towards North Beach. 'Let's go suss out the competition before everyone else wakes up.'

They strode along the front, past the King's Nose and The Pebble Street Hotel, and then Kate led the way down the little stone steps onto the large grey pebbles of North Beach.

Stanley followed, his pace slowing as he picked his way over the trickier terrain. There was no doubt about it - he preferred West Beach for haring around like a nutter - but North Beach *definitely* had all the great smells.

He promptly scuttled over to investigate a barnacle-covered wooden boat that was pulled high up the beach, away from the tideline.

Kate highly doubted that it was sea-worthy anymore as it had been sitting here on the pebbles for months now - but Stanley loved it and every time they came down here he snuffled around underneath it, getting bits of seaweed stuck in his coat.

Kate trudged across the pebbles, making the most of the relative privacy of the beach to eye what would become the new frontage of New York Froth. It was pretty unlikely that there would be any locals around at this time of the morning to spot her on her recce, but still, she didn't much fancy becoming the main topic of conversation for the next couple of weeks.

Once she had a good view of the entire front of the old surf shop, Kate paused. There was no doubt about it – this was going to be a serious bit of competition for The Sardine when it opened up – no matter what she'd been trying to tell herself the day before.

For a start, this place would be able to seat so many more people. Probably fifty – perhaps even more if they were clever when it came to the new layout. The Sardine had space for eight... or maybe a dozen at a push – and that was with people perched all over the place.

Kate sighed, wrapped her arms protectively around herself and chewed her lip. Serious, serious competition. Her original plan of staying the course and seeing what happened just wasn't going to cut it.

'Come on Stanley, let's go!' she clicked her fingers.

Stanley picked his way carefully back to her, but, at the last minute, Kate decided that she'd actually quite like a proper peep inside the empty shop – just so she knew what she was up against. There was no harm in that, was there? She wasn't doing anything wrong, even if someone *did* happen to spot her.

She climbed the steps up from North Beach and clipped Stanley's lead to his collar. With a quick look around her, she made her way across the road, around a couple of cars that were parked in the spaces outside and pressed her eye up against the window.

'It's bigger than I remember,' she muttered to Stanley, as he sat on her toes, panting. 'Gonna take him ages to sort out though – what a mess!'

She cupped her hands against the glass to get a better look. It was just a bare shell of a room, knackered, sun-bleached boarding on the walls with the occasional, empty clothes hanger, and some metal brackets that must have been used to hold up the surf boards for sale. It could be gorgeous – but boy, was it going to take some time – not to mention serious money – to get there.

'I don't think we've got anything to worry about for a couple of months. But still…'

Kate realised that she loved The Sardine way too much to just sit back and "wait and see" if the arrival of New York Froth was going to have an effect. Sure, there wasn't anything she could do about it opening - but she *could* make sure her business was in the best possible shape to withstand the competition.

What she needed was something special, something unique that would set her apart from the crowd. Right now – she had her delivery round on Trixie and the amazing cakes Ethel made – but somehow, she didn't think that was going to be enough. She needed a plan. She owed it to her regulars. Hell, she owed it to herself.

'Checking out the competition?!'

The nasal, female voice made Kate jump back and she stumbled as she got tangled up with Stanley and his lead.

'Veronica!' she squeaked. 'You're up early!'

'Well… the early bird catches the worm and all that. So – you've heard the news about your new rivals then?' she said, raising an eyebrow and fixing a beady eye on Kate.

'I'd hardly call them rivals. We'll be catering to a very different bunch of customers.' She knew she sounded defensive, but she really had to make sure she didn't show a single sign of weakness in front of this woman – if she did, the news that she was closing down would be all around the town before it was even breakfast time.

Veronica laughed, though it wasn't a particularly joyful sound. 'Yeah, well – you're right about that. He'll be catering to the general public, and you'll be left with the dregs. Very different customers.'

Veronica paused and sniffed as she looked Kate up and down, a slight sneer on her face. 'Mark my words – things are starting to change for the better here in Seabury. More visitors, more money, more business. I'd advise you to move with the times – otherwise, The Sardine's just going to become a quaint memory.'

'Erm, okay. Thanks for that,' muttered Kate, taking a couple of steps away from Veronica as if the extra space between them would stop her from catching the woman's sceptical outlook on life.

Veronica shrugged. 'Just trying to help. I've been talking to the council. It's the businesses that move with the times they'll be supporting, you mark my words.'

Kate swallowed. She didn't really know what to say. There was "moving with the times" and then there was "destroying the spirit of Seabury". From what she knew of the local council, they tended to err on the side of destruction.

'Have a good day,' she said blandly, flashing Veronica a tight smile. She really did need to get away from her before she said something she'd regret.

'Oh, I will. Mike Pendle's taking me out to lunch later. He wants my advice - business person to business person, you know? We're going to that snazzy new place down in Plymouth – after all,' she paused for effect, 'it's not like there's anywhere decent here in Seabury, is there?'

Kate swallowed down a bitter retort then simply raised her hand in a half-hearted wave as she led Stanley away along the seafront as fast as his furry legs would go.

CHAPTER 6

'Wow – you're here early!' said Ethel, a note of worry in her voice as she bustled into the café.

Kate had watched her approach, then pause at the door with a look of surprise on her face. The fact that all the lights were already on, and the door was unlocked was a rare enough occurrence, but the fact that Kate was ensconced at one of the little tables with a bunch of paperwork strewn about in front of her had clearly been enough to startle her.

Kate smiled at Ethel. 'I'm making plans,' she said as if that explained everything.

'Plans? Going on holiday or something?'

'Nope. Plans for this place,' she said.

'Oh Kate – you're not selling, are you?' said Ethel, dumping the bags she was carrying down on the floor so that she could grasp the back of one of the chairs for support.

'Hell no!' laughed Kate. 'That's exactly why I'm making plans. Between you and me, I got myself all wound up about New York Froth last night. This morning I went down there to check it out – it's going to be massive.'

Ethel nodded. 'Yes, and I see he's already been in and papered over the windows. I guess he wants to do a big reveal when it's all ready.'

'You're kidding me?' said Kate, raising her eyebrows. 'Well, he's been in and done that in the past...' she glanced down at her battered old watch that had once belonged to her father, 'hour. And there I was thinking we'd have at least a couple of months before he got that place ready.'

'Oh, I expect you still do,' said Ethel, gathering her bags up and taking them over to the kitchen, ready to set out today's selection of delicacies. 'He'll need to hire the builders and the people to fit a new kitchen. And I'm sure there are all sorts of things he needs to sort out with the council before he's allowed to swap from being a shop to a café.'

'Something tells me he's probably got most of that in place already – and the bits he doesn't he will do soon. He's taking Veronica out to lunch, you know.'

'Well, if he's looking for advice from that old ... *her*, then he's barking up the wrong tree, isn't he?!' growled Ethel.

Kate shrugged. 'In one way, maybe ... but she does seem to know what the council wants and gets her way in most things eventually. Oh my - I bet that's why he's papered over the windows so quickly too. I was having a look in there first thing this morning and Veronica caught me. What's the betting she sent him a message the minute Stanley and I were out of sight?'

'Oh, I doubt she even waited that long,' muttered Ethel with a tut as she placed a dozen perfect fruity scones onto the top tier of a cake stand. 'Anyway – that's enough about her. Tell me about these plans of yours.'

'So far, the plan is to come up with a plan,' said Kate, shaking her head and shooting a sheepish grin at Ethel.

'Well, that's always a good start,' said Ethel with a heroic effort at keeping her face straight.

'Problem is – this place is tiny, it's not like I can expand without leaving here – which I'm *not* prepared to do. The delivery round covers everyone I can get to without taking a car instead of taking Trixie – which I'm *not* prepared to do...'

'Okay – I think I see the problem,' said Ethel.

'You do?'

She nodded. 'Yes – you're focusing on the negatives rather than the positives. Stop dwelling on the things you *don't* want to do and start thinking about the things you *could* do. Even better – the things you'd *like to do!*'

'So, you mean...'

'It's just a matter of a change of headspace and perspective. Rather than saying "I'm not prepared to give up Trixie" you might say . . . "I'm going to use Trixie to do special coffee and cake deliveries to events." She's quirky and good-looking enough to get into those selfie things, isn't she?!'

Kate stared at Ethel with her mouth open.

'Don't look at me like that. I use the inter webs too, you know.'

Kate grinned and shook her head. 'Sorry. Just a bit mind-blown here. I've sat struggling since silly o'clock and you've just handed me a suggestion in seconds.'

'All a matter of perspective. Don't narrow down your thinking too soon. List everything that you *could* do, then when you've thought as far outside the box as you can, start crossing things off the list.'

'I think you deserve a cup of coffee,' said Kate, leaping to her feet.

'Don't mind if I do,' said Ethel. 'Hey – where's Stanley?

'Down with the Chilly Dippers – Paula's taking him out for a swim. It was as much as I could do to stop him heading for France when we were down there earlier.'

'Bless his heart,' chuckled Ethel. 'I'm surprised

Paula's going back in so soon after that funny turn she had though.'

Kate felt a sudden spike of anxiety hit her in the chest, and she busied herself loading the puck with freshly ground coffee, not wanting Ethel to catch the worry on her face.

'She's had some tests. She said she's feeling a lot better. Hopefully it was just a bit of an infection or something.'

Kate kept parroting this to herself whenever the image of Paula, looking pale and wan as she crashed to the floor of The Sardine a couple of weeks ago, flashed up in her mind. Kate had made her promise to go to the doctor, and Paula had been and got blood tests, but she swore it was nothing. Kate wasn't so sure. Her friend simply hadn't had the same bounce in her step for a while now.

Kate grabbed the milk jug and started to froth it as loudly as she could, just to buy herself a couple more seconds before she had to speak again.

'Here you go,' she said, placing the tall latte down in front of Ethel, and then gratefully accepting a cream and jam laden scone in return.

'Taste test,' laughed Ethel. It was a long-running joke.

Kate took a massive bite. There was nothing on earth as good as Ethel's scones … unless it was Ethel's Victoria sponge … or her flapjack.

'Yum!' said Kate. 'So, just going back to plans for

this place for a second – there is one thing I definitely need to do straight away.'

Ethel nodded. 'New member of staff,' she said around a sip of coffee.

'Right. Because trying any bright new ideas will take at least one extra pair of hands.'

'Well – count me in too, won't you? And you never know – this new person might have some bright ideas of their own to throw into the mix.'

Kate nodded. She knew what Ethel was saying, but it would have to be someone really special before she'd trust them enough to bring them right into the heart of her little world so quickly.

∽

'Come in, come in!' cried Kate, waving the mass of towel-clad women into the tiny café. 'Hands up for coffees?' she called, then quickly counted the raised hands. 'Teas? Anything else?'

'Hot chocolate times two.'

'Got any soup?'

'French onion,' called Ethel.

'Three please!'

It was always total bedlam when the Chilly Dippers piled in after a swim, and this morning was shaping up to be no exception. The windows steamed up in spite of the warmer weather outside, as much vigorous towel-drying, hair wringing and wrangling of warm post-swim hoodies and sweatpants took place.

'Hello boy, did you behave?' said Kate, patting Stanley's head as he trundled over to say hello, then promptly regretting it as he was drenched and covered in sand.

'He was as good as gold. Only one attempt at seal-watching,' laughed Paula, leading the soggy doggy back out of the kitchen and treating him to a vigorous rub down with the towel that Kate always had on hand for him.

'Thanks so much!' said Kate, peeping at her friend while she was busy, and letting out a secret sigh of relief to see that Paula was flushed from her swim and looking much happier and healthier than she had done in a while.

'We love having him! He's our honorary member, you know that.'

Kate grinned. She loved the fact that the locals were as much of a family to Stanley as they were to her. She really did live in the best place in the entire world.

'Oh - by the way,' said Kate, carrying a tray laden with hot drinks into the middle of the gaggle of damp women - who pounced as if their lives depended on wrapping their cold fingers around the warm mugs - 'if anyone's looking for a job, or knows of anyone who'd like to work here – I'm looking to find a replacement for Claire.'

'Have you got any fliers or anything? I can pass some around work for you,' said Paula.

Kate shook her head. 'I don't – but I could easily print some up before I deliver to you guys later?'

'Perfect!' said Paula.

Kate grinned at her friend. She worked in a large graphic design company on the outskirts of town . . . and Paula knew everyone.

'Drop some in to me too, love,' said Doreen, who owned the post office. 'I'll display some in the shop, and pop some in with the local paper deliveries too if you'd like?'

'Yes please!' said Kate, her heart filling with warmth. As usual, the people of Seabury were rushing to her aid. She made a mental note that both Doreen and Paula were on free coffees for the rest of the week.

'How'd it go?' asked Ethel as Kate and Stanley strode back into the café, Kate slightly breathless after what had felt like a particularly arduous sandwich round. Maybe when she found the new person, they'd be up for doing it occasionally, just to give her legs a break!

'Yeah – not too bad,' she said, having nodded a

greeting to the half a dozen regulars who'd pulled the two tables together and were sitting in one big group, munching on tea cakes.

'They take the fliers?' asked Ethel.

'Yeah – that was no problem. I just don't know if it's going to work – you know how picky I am.'

'I do. But that's not a reason to start discounting people before you've even met them,' laughed Ethel. 'The right person will come along, just you wait and see. I bet it's the last person on earth you'd expect, too.'

'You're probably right. Busy here?' asked Kate. It had really lifted her flagging spirits to come back to find the outdoor tables playing host to a whole gaggle of cyclists. Maybe she really did need to get over her dislike for visitors. After all, if she didn't live here herself, she'd definitely want to visit – take a holiday close to the sea and suck in all the beauty Seabury had to offer.

'Very busy here,' said Ethel.

Kate beamed. 'Not too much for you?'

'Course not,' said Ethel stoutly. 'Though I'm not pretending I won't be glad when you've got someone new to help take up the slack... I'll be falling behind on my cake baking and jam duties otherwise!'

'Can't have that!' said Kate, taking Ethel's hand and giving it a quick squeeze. 'But thank you. Really. I don't know what I'd have done without you. And

I'm not just talking about these past few weeks, either.'

'Get away with you girl!' said Ethel, giving her a friendly swipe on the arm and then feeling around in her apron pocket to give Stanley a treat.

Kate watched them fondly for a moment, a smile on her face. Ethel had been there as long as she could remember. She'd been her babysitter when her dad had needed a rare bit of grown-up time. She'd been there when Kate got a bit older and needed a female perspective. And now, here she was – still taking care of her, looking out for her, being her friend.

'Excuse me? Are you Kate Hardy?'

Kate spun around, turning slightly pink at being caught in the middle of such an unguarded moment. She usually kept a tight lid on her treasured memories – they were only to be pulled out and looked at in the sanctuary of her flat when she was alone.

'Yep. That's me,' she said, smiling at the young girl who'd materialised in front of her. 'What can I do for you?'

'Well … I wanted to ask about this,' she said, waving one of Kate's recently printed fliers. 'Is the job still up for grabs?'

Kate had to force herself not to laugh. 'Erm – very much so. I only handed those out about an hour ago.'

'Ah, brilliant!' grinned the girl.

'Hey – didn't I spot you in here yesterday?' said

Kate, suddenly recognising the young face as the girl who'd sat outside in the afternoon and had steadily worked her way through three pots of tea and sampled every single cake they had on offer.

She nodded and smiled. 'So ... I don't know what experience you're after?' she asked. Clearly she wasn't going to be derailed from her purpose.

'Well...' said Kate slowly. This girl looked to be quite a bit younger than she'd normally go for, but she had to be careful, she didn't want to crush her outright. 'I do need some decent experience in a café or something similar.'

'That's no problem – I've worked on and off at one every school holiday for the last two years where I used to live.'

'Are you new in town?' asked Kate, though in reality she already knew the answer – after all, she quite literally knew *everyone* in town, and she didn't recognise this girl's face – yesterday was the first time she'd set eyes on her.

'Yep. Just moved here. I'm Sarah, by the way,' she thrust a hand out for Kate to shake. Kate had to bite her lip to stop herself from letting out a giggle at the firm grasp.

'Well, it's really lovely to meet you, Sarah. So, do you mind if I ask how old you are?'

Sarah shrugged. 'Course not. I'm sixteen,' she said, glancing back over her shoulder towards the door.

'So you're still at school?' asked Kate, wondering who the girl was looking for.

She shook her head and turned her attention back to Kate. 'I finished my GCSEs at my old school. Now I'm here, I really want to go to college, but dad's being a prat about it – he says I have to take A levels and go to university.'

'And what do you want to do?'

'Bake,' said Sarah. 'I want to go to college and do a course that means I can train up as . . . I don't know . . . maybe a pastry chef?'

'Wow,' said Kate. She couldn't help but be impressed by the girl's ambition and the fact that she knew what she wanted to do at such a young age. 'Thing is, no matter if you go to school or to college – I really need someone who can work some weekdays for me too…'

'Oh…' Sarah chewed her lip and looked around her for a moment. 'Well – I wouldn't be starting back until September no matter what happens. If I get my way and go to college – it won't be full time, so I could do some weekdays with you – especially if you'd let me learn some of the baking. I might be able to count it towards the course then.'

Kate's mind was racing. She knew she shouldn't be jumping into anything too quickly, and the girl was so far from the ideal candidate it wasn't even funny . . . but she was getting a weirdly good feeling about her. Still, she needed a few seconds to think.

'Morning Kate!'

Kate glanced around to find one of her regulars waiting to be served.

'Sorry Mary!' she said quickly. 'Your usual?'

'Please! And a teacake. I'll be outside.'

Kate turned to Sarah. 'You used a coffee machine before?'

'Of course!' said Sarah, looking hopeful.

'Well, ours in ancient, Italian, and particularly temperamental. Two lattes – one for Ethel, one for me, and Mary will have a cappuccino. Let's see what you've got!'

Sarah plonked her bag down excitedly on one of the stools and pulled the sleeves of her long black tee-shirt up a bit before moving around to join Ethel on the other side of the counter – where she stopped dead.

'Oh my goodness!' she gasped.

'Okay, dear?' asked Ethel, raising a quick eyebrow at Kate.

Sarah dropped to her knees in front of Stanley and held out the back of her hand for him to sniff – he did so and then promptly gave it a great big lick, making Sarah laugh.

'What a sweetheart!' she said, stroking his head. 'Is he yours?' she looked up at Ethel.

'Kate's.'

'Ah – good point,' said Kate. 'Sarah – meet Stanley. If I'm here, he's here. So, being around him kinda goes with the job…' she said, watching Sarah closely for her reaction.

'Bonus!' said Sarah, beaming at her. 'Right. Sorry,' she got to her feet looking a bit embarrassed. 'Sorry,' she said again. 'I love dogs – I've always wanted one but … parents, you know?'

Kate grinned at her and nodded. This was looking more and more promising by the second.

She watched as Sarah moved to the sink and thoroughly washed her hands before drying them on some blue paper from the dispenser and moving over to the Italian Stallion. She looked so at home in the cramped kitchen, careful not to stand on Stanley or bump into Ethel as she went, that Kate could swear she'd already been working there for several months.

Now came real the test. There were very few people who could get that coffee machine to work with them rather than against them. Kate loved it – but it had taken both Ethel and Claire quite a while to learn its little foibles.

A minute later, Kate was looking down into a latte that looked just about perfect – especially as it had an absolutely adorable little bird swirled into the milk.

She took a sip with her eyes closed. Okay, it was official – if she hired this girl, she could retire from coffee making duties forever. Sarah not only had the knack – this coffee was better than the ones she made herself.

Kate didn't make a comment but instead opened her eyes to watch as Ethel took a sip of her own coffee. She raised her eyebrows and nodded her approval to Kate. Sarah didn't notice – she was fastidiously cleaning the steam spout and emptying the coffee puck ready for the next customer.

'Can you take Mary's out too?' she asked.

'Course!' said Sarah, gathering up the scone Ethel had prepared and scooting outside.

She reappeared with a smile. 'Mary's nice!' she said.

'Okay, Sarah – here's the thing…' started Kate.

'Uh oh,' said Sarah, suddenly looking nervous. 'Not the thing. The thing's never good, is it?!'

Kate chuckled.

'I'll do a trial, or I'll even work just to help you out until you find someone more permanent – whatever you need!'

Kate held up her hand and Sarah promptly put her hand over her mouth to stop herself from talking.

'How about we start by calling it a summer job? Work with me until September – then we'll figure out what's what?' she asked.

Sarah's lip quivered and for a moment. Kate thought she was going to burst into tears, but then she seemed to get control over whatever emotion she was grappling with and she nodded. 'Sounds perfect to me. When do I start?'

'How does tomorrow sound?'

Sarah reached out and shook Kate's hand again, then squatted down next to Stanley, who'd wandered over to sniff her trainers. 'You and me are going to be best friends!' she said, wrapping her arms around him in a giant hug.

CHAPTER 7

Kate passed the turning to the lighthouse and stopped for a brief moment to stare lovingly at her favourite spot. She'd like nothing more right now than to take a few minutes to sit there with Stanley and stare quietly out to sea – but today definitely wasn't the day for it. She needed to get back to The Sardine and take over the Sarah-sitting duties from Ethel.

The young girl had only been with them a few days, but Kate was pretty sure that she could already run the place all by herself whilst blindfolded if she needed to. Not only was she incredibly capable and soaking up every bit of new information like a sponge, but she'd also fitted in as if she'd been there for years. The customers seemed to like her, Lionel had given her his seal of approval, and she and Ethel had already become firm friends.

Kate loved how eager she was to learn. Sure, she was more than a little bit reserved when it came to talking about her home life and parents, but Kate wasn't going to push her on that – all in good time. She would rather that The Sardine was a sanctuary Sarah could count on if she needed it. After all, she could still just about remember how tricky being a teenager was!

In fact, as far as Kate could see, Sarah's age was the only drawback in the whole equation. She and Ethel had agreed that Sarah wasn't to be left to work alone – it wasn't that she wouldn't be able to handle it, but Kate would hate for anything to happen – whether a burn from the Italian Stallion or a run-in with one of the more stubborn customers who sometimes stumbled into their little world.

Kate wanted to make sure that Sarah would *always* have back-up if she needed it. After all – she *was* only sixteen.

To begin with, Kate had worried that this meant they were still at square one. After all, it was an extra person to pay, and it didn't give her or Ethel any more freedom to take time out than they'd had before Sarah had started. On top of that, she'd *still* need to hire someone else. But Kate quickly changed her tune. Sarah had already helped her to pack up the orders and load Trixie each day – giving Kate more time to focus on the customers in the café and Ethel more time to do some extra baking.

Suddenly, between the three of them, it felt like they might actually get some time to come up with some new plans to keep New York Froth off their backs.

In fact, it was the first thing she was going to do when she got back, before Ethel left for the day – arrange a bit of a staff get-together to pick their brains – the sooner the better!

With one last look out across the lighthouse and a quick check that Stanley was still sitting comfortably, Kate pushed off and freewheeled along until she was hurtling down the steep hill back into the heart of Seabury.

As she whizzed past, she couldn't help but notice how many of the outlying cottages had either been converted into B&Bs or holiday homes. In fact, she passed Stanley's old place on this part of her route - now a second home to some rich city types who only visited about three times a year.

Kate had always made it her policy not to deliver to the second homes and air B&Bs. She hated that the housing prices around here sky-rocketed because a bunch of rich idiots wanted a country bolthole for the occasional weekend. It had practically broken her heart when she'd had to sell her dad's house after he'd passed away. There had been no way that she could afford to take on the mortgage for such a large place. But the thing that really stuck in her throat was that it was now owned by someone who used it maybe two days a month at most.

Kate took a deep breath and shook her head so that the wind whipped through her hair as she tried to let go of her anger. Something good had come of it, after all. The swift sale had meant that she'd been able to buy The Sardine and her flat. But now . . . now that it came to shoring up the café against this new threat, perhaps it was time to swallow her pride - and her prejudice - for the sake of everything she held dear.

As usual, Kate slowed as she trundled into the heart of the town - passing *Nana's*, the little ice-cream parlour that had been going for as long as she could remember. Hm. Maybe that's where she should take Ethel and Sarah. What better way to get the creative juices flowing than a double cone with a good sprinkling of chopped nuts, or hundreds and thousands, or her personal favourite - hot fudge sauce?

Yes - they'd make a date, she'd cook for them and then they'd go out and take in the sights. After all, Seabury itself was the best muse she knew.

Letting out a little sigh of relief to find Trixie's yard wasn't blocked this morning, Kate indicated and pedalled the tricycle through the open gates. Then she hopped off, helped Stanley out of the trailer and loaded her arms with the empty bags and boxes from yet another successful delivery round.

'Need a hand?'

Sarah appeared at the entrance to the yard, and quickly took the stack of massive Tupperware tubs out of Kate's arms so that she could grab the last few bits from Trixie's trailer.

'Thanks Sarah!' said Kate gratefully.

'No probs - we saw you pull up. Round go okay?'

Kate nodded. She was wiped.

'Come on - I'll make you a coffee. Me and Ethel have tried out a new shortbread recipe for you to taste test!'

Kate's ears pricked up at this. 'Sounds good! Has it been quiet then?'

Sarah shook her head, expertly balancing the boxes with one arm while she opened the café door for them both with the other. 'Nope - it's been heaving. There's a bunch of new what-ya-call ems . . . erm . . . you know, *moth guys?*'

Kate snorted. 'We need a sign - "Moth Guys welcome here!"'

Sarah stuck out her tongue. 'You know what I mean!'

Kate nodded, chuckling as she made her way into the café and plonked her armload down onto the counter.

Sarah went straight over to the Italian Stallion to make Kate a coffee while her boss slumped into one of the chairs.

'Some days that hill out of town is a bit much for these old legs!' she sighed.

'You could always drive?' said Sarah, peeping back over her shoulder as she loaded the puck.

'Wash your mouth out!' said Kate with a grin.

Sarah rolled her eyes.

'I know I need to make some changes around here if we're going to be able to compete with the new boy, but that's not one of them.'

'It would be a lot faster – and you could go further-' said Ethel, in a gentle voice.

Kate stared at her, knowing full well that she'd never suggest such a thing if there wasn't the protection of the counter between them.

'Nope. Trixie stays. Our customers love her – and I might complain, but I love her too. Anyway – Stanley'd never forgive me.'

'Well …' said Sarah slowly, popping a perfect cappuccino down in front of Kate along with a piece of shortbread, 'if Trixie's staying, maybe you could make her work a bit harder for you?' said Sarah.

'How'd you mean?' asked Kate curiously.

Sarah shrugged. 'Not sure – but she *is* kind of your mascot. Everyone knows her, but she's hidden in the yard all day. Maybe you could use her as a bit of advertising somehow – a way to bring new customers in. Or, I don't know, visit events with her or something?'

Kate nodded slowly. 'Yeah . . . Ethel suggested

events too . . .' This was exactly what she needed – fresh ideas that weren't weighed down with years and years of "this is how I've always done it".

'Okay, you two – I'd like to cook a meal for you both. A kind of mini team-party.'

'Ooh,' said Ethel. 'That sounds lovely. I could bring a trifle!'

Kate grinned. Ethel never went anywhere empty-handed. 'How about Sunday afternoon – are you both free? We'll be closed here, so that makes it easier…'

'I'd love that!' said Sarah, looking thrilled to be included.

'Brilliant! Though I have to warn you that I've got an ulterior motive – I'm going to pick your brains remorselessly.'

'About…?' said Sarah.

'This place. It's time to shake things up a bit, and the only way we're going to do that is as a team.'

Sarah bounced excitedly.

'Oh – by the way Sarah, can you give me a number for your parents? Just so I can check it's okay with them?'

Sarah instantly stopped bouncing. 'I … erm … they'll be totally fine with it.'

'Okay,' said Kate, a bit taken aback. 'But I do need a number anyway – just for an *in case of emergency* contact, you know? I've got a form and because you're under eighteen, I'd prefer it if they could sign it and let me know how best to contact them.'

She watched as Sarah chewed her lip for a second, trying to hide her face as she started to wipe down the already immaculate counter. There was something else going on here, but maybe now, in the middle of the shift wasn't the best time to push it.

She glanced at Ethel to see if she'd picked up on anything, and her old friend instantly met her eye and raised a worried eyebrow. Uh oh – so it wasn't just her.

'What time on Sunday?' said Ethel to break the silence.

'I was thinking about five? We can eat early, throw some ideas around and then I'll treat you both to whatever you fancy from Nana's before they close?'

Sarah looked over at her and Kate was relieved to see a grin on her face. 'Perfect!'

∼

Kate grabbed one of the tables and hauled it towards the doors of The Sardine. She'd already sent Sarah home at three as she'd been there so early that morning. Kate could tell she was going to have her hands full with Sarah – but in the very best way. The customers adored her, and the young girl was so keen that it was practically impossible to make her take a break, let alone send her home at the end of her shifts.

Heading back outside for the other table, Kate wondered again about what the story with her parents was. She never talked about them, had shaken her head when she'd asked if she had any brothers or sisters, and Kate had found the 'In Case of Emergency' form she'd printed off abandoned in the kitchen after she'd left.

For whatever reason, Sarah really didn't want Kate to have anything to do with them … and she really didn't feel comfortable about that.

She pulled her mobile out of her pocket, intending to give Ethel a quick call. If she couldn't get Sarah to open up, perhaps Ethel might have more luck.

Just as she pulled up Ethel's number, her screen started flashing with an incoming call.

Kate grinned and ran her fingers through her tousled mop of hair as she answered and slumped down into the last chair left out on the pavement.

'Hello Kate.'

'Pierre!' she grinned. 'I haven't heard from you in forever!'

'I am sorry, ma chérie, it has been busy – for you too, yes?'

'Definitely!' laughed Kate.

'But – are you free ce soir?'

Was she free tonight? Hell yes! She couldn't imagine a better way to finish the day.

'Absolutely!'

'In… un heur?'

'Perfect!'

'I only stay one night. Tomorrow I must go back home.'

'Then we'd better make it count!' said Kate with a huge smile.

CHAPTER 8

Kate rolled over in her bed and reached a hand out, searching for the smooth warmth of Pierre's skin. Instead, all she found were rumpled sheets that were already cold. Shit – had she overslept?

She sat bolt upright and reached for the little alarm clock that sat on her bedside table. Six forty-five in the morning. Huh. So, where the hell was Pierre? Maybe he'd been unable to sleep and had decamped down to the living room so that he didn't disturb her... not that there would be much chance of him doing that after they'd finally curled up to sleep so late the night before!

After getting his call, Kate had hurried to lock up The Sardine, packed a massive picnic basket full of tasty leftovers, and then ran upstairs for a hasty shower. She'd even managed to add a quick slick of mascara and lip-gloss before the sound of the doorbell was met with Stanley's eager, booming bark.

Much to Stanley's disgust, Kate had whisked Pierre off for a romantic stroll, leaving him with an order to stay put in his bed. She did feel a bit bad about it – after all, Stanley was usually with her no matter what was going on - but this was different. He definitely wouldn't have been a good addition for what she had planned.

Kate had led Pierre to one of the secret coves just along from West Beach. She'd discovered this particular one when she was a teenager and had never yet met a single soul there when she visited. This might have been something to do with the fact that you had to scramble along a practically hidden path through a thicket of brambles and blackthorn, and then clamber down a steep, muddy cliff on your behind to get there – but boy, was it worth it.

Golden sand and the perfect, private place for skinny dipping. She and Pierre had made the most of it, and she thanked her lucky stars that she'd remembered to pack her tartan picnic blanket.

Kate rolled out of bed and snagged her silky robe off the floor where it had been unceremoniously tossed away by Pierre the night before. Slipping it on, she listened for any sounds in the flat, but everything was completely quiet.

She padded across to the bathroom, hastily wiped the smudged mascara from under her eyes (no point terrifying the poor guy!) and then silently made her way downstairs. She peeped into the kitchen, which was empty, then pushed open the door and made her way into the living room.

Stanley lifted his head from his bed and wagged his tail. At least it looked like he'd forgiven her for abandoning him the night before. But there was no sign of her visitor.

'Where's he got to then, Stan?' she said, bending low to tickle his ears.

Stanley let out a huge sigh and flopped back down onto his bed. His meaning was more than clear – he couldn't give a monkeys what had happened to the interloper that had cost him his evening walk!

Kate straightened up and went back through to the kitchen. As she was up, she may as well grab a cup of tea. She went to flick the kettle on and paused. There on the counter was a folded piece of paper with her name on the front. She grabbed it and unfolded the sheet that looked like it had been torn from the pad she used for her shopping lists.

Ma Cherie Kate,

Merci! I had an amazing time with you. Désolé. So sorry I have to leave early. I did not want to wake you – you need your sleep after last night! I closed the door so the dog did not follow me out. See you next time.

Pierre x

. . .

Kate stared at the note and for just a moment, a little wave of disappointment ran through her. Then she let out a sigh, popped the piece of paper in the bin and flicked the kettle on. She didn't have the right to be disappointed. This was how things were between them. It was what she *wanted*, wasn't it? They'd had a wonderful evening – and it was too much to expect breakfast together before he disappeared back to France, wasn't it? Anyway, she needed to get a wiggle on if she wanted to turn all the fish he'd brought her from his boat into a pie in time for the lunchtime crowd!

∽

'Oh my God, what's that amazing smell?' said Sarah, bowling into The Sardine with a Tupperware box clamped under one arm, followed closely by Ethel.

'Fish pie,' said Kate.

'Ah yes, the smell of a visit from a certain Frenchman,' laughed Ethel.

'Oi!' said Kate, letting out a laugh.

'You don't have to pretend it's not true,' said Ethel, eyeing her sternly. 'One look at that glow on your face and anyone could tell what you've been up to!'

'Ethel!' laughed Sarah in delight, turning to stare at her.

'What? I may be old, young lady, but I'm not past it.'

'Wouldn't dream of saying you were! Anyway – when do I get to meet the guy?' Sarah demanded.

'What? Kate's guy? You'll be lucky!' laughed Ethel. 'That man's like quicksand. I think I caught a glimpse in passing … maybe once?'

Kate shrugged. 'He's busy.'

'That's one way of putting it. I'm guessing he was gone before you even woke up this morning?'

Kate shrugged.

'Nothing changes,' sighed Ethel.

'That sucks,' said Sarah. 'How come you look so happy?' she said, turning back to Kate.

'Because I like things just the way they are,' she said decidedly. 'Anyway you two, enough of all that! What's in the box Sarah?'

'An experiment. I wondered if you'd let me know what you think?'

'And so it begins,' laughed Ethel.

'You don't have to!' said Sarah, looking a bit embarrassed.

'Oh, no lass, don't misunderstand me. You're just reminding me of myself. And Kate here too – when she started experimenting with pie fillings.'

'Oh!' said Sarah, looking between the two of them.

'Yeah – welcome to the club!' said Kate. 'And

gimmie! I could do with a pick-me-up before I head out.'

Sarah opened the box almost shyly as Kate strode over to join her and Ethel at the counter.

'Oh my,' breathed Ethel.

'Holy mackerel!' said Kate.

'I think you mean holy macarons, actually!' chuckled Ethel. 'May I?'

Sarah nodded, looking decidedly nervous.

Ethel reached in and gently lifted out one of the delicacies. Apple-shaped, the macaron was a rich red colour and glazed in a shiny red coating. A stalk crafted of chocolate stuck out of the side, a tiny leaf piped on in green icing.

'I hate to do this, but…' Ethel broke it in half to reveal a perfect, gooey centre. She popped half in her mouth and chewed.

Kate and Sarah stared at her, following her every move as if she was a *Bake Off* judge.

'Oh my!' she groaned.

'Right, my turn!' said Kate, nabbing one for herself and taking a bite.

'Cinnamon and apple?' she breathed.

Sarah nodded. 'Do you like it?'

'Mmmmmmm!' chorused the two women together.

'Alright back there, boy?' she called to Stanley over her shoulder as she pumped her legs for all she was worth, heading up the hill out of Seabury to her first stop on the sandwich round – the graphic design company where Paula worked.

Stanley seemed to grin at her from his perch, looking as happy as Larry. Kate laughed and stood up on the pedals to give her a bit of extra oomph to get to the top road.

Hearing a car coming up behind them, Kate kept pedalling as hard as she could. This part of the road was ridiculously narrow, and there would be no chance they could overtake here - but she knew that there was a decent passing spot she could pull into about fifty meters ahead. She started to pant with the extra effort. Not long now and she'd be out of their way.

Whoever was behind them started to impatiently rev their engine, making Stanley bark. Kate threw a cross look over her shoulder and swore. The car was mere feet behind Trixie, deliberately tailgating her, pulling closer then dropping back, then pulling even closer again. Kate squinted, but the light reflecting off the windscreen meant that she couldn't make out the driver's face.

Stanley was now on his feet, barking his head off, and there was quite literally nothing Kate could do because the prick wasn't even giving her enough space to slow down, let alone stop.

Letting a fluent stream of swear words flow from her lips as she pumped her legs even harder, Kate did her best to keep up the pace, heading as fast as she could for the pull-in and praying that Stanley didn't get so freaked out that he tried to do anything stupid.

The road started to widen slightly. Kate could just about see the pull-in up ahead when the driver decided that they couldn't wait any longer and swerved to the right, determined to overtake.

'What the hell?!' squealed Kate, steering Trixie in towards the spikey, thorned hedge on the left.

The huge estate car whizzed alongside her, coming so close that she had to wrench the handlebars and steer them right off the road onto the verge in an attempt to stop the car from clipping their side. The handlebars juddered and jerked in Kate's hands. Trixie's front wheel hit a rock and Kate fell off the saddle just as the trailer toppled onto its side.

'Stanley!' Kate screamed, scrambling on hands and knees around the back.

Stanley cowered away from her, backing in towards the hedge.

'It's okay boy, you're okay,' she crooned, her voice shaking with the shock of what had just happened. She managed to lay one hand gently on his head and get hold of his collar with the other. He let out a little whimper - a sound she might expect from a puppy rather than her great big bear of a dog.

'Don't be hurt, don't be hurt!' she muttered,

stroking him and trying to coax him forwards out of the hedge a bit. She really needed to get Trixie fully off of the road, but she didn't dare let go of Stanley in case he bolted in fright.

'Here,' she said reaching into her pocket with her free hand. 'Biscuit?'

Stanley's nose twitched and he moved closer to her to snaffle the treat. Kate groaned. There was no mistaking the fact that he was limping and trying to carry his front foot.

Kate did her best not to panic. The last thing she wanted to do was stress Stanley out even more. She reached into her cardigan pocket where she'd stashed the rope lead she always carried with her and gently clipped it onto his collar, then carefully stood up. *She* didn't seem to have hurt herself in the fall - at least that was something.

'Can you walk?' she said, trying to coax Stanley forward. She really did need to get Trixie out of this narrow part of the road before this disaster turned into something even messier.

Stanley stood up, took two limping steps and then promptly sat back down with a little whine.

'Oh, my poor baby!' she said, fighting back tears as shock started to set in. 'I'm going to kill that . . .'

She drew her mobile out of her pocket. Thankfully it was unscathed. She needed to call for some help. She was just about to dial The Sardine's number when she heard the sounds of an approaching engine. Balls!

She was just about to try yanking the trailer to see if she could slide it sideways when a white pick-up crawled into view.

'Kate love! What's happened?!'

Charlie's kind, worried face appeared alongside her, staring at her out of the window.

Kate felt her lip wobble as tears that were part-rage and part-shock threatened to spill over.

'It's okay, it's okay love. We'll get you sorted.'

Charlie popped the truck's hazard lights on and killed the engine. He hopped quickly down and made his way around to Kate.

'Did you crash?' he said in surprise.

Kate shook her head. 'Stanley's hurt!' was all she managed to force out around the massive lump of fear in her throat.

'Bleeding?' he asked quickly, bending down and stroking Stanley's head.

Kate shook her head. 'It's his front leg. It . . . it might be broken.'

'Okay. First things first. Come on lad.'

Charlie wrapped his arms around Stanley and with surprising strength, lifted him gently in his arms. Stanley let out a little yelp that turned into a pathetic whine. The sound nearly finished Kate off - but she just about managed to hold it together enough to open the truck's passenger door. Charlie gently placed Stanley in the footwell on top of what looked to be a fleece jacket.

'Let's get Trixie in the back - we can look at her later. We need to get the lad straight to the vet.'

Between them, they unhooked the little trailer from Trixie and managed to haul her into the open back of the truck.

'Right,' said Charlie. 'Let's go.'

Kate nodded, pursing her lips as she climbed up into the passenger seat, careful not to nudge Stanley with her foot.

'It's okay boy,' she said, gently stroking his head. 'You'll be okay.'

'What happened?' asked Charlie as he pulled out onto the top road.

'We got pushed off the road by a car,' said Kate, doing her best not to growl.

'What? That's terrible! And they didn't even stop?!'

'No,' said Kate, struggling to keep a lid on her anger as she fully realised this fact for the first time. 'No, he bloody well didn't, did he?'

'He? So you know who it was?'

Kate nodded. It had been the same estate car that had blocked Trixie's yard just the other day. 'That car belongs to Mike bloody Pendle.'

CHAPTER 9

'Are you okay?'
'Where's Stanley?'
'What exactly happened?'
'You've been gone for hours!'

Kate was greeted back into The Sardine by a barrage of worried questions from Ethel and Sarah. She'd called them from the vet's and told them there had been an accident. Ethel had agreed to call all her customers, but there hadn't been time to give her the ins and outs of what had happened. It had been as much as Kate could do not to dissolve into a puddle of tears on the phone. If she was honest, she wasn't far off it now, either.

'That Mike Pendle ran her off the road in his car,' said Charlie, a frown marring his usually smiling face as he followed her in and, seeing that the café was empty – it being long after the lunchtime rush by this point – shut the door firmly behind him and flipped the sign to "closed".

'*What?!*' squeaked Sarah, the colour draining from her face. 'But he *couldn't* have. I mean…' she paused, looking a bit like she was going to fall over. She looked to Ethel for some kind of support, but the older woman gave a little shrug and shook her head.

'Hang on, where's Stanley?' Sarah demanded. 'Oh my God. He's not…?'

Kate sank into one of the empty chairs. 'We had to leave him at the vet's. He needs an x-ray. He might have a broken leg – though the vet thinks it's probably just sprained. But she wants to check there's nothing else going on that we can't see.'

'Oh no, poor lad,' said Ethel, shaking her head, and bringing a cup of tea over to Kate. 'Charlie, what can I get for you?'

'Oh, nothing thanks,' he said, smiling at her warmly. 'I'll just get out of your hair.'

'Please Charlie, I insist!' said Kate, indicating for him to sit down with her. 'I've wasted your entire day running around after me like that.'

'Not wasted. I'm glad to help,' he mumbled.

'You're our hero, coming to the rescue like that!' said Ethel, her voice soft.

'Oh I don't know about that…' he said scratching his nose and turning red.

'You are!' said Sarah. 'Imagine if you hadn't come along!'

'I don't want to think about that, thanks,' said Kate, doing her best to suppress a shudder. 'Did you guys manage to call everyone?' she asked as Sarah hovered over her and Charlie while Ethel bustled off to make him a drink.

Sarah nodded. 'Ethel got straight on the phone to everyone – she worked through your delivery list and explained you'd had an accident and were stuck at the vet's.'

'Many complaints?'

'Are you mad?' said Ethel from the kitchen. 'Everyone was just worried about you and Stanley!'

'But no one got their deliveries,' she sighed.

'Most of them put in a new order over the phone and sent someone down to collect it. We nearly ran out of cake, so we sold all of Sarah's macarons too. Paula came down from their lot and even took some deliveries up to a couple of places that couldn't make it down into town themselves.'

Kate shook her head and tried to control the wave of emotion that ran through her. As usual, the kindness of the locals amazed her. Well – *most* locals. 'That must have been bedlam for you guys!'

'Busy, but it was okay – Sarah was amazing,' said Ethel, unable to hide the note of pride in her voice.

'Thank you both so much. I don't know what I'd do without you two. I think I'll have to make something special to take everyone when I get back to the round next week… you know, a little apology...'

'Next week?' said Sarah, sounding worried.

Kate shrugged. 'Luckily it's Saturday tomorrow, so no round anyway. Closed on Sunday. And maybe - hopefully - Trixie'll be fixed up by Monday... though I'm not sure how likely that is . . .'

'Oh no! Trixie's broken too?' said Ethel.

Charlie nodded. 'Needs a bit of straightening out after her tumble, that's all. I'm sure she'll be okay.'

'You know, Kate love, I think maybe we should shut up shop for the rest of the day. Or at least, you should take the afternoon off,' said Ethel, popping a small pile of post down in front of Kate and perching on the chair next to her for a moment. 'I don't mind working with Sarah until closing time. You've had a shock and you'll be worrying about Stanley until you know what's happening. The last thing you need to be doing is fielding customers.'

Kate started to shake her head, but fear about Stanley combined with bone-tired weariness made her want to curl up and go to sleep instead. She wasn't sure what to say, so she picked up the top envelope from the pile just for something to do and slit it open.

'You know, Ethel's right,' said Charlie.

'But... then he'll win!' muttered Kate, drawing the letter out.

'Who?'

'Mike Pendle. I can't let him win.'

'Love,' said Ethel in a gentle tone, 'I don't think he

did it on purpose. Yes, it was irresponsible and awful, but there's no way...'

'You didn't see what he was doing,' growled Kate.

'Well, no...'

'He wouldn't do that,' said Sarah in a decided voice.

'Well,' said Kate, trying to keep her calm, 'I'm afraid he did.'

'Actually,' said Sarah, there's something I need to talk to you about. Well, something I need to tell you...'

Kate looked up just in time to see Ethel shake her head quickly at Sarah. 'Maybe another time, love,' she said, a firm note to her voice. 'Kate's had a bit of a shock.'

'No, it's okay Sarah,' said Kate. 'Just give me a couple of minutes to land and go through this lot first and then . . .' she trailed off, glancing down at the piece of paper in her hand. 'Son of a b-!'

'What?' said Ethel, her eyebrows raised.

Kate looked up again to find all three of them staring at her in concern. She took a deep breath, trying to steady herself, trying to keep the well of anger that was building in her chest from breaking loose.

'You know what,' she said, her voice hard and low. 'I think I'll take you up on that offer of an afternoon off.'

'Good idea,' said Sarah, sounding relieved. 'Maybe a bath and...'

Kate shook her head. 'I'm going to go and pay Mike Pendle a visit. This,' she said, shaking the letter like she was trying to wring its neck, 'this means war!'

∽

Kate hammered on the locked and papered door of the old surf shop. She was shaking from head to toe as pure, unadulterated rage coursed through her veins.

Where the hell was he, the conniving, tailgating, backstabbing . . . ?

Kate banged on the door again, this time with both fists. She knew she should cool off, try to get into a calmer state of mind and think this through so that she could approach it rationally. She *knew* that she looked a bit like a rabid dog right now but-

'Mike Pendle!' she yelled. 'Get your arse out here *right* now!'

She knew there were people working in there. She could hear a radio and see shadows moving around behind the paper. It struck her, somewhere in the tiny part of her brain that was still clinging onto sanity, that Mike might not actually be here at all - but she ignored that thought. He *had* to be here.

She was just about to hammer again when there was the sound of a key being turned, then the door cracked open.

'Who the hell are you?'

Kate stared into the face of a huge guy she'd never set eyes on before.

'Kate Hardy. I want to see-'

'Mike Pendle. Yeah. We heard,' he said, raising a curious eyebrow. 'So did the rest of the bleedin' county. But he's upstairs.'

'Then let me up,' said Kate, taking a step forward.

'Can't do that love,' he said, blocking the whole doorway.

'Seriously. It's not the day to piss me off. Either let me in or get someone to fetch him. Now.'

The guy opened his mouth as if to argue, and then let out a huge sigh.

'Grey,' he called over his shoulder. 'Go tell his Highness that he's got a lady-caller gunning for his balls down here.'

If she wasn't so angry, that comment would have made her laugh. As it was, she just folded her arms protectively across her chest and tapped her foot.

'What the hell was that noise?' came a voice from inside. 'Stu?'

'He's all yours, love,' grinned the big guy, disappearing back inside and pointing Mike in her direction.

'Kate? This is a pleasant-'

'You *absolute* bastard,' she yelled, pushing forwards into the shop and poking him hard in the chest. She didn't care that there were half a dozen workmen she didn't know standing around them, staring at her like she had two heads. 'You could have seriously hurt us! You could have *killed* Stanley. You absolute, *absolute-*'

'Wow-wow-wow!' he said raising his hands in a small surrender motion and taking a couple of steps backwards. 'What are you going on about?'

'Don't pretend you don't know,' she spat. 'Stanley's still at the vet's. I've got to get Trixie fixed. I'm lucky I'm in one piece. And then I get back to The Sardine and you've complained to the f-' she paused briefly and took a breath in an attempt to stop her voice from going ultra-sonic and her language from descending further into the gutter.

'You complained to the council,' she said in a lower tone, 'about my outdoor tables.' She thrust the letter she was still clutching hard into his chest.

Mike flinched, grabbed the piece of paper and quickly scanned the letter from the council explaining that, following a complaint from members of Seabury's business community, it had come to their attention that Kate didn't hold the requisite licence to set up tables on the pavement outside The Sardine.

'I-' started Mike.

'No,' she said. 'No. You don't get to talk. I do. Play whatever stupid little games you want, but they won't work. You'll *never* kill off The Sardine. I've been here all my life - I'm not going anywhere. But if you *ever* do anything that puts me, my staff or my dog in danger again, then I will personally remove your balls and serve them to you for breakfast. Understood?'

Mike's mouth was hanging open, but he wasn't able to make any kind of sound. Good.

Kate snatched the letter back out of his hands, turned on her heel and, to the soundtrack of low whistles coming from the workmen, she stalked straight back outside.

Kate didn't slow her pace until she was back on the golden sand of West Beach. There was no way she was going to hang around near North Beach long enough for Mike Pendle to get over his shock and come up with some crummy excuse for his shitty behaviour. She'd just about managed not to take a swing at him back there, but she wasn't sure she'd manage it a second time.

Kicking off her shoes, Kate sank down into the sand and stared out at the sea. She just needed a moment to pull herself together before she headed back to The Sardine to face the inevitable questions from the others.

It felt so wrong to be down here on the beach without Stanley. She didn't know what she'd do if he was seriously hurt. What if she lost him? No, she couldn't even face that possibility.

Kate shook her head, trying to clear the bad thoughts as they crowded in on her. That wasn't going to happen. Stanley had a sore foot. She was just being dramatic. It was probably delayed shock from what had happened that morning - and that little scene back there.

She hated the fact that there was someone here in Seabury she now actively hated. She'd have to do her best to avoid bumping into him. Hell, in reality, that meant she'd have to avoid North Beach completely. This sucked!

Kate wiggled her toes in the sand then grabbed her mobile out of her pocket. It was time to act. She'd call the place they'd dropped Trixie off at earlier and find out if they'd had a chance to figure out how long the repairs would take.

Just as she pulled the details up on Google, the phone buzzed to life in her hands with an incoming call. It was the vet.

'Hello?' A cold drop of terror landed in her belly.

'Kate? We're all done with your boy.'

'Is he okay? Is it broken? Is there internal bleeding?' she gabbled.

'He's fine, Kate. It's a mild sprain. Nothing to be seen on the x-ray - better safe than sorry, though.'

'But all that yelping - are you sure he's okay?' she pressed, still not able to get the memory of Stanley's pathetic whimpering out of her head.

'Well, the poor boy had a massive blackthorn spike stuck in his paw!' said the vet. 'It was lodged right between his toes - that's why we missed it when we first looked him over. Very painful - but we got it out cleanly. They can turn really nasty, so I've given him a shot of antibiotics and I've given the area a good spray with antiseptic. You'll need to keep an eye on it for any swelling over the next few days, but it should be fine - it wasn't in there long.'

'So he's going to be okay?'

'He's absolutely fine. A couple of days taking it easy, and you won't even remember that it happened.'

Kate sighed. Chance would be a fine thing.

CHAPTER 10

Sunday. How was it Sunday already?! All Kate wanted to do was hide in bed all day watching romcoms and eating chocolate, but of course, she couldn't.

She knew that Sarah and Ethel would have both understood if she'd cancelled their plans for their get-together, but she just hadn't been able to bring herself to do it. If anything, they needed to re-group now more than ever.

After the initial shock of the accident had subsided a bit and Stanley was safely back in the flat - complete with extra treats and cuddles - it became apparent to Kate that Mike's move with the council was actually far more damaging than she'd first thought.

The letter demanded that she remove her external tables immediately and not replace them until she had applied for - and been granted - the proper licence. *If* she was granted the licence. This had halved her seating in one fell swoop.

Then, of course, she was still Trixie-less. The guys at the repair shop had said it would be about a week before they could fit the work in. That was a whole week without her delivery round . . . because, of course, she didn't actually *own* a car. What was the point when she never left Seabury?! It meant that she had to let her customers down yet again and, of course, it meant another cut in her takings. Quite a serious one.

So yes, today's meeting was far too important to cancel just because *she* needed a break. What The Sardine needed was some creative thinking, otherwise it would be in serious trouble before too long.

Kate knew that she needed to put on a brave face and a happy and enthusiastic front while the other two were here . . . but still, watching romcoms in her PJs really *was* very appealing right now.

She'd made one small concession to the fact that she was completely knackered, though. Instead of preparing an extravagant meal for the three of them as she had been planning to, she'd knocked up some pizza dough, whizzed up a batch of tomato sauce and gone to town with various toppings. Easy, delicious, and cooked in minutes rather than hours.

Kate hadn't actually seen Sarah since the day of the accident. The poor girl had been distraught about

Stanley being hurt and had practically sobbed in relief when Kate had returned from the beach to share the good news that it wasn't serious.

Luckily, Charlie had still been there chatting away to the pair of them and had gladly offered her a lift to collect the invalid. Although Kate was super-grateful and accepted without hesitation, she suspected that this particular favour was designed to win him another of Ethel's much-coveted soft smiles above any thanks she could offer him.

By the time they'd returned, Ethel had sent Sarah home for the day, and Kate couldn't help but feel bad for all the drama. The poor girl hadn't been with them for long - what would she think?

The trilling of the doorbell combined with a booming bark from Stanley roused her from her thoughts, and she hurried downstairs.

'Ethel!' she said, forcing a smile onto her face. 'You're a bit early.'

'Hi! Yes - sorry about that. I just wanted a quick word before Sarah came up,'

'Why's that?' said Kate in surprise as she followed her friend up to the living room.

'Hello, my gorgeous boy!' crooned Ethel as Stanley mooched over for a tickle. 'How're you doing?'

'He's fine. His foot seems to be all better, other than a bit of a scab where that thorn was.'

'Not nice!' said Ethel with a tut. 'I still can't believe someone paid that vet bill for you, though!'

'That's Seabury for you,' said Kate, her smile instantly turning into a genuine one.

'True, true,' agreed Ethel. 'I wonder who it was. Probably one of your sandwich round customers, I reckon.'

Kate shrugged. She still couldn't believe it, no matter what she'd just said. She'd arrived to pick Stanley up, mildly dreading the hit her credit card was about to take and cursing the fact she hadn't taken out pet insurance, when the vet told her the bill had already been settled by a "concerned friend." When she'd asked who'd done such a lovely thing so that she could thank them, the vet had shaken her head and said she simply couldn't tell her - it was confidential.

'Well, whoever it was, I'm really grateful,' said Kate with a sigh. 'Not that I would begrudge emptying every account I have - as long as my boy's okay,' she added, earning herself a pat from Ethel. 'Anyway - I've learned my lesson. Stanley's now insured!'

'That's a very sensible idea,' said Ethel.

Just then the doorbell rang again.

'Bother. Kate - just quickly before you answer that - Sarah's got something she needs to talk to you about today.'

'O-kay,' said Kate, heading towards the stairs.

'Seriously - just - go easy on her, okay?'

'Easy . . .? Wait, what's going on?!'

'She needs to tell you herself. But - remember she's just a child, okay?'

Kate nodded. 'Of course. Is this what she wanted to tell me on Friday?'

Ethel nodded. 'Yes. But you've got to agree, that wasn't the moment.'

'Not the moment for anything, really,' said Kate with a wry smile.

The doorbell rang a second time and Kate bounded down the stairs to answer. She had to admit, she was curious. What on earth could lovely young Sarah have done to require such dire warnings from Ethel?

'Hiya!' said Sarah, her nervous smile wavering above yet another massive Tupperware box.

'Oooh . . . what have you been up to?' asked Kate, her eyes lighting up. 'More experimenting?'

'Yup,' said Sarah, nodding. 'I had an idea for The Sardine. Actually - a couple of ideas. But I need to speak to you about something first.'

'No probs,' said Kate, keeping her tone deliberately light. 'Come on up and we'll get a drink.'

'How's Stanley?' asked Sarah, puffing up the stairs behind her.

'Almost fully mended.'

'Thank God,' breathed Sarah.

'He'll be glad to see you! He doesn't think much of

walkies being suspended,' laughed Kate. That was an understatement. Stanley had been going stir-crazy. The vet had advised her just to give him very short walks for a couple of days, and she'd been keeping him off the beaches - North Beach so that he wasn't scrambling over stones making his sprain worse, and West Beach so that he didn't get sand in the puncture left behind by the thorn.

Kate had been right. The minute Sarah stepped into the living room - before she'd even had the chance to put her box down - the big bear was there at her feet, leaning his weight against her legs and staring lovingly up at her.

'Here, let me take that so you two can hug it out,' laughed Kate, taking the Tupperware from Sarah's arms.

Sarah dropped down next to Stanley and wrapped her arms around him, and he leant his huge head on her shoulder.

Kate watched them for a moment. That's what Stanley always did to her when she was worried about something. Hm. Ethel was right. She needed to be gentle with Sarah - no matter what the girl was about to tell her, she was worried enough about it that Stanley had already picked up on something.

'Tea Sarah?' called Ethel from the kitchen.

'Please!' she called back, her voice muffled through a layer of hairy dog.

'Did you have a good day off yesterday?' asked

Kate, perching on the sofa. She was hoping this little opener might ease the way into the conversation.

Sarah shrugged. 'I'd have preferred to be at The Sardine!'

'Well . . . sadly the law says that I can't use you as slave labour!' laughed Kate.

Sarah smiled back at her.

'So - when I came back from all that chaos on Friday, you wanted to talk to me about something? Sorry I stormed out before we got the chance!'

Kate watched the colour leach out of Sarah's face, and mentally kicked herself. Maybe the blunt approach wasn't the best one. Still, she wanted to make the most out of this evening, and there was no way she was going to be able to do that while they were dancing around whatever this big revelation was.

Kate watched as Stanley scooted his bum around so he was practically sitting on Sarah, and the girl couldn't help but let out a small laugh as he nearly knocked her over.

'Okay boy, I'm okay,' she said.

'You want to tell me?' asked Kate gently.

Sarah looked at her directly. 'I wish I had told you straight away. But . . . well, I really wanted the chance to work for you. And I love it so much. But after everything that's happened . . . is happening. . . you need to know. But I . . .'

Sarah paused and Kate watched her closely. She

didn't have a clue what the girl was about to confide in her, but it was certainly costing her a lot to get it out.

'Look - I'll get it if you don't want me to work for you anymore,' she said, her voice sounding shaky.

'It's not going to come to that, lass.' Ethel's voice in the doorway made Kate jump slightly. She'd been so focused on the scared girl in front of her, she'd briefly forgotten that her old friend was there too.

'Okay,' sighed Sarah. 'Well, you wanted to know about my parents.'

Kate raised her eyebrows in surprise, but kept her mouth shut.

'I live with my dad now. My mum's with a . . . a . . . well, she's with this other guy. She's divorcing my dad, and it's . . . it's really bad for him.' Sarah paused and swallowed.

'I'm really sorry, Sarah,' said Kate. 'I get it. I don't know if Ethel told you, but I lived with my dad too. A bit different because I lost my own mum, but I know how hard this stuff can be.'

Sarah nodded. 'It's not just that though.'

'Oh?'

'God, you're going to hate me,' she said, earning herself a wet nose in the cheek from Stanley.

'I can promise you, there's no way that's possible,' said Kate gently, wondering what awful story this poor girl was carrying around with her.

'Okay, but I get it if you do,' she paused and took a deep breath. 'My dad's Mike Pendle.'

Kate froze. Sarah was Mike Pendle's daughter? As in - second-generation New York Froth? The guy who had attacked her business and run her and Stanley off the road?

'See. I told you you'd hate me,' said Sarah, her chin trembling with emotion.

Kate swiftly shook her head. 'I don't. Not at all. It's just a - surprise.' She paused and swallowed, trying to gather her thoughts. 'Can I ask you a question?'

'Course,' said Sarah in a small voice.

'What does he think about you working for me. Was it his idea?'

Sarah shook her head in surprise. 'Definitely not - he doesn't even know!'

'He doesn't *know*?!' echoed Kate. 'But you've been in The Sardine for hours every day - how'd you swing that?'

Sarah shrugged. 'He's been really busy trying to get the flat sorted for us and . . . the café,' she added awkwardly. 'He hasn't had time to notice much else, I guess.'

Kate blinked a couple of times, and then her behaviour on Friday came back to her in full force. The tirade she'd gone on. The things she'd said about Sarah's *dad*! If she'd have known, she would never, ever have said anything in front of the girl.

'Oh Sarah, I'm so, so sorry!' said Kate seriously.

'*You're* sorry? What for?!'

'For everything I said on Friday. About your dad!'

Sarah shrugged. 'You didn't know. And anyway, if he *did* those things - going to the council, I mean - then he's been well out of order.'

Kate frowned.

'But there's no way that was dad in the car - you know - with the accident.'

Kate shook her head. That had been Mike Pendle's car and no mistake. But it wasn't fair to discuss it with Sarah. Not at all. It hadn't been her driving, had it? It wasn't as though Sarah had any control over her dad's behaviour.

'Look. That's between me and your dad,' said Kate quietly. 'I'm really sorry you got caught in the middle.'

'It's my fault for not telling you,' muttered Sarah.

'Okay - well, you've told me now. The question is, do you want to carry on at The Sardine? Because I'd love you to stay.'

Sarah stared at her, wide-eyed. 'Seriously?'

'Seriously!' laughed Kate.

Sarah nodded. 'I really, really do.'

'Well, that's settled then. But there *is* one condition.'

'Anything,' said Sarah eagerly.

'You have to tell your dad you're working with me.'

'Aw, really?' sighed Sarah. 'He'll go totally mental.'

'He's going to find out sooner or later anyway,' said Ethel gently. 'That's just the way things are around here.'

'Ethel's right. It's a miracle he hasn't already found out. Better coming from you than someone like Veronica.'

Sarah nodded. 'Okay.'

'I can talk to him about it if you need me to,' said Kate. It really cost her to say that. Every ounce of her being wanted to keep as much distance between her and Mike bloody Pendle as possible. But she owed it to Sarah to make this as easy as she could.

'Really?' said Sarah, surprise on her face. 'You'd do that?'

Kate nodded firmly. 'If it means we get to keep working together, then yes - I'll answer any questions he's got for me.'

'Thank you,' said Sarah, grinning at her, relief flooding her face. 'You're amazing.'

'You're not so bad yourself, you know,' laughed Kate.

CHAPTER 11

'Well then,' said Ethel from the doorway, brushing a tear from her eye. 'If you two have quite finished?'

Kate laughed and threw a cushion at Ethel, who caught it deftly.

'Right!' said Sarah, pulling herself together and nodding at Ethel. 'Kate – we've got something to show you.'

'You have?'

They both nodded. Sarah scrambled up from the floor and made her way over to the doorway - Stanley glued to her side. The three of them then stood staring at Kate with identical grins on their faces.

'Come on,' said Ethel, 'we need to go outside.'

'Don't you want to make the pizzas?' said Kate, getting to her feet.

'This won't take long. And trust me – you're going to want to see it.'

The four of them made a procession down the stairs, led by Sarah with Ethel bringing up the rear.

'Where are we going?' said Kate as they spilled out of the side door.

'Follow me!' said Ethel.

She led them around to the front of the café. Kate paused, half expecting them to be going into The Sardine.

'You know, we should have blindfolded her,' muttered Sarah.

'Ha – she'd never have agreed,' said Ethel.

'I might have!' said Kate with a snort.

'Well, too late now!' said Sarah, coming to a stop in front of Trixie's yard and pointing.

Kate's heart leapt. Somehow, she half expected to find that the pair of them had managed to work a miracle and get Trixie fixed early - but it wasn't that. She was dumbfounded by the sight that met her eyes.

Trixie was still nowhere to be seen, but neither was her grubby, unloved little yard.

'What on earth...?' murmured Kate, taking a couple of steps forwards before stopping again and bringing her hand to her mouth.

The wrought-iron gate stood wide open and the dim, slightly dank yard had been transformed into something straight out of a fairy tale. There was a gaggle of small tables - complete with a couple of chairs apiece - all set with blue and white striped linen tablecloths. The old stone walls around the sides looked like they had been swept, and now glittered with an array of tiny lights that had been strung across their rough surfaces.

All the random tat she usually stored in the yard along with Trixie had miraculously disappeared, and the cobbles had been weeded and swept. There was even an old barrel over in the corner that looked like it had been turned into a makeshift station for cutlery and condiments.

'This is just to give you an idea of what it could be like,' said Sarah, sounding excited. 'We had to do it quite quickly - we didn't want you turning up and ruining the surprise - but of course, there could be loads more decorations, and proper place settings and everything.'

'You two . . . you two did all this on your own?' asked Kate, unable to tear her eyes from the scene.

'Well no - Charlie helped,' said Ethel with a smile.

'He's a keeper, that one!' said Kate.

'Well, he's not mine to keep,' said Ethel quickly. 'Anyway - what do you think?' she pressed, gesturing at the yard.

'I love it. It would never have crossed my mind to use it like this!' she said, wandering forwards and running her hand across the back of one of the chairs. 'I mean, *how* have I never thought to use it like this? It's perfect. It's beautiful . . . and doesn't it look like it's already been part of the café for years?!' she laughed.

Kate couldn't believe this. There was more than enough room to navigate between the tables comfortably, and the view out through the gate, right down across the beach to the sea was magical.

'Well,' said Sarah, 'we were trying to figure out what we could do about space for more customers until you get the outdoor tables sorted out, and this idea came up. Without Trixie in here, we thought it was the perfect time to give it a go.'

'All the tables and chairs fold up, so you can still move them out of the way to lock Trixie in overnight,' said Ethel.

Kate nodded. 'Erm, where did you get them?'

'Borrowed them from the town hall,' said Ethel. 'They don't mind - they're hardly ever used!'

'Plus,' said Sarah, 'like we were talking about before, Trixie's trailer is sign-painted for The Sardine - so she's like an advertisement on wheels. It makes more sense for her to be parked up somewhere where visitors can spot her - at least during the day when you're not using her.'

Kate nodded again. A strange tingling sensation seemed to be travelling down her arms. Excitement? Fear of all this change? She wasn't sure which!

'Of course, if you don't like it, it's not the end of the world,' said Ethel, quietly moving closer and linking arms with her. 'All it means is that this place has had a much-needed tidy-up!' she chuckled.

'No - I *adore* it,' said Kate, staring around her. She pulled out one of the chairs, sat down and watched Stanley as he snuffled around the edges of the newly cleaned yard.

It *should* feel cramped, dark and unappealing in here, but it was quite the opposite. You could smell the salty sea air, but the walls provided shelter from the breeze and the blazing sunshine alike. It felt cosy and cute, and . . . pretty much perfect.

'We could add a few little decorative touches here and there like Sarah suggested,' said Kate thoughtfully, 'some leafy plants hanging here and there on the walls and in those little alcoves?'

Sarah nodded, looking around. 'That'd look brilliant - and maybe bring in a couple of seaside themed bits too?'

'Nice!' said Kate, then shook her head in disbelief. 'You realise this has more than doubled the seating we already had?'

Ethel nodded, plonking herself down in the chair next to Kate. 'That's not the best bit, though.'

'It's not?!' laughed Kate.

'Well no. We were thinking you could get one of the local sailmakers to rig something up overhead. It would give you even more shade when the sun's high as well as shelter if it rains. Then in the autumn and maybe some of the winter, you could pop one of those outdoor space heaters out here.'

'And if it's a sail instead of a proper roof, you could still roll it up and pack it away like you do with the awning when there's going to be high winds or whatever,' said Sarah

'You two've thought of everything!' grinned Kate.

'You ain't heard nothing yet!' said Sarah, excitedly.

'Well . . . no,' said Ethel. 'But how about we go get that ice cream you promised us before we carry on?'

'Ethel Watts!' laughed Kate, 'pudding before the main course? You rebel!'

Ethel grinned, looking more than a bit naughty. 'All this excitement has got me feeling . . . adventurous!'

∼

'So, here's a question for you both,' said Kate, taking a massive lick of Black Forest Gateau ice cream as they wandered, three-abreast with Stanley ambling along ahead of them, back towards West Beach. 'Do you think it would be worth opening the café on Sundays?'

'Nope,' chorused the other two at exactly the same time.

Kate spluttered out a laugh. 'Jeez, don't hold back!'

Sarah shrugged. 'How many customers did you just see in Nana's?'

'Well - three,' said Kate, 'if you count us.'

'And how many people do you see pottering around right now?' said Ethel, waving her mint choc-chip cone at the deserted seafront.

'Just us,' sighed Kate. 'Oh wait - there's Lionel down there.'

'He's painting,' laughed Sarah, staring down towards the sea where Lionel had set up his easel. 'He doesn't exactly count as a potential customer.'

'I bet you he'd be in at some point in the day if we opened on Sundays.'

'Well, yes,' said Ethel again, 'but he might well be the only one. We just don't get the visitors in town on Sundays. Not that we get that many any day of the week. I've never understood why Frank opens Nana's for the entire afternoon and evening on a Sunday, other than to make new stock!'

'Dad never opened any of the cafes on a Sunday,' said Sarah, shrugging. 'Don't think he's planning on doing it here either. He always said the cost of staffing was more than the takings - and that everyone should have one day where there's no chance of getting called into work for some emergency or other.' She paused, and suddenly look freaked out. 'Sorry, I shouldn't talk about him.'

Kate glanced at Sarah and shook her head. 'Don't apologise - that's actually really good advice. I *do* forget about things like having a life - The Sardine *is* my life. But you're totally right - it's good to have a day I can tell Pierre that I definitely won't be working.'

'Pfft,' said Ethel. 'Not sure *he's* a good enough reason, to be honest.'

'Oi!' laughed Kate. 'I'm happy, okay?'

'Are you really?' asked Ethel.

'Erm - is Stanley allowed down onto the beach?' asked Sarah sounding awkward. She grabbed hold of Stanley's collar just in time to stop him from launching down onto the sand.

'Here!' said Kate, taking his lead from her pocket and tossing it to Sarah. 'We'll keep him on that to slow him up a bit - but I reckon he'll be okay! A bit of saltwater would probably be quite good for his foot to be honest.'

Kate and Ethel watched as Sarah clipped the lead to Stanley's collar and then head down onto the sand with him.

'Anyway,' said Kate in a low voice now that Sarah was briefly out of earshot, 'bit rich you having a go about Pierre when you're pining for a certain Mr Endicott, isn't it?!'

'Pining?!' grunted Ethel. 'I'm hardly pining. He's in the café most days.'

'Yes, and we all know why that is,' retorted Kate.

Ethel nodded, a mulish expression on her usually

serene face. 'Because he's delivering your veg - and because he's now addicted to your coffee.'

'Oh, give over,' laughed Kate. 'The man's head over heels in love with you . . . and I'm starting to wonder if you might actually feel the same way?!'

'What would make you say that?' said Ethel, pushing past her and climbing down onto the beach.

'Oh nothing, just that you go bright pink any time anyone mentions him, and when you see him, or when you're talking about him,' said Kate following her friend down onto the sand. She kept her voice light and playful, but there was no chance Ethel was going to fob her off so easily this time.

Ethel glanced down the beach towards Sarah and Stanley who were pottering together along the tideline, Sarah now carrying her sandals so that she could paddle with Stanley. Then she turned back to Kate.

'So what if I *do* have feelings for him?' she practically growled, looking decidedly uncomfortable all of a sudden. 'There's nothing to be done.'

'There's *everything* to be done!' said Kate looking thrilled.

'No,' said Ethel decidedly, 'there isn't. I'm too old for any of that nonsense. And besides . . .'

'What?' prodded Kate gently. 'Besides, *what?*'

'He has never *once* told me that he feels anything for me. At all. It's probably just all in my head.'

'I promise you it isn't,' said Kate carefully.

'Well - even if it isn't, there is *no way* I'm doing or saying *anything* - understand? It's up to him to make the first move - not that he ever will. But until that happens, can we just *drop it?!*'

Kate could see that the usually serene Ethel was getting more than a little worked up and felt bad. It hadn't been her intention to upset her friend - only to encourage her. After all, if two people loved each other, like these two clearly did (at least - it was clear to the entire town, even if it wasn't to them) then surely they should be together? *Deserved* to be together. Life was far too short to miss out on things like true love.

'Can I just say one more thing, then I promise I'll shut up?'

Ethel gave a curt nod.

'Charlie isn't really the kind of man who tells you what he's thinking or how he feels, is he? He's the kind of man who shows you.'

'And how has he shown me?' said Ethel, raising an eyebrow.

'Well . . . answer me this. Has he ever come into the café without bringing you a gift of some kind?' she asked. 'And the other day when he rescued me and Stanley doesn't count!' she added quickly.

'He . . .' Ethel paused, her eyes seeming to unfocus as she thought about it. 'I . . .'

'Exactly,' said Kate.

Ethel frowned and then shook her head. 'Come

on, let's go and join those two for a paddle - we've still got loads of ideas to talk about, and today was meant to be about The Sardine, not our love lives!

Kate chuckled. 'Okay, you're on,' she said, linking her arm through Ethel's as they strode down the beach towards the sea.

CHAPTER 12

Kate cursed. The knock on the flat door made her jump so much that the pages she'd been carefully setting out on her coffee table fluttered to the floor.

'Balls,' she muttered again, hastily gathering them back together and dumping them in a heap onto the table. She'd just managed to get them in some kind of order too.

Kate wondered who it could be. In theory, no one other than Sarah and Ethel knew that she was hiding out up in her flat. They'd agreed that while Trixie was off the road, Kate would cancel her sandwich round rather than trying to borrow a car and use the time to do some much-needed planning while Ethel and Sarah manned the café. Most of the businesses she delivered to had agreed to pick up orders directly from The Sardine as it was only a short-term break - which was a huge relief.

Kate was busy delving deeper into the ideas they'd all brainstormed the other night - and she had to admit, she'd spent quite a lot of time quivering with both fear and excitement. Of course, they wouldn't be able to run with everything, but the possibilities seemed endless. Cake baking and simple cookery workshops, cute hen-do evenings in the yard, afternoon teas delivered on Trixie, weddings, cake subscription boxes . . . "a taste of the seaside" . . . the ideas were bonkers and wonderful.

Now Kate was busy gathering quotes, crunching the numbers and doing some market research to see what had legs. One thing was for sure, the little yard was already a huge hit with customers, and her visitor numbers were already going up.

Whoever was at the flat door thumped again and the sound was met by an echoing bark from Stanley who'd been snoozing in his bed.

'Stay there, lad,' she said.

Another knock sounded and she tutted.

'Alright, I'm coming, I'm coming!' she yelled,

Kate hurtled down the stairs hoping there wasn't some kind of emergency in the café - though surely they'd have just called her mobile? Flinging the door open, she stopped dead. There, in front of her, was the last person she'd expected to find on her doorstep.

'I think we need to talk,' said Mike Pendle.

'O-kay . . .' said Kate. Ah. Of course. Sarah must have finally spoken to him about her job at The Sardine. She should have been expecting this really. She was just about to take a step backwards to let him in, then abruptly changed her mind. 'What about?' she asked. She didn't want to assume this was about Sarah, only to find out it was something else.

'Sarah,' he said, raising his hands in the kind of gesture that said *"duh, what else?"*

Kate nodded. 'Okay, shall we go to the café?'

Mike shook his head. 'Maybe somewhere a bit more private?' he said, his face deadly serious. 'Somewhere Sarah can't hear us, I mean.'

'Well, I *would* invite you up,' said Kate, 'but Stanley's up there.'

Mike swallowed. 'Okay, how about a stroll on the beach?'

Kate shrugged. It was definitely better than having to invite her least favourite person up to her little sanctuary. 'Sure.'

'So,' said Kate as she pulled the door carefully closed behind her, 'I'm guessing Sarah has told you that she's been working for me?'

Mike nodded and glanced at her as they crossed the little road and headed down onto the sand. 'She has. I have to say, I'm quite surprised that you haven't been in touch before now - just as a courtesy.'

Uh oh. So this was going to be one of *those* kinds of conversations, was it?

Suddenly she was very glad that they were outside on the beach, with the soft breeze blowing through her hair and plenty of space around them, rather than trapped together in her flat.

'Well, to be honest, I would have spoken to you as soon as she started, but Sarah didn't actually tell me she was related to you until Sunday.'

'Ah, right. That explains a lot.' Mike sighed and frowned at the sea.

He looked quite bizarre down here in the fresh air. With a crisp white shirt and suit jacket over dark chinos and silly, pointy dress shoes, he stood out like a sore thumb. Kate briefly struggled to contain a smile. He really did have a lot to learn about living in Seabury.

'Look,' she said, 'don't be too hard on her. I think she just felt really awkward and didn't want it to affect her chances of getting the job.'

Mike nodded, frowning, but didn't say anything.

'She's a great worker - makes a mean cup of coffee, the customers love her, she's bursting with ideas and her baking is incredible!'

'Of course she's a great worker,' Mike snapped. 'Sorry. What I mean to say is that she's been in and out of cafes all her life - and she's been working in New York Froth at weekends for ages.'

'That explains why she's such a natural, then.'

Mike nodded. 'She told to me that she wanted to work with you because of learning more about the baking side of things. From Edna?'

'Ethel,' corrected Kate. 'She's a genius - it's a great opportunity for Sarah. It sounds like she really knows what she wants to do.'

'But she doesn't. She's just a kid!'

'Which makes it even more impressive!' exclaimed Kate. 'Just imagine how far she could take it if she follows her dream now.'

'There'll be plenty of time for all that after A-levels and university. I don't want her wasting her brain, and I don't want her working in a café when she could be studying.'

'Unless it's your café!' muttered Kate.

'That's different. You just want her because she comes pre-trained,' he spat. 'And what a *great* chance for you to pick her brains about my business.'

'You really do think a lot of yourself, don't you?' said Kate, incredulously. 'Of *course* it's a massive bonus that Sarah knows what she's doing and knows how to deal with customers - but I hired her before I knew she had anything to do with you.'

'But *now* you know, it's got to stop.'

'No, don't say that!' She took a deep breath, trying to stay calm. 'Look, Sarah seems to be happy at The Sardine - surely that's important to you?'

'Of course it bloody well is,' said Mike, raking his hand through his hair.

'Well then - let her stay. She's getting to know the locals and finding her place here! I'd never dream of getting in her way if - when you've opened up New York Froth - she wants to come back to work for you . . .'

Mike let out a bitter laugh. 'But she won't. It's all about the bloody baking for her.'

'Then I promise she'll learn loads with us, but I'd never put her in a position where I ask about your business, okay? For the moment, we've said it's just for the summer holidays - until she knows whether she's going back to school or on to college in September. I said we'd talk things through again then.'

'She'll be going back to school,' he said, his voice flat and determined. 'But if it's just for the summer then . . . fine, I guess it's okay.' Mike scuffed his shoe through the sand. 'How's Stanley now?

Kate's spine stiffened. 'Mending.'

'Thank goodness,' said Mike.

She tried to bite down the retort - for Sarah's sake, more than anything - but there was no stopping it. 'Like you care,' she muttered.

'*Excuse* me?! Look, Sarah told me about your accident. Actually, she yelled at me for it.'

'Can you blame her?'

'If I really had done what you think I did, then no - I wouldn't blame her - *or* you! But I didn't.'

'It was your car!'

'It *was* my car. My ex-wife came to pick it up from me - she got it in the divorce. I was just using it to get Sarah's stuff moved down here. If it really *was* my car that caused that accident - then it was *her* driving that day.'

Kate opened her mouth to retort, then closed it again. Was he telling the truth? She jumped as his hand shot out and gently caught hold of her arm, pulling her around to face him. 'You *have* to believe me. I would never, ever have done that.'

Kate stared at him feeling like her world had just tilted somehow. 'Well then,' she blustered, trying to wrap her head around this, 'tell your wife-'

'Ex-wife!'

'Yeah, her. You can tell her she's not welcome back here. And it's not a good idea for her to come anywhere near me.'

Mike raised an eyebrow. 'Well, no. After witnessing your protective streak first-hand, I can see she'd have quite a lot to worry about.'

'Then tell her to stay away,' growled Kate.

'Nah,' said Mike, and for the very first time, Kate saw a tiny smile pull at the corner of his mouth, his eyes taking on a mischievous look. 'I'd actually pay good money to see you take her down.' He cleared his throat. 'For what it's worth, I'm *really* sorry that happened to you and Stanley and . . . Trixie?'

Kate raised an eyebrow. The fact he'd just called Trixie by her name rather than "that heap of rust" made her realise that he was trying to make an effort. Damn. It was much easier when she could just straight-out hate him.

'Well, I guess I owe you an apology,' she muttered, 'for yelling at you - especially in front of your staff.'

'Nah. The guys thought it was hilarious.'

'Oh.' Kate scratched her nose. 'Who were those guys anyway?'

'Why? Want to poach them to do some work on your place?'

'You don't give up do you?' she said, incredulously. 'For one thing, no, and for another, if I wanted work done on my place, I'd hire local builders from here in Seabury. You'll have put an awful lot of noses out of joint by bringing them in when we've got great guys here in town who *need* the work.'

Mike shrugged. 'That's business.'

'It's not how business is done in Seabury. We support our own. We try to keep cash *within* our community. It's how it works.'

'Well, these guys are from Plymouth. They're about half the price and hiring them means I can open up much sooner and give you a run for your money.'

Kate let out an exasperated sound.

'What?!' he demanded.

'Nothing. I need to get back.'

'Oh yeah - Sarah mentioned - you've gotta work

out a plan now the council's causing you problems, I guess?'

'I . . . you . . .' spluttered Kate.

'What?'

'Nothing. But if you *ever* need someone to tell you how things *really* work around here - you know, when you decide that you actually want to fit in rather than alienating everyone around you and getting the council to do your dirty work - *do* come and visit!'

'You know, you really need to get your facts straight!' said Mike, his eyes flashing.

'Are you or are you not employing a bunch of people to work on fitting up your café who have to drive in from Plymouth every day?'

'I am, but-'

'Instead of the local guys?'

'Yes and I already told you why - but-'

'Then I rest my case,' said Kate.

'Look. If you want The Sardine to survive, you need to open your eyes and accept reality!' he said, starting to raise his voice in agitation.

'And you need to stop being a . . . a . . .'

'A what?' he demanded.

'A grumpy badger!' she spat, turning on her heel and marching across the sand, putting as much distance between them as quickly as she could.

CHAPTER 13

'What happened, what happened, what happened?' chanted Sarah the minute Kate walked into the café.

Kate slumped into one of the chairs and Sarah followed suit in the one opposite her.

'Give her a second, girl!' said Ethel, tutting at her from the kitchen, and watching Kate in concern as she rested her head in her hands. 'Okay - that's a long enough second, Kate. What happened!'

Kate quickly looked around her. 'No customers?'

'Plenty,' laughed Ethel, 'but they're all out in the yard. 'Come on, quick. I've got a round of teacakes toasting.'

'Well,' said Kate, 'I'm guessing you know Mike - your dad, I mean - came up to see me.'

'Course we do,' nodded Sarah, 'we told him where you were!'

'Yeah - thanks so much for that!' muttered Kate.

'*Annnnnnd?*' demanded Sarah. 'Do I still have a job? What happened?'

'Well - I, erm, I just called your dad a . . . a . . . grumpy badger,' said Kate, wincing and burying her face in her hands.

Sarah let out a massive snort and Ethel started chuckling from behind the counter.

'Guys! It's not funny!!'

'Are you kidding? That's frickin' hilarious. Oooh, I'm never going to let him live that one down. It's going in every single birthday card, every-'

'Don't you dare, or you're sacked,' said Kate, glaring at Sarah.

Sarah, however, didn't even flinch. 'So, does that mean I've still got a job to be sacked from, then?' she asked.

Kate nodded. 'Yes. For the summer. As long as you don't tell me anything about his business!'

'Like I would anyway. Well, that's better than nothing,' said Sarah with a grin.

'Yep - he said you'll be going back to school in September . . .'

Sarah's smile dropped.

'Don't look like that. It gives us plenty of time to figure out a plan to convince him college is right for you - if that's what you want.'

'You'd help me do that?'

'Course we will,' said Ethel, 'on one condition.'

'Which is?'

'Take this lot out to table six for me!' she said pointing at a tray laden with buttery teacakes.

'You've got it!' said Sarah, leaping to her feet, grabbing the tray and heading straight outside.

'So, how'd it really go? From what you just told Sarah, that's a great outcome, so why the dramatics?' asked Ethel.

'Mike just told me it was his ex-wife who ran me and Stanley off the road,' she muttered. 'Not him.'

'Oh.'

'You already knew, didn't you?' said Kate, staring at her.

'Sarah told me this morning.'

'And you didn't think to warn me?'

'It was a bit late by then, love. Mike was already at your door!'

'I'm so embarrassed. I went absolutely ape-sh- . . . bananas at him the other day!'

Ethel bit her lip, clearly trying to stop herself from laughing. 'I know. But I'm sure he understood? I mean, you didn't know at that point if Stanley was going to be okay, did you? And you were in shock yourself.'

Kate nodded, cupping her face in her hands. 'He understood. And he did apologise for what his ex did - even though it had nothing to do with him other than happening in his old car. I mean, he brought the subject up to start with -

asked how Stanley was - and he doesn't even like dogs!'

'Who?' said Sarah, bouncing back through the door. 'My dad?'

Ethel nodded at her.

'Yeah, well - there's a reason for that. He'd hate me telling you though.'

'Better not, then,' said Kate, though she was definitely intrigued.

Sarah shrugged. 'Okay. It's pretty nasty, actually.'

Ethel raised her eyebrows at Kate, who subtly shook her head. She was going to start as she meant to go on - she was *never* going to put Sarah in the position where she felt like she was snitching on her dad.

'Oh,' said Sarah, 'one thing I did find out that I think you should know - and then I promise we'll go back to pretending that I don't even know him - he's the one who paid Stanley's vet bill.'

'He *what?!*' said Ethel and Kate at the same time.

'Yup. Sounds like he was so worried after you'd been to see him that day, he called to find out if Stanley was going to be okay and paid for the x-ray and everything.'

'But why?!' said Kate. 'He didn't even know that . . . that . . . erm . . .'

'That my bitch of a mother was responsible?' said Sarah. 'He'll have put two and two together.'

Kate flinched and she saw Ethel nearly drop the

teacup she was holding. It was the first time Sarah had ever mentioned her mum. She looked at the girl's face, trying to judge whether this was something they needed to talk about or brush straight past for now.

'It's okay,' said Sarah. 'I know what she's like. Always have. She's a nasty piece of work and I've had to put up with her for years. She only had me because dad wanted kids. *She* told me that. When I was about six. That's why I'm so happy dad's finally away from her and I get to live with him!'

'Oh. Okay,' said Kate, thrown by the matter-of-fact way the girl had just delivered these heartbreaking titbits. *Poor Sarah!*

'Look, dad's been through the shittiest of shit times,' said Sarah in a low voice. 'I *know* he can be a bit of a prat. He's like captain awkward when it comes to change, and making friends, and talking to new people. But underneath everything, he's actually really kind. A good guy.'

Sarah paused and Kate watched her try to regain full control of her feelings a moment.

'Though,' said Sarah, raising an eyebrow as a smirk appeared on her face, 'I think Grumpy Badger is still going to be his name from now until the day he dies!'

Spotting an elderly couple in the doorway, Sarah quickly plastered a professional smile on her face. 'Good morning! We've got seats in here or there are still tables available out in our gorgeous courtyard if you'd prefer?'

This transition to smooth waitress-mode almost made Kate laugh out loud.

'Ooh, courtyard please!' said the elderly woman, beaming at Sarah.

'Of course, let me take you to a table and we'll bring your order out to you.'

Sarah led them back outside and Kate turned, open-mouthed to Ethel who was standing in the kitchen with her hand over her heart.

'Well I never!' said the older woman. 'He paid for Stanley!'

'Right?' said Kate. 'Now I feel even worse!'

'Nothing that can't be solved by a proper, calm apology at some point, love,' said Ethel. 'But I have to ask, what's with the Grumpy Badger bit?'

'He was being a prat about business stuff, and the issues with the council - which *he* caused - and about using that company from Plymouth instead of the guys from Seabury! And I just lost it and told him that when he wanted to find out how things worked around here, he should come to me, as long as he'd stopped being-'

'A grumpy badger?' snorted Ethel.

'Precisely.'

Sarah's bombshell had completely derailed Kate's day, so when Charlie turned up with several extra crates laden with soft fruit, it took her a moment or two to figure out what was going on.

'Yer order, Kate! I have to say, I'm *that* excited about the idea of being able to get a box of cakes every week. And everyone up at the allotments loves the idea of your cream tea packs too!'

Kate shook her head and forced herself back to life. The cake boxes - of course! That's why she'd ordered so much fruit! She, Ethel and Sarah had decided to trial the cake subscription boxes locally - as well as another gem of an idea - cream tea in a box. Scones, jam, cream and some fancy-pants, individually wrapped teabags. Ethel had promptly declared that she'd better get more jam made, so Kate had asked Charlie to help her out.

'Couldn't grab a cuppa and a cheese toastie while I'm here, could I?' he asked.

'Of course,' said Ethel.

'Thanks. Tis hot work picking these blighters,' he said, pointing at the plump gooseberries.

'Just you wait until I've had my way with them,' she beamed, 'I'll save a jar for you.'

'Much obliged,' he murmured turning pink. 'Oh. Wait a sec - I'll be right back.'

He scuttled back out of the café and Kate, who'd started ferrying the crates of fruit into the tiny, cool store cupboard at the back of the café to keep them fresh for later, raised her eyebrows. 'What was all that about?'

'No idea,' said Ethel, starting to grate fresh cheese for a toastie with a little smile on her face.

'*I* know!' said Sarah, nodding at the door.

The other two turned just in time to see Charlie reappear with a huge bunch of flowers in his arms.

'I brought these for you, Ethel, from the allotments.'

'For me?'

Charlie nodded.

Ethel dumped the block of cheese back onto the chopping board and hurried around the counter towards him.

Kate paused in the kitchen, not wanting to interrupt by going over to fetch the last crate of fruit.

'I thought you might like 'em?' said Charlie, thrusting the flowers into Ethel's arms.

'They're beautiful!' she breathed, inspecting the different blooms.

'Tha's larkspur, and that deep purple is-'

'Dahlia!' she said with a sigh of happiness. 'My-'

'Favourite,' said Charlie, nodding. 'And then those white ones are campanula.'

'Oh Charlie, they're gorgeous, thank you!'

'Tis my pleasure. Picked 'em mesself.'

Kate jumped as Sarah squeeze her hand in excitement. The two of them were now standing, watching the little scene unfold in rapt silence.

'So - what was it you wanted to drink with your toastie?' asked Ethel lightly, unable to take her eyes off the flowers, but clearly making a valiant attempt to get back onto more familiar ground.

'Tea please.'

'Tea?'

Charlie nodded. 'Tea. I'll take a pot if you care to share one?'

'I . . . well . . . we're quite busy . . .' she said, flustered, turning to Kate as if looking for help.

'You're due a break!' said Kate.

Ethel glared at her. Clearly that wasn't the response she'd been looking for.

'I'll finish off Charlie's toastie and bring it out to you, if you'd like to sit outside?' said Sarah, a mischievous grin on her face.

'Tha's right kind of you,' said Charlie, smiling at her.

'I'll get these in some water and be out in a mo,' said Ethel, ushering Charlie back out of the café. As soon as he was out of sight she turned to the pair of them in the kitchen. 'Interfering wenches,' she spluttered, making them both laugh.

'I'll take those,' said Kate, grabbing the flowers from her friend. 'I'll pop them in some water and stand them out with the fruit to keep them cool.'

Ethel was still glaring back and forth between the two of them.

'Why are you still here?' laughed Sarah. 'Your

date's waiting!'

'I . . . I . . .' Ethel cleared her throat. 'He knew my favourite flower,' she finally managed to say.

'I know - how cute!' said Sarah, not looking at her as she carefully moved Charlie's toastie onto the grill.

'I'm nervous,' said Ethel in a quiet voice.

Kate stared at her, open-mouthed. 'Why? It's just Charlie. You've known him forever.'

'But . . . he knew my favourite flower,' she said again, wonder in her voice, as if she was confirming the fact to herself rather than speaking to Kate. 'This changes *everything!*'

'It's a cup of tea with a friend,' said Kate stoutly, watching Ethel carefully now. She'd never seen her like this before, and Kate wondered if Ethel was considering making a dash for her cottage instead of joining Charlie outside. 'Just a cup of tea with lovely Charlie,' she repeated.

'Right. You're right,' said Ethel, giving herself a little shake. 'I won't be long.'

'Take as long as you need. Oh - and invite him to the party while you're out there? I forgot earlier!' said Kate.

They both watched her march out of The Sardine and turn towards the yard, and then Kate turned to look at Sarah.

'Well!' said Kate.

'I *know!*' said Sarah with a huge smile on her face. 'Charlie's about to get *so* lucky!'

CHAPTER 14

The rest of the week disappeared in a haze of preparations for the party. It had been Sarah's idea to get a bunch of their regulars together one evening, make use of their gorgeous new courtyard, and have a tasting session for their various cake-box recipes.

'I mean, who can say no to free champers and cake, right?!' she'd said with a grin.

Kate and Ethel had both agreed that it was a great idea - but that had been when it had been a theory rather than a reality. But the incredible summer weather they were experiencing in Seabury brought a wave of new visitors to the town - and as most of them were staying with Veronica at The Pebble Street Hotel, they invariably ended up at The Sardine for a much needed second breakfast - and tended to come back for lunch as well.

Kate had now lost count of the number of times she'd been asked if they did evening meals at The Sardine, and she was starting to seriously consider it as an option.

'One new idea at a time!' was Ethel's wise warning the day before, when she'd floated the idea past her.

Kate couldn't blame her. Ethel's workload had just skyrocketed due to the cake-box plan - and she was in full-flow, perfecting the samples for the party on Saturday night.

Sarah, who'd proven herself to be the perfect right-hand-man for Ethel on the baking front, had begged for the previous day off. She'd been invited to go shopping with her friends over in Plymouth, followed by what sounded like a very giggly, girly sleepover. Of course, Kate had agreed immediately. Trixie was still out of action, so Kate had covered the café herself, leaving Ethel free to obsess about tweaking cake recipes.

'Usual, Lionel?' said Kate as he strode into the café with a beaming smile.

'Yes please! No Sarah again - is she well?'

'She's due in any moment!' said Kate, firing up the Italian Stallion for what already felt like the thousandth time that morning. 'She had a well-earned day off to hang out with her friends yesterday, and she'll be in to help Ethel with more party preparations this afternoon, while I man the fort here.'

'Jolly good!' said Lionel. 'I've grown quite fond of

that little firecracker already. Shame her father's such a... well, you know.'

Kate bit down on an uncomfortable smile. 'I hate to say it, but I don't think he's quite as bad as he seemed at first.'

'How so?' demanded Lionel. 'Charlie told me about your accident. Surely you haven't forgiven him for hurting our boy?' he said, laying his hand on Stanley's head - because, of course, he was already under the table. Stanley knew that if Lionel was here, that meant toast-treats at any moment.

'Well, I'm afraid I was mistaken there,' said Kate, now feeling decidedly awkward. 'It wasn't him driving. Apparently, it was his rather unsavoury ex-wife.'

'Oh. Well! That's quite a turn up for the books.'

Kate nodded, piling Lionel's toast onto a plate and bringing it over to his table.

'Thank you,' he said with a grateful nod. 'Well, I do have to say that I'm relieved in a way - it felt pretty uncomfortable having someone that inconsiderate living with us here in Seabury.'

Kate nodded again. She knew what he meant. Her own feelings about Mike Pendle were now so muddled, she didn't know what to think. On one hand, he'd been so concerned to hear that Stanley had been hurt that he'd called the vet himself to check up on him and then anonymously covered the bill. But, on the other hand, he'd complained to the council about The Sardine and had her outdoor tables removed. Add to that the fact that he'd generally been a bit of a . . . well, a bit of a Grumpy Badger about Sarah . . . she really didn't know what to think anymore.

The picture Sarah had painted was of a kind and considerate father who she'd actively wanted to live with after the divorce. A little strict and blinkered when it came to the possibilities for her future perhaps, but certainly a parent who doted on his daughter.

'Earth to Kate?' laughed Lionel.

'Sorry Lionel!'

'Where were you, anywhere nice?'

Kate smiled. 'Just trying to work out our Mr Pendle, if I'm honest. He's still a bit of an enigma!'

'Ah, the joys of new blood in a town as small as ours, eh?' chuckled Lionel, taking a sip of his coffee. 'Nothing like a new character to study.'

Kate nodded, wondering if she should tell him about the fact that Mike had paid Stanley's vet bill, but promptly decided against it. Something told her that he hadn't done it for praise and might not like that particular bit of information bandied around.

'So, have you asked him to the party?' said Lionel. 'Charlie and I can't wait!'

Kate's mouth dropped open. 'You know, I haven't,' she said, suddenly feeling bad. It wasn't that she'd actively decided against it, she just hadn't even considered it in the first place. 'How awful of me! I'll make sure I send an invitation back with Sarah this evening.'

'Good girl,' he said approvingly. 'You know, your dad really would be proud of the woman you've become.'

Kate smiled at him. 'That means a lot. Though I somehow doubt he'd have approved quite so much if he'd seen me screaming at the poor guy after Stanley got hurt, and then calling him a grumpy badger last time I saw him!'

Lionel chuckled. 'Oh I don't know, even your gentle old dad could be quite peppery when roused.'

Kate laughed, nodding. She loved the fact that she lived in a town where every single local helped her to keep the memory of her wonderful dad alive. When he'd died, so many people had asked her if she was going to move away from Seabury "for a fresh start" and "to escape the memories" - but being here, where her history was known and cherished by so many people, was one of the biggest comforts of her life.

'So,' said Kate, plopping down into one of the empty chairs for a brief moment's respite, 'while she's not here, any gossip on the Ethel and Charlie front?'

'Only that I don't think I've seen Charlie smile so much in his entire life,' said Lionel, feeding Stanley a toast crust, which disappeared in record speed.

'But what's been said?' prodded Kate, excitedly. 'All I know is that he brought her the most beautiful bunch of flowers, Ethel went all mushy because he knew what her favourites were, they shared a pot of tea while Ethel had a break and that was that!'

Lionel shrugged. 'Yes, but it meant far more than that, I think. Ethel asked Charlie to the party.'

'Because I told her to!'

'Yes, but Charlie saw it as a sign - a good sign.'

'Well, I really hope he makes the next move, otherwise they're doomed to remain friends forever!' said Kate, shaking her hair back and heaving herself to her feet again.

'Would that be so bad?' asked Lionel.

'Not bad - but when they both love each other...'

'You think Ethel returns his feelings then?' asked Lionel, his eyes shining.

'Actually, yes - I do.'

'Then, my girl, we shall watch with interest, won't we?!'

'What'll we watch with interest?' demanded Sarah, bouncing into the café and promptly dropping to her knees to give Stanley his customary cuddle which he returned with interest. 'Morning gang!'

'Ah, there's our girl,' smiled Lionel. 'Just in time to make me coffee number two. I've got a painting to finish off today, so I need my go-go juice!'

'Coming right up,' said Sarah, hauling herself to her feet and heading to wash her hands. 'Anyway - what are we watching with interest?' she said again, going to the fridge for the milk and pouring it into a frother jug.

'Oh . . . erm . . .' hedged Lionel.

'Just which cake combinations will prove to be the favourites at the party!' invented Kate quickly.

'My money's on the rhubarb streusel cupcakes!' said Sarah. 'They're still my faves.'

The landline started to ring, making Kate jump. The thing virtually never rang, and the sound sent a nervous thrill through her for some reason.

'Sarah, mind doing a quick tour around the yard to check everyone's okay once you've done that?' she asked, reaching for the receiver.

Sarah gave her the thumbs up, delivered Lionel's fresh coffee, then headed straight outside.

∽

'Well, that's good news - in a way,' said Kate, replacing the receiver just as Sarah strode back into the café with three new orders to work through.

'What's happened?' she asked.

'Trixie'll be ready to pick up on Friday.'

'How's that "in a way" - surely that's brilliant news?'

'Well yeah - but typical because we've got the party the day after, so I'll have nowhere to park her!'

'Just bung her on the pavement outside until we're done!' shrugged Sarah.

Kate huffed. 'Not with-' she stopped abruptly, looking awkward. 'Not with the *council* looking to find fault,' she amended quickly. She'd been about to bad-mouth Mike, and she'd sworn not to do that in front of her.

'Okay,' said Sarah, 'so park her in one of the spots in front of dad's place. They're public spaces, and she should be safe there - you've got a chain for her and that weird lock thing for the trailer, haven't you?'

Kate nodded. She hadn't even thought about one of the public parking spots. They were free . . . but it really was *super* cheeky to park right outside her new rival, wasn't it?!

'Wouldn't your dad mind?' she said.

Sarah shrugged. 'He's not even open yet. It won't be for long - and not like it's on his launch day or anything!'

'Sarah makes good points,' put in Lionel. 'I think you're worrying too much!'

Kate shrugged. 'Great. Well, that's sorted then!'

'Right ladies, I'm off. Give my best to Ethel when she comes in, tell her not to overdo it before the party! She's got to be fresh and all bright-eyed and bushy-tailed for her date with Charlie.'

Kate nodded. 'I'll give her your love - but there's no way I'm saying the rest of it - I value my life too highly!'

Lionel saluted, gave Stanley a last pat and they waved him off.

'Is Ethel okay?' asked Sarah.

Kate nodded. 'She's fine - may be getting a *little* bit stressed. She missed your help yesterday, I think.'

'God, I'm really sorry,' said Sarah looking anxious.

'No, I didn't mean it like that! You deserved a day off after everything you've been doing! What I meant was - I think you two make an excellent team. But I do think we need to consider another member of staff, don't you?'

Sarah cocked her head thoughtfully and then nodded. 'Yep. I mean Ethel's amazing, but she's only meant to be doing your cakes and just occasionally helping out, isn't she? And she's been pretty much full-time since I started.'

Kate nodded. Sarah was right. Ethel was so feisty and quick to offer her help, it was too easy to forget that she was in her seventies. She'd taken on a lot to help her out - especially since the accident - but Kate didn't want to take advantage of her.

'Let's get this party over and done with and then I'll start looking for someone else. I got way too lucky with you, you know - you breezed in and spoilt us!'

Sarah blushed and kicked the heel of her converse against the floor. 'Thanks, Kate.'

Kate gave her a friendly nudge with her elbow.

'One thing,' said Sarah, 'when you do get someone new - make sure they're into baking too.'

Kate raised her eyebrows. 'Really? Surely that's your thing . . . and I'd never replace Ethel's cakes . . .'

'Yeah - but if you want the cake boxes to take off, it just makes sense to bring in someone who's at least got a passion for that side of things. I mean, even if you decide against carrying on with the cake subscriptions at some point - a baker's never going to go to waste here, are they? Plus - it's an added bonus for me if there's someone else's brain to pick!' she laughed.

'Okay, you've got it!' said Kate. 'So, how was your sleepover?'

'Epic!' grinned Sarah. 'It was like being a little kid again. We got pizzas and pick'n'mix and did face masks and watched cartoons!'

'You're not a normal teenager, are you? You're an alien!'

Sarah giggled. 'The only gross bit was when Tina's mum came home. We were all hanging out in the living room, and she didn't realise, and her and her boyfriend came in glued to each other's faces like limpets!'

Kate snorted. 'Did they see you?'

'Only when Tina started making puking sounds. I think they'd have ended up naked before they realised there were six teenagers in the room otherwise. Then they disappeared upstairs. One guess where they were going!' she paused for a moment and sighed. 'Tina hates it. This guy just drops in like once a week and then disappears, and then turns up again when he wants another shag. She thinks he's using her mum because she's a bit . . . you know . . . vulnerable. Because Tina's dad left.'

'That sounds horrible!' said Kate.

Sarah shrugged. 'Total slimeball. Made me feel really lucky that dad's pretty cool. He'd never do something like that.'

'Ooh - well reminded!' said Kate. 'Sorry to change the subject, but before I forget, would you mind if I invite your dad to the party?'

Sarah smiled at her. 'No. Course not. Actually, I bet he'll be chuffed. Ever since he found out I work here, he won't shut up about you.'

Kate's smile froze on her face. 'What do you mean?' she asked, trying to keep her tone light.

'Oh, you know - tons and tons of questions! Don't worry - I never tell him anything.'

'Right,' muttered Kate as Sarah rushed off to serve a couple of women who'd just come in.

She couldn't believe it. He'd been so worried about the possibility of Sarah discussing New York Froth with her - now here *he* was, questioning Sarah about The Sardine! So much for grumpy badger - hypocritical badger might be closer to the mark. And now she'd told Sarah about inviting him to the party, there was no way she could do a U-turn.

Balls. Bloody Mike Pendle had struck again.

CHAPTER 15

'Paula - you're early!' said Kate, rushing over to give her friend a hug then realising that she was still carrying a pile of Tupperware. 'Two secs,' she laughed, heading into the yard and handing the boxes over to Sarah.

She couldn't believe how fast the weekend had arrived, but now that the party was almost here, Kate was a mixture of anxiety and excitement. She quickly handed over the last batch of cakes to Sarah, who was busy setting up the stands and setting out the goodies - one variety per table - along with voting slips so that everyone could leave comments and vote on their favourites.

'Right - come here,' she said, turning back to Paula and pulling her into a massive hug. As she stepped back, Kate subtly looked her friend up and down. She was pretty sure she'd lost weight, but at least she looked alert and a lot healthier than she had a couple of weeks ago. 'You're looking gorgeous!' she said.

'Thanks, Kate,' said Paula, giving her a soft smile. 'So - who're you expecting this evening? Blimey, it looks like you've invited half the town if those piles of cakes are anything to go by.'

'Half the town?' laughed Kate, 'I think I invited pretty much the *whole* town, to be honest!'

'Of course you did,' chuckled Paula. 'That's so like you!'

Kate shrugged. 'Well - I think everyone from the allotments is coming, all the Chilly Dippers of course, Veronica, Lionel, some of the town councillors-'

'Good move,' said Paula, pinching one of Sarah's now-famous apple macarons off the top of the nearest pyramid and taking a bite. 'Oh my sainted aunts - that's *heavenly!*'

'Sarah's a genius!' said Kate with a shrug.

'Really good call on inviting the council though - shows no hard feelings on the whole table licence thing.'

'Yeah, well,' said Kate frowning, 'I should have made sure I'd covered my backside, shouldn't I? I've invited Mike Pendle too,' she added in a low voice so that Sarah didn't hear her.

'You have?' said Paula. 'That's very forgiving of you!'

'Have to admit I regretted it pretty much straight away.'

'Well - he's part of the town now. You may as well try and get on, right?'

Kate nodded. 'That's basically what Lionel said too.'

'Well - he's pretty wise,' she grinned.

'Yeah, but Sarah said he's been asking loads of questions about The Sardine!' muttered Kate.

'But you've got nothing to hide.'

Kate stared at her friend for a second then laughed. 'Trust you to give me a new perspective so easily. You're right! Thanks.'

'You're welcome! Hey, Kate . . . do you reckon we could go for a walk, just us two - and Stanley, of course - and maybe have a bit of a picnic? Soon?'

Kate frowned at her friend, a spike of concern going through her again. It wasn't that she didn't want to spend more time with her friend - of *course* she did. But the way she'd just asked felt so . . . formal.

Paula laughed. 'Don't look at me like that! You've just been mega-busy recently, and the selfish being that I am - I'd really like some "Kate-time"' she grinned.

'You know, I'd really love that,' said Kate, nodding. 'You're right, we've barely had a chance to chat, have we? Time just seems to disappear, doesn't it?'

Paula nodded, and Kate could swear that a tiny

flash of sadness crossed her friend's face before being quickly replaced by another smile.

'Now - what can I do to help,' asked Paula.

'Just chill?' said Kate, knowing full-well this wouldn't cut it.

'Kate Hardy - give me a job to do this instant!'

'Okay, okay!' laughed Kate, holding up her hands in surrender. 'Well, if you wouldn't mind - could you pop into the kitchen and check if Ethel needs a hand with anything, while I help Sarah finish off out here? I need to get the champagne glasses lined up and ready to roll!'

'You've got it!' said Paula, giving her a quick kiss on the cheek before heading towards The Sardine to check on Ethel.

Kate knew that the older woman would have everything perfectly under control - as usual - but she might welcome an extra pair of hands, nonetheless.

She made her way over to Sarah, who shot her a quick grin before looking back down at the paper napkin she was folding. She'd finished setting out the cakes, and the gorgeous stands with their mountains of sweet treats looked really rather special. Kate couldn't wait to see what everyone's favourites were.

'Paula loved your apple macarons!' she said, settling in to help Sarah.

'Yay!'

'Where's Stanley?' Kate asked, glancing around.

Sarah had been left to keep an eye on him as Kate had been rushing back and forth between the kitchen and the yard for the past hour or so, ferrying boxes and tables, chairs and cake stands, and bottle after bottle of champagne.

Sarah pointed to the corner, and Kate looked over and spotted a pair of furry hind legs sticking out from behind one of the trestle tables.

'He had a good snuffle around, checked for any crumbs we'd missed, and now he's having a pre-party nap,' laughed Sarah.

'Gathering his strength - he'll be petted to within an inch of his life later,' laughed Kate, 'but on the plus side, we won't have many cake crumbs to clear up afterwards! Oh crikey, I hadn't thought - will your dad be okay with Stanley being here?'

'I guess he'll just have to keep his distance,' said Sarah.

'It's such a shame,' said Kate quietly.

'Yeah,' said Sarah, grabbing another napkin and folding it carefully. 'See, his dad - my grandad - really wasn't a nice guy. Used to own this Alsatian when dad was a kid, and it sounds like he was absolutely vile to it. Made it really aggressive. Then if dad was ever naughty, he'd basically use the dog to punish him.'

Kate froze, a look of horror on her face. 'You're joking?' she said.

Sarah shrugged. 'He didn't make it actually attack

him, I don't think,' said Sarah, 'but he'd send dad to his room and then basically set the dog at the open door to stand guard. If dad got too close, it would snarl and snap - bare its teeth - that sort of thing.'

'No wonder he reacted badly when he first saw Stanley.'

Sarah shrugged again. 'It's not so bad if he gets some warning. Like, he knows Stanley might be around tonight, so he'll be expecting it and will have the chance to prepare.'

'But he *is* definitely coming?' said Kate.

Sarah nodded. 'I think he's looking forward to it. Hopefully, he might have stopped muttering about Trixie by then,' she laughed.

'Ah. So - the parking spot didn't go down too well then?' said Kate, pulling a face.

'Not so much - as we expected. Nothing he can do about it though, is there?!' said Sarah.

'I'll be sure to tell him I won't make a habit of it once he's open,' laughed Kate.

'I wouldn't worry - he'll be on his best behaviour tonight. He's probably pretty nervous.'

'Nervous?' laughed Kate. 'Your dad?'

'You know, I still think you might have the wrong impression about him,' said Sarah quietly.

Kate wasn't sure what to say. She really didn't want to upset Sarah.

'Well, it'll be nice to have him here,' she said, hoping it was a gentle full-stop on the conversation for now. Because, really, Kate no longer knew what to think about Mike Pendle, and every time he was mentioned a strange little fluttering sensation hit her in the chest. She had no idea if it was caused by a bit of left-over anger towards him or . . . perhaps something a bit more troubling!

Half of her was still livid with him for being an interfering, council-dobbing know-it-all, and the other half now really felt for the scared little boy Sarah had just told her about. And - even though the maths didn't add up - the third half of her admired his generosity and his love for his daughter. Mike Pendle was a conundrum.

∼

'Thank you all so much for coming!' said Kate, addressing the crowd filling their little yard. She usually hated any kind of public speaking, but this was different. Yes, there were so many people crammed in here that they spilled out onto the pavement - but every single person here was familiar to her. This was her family - her beloved Seabury - who'd come out en masse to support her.

'I'm not going to keep you. Go forth and drink all the bubbly, try all the cakes, and don't forget to leave us your comments and vote for your favourites. You'll be able to sign up for one of our weekly cake subscription boxes or treat yourself to a cream-tea pack - from Monday!'

A massive cheer went up, complete with loud pops as Charlie and Ethel sent the corks flying on a couple of fresh bottles of bubbly. Kate was about to go over and give them a hand to pass out the glasses when she felt a hand on her arm. She turned to find a short, rather dumpy woman with a shock of white-blond hair and bright fuchsia lipstick smiling at her.

'Councillor Jones!' said Kate in surprise. 'So glad you could make it.' She'd invited all of the town councillors, but she'd hardly expected any of them to turn up.

'Well, thank you for inviting me!' said the councillor, bending over to ruffle Stanley's ears. 'Hello boy!' she crooned. 'I heard about your accident. He's all better I hope?' she asked, straightening back up.

'Yes - he's fine now, thank goodness.'

'Good. So - congratulations on your wonderful new ideas,' she said. 'I've already tested the macarons, the mini-fudge-flapjacks and, of course, I'm no stranger to Ethel's scones!' she laughed. 'You can count on me as one of your first customers.'

Kate smiled warmly at her. 'Thank you so much. I really appreciate your support.'

'Not at all - I love my cake,' she laughed. 'And it will be a real boon for the town too. Now then, have you thought about building your social media presence?' she demanded.

Kate shook her head, feeling slightly bewildered. 'Not really. All my customers are locals, other than the random visitors who stumble in, of course!'

'Well - you should. It would be great for The Sardine and could bring more visitors to the town too, make it a bit of a destination . . . think about it!'

Kate nodded. The idea made her shudder slightly, but maybe there *wouldn't* be any harm in sharing a few photographs of her favourite place in the entire world - and mix in a bit of cakey-goodness while she was at it! 'Okay - I'll have a chat with the others and see what they think.'

'Wonderful. Oh, and Kate,' said the councillor, now eyeing a mountain of gooey chocolate brownies on a nearby table, 'the licence for your outdoor seating is in the post. Should be with you on Monday.'

Kate beamed at her. She might not be *quite* so desperate for it now that she had the yard set up, but it would be good to have that spot back too. Her two little tables under the awning had been there ever since she'd first opened the café. Now that Trixie was back in action as well, it really felt like everything was falling into place again.

'Thank you,' she said warmly.

'Congratulations again,' smiled the councillor. 'The Sardine is a real asset to Seabury, as are you.'

Kate watched her move away towards the brownies, then bent down to give Stanley a hug.

'Hear that, boy?' she whispered, burying her face in his soft fur for a moment. 'We're an asset.'

'Don't get used to it. They're a fickle bunch.'

The voice from above made Kate's jaw clench in spite of her happy mood. She stood back up and plastered a fake smile on her face.

'Veronica,' she said. 'Thanks for coming.'

Veronica simply sniffed.

'Do help yourself to a glass of bubbly,' said Kate.

'I don't drink that cheap supermarket stuff,' she huffed.

'Oh,' said Kate, and watched as Stanley disappeared off through the crowd again, making his way determinedly towards Ethel and Charlie who were busy chatting in the corner with eyes for no one but each other. She forced her attention back to Veronica. 'Well, this stuff's from that vineyard over near Little Bamton, but if you don't like it, I'm sure Sarah can help you to some elderflower bubbly instead.'

'I'll wait until I get home, thanks. I just wanted to let you know that I think your idea is ridiculous. All style, no substance,' she said, pointing at one of the cardboard cake boxes that Kate had had printed up with The Sardine's logo. Each one had six little inner compartments, all ready for the individual cakes to sit in.

'I'm sorry you feel that way,' said Kate, fighting not to roll her eyes. She loved her new cake boxes, and she was buggered if she was going to let this miserable old trout spoil such a happy evening.

'Smells of desperation, Kate, to be honest. Though I *do* understand where you're coming from. I'd be worried too if I were you. I guarantee the minute New York Froth opens up, you'll be out of business.'

'Well, *do* be sure to support Mike when he opens, won't you? Life's about supporting each other, after all,' she said with a syrupy smile. Kate couldn't actually remember the last time Veronica had spent a single penny at The Sardine, and she'd be more than happy if she never appeared in the café ever again. 'Enjoy your evening' she added smoothly.

Veronica, however, didn't seem to want to take the hint to clear off. Instead, she grabbed at one of the nearest lemon-drizzle cupcakes - complete with exquisite icing piped on by Ethel (watched closely by Sarah) - and shoved half of it in her mouth, chewing noisily.

'You'll never make this stick,' she said, swallowing, then pursing her mouth into a little cat's bum. 'Too expensive. Too *look at me*.' She paused, took another bite then shook her head. 'Honestly, you don't have a clue what you're doing here do you? Thank heavens I told the council you didn't have a permit for those tables outside - you could have got into some real trouble there.'

'I'm sorry - *what?!*' spluttered Kate.

'Those blasted tables you had outside, cluttering

the pavement. Honestly! Much safer without them. Though,' she said, licking the remaining icing from her fingers while Kate winced at the sight, '*why* Mike suggested you use this yard instead is anyone's guess. Not the sharpest knife in the drawer, that one! Seems his ex-wife was the brains in that outfit!'

With her piece said, Veronica wandered off at last. Kate balled her hands into fists as she watched Veronica load cake after cake into a serviette then place them into her capacious handbag. Kate would bet pretty much anything that they'd be served up at The Pebble Street Hotel the next day.

Right now though, Kate didn't really care. Her whole world felt like it had just shifted on its axis. *Veronica* had set the council on her? *Mike* had been the one to come up with the idea of using the yard? What was this world coming to?

She looked around her, desperate for someone to talk to - someone who'd help her make sense of these strange things - and came face to face with Mike.

CHAPTER 16

'Congratulations. This place looks amazing,' he said with a smile.

Kate opened her mouth to thank him but paused.

'Kate? Are you okay?'

'This was your idea?' she said, sounding like she was surfacing from deep water.

'Huh?'

'Using the yard as extra seating for The Sardine was your idea?' she said in a low voice.

Mike shrugged. 'Well, yeah, I might have mentioned in passing that it seemed like a good idea.'

'But you didn't even know Sarah was working for me when she surprised me with the idea!'

'No, I know. But I said something about it to her when we went for a stroll together around the town one evening,' he laughed. 'I'd noticed that you hadn't put the tables outside that day, Sarah muttered something about the council stopping you, and I said I was surprised you didn't make better use of Trixie's yard. That's all there was to it'

'Oh . . .' Kate shook her head, looking like she was trying to clear water from her ears as she struggled to get her head around this.

'I promise, it wasn't anything weirder than that. It was Sarah who ran with the idea. And it's worked out brilliantly by the looks of it - though I *would* be happier if you'd chosen literally *anywhere* else to dump Trixie.'

Kate let out a snort of laughter. 'Don't worry - I promise that's a one-off unless I really need to torture you for something!'

'Much obliged!' said Mike with a little nod.

'Tell me, though,' said Kate, 'how *exactly* did Veronica know it was your idea to use the yard?'

Mike's face fell. 'Well, I picked her brain a bit when I first arrived.'

'Yes, I know. She told me you'd taken her to lunch.'

'The one and only time I'll ever fall into that trap,' he muttered. 'Anyway, I was trying to find out more about you after I'd blocked your yard that first morning - so I asked her about you. I think I might have asked her about the yard too.'

'So, you were trying to get the inside scoop on the enemy, hey?' said Kate, her voice coming out a bit harsher than she'd intended.

Mike raised his eyebrows and shook his head. 'No. Just trying to find out more about the beautiful woman who was single-handedly running a thriving business in such a small town - the one who was more than a little bit fiery.'

Kate's mouth dropped open and she watched as Mike flushed. It *was* quite packed in here - but she was pretty sure that was a blush rather than him being too hot. *What* was going on here this evening?!

'Erm - is Stanley around?' he asked, clearing his throat and awkwardly changing the subject.

'Yes - but it's okay - he headed over to Ethel and . . . oh, goodness!' she said with a gasp. Her eyes had sought Ethel in the crowd only to find her standing with Charlie's arm around her shoulders.

'Well, looks like those two are getting on!' said Mike with a gentle smile.

'It does, doesn't it!' said Kate. 'Anyway, you're still safe - Stanley's over with Sarah,' she added, giving Sarah a little wave and getting a thumbs-up in return. It looked like she'd clipped Stanley's lead on to keep him with her. Thoughtful girl.

'It's okay,' said Mike. 'I actually brought him something . . . I'd really like to . . . well, to get to know him a bit better. If that's okay, of course?'

Kate watched as Mike reached inside his posh suit jacket and drew out a brown paper bag. He handed it over to her. Inside it was a large, knotted hide-bone.

'Mike!' she said in surprise, 'this is so kind of you!'

'Well,' he said, looking a bit embarrassed, 'I thought he might like it to wash down all the cake.'

'He'll love it. Do you want to give it to him yourself?'

Mike shook his head. 'Nah, I'll leave it for you. But I meant what I said, I really *would* like to get to meet him properly - but maybe when things are a bit quieter?'

'Come here!' said Kate, and without thinking about it too hard, she reached forward and drew a very surprised Mike Pendle into a warm hug.

After a second, Kate felt him relax against her. Mike's arms softened around her, drawing her closer. Kate felt something deep inside her chest shift. She didn't want this hug to end - she didn't want to draw away from him.

'You know,' said Mike quietly in her ear, 'I'd really like to get to know you better too . . . maybe I could take you up on that offer of finding out how things *really* work here in Seabury?'

Kate pulled back and his eyes locked onto hers. There seemed to be something warm and hopeful in his face, and for just a second, it was like someone had hit the mute button on the sounds of the party going on around them. For just a second, she wondered if he was going to kiss her . . . or maybe . . . if she was going to kiss him . . .

'Kate?'

The low, accented male voice made her jump away from Mike as if she'd received an electric shock.

'Pierre?' she squeaked, trying to smooth her hair back away from her face, then realising she was waving the paper bag with Stanley's bone around wildly in the process. She shoved it into her pocket. 'Erm, hi! This is a . . . surprise!'

'So I see,' he said, raising his eyebrows and shooting a look from her to Mike.

'No - oh, noooo!' she laughed, the giggle sounding a little manic. 'This is Mike. He's opening a café over on North Beach. He was just giving me the bone . . . I mean, *a* bone - for Stanley.'

Kate was gabbling and she knew it. She shot a quick look at Mike, who appeared to be struggling to swallow a giggle. She looked around her for help, only to find Sarah staring at her across the yard, a horrified look on her face.

Ah shit - had Sarah just spotted what happened with her dad? Or what *almost* happened. . .

'Good to meet you,' said Mike, holding out his hand to shake Pierre's. 'You are?'

'Kate's boyfriend,' replied Pierre, not taking Mike's hand but instead winding his arm protectively around Kate's shoulders and kissing the top of her head.

'Oh. Right,' said Mike, the smile dropping from his face. 'Erm, I should . . . erm . . . cake,' he pointed over towards Sarah and moved away through the crowd as fast as he could.

Kate stared after him in surprise. *What exactly* was happening here? She craned her neck to look over at Sarah again. She needed to check that she was okay - but Pierre had her clamped to his side.

'You are not happy to see me?' he laughed, clearly not believing a word of it.

Kate looked back to him and gave him a little smile. 'Of course I am - just surprised! I didn't even know you were in the country!'

'I could not go too long without seeing you again,' he said, pulling her around and landing a huge kiss right on her lips.

Kate couldn't help it, she squirmed away from him slightly. She really wasn't particularly keen on canoodling in public - especially at what was essentially a work do.

'What? You go off me?' he said, with a fake pout.

'Course not,' said Kate in a low voice, shaking her head. 'But I have guests.'

'It is someone's birthday?'

'No - we're taste-testing cakes and launching a new bit of my business.'

'So, it's work,' he said with a nod.

Kate felt her shoulders relax a bit. He understood. Thank heavens for that.

'Yes, it's work,' she smiled.

'So - you can hand over to your staff and come

away with me!' he said, getting a firmer grasp on her waist and pulling her so close to him it almost hurt.

'I can't!' she said, with a light laugh. Again, she struggled away from him. 'Sorry. We've been planning this for a while - it's too important!'

'So, you don't want to spend time with me?'

This was getting ridiculous. Kate struggled to reign in her growing impatience. This wasn't how it was meant to work between the two of them! She thought they had an understanding.

Of course, he *was* welcome - but welcome to eat cake, chat to her friends and *let her get on with her business!* He wasn't welcome to try guilt-tripping her out of her own party just because he'd decided to turn up out of the blue. But right now wasn't the moment to tackle that particular problem. Not in front of the whole of Seabury!

'Look,' she said, forcing a smile onto her face, 'let's just-'

'Ooh Kate!' said Paula, materialising at her side and eyeballing Pierre. 'Is this your mystery man? Are you going to introduce us?'

Perfect. Paula to the rescue!

'Pierre, this is my best friend Paula. Paula - Pierre.'

'Enchante!' said Pierre, grabbing Paula's hand and kissing the back of it.

'Oh my,' she giggled.

Kate rolled her eyes good-naturedly. Pierre *did* tend to have that effect. She remembered it well.

'Paula - can you help Pierre to some bubbly and your favourite cake?'

'But chérie-' Pierre began to argue.

'I'll be right back!' said Kate, struggling to stop an eye roll from slipping out. 'I just need to check in with Ethel and Sarah!'

Kate headed over towards where Ethel and Charlie were still standing in the corner. They didn't seem to have budged all evening, and Kate hated to break into their cosy little bubble, but she really did need to check Sarah was okay. She couldn't see her or Mike anywhere.

'Hello love!' said Ethel, her eyes sparkling.

'Hi you two!' she said. 'Having fun?'

'A lovely evening,' grinned Charlie. 'Thank you for all the cake.'

Kate smiled and watched as Charlie took hold of Ethel's hand. She wanted nothing more than to find out *exactly* how this miracle had come about, but first, she had to check that Sarah wasn't too freaked out by witnessing the almost-whatever-it-had-nearly-been between her and Mike. Before Pierre had interrupted.

'Good. Good. I'm glad,' she said distractedly. 'Have you seen Sarah?'

'Didn't she find you?' said Ethel.

Kate shook her head. 'No, why?'

'She's had to go. Wasn't feeling well. Mike took her home I think.'

'Oh *no!*' said Kate. This was not good.

'She had a sudden headache or something,' said Ethel. 'She *has* been working hard, and between you and me I think she might have got a bit overexcited by the whole thing. Looked very pale and couldn't hold back the tears when Mike came to the rescue.'

Kate pulled a face. Headache? Yeah right. Total horror was more like it. 'Maybe I should go over, or call Mike, or-'

Charlie shook his head. 'She'll be okay, don't worry. She's with her dad. I'm sure he'll let you know if it's anything serious.'

'But-'

'Kate?'

Kate clenched her teeth. *God save her from clingy Frenchmen!*

'Pierre,' she said, turning to him.

'Are you ready to come away now?'

'No. I told you, I-'

'Pierre?' said Charlie, a massive grin spreading across his face. 'So you're Kate's chap?'

Pierre held out his hand and shook Charlie's.

'Pierre,' said Kate, feeling forced into it, 'this is Ethel who bakes all the cakes for The Sardine and works with me, and this is Charlie-'

'Ethel's chap!' said Charlie, pride beaming from his face.

Kate raised a delighted eyebrow at Ethel, who

gave her a little shrug, unable to keep a huge smile from spreading across her own face.

'Delighted to meet you both,' said Pierre. 'I had hoped to . . . how do you say . . . whisk Kate away? But she will not be moved.'

'Well, no, I should think not,' said Ethel a tight little laugh. 'I'm not tidying this lot up on my own.'

'No fear of that, don't worry,' said Kate, rolling her eyes at Ethel, who had to hide her expression behind her hand. 'Erm, have you guys seen Stanley? Last time I saw him Sarah had him on a lead to keep him away from Mike!'

'Well, you won't believe this, but Mike himself took the lead from Sarah and managed to hand him over to Doreen from the post office to look after. Last time I saw him they were sitting at that table over there with Councillor Jones,' said Ethel, pointing at the table closest to the gate.

Kate nodded. 'I'll be back in a bit,' she muttered, and feeling slightly guilty for dumping Pierre on Ethel and Charlie, scooted through the crowd to check on Stanley.

CHAPTER 17

Kate glanced down at her watch and sighed. It was only just gone nine in the evening, so why did she feel so exhausted?

'You look like I feel!' laughed Ethel, stacking the last few empty Tupperware boxes onto the trestle table. There had been very little cake left over by the end of the party, and she'd sent anything left home with the stragglers to enjoy tomorrow.

'Knackered?' laughed Kate.

Ethel nodded. 'But it was good, wasn't it?'

'Well, these certainly say so,' said Kate with a weary smile, wafting the huge stack of completed comment sheets at her. 'I'm looking forward to having a good look through them tomorrow. Thank you so much for helping tonight!' she added gratefully.

'I wouldn't have missed it for the world,' said

Ethel lightly. 'Hey, where's your man and Stanley? Didn't they fancy helping with the clear up?'

Kate shook her head as she tucked the forms carefully into a plastic folder, then glanced around at the yard. Not too bad. The rest of this could just wait until tomorrow.

'I sent them upstairs while you were saying your goodbyes to Charlie,' she said, watching Ethel as she squirmed slightly. 'Stanley - because I think one more cake crumb would have made him explode, and Pierre - because he was doing my head in!'

'Really?' said Ethel lightly. 'He seemed quite charming, in an . . . *insistent* sort of way.'

'That's one way of putting it!' sighed Kate. 'I don't know. Maybe it was just because I wasn't expecting him here tonight, or because he seemed to think I'd just drop everything because he'd turned up - but, well . . .' she stopped and made a frustrated gesture.

Ethel winked at her. 'Well, go easy on him. Or not. What did Sarah say to me the other day . . . oh yes - *you do you.*'

Kate snorted. 'We'll see. Anyway, I just needed a couple of moments to sort everything out down here and say goodbye to everyone properly, without tripping over him every time I turned around.'

Ethel nodded. 'Fair enough. Now then, is there anything else I can do?'

'Yes,' said Kate, stifling a yawn, 'you can take this,' she grabbed one of the last bottles of bubbly and handed it to her. 'Take it home, pop it in the fridge, and share it with your new man when you fancy it.'

'*New man,*' breathed Ethel, shaking her head. 'Who'd have thought?!'

Kate grinned at her. She seemed to be floating on cloud nine. 'Actually - I think the whole of Seabury's been waiting for it to happen.'

'Thanks Kate. We'll enjoy this - maybe with some strawberries up at the allotments' said Ethel, placing the bottle carefully into her bag and hoisting the whole thing onto her shoulder.

'Oh hush,' said Kate. 'You're making me jealous!'

'Hardly! You've got your very own international man of mystery waiting for you upstairs - and tomorrow's Sunday. Anything could happen!'

'Maybe,' said Kate. She didn't want to put a dampener on Ethel's mood by telling her that somehow, she didn't think Pierre was going to be around by tomorrow morning.

Waving her friend off, Kate summoned her last ounce of energy to haul the heavy gate to the yard closed. She would just shut the remainder of the party away for tonight and finish off the tidy up in the morning.

She clicked the padlock closed and then paused to stare out to sea for a moment, listening to the peaceful waves as they lapped at the golden sand of West Beach. If only she could take Stanley for a gentle wander along the shore to finish her evening off, rather than having to retreat to her flat and deal with the attentions of a weirdly clingy Pierre!

'Kate!'

The sharp call made her turn, only to find Mike striding towards her.

'Mike!' she said in surprise. 'Hi! Is Sarah okay? I wanted to check with you earlier, but-'

'She's in pieces!' he said, his face deadly serious and a frown firmly in place.

'Oh no! Is she really ill or . . .' she wasn't sure how to put this next bit, 'erm - did she spot us?'

'Us?' he said, confused.

'You know . . . whatever almost . . . nearly happened.'

'What, Kate? What nearly happened?'

He'd come to a halt so close to her that she could feel the heat radiating off him. He'd changed and was now wearing jeans and a soft, slouchy grey tee shirt. The sight was doing something very strange to her. She swallowed, doing her best to look him in the eye.

Did he *really* not know what she was talking about? Was it just her over-active imagination that had convinced her they would have kissed if Pierre hadn't turned up at exactly the wrong moment?

Or - *the right moment* - she quickly amended. Because she shouldn't be thinking about kissing Mike. He was her rival. Sarah's father. A grumpy badger.

No, she definitely shouldn't be thinking about

kissing him, especially with him standing so close to her, waves of anger and worry rolling off him.

'Where's the arsehole, Kate?'

'Excuse me?' she said, taking a step back and crossing her arms protectively across her chest.

'The guy who turned up. Your lover!' he spat.

'Pierre?'

Mike nodded, and Kate watched in confusion as his anger suddenly and inexplicably seemed to drain from him again. 'Yeah, him,' he sighed.

'I don't get it. What's Pierre got to do with Sarah not feeling very well? Oh my . . . nothing *happened* did it? He didn't-?'

Mike quickly shook his head. 'Look, can we go up to your flat a minute?'

'No,' said Kate, 'Pierre's taken Stanley up for me. Just tell me what's going on, Mike!'

He sighed, running his hands through his hair. 'Okay, look. Sarah's met Pierre before.'

Kate shook her head, frowning, trying to make sense of this. 'Where?'

'At that sleepover she went to. Kate - he's the mum's *boyfriend*!'

Kate's mind started racing. The guy who'd been all over Sarah's friend's mum? 'He can't be, he lives in France,' she said.

'Well, apparently not. From what Sarah told me, he turns up every week or so - for a night or two.'

Kate swallowed, suddenly feeling sick.

And he turns up here about once or twice a month.

'Are you okay?' said Mike, reaching out a hand to pat her on the arm, then thinking better of it and dropping it down next to his side again.

'EEEEW!' groaned Kate, giving a full-body shudder.

Mike's face went from anger to concern to slight amusement.

'And he's up in my flat!' she added, wringing her hands. 'Wait though - why did Sarah leave so suddenly?!'

'She couldn't tell you herself! She's terrified you'll hate her. I knew something was seriously wrong, but it took me ages to get the story out of her once we got home! I left her sobbing her heart out!'

'Why would I hate her?!' said Kate.

'Because she's worried she's just broken your heart!' said Mike. 'She said - if she hadn't been there and seen him-'

'Then I'd never have found out!' said Kate, giving another shudder of disgust. 'Tell her thank you. For saving me from - that! I'll tell her myself as soon as I get this . . . *situation* . . . under control.'

'So . . . you're okay?' asked Mike gently.

'I will be as soon as I get him out of my flat!' said Kate.

'Do you want me to stay? I can help,' said Mike, looking concerned.

'No,' said Kate. 'No - go back to Sarah.'

'You sure?' said Mike, uncertainty clouding his face. He was clearly torn between the desire to get back to make sure his daughter was okay and not wanting to leave Kate on her own to deal with Pierre.

Kate nodded. 'Seriously, go. Sarah's more important.'

'Okay - I will. Good luck!' he said, moving away from her as if to head back in the direction of North Beach. Then he paused and turned back to her. 'Look. Can you at least call me when you're done? I need to know he's gone and that you're okay. Come over afterwards if you want.'

Kate shook her head, knowing she wouldn't. 'I'll call you though,' she said.

'Here's my number,' said Mike, rummaging around in his pocket then handing her a decidedly crumpled business card.

'Okay,' she said, putting it in her pocket. 'And Mike - thank you!'

Mike shrugged, clearly still struggling with the idea of leaving her to deal with the mess alone.

'Seriously, go!' she laughed. 'I've got a letch to get out of my flat. Don't worry, Stanley will look after me.'

~

'Where's my dog?!' Kate demanded.

She'd shot straight up the stairs, wanting to get

this scene over and done with before the pounding anger and disgust that was coursing through her system wore off and left her with the inevitable dollop of sadness that was bound to follow.

She'd just crashed into her little living room and stopped dead.

Pierre had lit every candle in the place, and the small room glowed with golden, flickering light. Pierre himself was stretched out on her squashy sofa, stark-bollock-naked.

Kate fought the urge to heave at the sight of him. He really *had* just turned up and expected sex, hadn't he? But then, why was she surprised? Clearly this was the way he operated. Right now, though - she had more important things to worry about. Stanley's bed was empty, and he was nowhere to be seen.

'Kate, chérie, come,' Pierre grinned, opening his arms.

Kate swallowed hard. 'Where. Is. My. Dog?!'

Pierre shrugged. 'I shut him in the Salle de Bain. Out of the way so we can-' he gestured at his lap.

'You did *what?!*' she said, desperately trying not to puke as she turned on her heel and headed back out into the hallway.

She could hear Stanley whining and scratching at the closed bathroom door on the next floor.

'It's okay, boy!' she called, running up the stairs. The sound of her voice was met with a loud thump. It sounded like Stanley had just thrown his whole weight at the door.

She flung it open, and Stanley flew out onto the landing, burying his face in her front as she dropped to her knees and threw her arms around him.

'It's okay, boy,' she crooned into his fur. 'You're okay. I'm here.'

Stanley straightened up and started to lick her face, making Kate splutter.

'I'm okay, I'm okay, you idiot!' she laughed, trying to avoid being drowned by doggy kisses. 'Come on. Let's go and get rid of that bastard.'

She got to her feet headed back towards the stairs, flanked by Stanley. As she reached the top, Pierre appeared at the bottom, still without a stitch on.

'Kate, chérie - come!'

Kate pulled a face. 'You'd better cover *that* up,' she said in disgust, 'before I ask Stanley to remove it for you.'

Much to her amusement, Pierre took a step back, covering his privates with his hands.

'Get your shit together and get out,' said Kate, walking slowly down the stairs towards him.

Pierre backed away into the living room, not taking his eyes off of Stanley.

'Kate? I do not understand. I came to see you, so we could spend time together. I lit candles. I brought you presents . . .'

'How many others *are* there?' said Kate, tilting her

head curiously as she followed him into the living room.

'Others?'

'Yes, *others* you little sh-!' Kate took a deep breath. 'I know there's at least one just along the coast who you visit a couple of times a week. Then there's me - a couple of times a month. That leaves *poor old Pierre* many lonely nights to fill, doesn't it?!'

She didn't expect an answer out of him, but it was quite satisfying to see a look of panic kindle in his eyes as he realised that he'd been busted.

'How . . . how did you-?'

'Oh, I have my spies,' snarled Kate.

Stanley took a couple of steps into the room, eyed his bed, and then ignoring it, continued to move towards Pierre.

'Get away from me!' said Pierre, taking another step backwards.

'*Wow!* said Kate, her mouth dropping open. 'Where'd your accent go?'

'Oh sod off!' he said, sounding about as English as it came. 'Like *you* didn't know. Deep down. It's all part of the mystique, innit?! All part of the *fantasy*.'

'Fantasy?' spluttered Kate.

'French fisherman? Bringing you sodding *fish?!* I mean, *Pierre?!*' he laughed. 'My name's Ian, you feckin' knob.'

Oh god oh god oh god!

She needed him out of here. She needed a shower. The longest, hottest shower in the entire world.

'Stanley?' said Kate, her voice shaking.

The big bear glanced up at her in concern, then advanced on "Pierre" with the kind of low rumble Kate had never heard him make before.

Pierre took a terrified step backwards, his ankles caught on the base of the bookshelves and he let out a high-pitched squeal as his bare bum-cheeks got a bit too close to a candle for comfort.

'Get out get out get out GET OUT!' yelled Kate, grabbing his bundle of clothes off the floor and lobbing them at him.

Pierre caught them in a messy heap and finally took the hint. Clutching the bundle, he scrambled up and bounded over the sofa cushions to avoid having to get too close to Stanley, dropping one of his trainers in the process. He shot out of the room and down the stairs towards the front door, where he paused to yank his jeans on.

Kate grabbed the trainer and followed.

'GET OUT!' she yelled, lobbing the shoe at his head from the top of the stairs. Even in her rage, she couldn't help but be impressed with her aim.

That did it. "Pierre" fumbled with the door catch and promptly disappeared - half-dressed - out of her life.

CHAPTER 18

Kate stomped around the living room, snuffing out candles. She couldn't *believe* what had just happened! Another little shiver of disgust ran through her.

Ian? English Ian?!

What had he done - visited the fishmongers to buy something to bring her from his "boat" every time he came to see her?

Eeeewwwww!

Kate threw open the sash window to let the soft salty evening air cleanse the room of *Ian* and the stink of candle smoke.

What else?

She looked around the room, searching for any remaining traces of his visit. Her eyes rested on the sofa cushions. Yuck. There was no way she was sitting on *them* until all vestiges of his bare, cheating butt-cheeks had been washed off. She quickly stripped off the covers then took them straight through to the kitchen and bundled them into the washing machine.

Heading back into the living room, she knelt down next to Stanley, who'd been watching her with interest from his bed.

'You were *brilliant!*' she said, stroking his head. 'Oh - I nearly forgot . . .' she reached into her pocket and pulled out the paper bag Mike had given her earlier. 'This is from Mike. I think we like him, okay? What do you think?' she said, offering him the end of the bone.

Stanley sniffed it then took it gently from her.

'Thought so!' she laughed, as he settled down to give it a good chew. 'Actually, I'd better give him a call, hadn't I? Tell him you got rid of *Pierre*,' she sighed.

Kate struggled back to her feet and was about to plonk down onto the stripped sofa when she changed her mind and perched on the wooden bentwood chair by the open window instead.

Drawing out the card Mike had given her earlier, she flipped open her mobile.

'Uh oh,' she sighed. There were twelve missed calls and four new voicemails - all from the same number. A number she knew way too well. What did that plonker want from her now? Whatever it was, he could wait until she was in the mood to talk to him. Right now, she needed to call Mike.

But it was too late. Her phone lit up with a silent, incoming call. It was his number - again. Well - it wasn't like he could make her mood much worse than it already was!

'What?' she spat, answering the call.

'That's no way to speak to your husband!' slurred Tom's voice at the other end of the line.

Why oh why was she so bad at picking men?

'You're not my husband. At least, not for much longer,' she sighed.

'Kate. If you want this divorce to actually go through, you should start responding to my solicitor.'

Kate frowned. Tom sounded drunk. Very drunk. She really wasn't in the mood for this.

'Whatever. I sent the papers back.'

'You didn't respond to my solicitor,' he slurred again. 'You didn't answer the letter, Kate. And now it's going to be mine.'

He was starting to sound like a pantomime villain, he was that plastered. So why did something in what he just said send a tremor of fear through her? A letter? Shit. The letter!

The vague memory of an envelope being whipped out of her hand, folded and slipped into Ethel's apron pocket came back to her.

Shit, shit, shit! It was time to bluff.

'I've not received any letters,' she said.

'Well, that's your tough luck, isn't it?' he said. 'You had a week to respond.'

'To what?' she demanded.

'The Sardine!' he said.

Then there was a crash on the other end. It sounded like he'd just walked into something. Kate didn't particularly care. She was desperately trying to piece together whatever the hell he was trying to say.

'What are you on about?' she said.

'You need to sell The Sardine so that you can split it in the divorce. Or just give it to me.'

'Bullshit,' she said firmly, though she could now feel her hand trembling around her phone. 'This place is mine. I bought it with money from my dad's house. I owned it before we met.'

'And now you have to support me because we're getting divorced, and you've left me with nothing. Oops!'

There was another crash and a bit of swearing before he focused on her again.

'You deserted me, Kate. You owe me.'

'No - this has already been decided. The Sardine has nothing to do with the divorce.'

'Well, my solicitor says it does.'

'No!' she said again, feeling tears prick her eyes.

'Keep saying it,' he laughed. 'Won't make it come true. See you in court - *wifey*!'

The line went dead. Kate flung her phone away from her as she felt a weight land in her lap. Stanley had plonked himself down at her feet and rested his large head on her knees. She looked down at him, took a huge, shuddering breath . . . and then the dam broke. Kate flopped forward and soaked her big bear's silky head with her tears.

∽

The sound of hammering at the front door made Stanley bark and struggle away from Kate's tight cuddle. She'd lost track of how long the pair of them had been curled up together on the stripped sofa - her crying what felt like a never-ending river of tears into Stanley's coat. She wriggled into a more upright position as he jumped down and tilted his head, booming out another bark as another round of hammering started.

Kate roughly scrubbed at her sore, swollen eyes with her sleeve and peered down at her watch. Shit, it was really late. Who on earth was hammering at her door at this time of night?!

She got to her feet, wrapped her cardigan around her more snugly and headed down towards the door.

'Kate? Kate!' came a muffled call, followed by more hammering.

It was Mike. Crikey, he'd wake up the entire town

if he carried on like that! She quickly opened the door.

'Mike . . . what . . .?'

'Oh, thank goodness! You didn't *bloody* call me - I had to check you were okay.'

'It's nearly midnight!' said Kate, rubbing her face again.

'I know it's nearly bloody midnight - I-' he paused. 'Oh shit, Kate. Did he hurt you?' he demanded, now staring at her swollen, tear-stained face. 'I *knew* I should have stayed. I'll get that little-'

'It's fine,' said Kate in a flat voice. 'He's long gone. Won't be back in a hurry either!'

'So - what's . . . I mean . . . you've been crying?' he said, his face creased with worry.

The words were like a switch. Kate's chin instantly started to quiver, and the tears started to fall again.

'Hey, hey - it's okay!' said Mike. He reached out and gently laid a hand on her shoulder. 'Do you want me to come up for a minute?' he asked, looking bewildered.

Kate nodded, then shook her head. 'Stanley!' she sobbed.

'What's happened to Stanley!' demanded Mike.

'No . . . Stanley's up . . . up there,' she sobbed.

'Oh. Well. That's okay. We had a chat earlier. We're cool!' said Mike, a determined set to his chin.

Kate couldn't do anything other than nod and

turn to head back up the stairs. Mike followed her inside, closed the door behind him quietly and then trailed up the stairs behind her.

Stanley was standing at the living room door on lookout duty.

'It's okay boy,' said Kate, patting him on the head. 'Come on!'

Stanley eyed Mike, who'd paused at the top of the stairs.

'Hey, Stanley,' he said, holding out his hand.

Stanley stepped forward, sniffed Mike's hand, gave a soft wag of his tail then turned and retreated onto his bed.

Mike followed him into the living room, taking his time to look around the cosy space and admire Lionel's paintings. Kate watched him, trying to get a hold of herself and stop her tears from flowing. She had a sneaking suspicion he was trying to give her a moment to pull herself together.

'Gorgeous room you've got here.'

Kate nodded. It *was* gorgeous. And she was going to have to sell it. Because she'd married an idiot! She started to sob harder than ever.

Mike looked horrified and dropped down onto the sofa next to her.

'What *is* it, Kate? What's happened? Was it Pierre?!' he demanded again.

'My ex . . .' she managed to stutter. 'Ex-husband.' She swallowed. 'Well, not yet.'

'I didn't know you were married,' said Mike quietly.

Kate nodded. 'Not for much longer.'

'I know the feeling,' sighed Mike. This made Kate laugh at the same time as another sob burst out of her, and she let out a strange honking sound that caused Stanley to cock his head.

'Here,' said Mike, reaching into his pocket and handing her a pristine cotton hanky. 'It's clean, I promise!'

Kate mopped at her face and swallowed hard.

'So, what did this ex do?' asked Mike.

'Nothing. I . . . I left him.'

'Right?'

'I wanted the divorce.'

'Okay?'

'He countered it - so he's divorcing me. For desertion.'

'But . . . that doesn't change anything, does it?' said Mike, desperately trying to piece this puzzle together as fast as possible. 'That's just words on a form!'

'He . . .' Kate's lip started to tremble again, and she fought with another wave of emotion as it threatened to crash down on her. 'He called me this evening. He's going to take The Sardine from me!'

That was it. That was all she could tell Mike before she was crying so hard that words were no longer possible. She simply dissolved, and every time she tried to get it under control, the thought of having to leave her sanctuary - the one place in the world that she felt safe - set her off again.

At some point, Stanley came closer and plonked himself down directly in front of the two of them, staring at Kate. Every now and then, he placed his paw on Kate's lap, and when he got no response from her, he glanced at Mike as if asking him to do something about the fact that his best friend was still howling.

The third time he did this, Mike reached out and very gently, very carefully, laid his hand on Stanley's head. 'It's okay lad,' he said softly. 'Your mum'll be okay in a minute.'

It took a good ten minutes for Kate to cry herself out, at which point Mike got to his feet and without saying anything, went through to the kitchen and returned in a couple of minutes with two mugs of peppermint tea.

'Here,' he said, handing one to Kate. 'Hope you don't mind, I helped myself.'

'Thanks,' she said with a shuddering sigh. She balanced the mug on the bare arm of the sofa with one hand and stroked Stanley's head with the other. 'What am I going to do, Mike?' she said in a tiny voice.

'First, you're going to get some rest. You're exhausted. And then, when you've had some sleep, you're going to tell me everything, and I'm going to help you.'

'How?' said Kate, leaning her head back and covering her eyes with her hand. She was struggling to fight the waves of drowsiness that were setting in now she'd stopped crying.

'I've just been through this too, remember?' said Mike, carefully placing his mug down on a side table. 'I've got a really good guy who can help you - or at least give you some advice if you'd like it.'

'But you lost your cafes,' she said, her exhaustion making her blunt and unfiltered.

'Yes - but I got to keep Sarah. And that's what I was fighting for. That was the only thing that mattered to me.'

Kate turned her head to stare at him. How wrong had she been about this guy?

'How about this,' said Mike, 'maybe we can meet up for lunch tomorrow - after you've had a rest and a lazy morning to yourself. I know Sarah would really like to talk to you - she's worried sick about you too. I'll pack us all a picnic and you can choose where to go?'

Kate nodded, her mind instantly going to the lighthouse. 'That sounds great,' she said, 'But - would you be okay with Stanley coming too?'

'I - oh!'

Mike followed her gaze down to his left hand, which was resting on the big dog's head. He had no idea how long he'd been absentmindedly stroking Stanley's ears.

'Erm,' said Mike. 'Yes. Why not? I think . . . I think we're friends, aren't we?' He looked back at Kate and their eyes locked. Her hand found his on the sofa, and she squeezed his fingers.

'Yes. I think we are,' she replied.

THE END

TROUBLE IN SEABURY

SEABURY - PART 2

CHAPTER 1

Kate peeped through the window of the taxi as it drew to a standstill and breathed a sigh of relief. The Sardine looked quiet. Although there was light spilling from behind the closed blinds, the outdoor tables had been moved inside and it didn't look like there were any customers lingering in the yard like they did some evenings after closing time. Good. This was one night she'd be grateful to slip inside quietly without her arrival becoming instant gossip-fodder.

'Thank you!' she said, leaning forward and handing the driver what felt like a small fortune. She grabbed her bag and quickly hopped out of the cab before he could add any more to her bill. If she'd been off on a jolly she wouldn't have minded so much but given that it had been such a miserable trip, it felt a bit like daylight robbery to cough up so much cash. It was her own fault really - several people had offered to pick her up from the train station in Plymouth, but she'd turned them all down. This was a trip she'd felt she had to face alone.

Even though it had stung, the cost of getting to London and back would have been a small price to pay if it had meant that her beloved Sardine was safe.

Kate let out a massive sigh as she watched the taxi drive off, slowly navigating the narrow, seafront road. She turned to stare sadly at the front of her cafe. Her home. She couldn't believe today had gone so badly wrong. She'd really thought that by the time she got back from London, everything would be sorted out and she'd be happy in the knowledge that The Sardine was safe. Sadly, she hadn't factored Tom into that particular equation.

The man was a first-class prick, and today had just ended up being a very expensive reminder of the many (*many!*) excellent reasons she was divorcing him in the first place.

Kate hauled her overnight bag more firmly onto her shoulder. All this could wait until she was safely back upstairs in her flat with a glass of wine in hand. She couldn't stand here staring at The Sardine all evening. She just needed to pop into the cafe, pick Stanley up from Ethel, and make sure nothing major had happened in the day and a half she'd been away.

This whole trip had been terrible timing. The new cake subscription box for October was launching in just a couple of days - with a record number of orders to fulfil. She'd felt terrible leaving Ethel, Sarah and Lou to run the place.

Lou was still pretty new, but just like Sarah, she'd fitted in instantly. She also happened to be a keen cyclist, and it had been music to Kate's ears when she'd declared that she was more than happy to step in and cover the rounds on Trixie, The Sardine's delivery tricycle, whenever Kate needed a break. Or whenever she was forced to travel to London for a mediation session with her stupid, soon-to-be ex-husband.

There was a tiny, secret part of Kate that felt immensely guilty about hiring Lou. What if Tom managed to get his way? What if she had to sell The Sardine to give him his half? She'd have to let Lou go . . . Ethel and Sarah too, come to that. Add into that little soup of misery the fact that she'd be homeless as well as losing her beloved business, and Kate felt a bit like she needed a damn good sob.

No. She wouldn't give in to that right now. All she needed was a Stanley cuddle. She'd loathed leaving him behind, but Stanley would have hated London, so he'd gone for a sleepover at Ethel's instead.

Kate sucked in a long, deep breath, filling her lungs with as much of Seabury's fresh, sea air as she could hold. She was home. She quickly made herself a promise that, no matter what happened with The Sardine, she'd find a way to stay in Seabury. She'd find a way to start again. Everything would be okay. Somehow.

Finally, she strode across the road and let herself into The Sardine - only to be met by an entire table full of people waiting for her.

'Hello, you lot!' she laughed in surprise. They'd clearly been camping out in the cafe awaiting her return for some time. The table was groaning with empty coffee cups and crumb covered plates.

'So-?' said Ethel, bustling over and somehow managing to take her coat, remove the bag from her shoulder and draw out a chair all in one fluid motion.

'So?' sighed Kate, sinking down gratefully.

'How did it go?' demanded Lionel, staring at her across the table.

'Don't keep us all waiting!' said Mike.

'Was it horrible?' said Charlie, earning himself a swat on top of the head from Ethel as she returned to the table.

'I . . .' Kate looked around at them all. She was incredibly grateful that they were here for her - but right now, all she really wanted was a coffee and-

'Where's Stanley?' she asked.

'On his way!' said Lou from her spot behind the counter. 'I think he's only just realised you're back!' she said with a grin. 'You look like you could do with a coffee?'

Kate nodded gratefully, then looked down with a

smile as Stanley's huge head landed heavily in her lap.

'Hello beautiful boy,' she said, softly stroking his ears. 'Sorry I was gone so long.'

'He's been as good as gold,' said Ethel with a smile. 'Sarah popped in before she had to head off to college and took him for a nice long walk along the beach, and Mike took him out again about an hour ago.'

'Thank you,' said Kate, turning to smile at Mike.

'It was nothing,' he said, smiling back. 'Now - please, put us out of our misery!'

For a split second, Kate wished that she'd arranged to meet Ethel and Stanley up in her flat instead of down here. At least that way there wouldn't have been an entire welcoming committee waiting to interrogate her the minute she got back. She looked around and gave herself a little shake. They were only here because they cared about her so much.

'I'm afraid it didn't go to plan,' she sighed.

'What do you mean?' said Lionel, frowning at her. 'Did they not do the job properly?'

The last thing she wanted to do was re-live the mediation session with Tom, but right now, she couldn't see a way out.

'It wasn't the firm's fault,' said Kate, shaking her head. 'They were brilliant. Really professional. Tom just behaved like a toddler. He didn't bring all the financial paperwork he was supposed to, he stomped his foot at every available opportunity and basically acted like a brat. It was a waste of time and money, and now I'm going to have to go up again for another session because we didn't get to the bottom of what we're going to do about this place.'

'Did you manage to agree on anything?' asked Ethel.

Kate nodded, then added a shrug. 'Just the stuff that had already been agreed by the solicitors. Tom still wants half of The Sardine, and I completely refuse to back down. I mean - I'm already paying him flippin' spousal support because he's such a lazy little-'

'You're *what?!*' demanded Lionel.

'I know, I know. But it's not very much and it's only for a few years, and it's my fault that we didn't work out. I mean, I *did* leave him.'

Lionel shook his head. 'But that's not how this works! There's no *way* that should be going on. I think you need a new solicitor,' he growled.

Kate nodded. 'I might have to at this rate. The thing is Tom's adamant he's going to take me to court for The Sardine. It's like he's been watching too much daytime TV or something - he was playing some kind of "big baddie" role the whole time. The poor mediator didn't know what to do with him. It was embarrassing.'

'But surely the courts won't touch this?' said Lou from the kitchen.

Kate shrugged again. 'They certainly wouldn't without this mediation malarkey. You've got to prove that you've done this bit first. That's why I went up there. I thought we might be able to get ourselves sorted out without taking it that far, but he just kept saying *"I'll see you in court!"* like a bloody pantomime villain!'

'Does he even realise how much a court case would cost?' asked Mike quietly.

'I doubt it,' said Kate. 'He reckons he's going to make me pay for his share of the mediation by the time this is all over too.'

'Well, that's *definitely* not how it works,' said Lionel, his bushy silver eyebrows now positively bristling.

Kate picked up her coffee, took a sip and then promptly plonked it back down on the table. It was delicious, but she didn't have the energy for it right now. She didn't have the energy to think about Tom any longer either. She needed a shower, and then she needed to go to bed early and pretend this mess didn't even exist. She would think about solicitors and letters, court cases and divorces once she'd had a good, long sleep.

'You know,' said Charlie, 'I've got one of me feelings about all this. I reckon it'll all sort itself out. Just you wait.'

Kate smiled at him weakly. 'I really wish that was true.'

'Well, true or not Kate love, you've done what you can for now,' said Ethel kindly. 'You look like you need a rest. Perhaps a shower and a glass of wine? I've left you a shepherd's pie in the fridge, and then maybe you should go to bed early?'

All eyes around the table swivelled to stare at her, and Kate nodded. 'Sorry, guys. I'm wiped. I'll fill you in a bit more when I've had a rest?'

She got to her feet and grabbed her coffee to take with her. 'Lou - are you okay to lock up for me if I disappear upstairs?'

'Go on, boss - get out of here! We've got this.'

∽

Kate was just turning the key in the lock to let herself into her little flat above The Sardine when she felt someone watching her. She peered over her shoulder only to find Mike looking at her awkwardly.

'Hey,' he said with a smile. 'I know you've got Stanley, but I was wondering if you'd like some company - or if there's anything I can bring you? Takeaway? Fish and Chips? Wine?'

Kate smiled at him. 'Thanks Mike, that's so lovely of you but I'm good. I've got Ethel's shepherd's pie waiting for me, and I'll probably just crash out after that. Sorry!'

'Don't apologise!' said Mike quickly. 'I just realised that we rather ambushed you in there - but it's only because we . . . because we care?' he shrugged, looking awkward.

If Kate wasn't so knackered right now, the sight of Mike Pendle, businessman extraordinaire, scuffing the toe of his trainer into the ground and looking more like a shy teenager than a grown man would have melted her heart. As it was, all she could really focus on was the siren call of her pyjamas and the numbing effects of the bottle of red she'd stashed for the occasion.

'I know you care,' she said at last, as Stanley gave a little whine, waiting for her to hurry up and open the door so that he could trundle up the stairs and get into bed. 'Let's catch up properly when I'm more with it?'

'Sounds like a plan,' said Mike, smiling at her.

'Great. Tomorrow evening? At the lighthouse? Leftovers picnic?'

'It's a date!' said Mike. 'Have a good evening, Kate.'

'You too,' said Kate.

She stood and watched as he wandered towards the seafront, turning in the direction of North Beach rather than back towards The Sardine.

'It's a date?' she muttered to herself, finally opening the door and letting Stanley amble past her before closing it firmly behind them both. 'I like you, Mike Pendle, but right now - after everything that's happened - the last thing I want is a date!'

CHAPTER 2

'Morning boss!' grinned Lou as she bounced into the cafe. 'How're you doing this fine morning?'

'Much, much better for a sleep and a shower to wash all that London grime off!' she laughed, adding the last order to the stack already waiting to be loaded onto Trixie ready for her morning rounds.

'I know what you mean. It does something funny to your skin, that place. Still, I love it,' said Lou, taking off her long, red coat. 'Don't think I'd want to live there, though,' she added decidedly.

'I hated living there,' said Kate, scrunching up her nose.

'I didn't realise you had! I had you pegged for someone who never left Seabury unless forced - like yesterday.'

Kate let out a delighted laugh. 'Then you've got

me pegged just about right. But when I lost my dad I thought it'd help to have a complete change. Turns out I was just trying to run away from how much it flippin' hurt.'

'Did it work?' said Lou.

'Nope. I was back here within three months leaving a disgruntled, jilted husband behind me. It just added to the pile of trouble really.' Kate paused and shrugged. 'Still, I had Seabury to help me get through it.'

'And Stanley, of course,' laughed Lou, bending down to pet the big hairy bear who'd just wandered over to demand a treat from his new friend.

'Stanley turned up not long after I'd come back actually. We kind of saved each other,' said Kate, smiling as she watched Stanley munching happily on one of his biscuits.

'So, do you want me to do the delivery round again today?' asked Lou, as Kate fired up the Italian Stallion, ready for their customary early morning coffee fix.

Kate shook her head. 'Nah - I'm actually looking forward to the exercise for a change. After sitting for so long on a train, I think a bit of pedalling will do me good.'

'Okie dokie!' said Lou cheerfully. 'Offer's always there, though.'

'Thanks Lou - you're a saint.'

Lou grinned at her.

'Oh - did Sarah mention how she did on that last assignment when she popped in yesterday?' asked Kate.

Lou nodded. 'You know our girl, she aced it! She was quite modest but reading between the lines it sounds like her tutors are thrilled with her. Anyway, I'm sure she'll tell you all about it - she's due in this morning, isn't she?'

Kate nodded. 'She's going to go far, that one,' she said, totally unable to stop a proud smile from spreading across her face.

Helping Sarah to get into college was something Kate was incredibly proud of. It had been quite the battle to convince Mike to let his daughter follow her passion. All Sarah had wanted to do was study professional patisserie and confectionery at college, but Mike had been adamant that she should stay in school and take her A levels instead.

Sarah had worked hard in The Sardine all summer, doing her best to prove to her dad that her interest in all things baking wasn't just a whim. Eventually, with a little added nudging from Ethel, they'd managed to win Mike over with a compromise. Sarah was allowed to take the baking course provided she also studied business management alongside it.

Kate suspected that the whole issue had had rather a lot to do with added pressure being applied behind the scenes by Sienna, Sarah's mother - and

Mike's ex - because as soon as he'd made the decision to let Sarah go to college, Mike had been incredibly supportive about the whole thing.

Kate didn't usually take against someone so completely. It had always been in her nature to believe that there was some good to be found even in the most difficult of characters. Not Sienna though. She'd never actually met the woman, but Kate loathed her. The moment she'd caused injury to her darling Stanley by running them off the road during one of their delivery rounds, Sienna had earned herself a place on Kate's shit-list. It was quite an exclusive list - the only other person currently on there was Tom.

'You okay?' asked Lou, taking her fresh cup of coffee from Kate with a frown. 'You were all smiley two seconds ago but I swear I just heard you grinding your teeth.'

Kate rolled her eyes. 'Unfortunately, even fleeting thoughts of my ex tend to have that effect on me at the moment.'

'I know what you mean,' said Lou.

'Were you married before coming to Seabury?' asked Kate, curiously, taking a sip of her own coffee.

Lou had been with her for several weeks now, but she didn't tend to talk about herself much. She'd arrived in Seabury at the end of the summer holidays "looking for a new start" as she'd put it, and rented the cutest little place on the hill just below the allotments. She'd bounced into the cafe on her second day in town, and Kate had instantly known that she'd be the perfect fit for The Sardine.

'Nah,' said Lou. 'Not married, but I'd been with the same guy for years. We lived together - but no kids, thank heavens!'

'What happened?' asked Kate.

'Younger model,' muttered Lou. 'I mean, I wouldn't mind . . . but it's such a cliché!'

'I'm really sorry,' said Kate.

Lou shrugged. 'His loss. If he can't see that spending his life with forty-two years worth of awesomeness is far better than babysitting a teenager, that's up to him.'

'*That* young?' asked Kate.

'His new bit? Yep - just nineteen. I'm sure she's a lovely girl, but there was no way I wanted to hang around and be compared to that all day, every day. As *if* there's any kind of comparison, anyway!' she smirked. 'I was *always* going to win that competition. Just wasn't fair on the poor lamb!'

Kate smiled at Lou. She didn't believe for one second that it had been as easy to deal with as she was making out right now, but she couldn't help but admire her attitude.

'Morning dearies!' came Ethel's cheery voice as a large pile of Tupperware walked through the door.

'You behind there, Ethel?' laughed Lou, rushing

over to remove the top layer of boxes so that Ethel could see where she was going.

'Thank you, love!' she smiled. 'I was *that* worried I was going to drop the lot - it's getting really windy out there this morning!'

She popped the rest of the boxes on the counter and did her best to smooth her hair back into place.

'Well, Kate - I have to say you look a lot more human this morning!'

'Erm, thanks . . . I think?!' laughed Kate.

Lou snorted.

'You know what I mean,' tutted Ethel.

'Yep, I do,' said Kate, giving her a reassuring smile. 'Everything feels a lot better for a good night's sleep - mind you, it was a bit more like passing out rather than sleeping, I was that tired!'

'Did Mike manage to catch you before you disappeared upstairs?' asked Lou lightly, ignoring Ethel as she dug her in the ribs with her elbow.

'Yes, he did,' said Kate raising an eyebrow.

'Well, that's nice,' said Ethel blandly. 'At least you had a bit of company.'

Kate rolled her eyes and shook her head. 'He just asked if there was anything I needed and then headed off home.'

'What?' said Lou. 'No cosy little chat upstairs?'

'Honestly, you two are impossible!' laughed Kate. She could sense that they were nearing their favourite topic of conversation - why she wasn't dating Mike - and she really could do without it this morning.

'No, Lou,' she huffed. 'You saw what I was like - I was good for nothing last night. I just stuffed my face and then crawled into bed.'

'Shame,' pouted Lou.

'Not at all,' said Kate. 'Ethel's shepherd's pie was just what the doctor ordered. Thank you, by the way!'

'No problem, my love. I'm just sad it wasn't a meal for two.'

'Okay, you two, quit it!' laughed Kate, just as the bell above the door sounded again.

'Quit what?' demanded Sarah, bowling into the cafe and instantly dropping to her knees to give Stanley a cuddle. 'Morning fluff-hound,' she murmured into his fur.

'We were just talking about Kate and your dad,' said Ethel.

'Ooooh!' squealed Sarah, causing Stanley to let out a little *wuff* of surprise. 'Are there developments? Have you two finally snogged? Can I be maid of honour?!'

'No, no and nope!' said Kate, covering her face with her hands. Honestly, these three would be the death of her!

'Aw - come on Kate, get a move on and ask him out already!' pouted Sarah. 'I'm totally shipping you two!'

'Shipping?!' demanded Ethel, looking confused.

'Yeah,' said Kate, 'I second that. Shipping? Explain!'

'Honestly, you two old fogeys!' laughed Lou, 'get with the program!'

'Exactly!' Sarah grinned at her. 'Shipping is when, like, you're totally into a couple. Like - my new friend Rhona at college is a total Harry Potter fanatic - and she ships Hermione and Harry!'

'As a couple?' said Lou, pulling a face.

Sarah grinned and nodded.

'Well, sorry to disappoint you,' smirked Kate, 'but I'm happy just the way things are, thanks.'

'What,' said Sarah, shooting her a sly look, 'him eyeballing you longingly and you pretending not to notice?'

'GAH! Look - we're both in the business community together - we're friends . . .'

'Friends with benefits,' chuckled Ethel.

Sarah gave a half horrified, half delighted squeak and Kate's jaw dropped.

'Do you even know what that means?' hooted Lou, wiping away tears of laughter.

'Shared picnics?' said Ethel innocently.

'I think you and I need to have a little chat about the birds and the bees,' said Sarah, laughing so hard that Stanley stuck his nose right in her face to check she was okay.

Kate was fighting the urge to join in. She crossed her arms and glared hard at her three troublesome members of staff. 'Ethel - please don't say that in front of anyone else, I'm begging you!'

Leaving them all guffawing in her wake, Kate grabbed the first pile of deliveries and took them out to the yard to get Trixie loaded up. The sooner she got out of the way, the sooner the others could set up for their first customers.

She hadn't expected the yard to remain as popular as it had been in the summer, but they were already in October and it was still proving to be a hit - with locals and visitors alike. She'd managed to get the local sailmakers to create a beautiful cover for the space - which seemed to enhance the feeling of being outside near the sea, rather than making it feel enclosed. She'd also gone to town and purchased three outdoor heaters. She hadn't had to use them much yet, but she knew they'd come into their own very soon.

'Right Trix!' she said, patting the bright red handlebars. 'Let's get ready and get out on the road - we've got a busy one today. At least I know you and Stanley won't give me a hard time about boys!'

'Who's been giving you a hard time about boys?'

Kate cringed. It was never great getting caught in the act of talking to your delivery tricycle, but considering the topic of this particular one-sided chat, things were shaping up to be even more embarrassing than usual.

'Morning Lionel,' she muttered, turning red-faced to greet him.

'Don't take any nonsense from those three troublemakers you call staff,' he chuckled. 'I think they make each other worse when they're together.'

'Worse. Better. Depends on how you look at it,' sighed Kate, giving him a wry smile.

'Well, don't worry. I won't poke my nose in. It's none of my business why you and Mike aren't all loved up like you should be.'

'Lionel!'

'Okay, okay!'

'What brings you here so early in the morning anyway?' said Kate, desperately wanting to get off this topic of conversation.

'Well, I wanted to talk to you about your ex-husband and The Sardine.'

Kate flinched, suddenly wishing they were back on the previous topic. At least that didn't make her want to sob.

'Now, don't look at me like that,' he said, reaching out and giving her a gentle pat on the shoulder. 'It's just that I think I might be able to help.'

'Really?' asked Kate, her voice flat.

'Absolutely. Perhaps we could meet this evening after you've closed up for the day?'

Kate bit her lip. Damn. She either had to cancel on Mike or admit that she was otherwise engaged to Lionel.

'Erm . . . I can't tonight, sorry Lionel.'

'Of course, no problem. Hot date?' he asked with a grin.

Kate rolled her eyes. 'I'm meeting Mike for tea - but definitely *not* a hot date.'

'How nice,' said Lionel switching to an impressive poker face.

'Yeah. Erm. Any chance you could keep it to yourself though? Not sure I'll live it down with the coven in there otherwise,' she sighed, nodding at The Sardine.

'Mum's the word. And how about tomorrow morning instead - before you open? It won't take too long.'

'Okay, thanks Lionel,' said Kate. 'Come up to the flat though - I think I'd prefer to keep all things *Tom* out of the cafe from now on.'

CHAPTER 3

'I've brought a treat for pudding!' said Kate, puffing a bit as she fought to get her breath back. Pedalling Trixie up the hill towards the lighthouse for the second time that day had almost proved to be more than her poor calves could handle. The minute she'd spotted Mike waiting for her on the far side of the old lighthouse - perched on a tartan picnic rug with two glasses of red wine poured and ready to go - she knew it had been worth it.

In fact, if she was being completely honest, she wasn't sure that her racing heart was entirely down to the steep hill. Mike was wearing a slouchy old pair of jeans and a cosy, soft grey sweater. For a fleeting moment, all she wanted to do was snuggle into the faded cashmere and feel his arms around her. She swallowed hard. Blimey, the constant jokes and wiggling eyebrows of Ethel, Lou and Sarah were definitely starting to wear off on her.

She took a second to lay her hand against the old stone side of the lighthouse, sending it a quick greeting as she did every time she came up here. It had nothing to do with the fact that she needed to calm herself down before she got too close to Mr Pendle! She took in a deep breath of the chilly evening air and watched Stanley trudging around the bushes, sticking his nose into them and checking the perimeter.

There. Calm. She was calm. She wasn't about to jump on the poor man. Nope. Not at all.

'Here,' she said, walking towards Mike at last and awkwardly passing him one of The Sardine's new cake subscription boxes.

'This month's new selection?' he asked, flipping open the lid and inhaling deeply.

Kate smiled and nodded. 'And just so we don't have any disagreements, I've pre-chopped them all in half.'

Mike laughed. 'Good thinking, girl wonder!'

The first time they'd shared one of the boxes, they'd had quite a heated scuffle over the carrot cupcake which had resulted in rather a lot of icing ending up in her hair and all over his face.

Kate placed her basket onto the tartan rug and dropped down next to it, glad to finally sit down. Mike quickly grabbed the two wine glasses to save them from getting toppled by Stanley as he ambled over to join them.

'Here,' he said, handing one to her as soon as she'd made herself comfy. Then he reached out to ruffle Stanley's ears as he flopped onto the rug next to him. 'Hello, you.'

As Kate watched Mike smiling down at her already-snoozing dog, her heart did something funny in her chest.

Ah, crap. This wasn't good.

This was the exact same feeling she had to ward off every time she bumped into Mike, and it was getting harder and harder to do. She was a sucker when anyone fell for Stanley, and seeing Mike be so gentle with him meant even more because she knew just how scared he was of most dogs.

She could trace the moment things had started to get worse back to the grand opening of Mike's cafe, New York Froth, just a few weeks ago. She reckoned it was the sight of him in a suit that had done it. But then, if she was honest, his scruffy down-time look made her knees go all wobbly too.

Kate cleared her throat. She needed to get her mind off of how bloody good Mike looked. It wasn't helping matters that right now, his dark hair, threaded with little tufts of silver here and there, was flopped forward onto his forehead as he petted Stanley. She stomped hard on the temptation to reach out and brush the strands back off his face.

'Cheers,' she said, awkwardly, reaching out and clinking her glass against his.

'Cheers!' said Mike in surprise, straightening up and grinning at her. 'So - how're you doing today?' he asked after taking a swig of wine.

'Better than yesterday,' sighed Kate, staring out at the sea. 'I mean - I'm back home, and I haven't just spent hours cooped up with my ex, pointlessly arguing in circles - so yeah, definitely better than yesterday.' She gave him a rueful smile.

'I keep telling you, I know a great solicitor if you need-'

Kate shook her head. 'No. Thanks, but no. I'm fine.' She didn't quite know why, but she'd made a decision early on that she wasn't going to accept any help from Mike when it came to anything to do with Tom. It just felt . . . wrong.

For one thing, Mike was a business rival. Sure, things were more than amicable between them at the moment, but considering the issues she was having with Tom were all about whether she stood to lose The Sardine or not, turning to Mike for help just felt . . . wrong. There wasn't any other word for it. For another thing, something was telling her that it was a bad idea to get help in dealing with her ex from the guy she was pretty sure she was starting to fall for. Not that she was ever going to do anything about that, but still . . .

'You keep saying you're fine but-'

'Do you mind if we talk about something else?' she said, smiling gently at him. 'Anything else?'

'Of course. I get it. Sorry.' Mike grinned back at her and Kate let out a sigh of relief. She *knew* he wanted to make this all better for her, but right now the best way he could do that was to help her forget there was anything to worry about in the first place.

She quickly drew the tea towel off the top of the picnic basket and pulled out the food she'd hastily packed for them.

'Brie and grape or chicken?' she asked, waving two wrapped baguettes at him.

'Did you cut those in half too?' he asked hopefully.

She grinned and nodded.

'Thank goodness for that. Share?'

'You've got it!' she said, opening both packages and placing them between them on the rug.

'So,' he said, grabbing half of the brie and grape sandwich and taking a massive bite.

She waited while he chewed with his eyes closed and swallowed the mouthful with a groan of delight. Surely watching someone eat shouldn't be making her toes tingle? She gave herself a quick shake, trying to pull herself together.

'So?' she said, cursing herself when she heard a little quiver in her voice.

'I've got some Seabury-style gossip for you if you want to hear it?' he said, turning to her with a glint in his eye that had nothing to do with the last rays of the evening sunshine bouncing off the sea.

'Ooh!' she said in excitement. 'Spill!'

'Veronica's decided to take The Pebble Street Hotel upmarket.'

'Yeah right,' laughed Kate around a mouthful of chicken. 'I've heard that before. What's she going to do, add an extra egg-cup full of cereal to the guest breakfasts and charge them an extra tenner for the privilege?'

Mike shook his head. 'Better than that, she's decided to start holding wedding receptions!'

Kate snorted.

'I'm serious!' said Mike. 'She's updated her alcohol licence, and even has her first wedding booked in - apparently it's just a couple of weeks away.'

Kate stared at him, wide-eyed. 'Well, all I can say is that I feel sorry for the couple.'

'Aw. Poor Veronica!' chuckled Mike.

'But Mike - ignoring the fact that the hotel's not exactly wedding-ready - *imagine* having Veronica in charge of what's meant to be part of the happiest day of your life! Talk about an ill wind wafting around!'

'The hotel could be beautiful if it was properly maintained,' said Mike. 'Maybe she's turning over a new leaf? Maybe she's decided to live out her dream?'

'You think?' said Kate, suddenly feeling a bit bad.

Mike let out a gleeful hoot. 'No, I don't think! She's probably come to the conclusion that she can charge a fortune for a wedding and do it as cheaply as possible!'

Kate nodded. Sadly, that *did* sound a lot more like the Veronica they all knew and didn't love.

'Well, I wish her all the luck in the world with it,' she said.

'You do?' said Mike in surprise. 'Really?'

Kate nodded. 'For the bride and groom's sake, if nothing else.'

'Good point. Well, I've heard she's getting some work done on the place before then - so I guess she's taking it seriously,' said Mike, reaching down and grabbing another piece of baguette.

'Well, she won't be using anyone local!' said Kate.

'I'm guessing you'll be around there to read her the riot act like you did to me, then?' said Mike with a laugh.

'Nope. No point.'

'Ah, come on Kate, play fair. You gave me a roasting about that!'

'For good reason!' said Kate.

'Okay - yes - I guess I understand that better now . . . but it's only fair for you to light a fuse under old sour-puss too!'

Kate shook her head. 'No, I'm serious - there's literally no point. None of the local firms will work for her anymore. She owes them all money.'

'You're kidding me?'

'Nope, afraid not. The woman's notorious for nitpicking about jobs and then refusing to pay on the back of it.'

'But surely they chase it up and force her to cough up?'

Kate shook her head again. 'See, that's her superpower. She's such a royal pain in the arse that every single one of them gives up before extracting the cash. It's almost like they decide it's worth the loss of income just so that they don't have to deal with her anymore!'

Mike spluttered a laugh. 'Superpower? The woman's a crook!'

'Pretty much. But it means that there isn't a tradesperson around here who'll do anything for her. She'll have to go to Plymouth - or maybe even further by this point!'

'You know, I'd almost admire her if she wasn't so despicable!' laughed Mike.

Kate shook her head. 'What a way to live, though. I swear I've never seen her be cheerful about anything, and she's never got a good word to say about anyone.'

'Maybe having all those joyful weddings at the hotel will cheer her up a bit,' smirked Mike, taking a swig of wine.

'Hah! Maybe.' Kate glanced sideways at him. 'You know - it's something we threw into the mix when we were all coming up with ideas for The Sardine.'

'What, weddings?' asked Mike, looking interested.

Kate nodded. 'Catering the receptions using Trixie. I mean, it would have to be for people who were after something a bit different - maybe vintage themed, or looking for a quintessentially English afternoon tea. We thought it would be fun to rock up at the reception venue on Trix and dole out finger sandwiches, cream teas and lashings of ginger beer - or tea - or champers!' said Kate with a grin.

Mike nodded, his eyebrows still raised. 'You know, I can just imagine that! It'd be something really different, and you could tweak it to fit each wedding.'

'Exactly,' nodded Kate. 'But - luckily for me - Ethel sensibly suggested that perhaps starting one new venture at a time would be a good idea!' she chuckled, patting the top of this month's cake box.

'I *do* see where she's coming from,' said Mike, 'but keep revisiting those new ideas, Kate - you never know what might be the next big thing for your business.'

Kate grinned at him. She'd not known Mike that long, and you couldn't say their friendship had had the most auspicious of starts - but she was constantly surprised by how generous he was when it came to discussing ideas, sharing thoughts and generally being a really kind friend.

Uh oh, there were those warm, squishy thoughts again!

'So,' she said, hastily hunting around for a safe topic of conversation, 'how's Sarah doing with college?'

'You tell me?' chuckled Mike. 'I think you see her more than I do these days.'

Kate frowned across at him. 'Do you think it's too much? The hours at the cafe as well as college?'

Mike shook his head quickly. 'Honestly, when I do catch a glimpse of her over breakfast or just before we both head to bed, I swear I've never seen her this happy. From what I can tell, she's doing great at college and she adores being at The Sardine with you guys. She's learning so much.'

Kate smiled. 'She does seem to have a spring in her step, and she's got so much talent. At this rate, I'll end up making her a partner in the cake-box business! She's so full of ideas.'

Mike sighed. 'I know. I just wish . . .' he pulled a face and went quiet.

Kate glanced at him. He was frowning down at Stanley, slowly stroking his finger down the big bear's nose, clearly trying to work through something.

'What do you wish?' she prompted quietly.

Mike let out a long, slow breath. 'I wish I could get her mum to see how happy it's making her.'

'Sienna's not playing ball?' asked Kate, doing her best not to growl.

Mike shook his head. 'She's livid that I let her leave school without talking it through with her first. I'm dreading her saying something to Sarah. I don't want her to dent that kid's confidence any more than she already has.'

Kate laid her hand on Mike's arm, and he looked at her in surprise.

'Sarah seems to be doing okay. Seriously. She loves living with you and she adores her life at the moment.'

'I hope she loves living with me, but sometimes I wonder-'

'Trust me, she does. She tells us often enough!' laughed Kate.

'Really? She actually says that?' said Mike, a look of delight crossing his face.

'Oh yes. Amongst her other wonderful qualities, your daughter doesn't have much of a filter!' laughed Kate.

'You get to see such a different side of her,' he sighed. 'Don't get me wrong, I love the fact that she has you guys at The Sardine - I just wish she felt as comfortable chatting with me. She's still being careful with me - it's like this long-lasting hangover because I was so miserable when I was with Sienna. I hate the fact that Sarah lost so many years of being a carefree kid because she was stuck in the middle of it all.'

'She just wants you to be happy, and to make you proud of her,' said Kate gently.

'Well, the first part's coming along nicely, and she's definitely got that second one sorted.'

'Aw Mike!'

'Now - don't try to change the subject - what else has she told you with this missing filter of hers?'

Kate sniggered. 'You don't expect me to give up all our girly secrets do you?'

Mike shrugged. 'Fair enough.'

Kate grinned but secretly breathed a sigh of relief that he wasn't about to chase that particular rabbit. Because the idea of telling him that Sarah couldn't stand her own mother didn't really appeal. Neither did she want to tell him that his own teenage daughter had declared that she was "shipping" the two of them. Talk about complicating things!

CHAPTER 4

'Morning Kate!' beamed Lionel as soon as she opened her door.

'Hi!' she yawned. 'Sorry, sorry. Come on in'

Lionel followed her up the stairs and into the cosy, light sitting room.

'Tea? Coffee?' she asked.

'Cup of tea would be wonderful if you don't mind?' he said, beaming at her.

Kate nodded and left him to greet Stanley - who was clearly very excited about having a visitor this early in the morning. She shuffled into the kitchen and flicked the kettle on - anything to buy a little bit of time before having to talk about the mess her life was in right now.

Her evening with Mike had proved to be exactly what she'd needed. They'd laughed and joked and gossiped, and it had all felt incredibly easy, as long as she firmly ignored the large, multicoloured elephant in the room - the fact that every time she looked at him, she wanted to kiss his face off.

Still, it had served to take her mind off of everything else, and all the good food, a glass of wine and tonnes of fresh air had meant she'd slept well for the first time in weeks. So well, in fact, that she'd really struggled to get herself out of bed and dressed in time to let Lionel in.

Part of her wished she hadn't agreed to this - but then, she owed it to The Sardine. Hell, she owed it to herself to do everything in her power to make sure that she didn't have to put her beloved life up for sale.

'Here you go,' she said, padding back into the living room and popping Lionel's mug down on a coaster.

'Thanks!' he smiled at her. 'You know, I didn't realise you'd bought so many of my original paintings!' he laughed, peering around at the walls, which were dotted with his stunning work - all depicting Seabury at its finest.

'I adore your work,' said Kate, following his gaze. 'And don't ask me to pick a favourite, because I've tried and it's completely impossible.'

'Well, it's a huge compliment,' he said, his voice sounding quite gruff.

Kate smiled at him. 'Have you always painted?'

Lionel was a bit of a mystery - no one really knew much about his history. There were plenty of rumours and guesswork going around Seabury, but she'd had first-hand experience of just how unreliable that could be!

He shook his head. 'Not always, no - but it's been my hobby for several decades now.'

'More than a hobby!' said Kate warmly. 'These paintings should be in galleries across the world!'

'You're too kind,' he chuckled in delight. 'But no - for me, they are my way of relaxing, of letting go of stress and making sense of the world.'

Kate nodded. Blimey, if only she could paint - that sounded *exactly* like what she needed right about now!

She glanced at Lionel. 'When did you start? I mean - were you living here, or . . .?'

'I was living in London.' He let out a sigh. 'I was quite a high-powered lawyer at one point. Dealt with some pretty nasty stuff along the way. And that only seemed to get worse when I became a judge.'

'Wow!' said Kate. 'I had no idea that's what you were!'

'Well no,' said Lionel. 'It's not something I tend to talk about . . . or think about very often, come to that.'

'Oh - I'm sorry,' said Kate, instantly feeling bad.

Lionel just shook his head. 'Not for any particular reason other than it filled my entire life with some of the worst moments mankind has to offer. I hope I did my bit. That's all anyone can hope. But yes, the painting - capturing beauty and kindness and friendship - was a way of balancing things up a bit for me. Now that I'm retired - it's the side of things that I wanted to keep in my life!'

Kate smiled at him. 'As a fan - can I just say, thank heavens.'

Lionel grinned at her. 'Anyway - all that does rather lead me to why I'm here, dragging you out of bed at such an ungodly hour!'

'Right,' said Kate, suddenly feeling a bit nervous.

'Look. You don't have to tell me anything, agree to anything or do anything you don't want to do. But I think I can help.'

'With The Sardine?'

'With this whole mess your incompetent solicitor seems to have left you in,' he huffed.

'The divorce,' said Kate.

'The divorce,' nodded Lionel. 'Or lack of divorce, in this case. By the sounds of it, it should have been done, dusted and tied up with a bow by now!'

'Well, it's complicated . . .' said Kate.

'Do you mind if I ask you a few questions?' said Lionel, pulling a spiral notepad and fountain pen out of his jacket pocket.

'Of course not!' she said, even though a voice in her head was screaming the exact opposite.

'So - let me just say - as a retired judge, I cannot represent you, so this is advice as a friend, okay?'

Kate nodded. 'Understood.'

'The fact that I have several friends who are still

practising solicitors - one of which owes me several favours - doesn't come into the equation right now,' he laughed.

Kate swallowed. She'd answer his questions, hear him out and see what he had to say - but she wasn't going to be taking handouts. It just wasn't the way she operated.

'So - how long were you married to Tom for before you returned to Seabury?'

'Three months,' said Kate, shifting awkwardly.

'And had you lived together before then?'

Kate shook her head. 'He stayed here some nights - but not often. Sometimes I stayed in the place he was renting nearby.'

'But you weren't actually living together - sharing bills, that kind of thing?'

Kate shook her head.

'And when you got married - who did the place in London belong to?'

'It's a rented place. Tom had been subletting it while he was down here. I moved in with him when we went back to London - and I covered all the rent for those three months - plus the following three months as I was leaving him in the lurch.'

Lionel blew out through his nose, sounding a bit like an irritated horse as he scribbled on his pad.

'I'm assuming the answer is "no", but do you have any children together?'

Kate shook her head, doing her best to suppress a

shudder that appeared out of nowhere. It wasn't the idea of having kids she had an issue with - just the idea of having kids with *that* idiot.

'And do either of you have children from a previous relationship?'

'No,' said Kate. 'At least - I don't, and he never told me about any.'

'And why did you leave him? Was there any foul play on either side?'

Kate's heart sank, this was the bit that made her feel like a totally heartless bitch. 'No. He never cheated. Neither did I. I realised I didn't love him - I was just trying to escape my grief at losing my dad.'

She paused and swallowed the thick lump of emotion that had just lodged itself in her throat. She glanced at Lionel, but he was still jotting down notes on his pad. She took a deep breath before continuing. 'I needed to get away from Seabury - it felt like I was trapped here after dad died. It took me leaving and moving all the way to London to realise that this was *exactly* where I needed to be.'

'And Tom?'

'He was a distraction from my grief. I threw myself into the relationship in the hopes that I could forget how broken I was. Then, the entire time I was in London, he badgered me to sell The Sardine so that I could contribute more to our life together. He wanted a new car, he wanted our own place, he wanted to eat out all the time. The list of things he wanted was huge. Still is, by the look of it.'

'So you left,' said Lionel.

'I left and came straight back here. I filed for divorce as soon as I legally could. Tom countered it - he wanted to divorce *me* - for desertion.'

'Unusual,' muttered Lionel.

'I think it was a pride thing for him. Anyway - of course, I agreed - because that's basically what I did.'

'Just words on a form,' said Lionel. 'The reason shouldn't make any difference to proceedings after that.'

'I know. But that's why I've agreed to pay monthly spousal support for the next few years. It's my fault this has happened. I should never have agreed to get married in the first place.'

'And this is why I'd quite like to dismember whichever idiot you've been using as a solicitor,' said Lionel, his voice unusually grim. 'That shouldn't have been agreed at all.'

'But-'

'No buts, Kate. In the eyes of the law, this should have been very straightforward - what's known as a "short term marriage divorce" - and there are no children and no dependents to take into account.'

'But I just deserted him.'

'It doesn't matter. After such a short period, you should both be leaving the marriage in the same financial standing as when you went into it. You didn't buy a house together, or anything else by the sound of it?'

Kate shook her head. 'No. But I made my last payment on this place while we were married, so technically-'

Lionel shook his head. 'He hasn't got a leg to stand on.'

'But he's taking me to court. That's why he's determined to mess up the mediation.'

'Kate - the courts would chuck this out in seconds. But if he's allowed to carry on and force everything to go that far, it'll cost you both a fortune for no reason!'

'Right,' muttered Kate. 'Just like the mediation.'

'No - not just like the mediation. That's nothing in comparison. We're talking thousands, here - possibly tens of thousands. Each.'

Kate could feel herself going pale. She couldn't afford that. Hell, by the sounds of things, if Tom got his way she'd end up having to put The Sardine on the market no matter what happened - just to cover legal proceedings.

'Kate - are you feeling quite well?'

She shook her head, looking guiltily back into Lionel's concerned eyes. 'Sorry. This has all been an absolute nightmare - and I had no idea that it's going to cost that much!'

'But it's not. That's what I'm telling you. I would say that Tom's solicitor is only pushing things this hard because yours hasn't been doing their job properly.'

'But-'

'But that's despicable? Yes. It is.'

'But what can I do? Mediation isn't working because Tom's hell-bent on getting his hands on half of this place.'

'Take a breath. We can sort this out. The question is - will you let me pull in one of my favours? I swear old Philip would love nothing more than to sort this out for you.'

'I can't ask him to represent me in court for no fee!' spluttered Kate, now feeling decidedly sick.

'Represent you in court?' hooted Lionel. 'This won't go anywhere near court if he gets his hands on it. A properly worded letter or two and we'll have this all ironed out and your divorce will be sorted, you mark my words. And if I know Philip - which I do and have done for more than half a century - it'll be done in a way that'll make sure that it's final. No ongoing payments and *definitely* no chance that Tom will be able to crop up in the future, rattle his chains and demand anything else from you. How does that sound?'

Kate nodded, staring at Lionel with eyes full of unshed tears. How did that sound?

'Can I think about it?'

Lionel nodded. 'Of course.'

'It just . . . it's too much to ask of you. I can't . . .'

'It's nothing - and if it means you can put this all behind you and get on with your life, it's worth it!'

Kate shook her head. She didn't really know what to do. It sounded too good to be true and every fibre of her being wanted to say yes, but it was too much to ask.

'I promise I'll think about it,' she said, her voice cracking. 'Lionel - can I give you a hug?'

Lionel smiled at her gently. 'Here,' he said, getting slowly to his feet. He opened his arms and Kate got up and wrapped her arms around the old man's waist, willing herself not to cry into his shoulder. 'Just give me the nod, and we'll get this mess sorted out,' he said, patting her back gently. 'Just don't leave it too long.'

For a moment, Kate felt like she was a little girl again, being comforted by her old dad. She swallowed hard before pulling back from Lionel.

'Thank you for offering to help me,' she said, her voice wobbling.

'It's what friends do. And when you're friends with someone in Seabury - it means you're family.'

CHAPTER 5

After her chat with Lionel that morning, Kate's delivery round felt like just what the doctor ordered. For the second day running, she pedalled with determination up the hill out of Seabury towards her friend Paula's graphic design office where she always made her first stop.

As usual, Stanley was happily ensconced in the trailer, and she was glad of his quiet company. That was the amazing thing about her best friend - he was always there for her but never asked her difficult questions or teased her about men she had the hots for even though she shouldn't. Stanley's company was exactly what she needed this morning.

Before Kate reached the Graphika offices, she'd made the executive decision not to share the news about Lionel's offer of help until she'd decided what to do. Lionel's certainty that Tom didn't have a leg to stand on felt too good to be true after the months of worry.

Even so, for the first time since that letter from Tom's solicitor demanding that she sell The Sardine and split the proceeds - she felt a bubble of hope. She almost didn't dare to think too hard about it. If she accepted Lionel's help, maybe, just maybe, this whole thing would be over and she could get back to enjoying her life without the threat of this great loss hanging over her.

By the time she pulled into the Graphika car park and drew Trixie and her trailer to a halt in front of the glass-fronted building, Kate had a big smile on her face – which was definitely a good thing as Paula and several of her colleagues were already outside, eagerly awaiting her arrival and enjoying a bit of Autumn sunshine while they were at it.

'We could set our clocks by you!' laughed one of the guys - who Kate was pretty sure was called Greg. 'I don't know how you do it, pedalling Trixie around!'

Kate grinned at him and hurried around the back to let Stanley down so that he could make his usual rounds and give hugs to everyone who needed them. As soon as he hopped down, she watched him make a beeline straight for Paula.

The big bear plonked his furry behind down onto her posh shoes and leaned back against her legs, staring up at her. Paula grinned at him in delight and promptly lowered herself into a squat so that she could wrap her arms around him.

'I *am* honoured,' she laughed, 'but I know it's only because I've got one of your faves in my pocket!'

Kate watched as her friend drew out a Rich Tea biscuit, snapped it in half and fed a piece to Stanley. He took it from her gently and it was gone in seconds. He quickly resumed his leaning and ignored the proffered second half.

Kate did her best to hide her frown of concern. Stanley only tended to ignore food and glue himself to someone when he sensed they were worried, upset or poorly. She made a mental note to check in with Paula when she wasn't surrounded by her colleagues. She'd seemed a lot better recently after her strange bout of ill-health back in the summer - but Kate had learned to trust Stanley's intuition when it came to people needing a little bit of extra TLC.

'So,' said Greg, snapping her attention back to him, 'are this month's cake boxes ready?'

Kate couldn't help but smile at his boyish excitement as she nodded.

'Yep - I've got everyone's orders here, and the three boxes you ordered for the office too!'

There was a general cheer at this, and it made Kate's heart sing. She was so proud of what her little team had achieved in such a short time. This month's boxes had a special autumn theme - so there was plenty of orange icing, cinnamon and spiced flavours, and the most divine little pumpkin cake-pops that Sarah had designed, complete with a salted caramel centre.

Kate busied herself doling out sandwiches and cake boxes until everyone had what they'd ordered and had disappeared back inside, shouting their thanks to her. Kate turned to have a few words with Paula before setting off for her next stop, only to find her friend still sitting with her arms around Stanley.

'You two okay down there?' she smiled.

'Erm, yes . . . but I think my feet have gone to sleep. Your pooch is quite heavy!' laughed Paula. 'Give me a hand?'

Kate grinned at her friend as she reached both hands down to her. The strange feeling she'd had five minutes ago cleared as she hauled her, laughing, up from the pavement. Stanley clearly thought that his hug had done the business too as he quickly snaffled the second half of the biscuit that Paula had left on the pavement.

Paula leant on Kate's shoulder as she stomped her feet, desperately trying to get some feeling back into them.

'So,' she said, 'dare I ask how it went with Tom?'

Kate pulled a face. 'Even worse than we were joking about!' she muttered.

'Ah crap, I'm sorry. What'll you do next?'

Kate shrugged, suddenly feeling a bit bad about her decision to keep Lionel's offer of help to herself, but she stuck with it.

'I'll just have to wait and see what happens next, I guess. Tom's not known for being a man of fast and decisive action,' she said with a grim smile.

'Ain't that the truth!' muttered Paula, reaching out and giving her hand a squeeze. 'You okay?'

Kate smiled at her and nodded. 'Yes. I'm okay. I'm just going to focus on enjoying autumn in Seabury. The rest will just have to work itself out.'

Paula smiled at her. 'Sounds like a plan to me. And . . . dare I ask . . . any progress with Mike?'

Kate groaned. 'Not you too?! That's all I'm hearing at The Sardine at the moment!'

'Oops. Sorry,' said Paula, but Kate noticed that she was looking anything but sorry. 'Us old married types have to get our kicks somewhere!'

'You're not old,' said Kate, desperately clutching at straws to change the subject. 'Fifties are the new twenties!'

Paula snorted. 'Tell that to my knees! Anyway - I've been married to Ryan since the dawn of time. Let me live vicariously!'

'I would if there was anything to report - but there isn't. We're friends. We had a lovely picnic last night up at the lighthouse.'

'How romantic!' sighed Paula, clearly choosing to ignore the bits she didn't want to hear.

'Hardly! We just talked about our twattish exes and Seabury gossip.'

'Don't tell me you're not attracted to him,' said Paula, wiggling her eyebrows.

Kate went quiet and frowned at her friend for a minute. 'Okay, I won't,' she said at last, causing Paula to squeal with excitement. 'Seriously though - with everything going on with Tom, and The Sardine, and Mike's business just getting on its feet - this isn't the right time. It might never be the right time . . .'

'Never say never!' was Paula's infuriating reply as she grabbed her own cake box along with a baguette from Trixie's trailer. 'Sorry lovely, I need to get back inside - conference call coming up. Urgh. Whoever invented video calling should be shot.'

Kate laughed. 'Catch up soon?' she said.

'I'll be in with the Chilli Dippers on Wednesday morning. We do need a proper catch up over a glass of wine soon though!'

'Sounds perfect,' said Kate, opening the back of the trailer so that Stanley could hop back in. Paula gave him one last tickle behind the ears, kissed Kate on the cheek and then headed back into the office.

'You'll never guess who's staying in that holiday cottage that ordered the two cake boxes out of the blue,' said Kate, striding back into The Sardine after parking Trixie up outside.

'Who?' asked Ethel, instantly firing up the Italian Stallion. 'And whoever it was, I hope you were nice to them young lady!' she frowned, making Lou chuckle over the teacakes she was busy laying out under the grill for toasting. 'I know you don't approve of second homes and all that, but paying customers are exactly what we need!'

Kate smirked. Ethel never would give up scolding her now and then when she was being stubborn about something.

'Of course I was nice!' she said. 'Actually, it was kind of hard not to be - they were so grateful for the treats. I don't think they've been having the best time.'

'Well,' said Lou, 'tell us. Who is it?'

'It's that couple who're holding their wedding reception in The Pebble Street Hotel in a couple of weeks,' said Kate. 'They've decided to rent that place until the wedding - a bit of a pre-wedding holiday so that they're close by!'

'How lovely!' said Ethel in surprise. 'But surely they should be having the time of their lives!'

Kate shook her head. 'Annabel - the bride-to-be - actually seemed quite down when she first answered the door. We got talking and I could tell she was trying to be a bit discreet and everything, but . . . reading between the lines, I'd say Veronica's already giving them the runaround!'

'Why doesn't that surprise me?!' huffed Ethel. 'There should be a law against that woman being allowed anywhere near someone's big day.'

Lou nodded. 'Yeah - she doesn't really seem the type that should be in that line of business, does she?'

'You've met her, then?' asked Kate, taking a coffee from Ethel and gratefully flopping down into one of the chairs for a moment while the cafe was quiet.

'Erm, yeah.'

Kate raised her eyebrows as a decidedly sheepish look crossed Lou's face.

'What's happened?' said Kate suspiciously.

'First of all - I'm really sorry, I didn't realise what she was like.'

'How could you, love?' said Ethel. 'You're new in town. I shouldn't have left you on your own for so long. It's my fault.'

'Alright you two, what's the wicked witch of Pebble Street been up to now?'

'Well, she came in when Ethel was having a chat with Charlie out in the yard. I told her to take a bit of a break, and Veronica came in.'

'In here?' said Kate in surprise. 'Blimey, that's the first time in months.'

'Yeah, well, we think she clocked that you and Ethel were both out of the way,' huffed Lou.

'So what's so bad?'

'She wangled a free coffee out of Lou for a start,' huffed Ethel. 'Told her you always ran a tab for her.'

Kate chuckled. 'She's incorrigible, you have to hand it to her.'

'I can think of ruder words that suit her better!' said Ethel.

'I did run a tab for her, years ago,' said Kate.

'Until we realised that she never ever coughs up,' said Ethel.

'Indeed,' said Kate raising a bemused eyebrow. 'So I'll just add another cappuccino to the dozens lost in that direction. Seriously Lou, don't worry about it. No big deal.'

'The coffee might not be, but-'

'Uh oh, this doesn't sound good!'

'That's because it's not,' scowled Ethel. Lou flinched and Ethel quickly patted her on the shoulder. 'Not you love - her!'

'She's ordered twenty-five cake boxes for that wedding,' said Lou quickly, like she was yanking off a plaster.

'Uh huh?' said Kate, a sinking sensation hitting her in the pit of her stomach.

'I asked her for payment upfront - like we've been doing all along - and she said that you always give her a fifty per cent discount for bulk orders for the hotel.'

Ethel let out a rumbling growl which was quickly echoed by a surprised Stanley.

'Sorry boy!' said Ethel, quickly feeding him a biscuit from her apron pocket to make up for scaring him.

'Oh. She did, did she?' said Kate.

Lou nodded. 'I'm really sorry.'

'She's paid for half already?' said Kate, mildly surprised.

'A cheque,' said Ethel shortly.

'Ah. She's back at that old game, is she?' said Kate lightly.

Lou nodded. 'Ethel told me they always bounce.'

'Always,' said Kate.

'I'm so sorry.'

'It's not your fault. I'll sort this one out - she was trying it on because you're new, that's all.'

'I can't believe she'd do that,' said Lou, looking hurt.

'Don't take it personally, love,' said Ethel. 'That old witch is an equal opportunity piss-taker.'

'Sadly, Ethel's right,' said Kate. 'And Lou - please don't worry! I should have told you about her, but she hasn't set foot in here for months, so I didn't really think about it.'

Lou nodded. 'Thanks Kate. And sorry.'

Kate just shook her head. 'Just for future reference - she has to pay for everything upfront when she orders - whether that's a coffee, breakfast or even a massive order for the hotel. But don't worry, I doubt you'll be seeing her in here again anyway. I'll be having words.' Kate paused and blew out a breath impatiently. 'In fact, I think I'll go pay her a visit right now. Pass me that cheque and keep an eye on Stanley for me!'

CHAPTER 6

Kate stomped along the seafront towards where The Pebble Street Hotel stood on the border of The Kings Nose - the grassy, rocky outcrop which speared out into the bay and separated West Beach from North Beach.

The hotel had been a really beautiful building in its heyday - it still was, if you could see past the peeling paint, windows that desperately needed repairing or replacing, and the general air of unkemptness that seemed to linger around it. It was a real shame that Veronica had let it get this scruffy - it was in a prominent position and could be a jewel in Seabury's crown if it was properly loved and looked after.

As Kate let herself into the narrow, weed-filled front garden, she wondered how Veronica had managed to bag herself the wedding booking in the first place with the hotel in such a state. The reception was due to take place in just a couple of weeks so it wasn't as though she had much time to get it spruced up before then. Not that Kate could believe the old skinflint was planning on spending a penny more than she had to on the event.

She paused at the front door, unsure for a moment whether she should knock or just wander straight in. She shrugged. If she were a guest, she'd just let herself in and head to reception, so she decided to do just that.

Turning the large brass knob, she pushed hard and found herself in the foyer. It had been years since she'd stepped foot in here - not since before her dad had passed away - and the sight of just how grubby and unloved the foyer looked made her quite sad. The parquet floor was still there, and would no doubt still be very beautiful if it was given a tiny bit of love and attention. As it was, it was filthy and didn't look like it had seen a mop in years - let alone any polish.

Over to the right stood a large oak reception desk, piled high with what looked to be an entire year's worth of paperwork, and at least several days' worth of old coffee cups. Kate wrinkled her nose and read the sign. Well, she *would* ring the bell for attention if she could see the bell, but she had a sneaking suspicion it had probably been covered up some time back in the spring - and it might take several hours of shifting papers around to unearth it.

Sod it - she'd have a little snoop around while she was here and see if she could find Veronica while she was at it.

Ignoring the sweeping staircase with its moth-eaten carpet, Kate headed towards the back of the building where she knew the guest lounge and dining room lay. She peeped into the lounge first and wrinkled her nose again. It smelled a bit like old cabbage. The little tables still held the remains of guest breakfasts - though they didn't look like today's. Partially empty bowls with dregs of old milk and a few cornflakes that had been left to weld themselves onto the china lay scattered on the tables. Discarded paper towels littered the floor and several cups boasting the cold, scummy remains of un-drunk coffee lay abandoned here and there.

Kate drew back into the hallway and made her way through to the dining room instead. She had to admit, she'd had no idea how bad things really were in here. She hadn't really given much thought to how Veronica was managing, considering she had no staff left.

For a moment, Kate was overwhelmed by a wave of pity - but that promptly disappeared when she remembered that Veronica didn't have any staff because she never paid their wages on time - if ever -

treated them appallingly, and had basically earned herself the title of Boss From Hell.

Kate wrapped her arms around herself, not really wanting to touch anything. It was all just so . . . grubby! Sure, she could still just about make out the forgotten splendour of the building buried under the layers of grime, but she couldn't for the life of her imagine why anyone would want to hold their wedding here!

Reaching the dining room, she let herself in. Ah. Okay, this might go some way to explaining it!

Mike had mentioned that Veronica was getting some work done on the place - and by the looks of things, she'd found that work in progress. The room had been newly painted in a soft, vintage eggshell. A couple of the windows had been re-glazed and it looked like there were new light fittings in the works too. The mangy carpet that was in evidence everywhere else had been removed, and she could see that certain parts of the parquet had already been beautifully restored.

'Can I help you?' asked a guy who was on his hands and knees, clearly hard at work in the far corner, laying a new section of floor with painstaking precision.

'Oh hi!' she smiled. 'This looks amazing!'

'Thank you. These old floors are a bit of a labour of love, but so worth it. I'm sorry, though - this room is closed to guests at the moment. We're doing it up for a wedding in a few weeks.'

Kate nodded. 'Yeah, sorry - I'm not a guest - I was looking for Veronica? It's about the . . . erm . . . catering for the wedding,' she invented quickly. Well, it was *kind* of true, wasn't it?

'Oh. Well, she went to get me a cup of coffee about an hour ago,' he said with a rueful smile. 'Between you and me though, the one she brought me yesterday was foul so I'm not too bothered!'

Kate laughed. 'Do you get a lunch break?' she asked.

The guy nodded. 'I'm pretty sure she'd quite like me to work straight through, but a man's got to eat! I asked my wife to pack something for me today though - Veronica's sandwiches have proven themselves to be . . . inedible?' he chuckled.

'Tell you what,' said Kate, instantly taking pity on the poor man, 'why don't you pop over to my cafe when you stop for your break? I'll treat you to lunch on the house!'

'You don't need to do that,' said the guy with a shy smile.

'It'd be my pleasure,' she said. 'I'm Kate, by the way.'

'Ken. And you've cheered me right up, Kate. Thank you!'

'I'm just a couple of minutes away, overlooking West Beach - at The Sardine?'

'I know it! I spotted it on my way in.'

'Great. See you for lunch, then. Right, I'd better go and hunt down Veronica.'

'Good luck!' he laughed.

Kate grinned at him and left him to it. She hated the fact that the poor guy was probably never going to see the money for such a huge job. She just hoped that he'd had the sense to get some of it paid upfront - but somehow she doubted it - that would be one of the reasons Veronica would have chosen him for the job in the first place.

Kate made her way back towards the kitchen, pushed at the swing door and was met with a screech.

'What on earth are *you* doing here?' demanded Veronica. She had a pair of rubber gloves on and was busy scraping mouldy food off of plates into a massive bucket - which looked like it hadn't been emptied in weeks.

Kate did her best to breathe through her mouth. The room smelled *bad*. Really, really *bad*. The kind of bad that a health and safety inspector would take one sniff of and have a fit.

'Can I have a word,' said Kate, doing her best not to choke. 'Maybe . . . not in here?'

'I don't have time,' said Veronica, curtly.

'It'll take thirty seconds.'

'Fine!' huffed Veronica, yanking her marigolds off with a double rubber snap and tossing them on top of the ginormous pile of washing up. 'Follow me.'

She pushed open a door that led out of the back of the building and Kate followed, hot on her heels, desperate for some fresher air.

'Wow!' she said, as soon as she'd escaped the stench. 'What a view!'

They were at the back of the hotel, overlooking The King's Nose and the sea beyond. Kate took a couple of steps away from the hotel and turned to peer around her. Over to her left was a beautiful, paved patio area that had obviously been newly cleared, cleaned down and repaired. The large flagstones were even and new sand was in evidence between them. There were even brand new planters around the edges of the space, with large sacks of compost standing ready in front of them. A set of glazed, double doors currently stood closed, but she'd bet anything that they led back into the dining room where Ken was busy at work.

'That looks amazing,' she said sincerely. 'What a beautiful space!'

Veronica snorted. 'A wedding reception with a sea view. That's a premium product. Idiots will pay through the nose for that.'

Kate bit her tongue. Of *course* Veronica wasn't one to see the romance in the place. She sighed. It was so, so sad that such a special place belonged to someone without the tiniest drop of magic in her soul. Ah well.

'Look, what do you want?' huffed Veronica. 'I've got a lot to do, and I don't trust that bloke not to rob me blind, neither.'

'What bloke?' said Kate in surprise. 'Do you mean Ken?'

'Ken? I don't know about that. The chippie in the dining room. Never trust a tradesman. All crooks,' she said.

Kate heaved a sigh. There really wasn't any point in arguing with Veronica - and yet-

'He seems like a lovely man,' she said stoutly. 'And he's doing a beautiful job on that floor.'

'Ruddy well should do too, the price he's charging.'

Kate raised her eyebrows. 'Well, it's specialist work.'

'It's a few bits of wood in some bleedin' holes,' grumbled Veronica.

'Well - you *are* going to pay him, fair and square, aren't you?'

Kate watched Veronica turn an interesting shade of puce and was suddenly very glad that they were outside. She could always make a hasty getaway onto The King's Nose if Veronica went supernova on her.

'What exactly are you insinuating?' she finally hissed.

'Oh nothing,' said Kate breezily. 'Anyway. Let's talk about why I came to see you. You wanted twenty cake boxes?'

'That's what I told the idiot you've got working for you. I've paid up too.'

'No, you haven't,' said Kate. 'You gave Lou a cheque. You *know* I don't accept cheques.'

Veronica shrugged. 'She said it was fine, so it's done now. You can't back out, we've got an agreement.'

Kate laughed. 'Veronica, we both know your cheques are made of rubber! Plus - it wouldn't be enough anyway. I don't know where you got the idea I'd give you a fifty per cent discount?'

'That was the girl!' said Veronica, crossing her arms. 'She offered. I'm not going to say no, am I? Anyway, you can't change your prices after the fact!'

Kate rolled her eyes and held the cheque up in front of Veronica. She proceed to tear it into strips, then into little squares, until she had a pile of pieces in the palm of her hand.

'Here!' she said with a wide smile, holding her hand out.

Veronica instinctively reached out, and before she knew what was happening, Kate had poured the torn pieces of cheque into her open palm.

'I . . . you . . .!'

'There's your confetti sorted at least,' said Kate, fighting to keep her face straight. 'Now then - I'll be glad to make up the cake boxes for you, and I'll even happily offer you a ten per cent discount as a local business. But you'll need to pay in advance, in full, by the end of the week if you would like us to add your order to the book.'

'You can't . . .' spluttered Veronica.

'You can apologise to Lou while you're at it too.' Kate smiled sweetly at her then stepped back towards the hotel, preparing to hold her breath for the dash back through the kitchen. 'Oh,' she said, turning to Veronica one last time before making her escape, 'we take cash or card, your choice.'

CHAPTER 7

Kate was partway back towards The Sardine when she paused, changing her mind. Quickly whipping out her phone, she pulled up Lou's number and sent her a text, letting her know that she was nipping over to New York Froth to warn Mike not to take any shit from Veronica.

She could only imagine that he'd be next on her list - not that he did fresh cakes, but she wouldn't put it past Veronica to get him to bulk-order something just for her. She quickly added a note about making sure that if a guy called Ken came in before she got back, he was to be treated to the royal welcome as well as a hot drink and whatever he fancied for lunch.

I'll explain when I get back. K x

Kate quickly hit send, pocketed her phone and

strode back in the opposite direction, making her way towards North Beach and the beautiful, newly opened New York Froth.

When she arrived, she paused briefly outside. How ridiculous - she had butterflies, and she knew they had nothing to do with warning Mike about Veronica. They were just about Mike himself. This crush - or *whatever* she had going on - was getting silly. In fact, it was time to get over it. Seabury was too small a town to avoid someone, and besides, she didn't want to avoid Mike. She loved spending time with the Grumpy Badger. He was excellent company. The fact that she had to spend her entire time focusing on not jumping on him . . . *that* was a bit of a problem.

Kate gave herself a little shake. This happened every time she tried to give herself a pep-talk - she just ended up listing the reasons why she liked Mike in the first place. It really didn't help matters in the slightest!

'Come on, Kate!' she muttered.

'Yeah, come on Kate!' came a chuckle from behind her.

She whipped around to find the man himself standing, holding open the door to the cafe, laughing at her.

'Hello!' she said with a grin that she hoped might cover up the pure mortification going on underneath.

'Hello yourself! What's up? You've been standing there muttering to yourself for ages!' he laughed.

Kate straightened her shoulders. Sod it, she'd just gloss over that little comment and cut to the chase. 'I've come to warn you about Veronica!' she said.

'Uh oh. That sounds like a job to do over a coffee - fancy one?'

Kate nodded and Mike grinned at her, indicating for her to follow him into the cafe.

He made his way around the other side of the counter, clapping his barista on the shoulder. 'I've got this one, Robbie,' he grinned.

'Okay boss - just remember Kate likes a double dose of hazelnut - and don't be stingy on the froth!'

Mike snorted and raised his eyebrows at Kate. 'Do I detect a regular in our midst?!'

'What?' demanded Kate, blustering and trying to cover up her blush. 'So I like to support other Seabury businesses . . . and sometimes it's nice to grab a coffee at a different beach!' she winked at Robbie.

'Right you are,' laughed Mike.

Plus, there's more chance I'll bump into you over here!

Kate scrunched up her nose and turned away from the counter to stare around the space that used to house the town's surf shop. It had gone out of business ages ago and had been such a sad, empty space right in the heart of Seabury before Mike had come in and worked his magic on it.

It was absolutely gorgeous in here - though a small part of her really did hate to admit it! It couldn't be more different from The Sardine if it tried. Whereas her place was tiny, eclectic and filled with seaside charm, New York Froth was a bit like having coffee in a beautiful old public library. The dark wood interior was lit with the warm glow of golden wall lights and quirky pendulums.

Several walls were papered to look like they held massive bookshelves, groaning with vintage volumes, but Mike had made sure to include several real bookshelves around the space too, and had even set up a book-swap in one of the back cabinets that was proving to be incredibly popular.

Sure - Kate came in here to hang out with Mike and to grab a coffee at a different beach. But she also came in here because it was simply a lovely place to spend time away from work. There had been quite a lot of muttering around town to begin when she was spotted drinking coffee in here - but then, as Mike spent just as much time hanging out at The Sardine, it soon blew over.

Right now, there was a gaggle of young mums taking over most of the back of the cafe. Their fleet of giant buggies was parked along the wall and they had an entire table groaning with coffees, pastries and sippy cups for the gang of rampaging toddlers who were clambering all over the leather sofas with gleeful abandon.

'Right. One very frothy hazelnut latte. Anything else?' asked Mike, popping the tall mug down on the counter next to his own minuscule espresso cup.

'Don't forget her biscotti or you'll be in trouble!' chuckled Robbie, grabbing the metal tongs and placing one on her saucer for her.

'Cheers Robbie!' she grinned.

'Outside or inside?' said Mike, as she picked up her cup and he followed her with his own.

'Inside. By the window?' said Kate. As much as she loved seeing the toddlers having fun on the sofas, she could really do with Mike being able to hear what she had to say!

'So, what's up?' he asked, smiling at her as he took the chair opposite hers.

'Veronica,' sighed Kate.

'Mm-hmm?'

'It's that wedding. She just tried to wangle twenty cake boxes. She got Lou to agree to a fifty per cent discount and then paid by cheque.'

'Ah. Not great.'

Kate smiled ruefully and shook her head. 'I've just been round there to warn her not to strong-arm my staff.'

'You know, I love your protective side!' laughed Mike.

Kate felt that treacherous blush rise to her cheeks again so she grabbed her coffee and took a sip. Not bad at all! Mike Pendle knew his way around a coffee machine, that was for certain.

'So?' said Mike, 'what happened?'

'Not much. I told her I'd give her a ten per cent discount - because I'd give that to any local business. And I told her she'd need to pay in full by cash or card by the end of the week.'

'And you don't think she'll do that?'

Kate chuckled. 'Not a chance.'

'I'm sorry you lost the order, though.'

Kate shook her head. 'I'm not. She'd be a nightmare from beginning to end. I just feel sorry for Annabel.'

'Whose that?' said Mike, looking confused.

'The poor bride. I met her on my delivery round. Her and her other half seem really lovely. I hate that they're going to be so disappointed.'

'You don't know they will,' said Mike gently.

'I've just been in there. The place is a biohazard, Mike!'

He wrinkled his nose. 'That bad?'

'I'm surprised she hasn't been shut down,' she said seriously.

'But surely this couple must have looked around before booking?'

Kate shrugged. She wouldn't have put it past Veronica to get around that somehow. 'She *is* doing up the dining room though. It's looking really nice, actually, but the rest of the place is awful.'

'I feel a bit sorry for her. Sounds like she's struggling,' said Mike looking thoughtful.

'I know,' sighed Kate. 'I do too . . . only . . . I would probably feel worse if she hadn't just tried to diddle me out of a bunch of money.'

Mike snorted. 'Good point! But wait - you said you wanted to warn me?'

Kate nodded, taking another comforting sip of coffee. 'She's going to be getting desperate. I can't believe she thought she'd manage to squeeze that little ruse past me . . .'

'She was relying on your soft side,' said Mike with a gentle smile.

'I'm afraid I don't have much of one of those anymore,' sighed Kate. 'Not after everything that's happened recently.'

Mike raised his eyebrows. 'You do. You're just a little bit more protective of it, that's all.'

Kate looked down at the table where her hand lay. Without thinking, Mike had just laid his own large paw over hers, and the feeling of his warm skin against hers was making her tingle.

Get a grip, Kate!

She forced a smile at him, and then as naturally as she could, took her hand away to pick up her mug.

'So,' said Mike, draining his own coffee as if nothing untoward had just happened, 'you think she might move on to me?'

Kate nodded. 'I wouldn't put it past her.'

'But I don't do cakes.'

'You do pastries - plus, she might try to get to Sarah through you rather than me,' she said, suddenly realising that she wouldn't put that past Veronica either.

'Would you mind if I did something for her - I mean, if she does ask?' said Mike.

'Not at all,' said Kate in surprise. 'I guess I just don't want her taking the piss out of anyone! Most of the stalwarts in town know exactly what she's like - that's why she waited until I was out on my rounds to approach Lou.'

'And that's why you think she might try to rope me in,' Mike nodded. 'I just hate the thought of that couple being let down, that's all.'

'I know what you mean,' sighed Kate. 'Just make sure you get paid upfront, that's all.'

'Got it!' said Mike. 'I'll make sure the staff know too - just in case. And thanks for the heads up!'

'Of course,' said Kate, smiling at him. 'It's what friends do, right?'

'Friends,' echoed Mike quietly, looking out of the window across at the sea. 'Right.'

'I guess I'd better-'

'Kate?' said Mike, suddenly turning back towards her and fixing his gaze on her. 'Do you think . . . I mean, would you like . . . no, never mind.'

'Mike, what?' She let out a little laugh, trying to brush off his awkwardness, but she suddenly had a strange sensation in her chest. It was like a cross between excited butterflies and impending doom.

'I just . . . I'd really like to . . .' he paused again and ran one hand through his hair making the dark strands stick wildly up in the air. Kate had the sudden urge to reach up and smooth them back into place. Instead, she firmly wrapped her hands around her almost-empty mug so that she wouldn't be tempted to do anything stupid without thinking about it.

'Man, this used to be so easy when I was a teenager,' laughed Mike. 'Kate, would you like to come out with me for a meal one evening?'

Kate smiled at him uncertainly. 'What, with you and Sarah?' she said lightly. She had a pretty good idea that this wasn't what he was asking at all, but she needed to check.

Mike shook his head. 'No, I mean just with me,' he paused and cleared his throat. 'Like - a date. I'd really like to take you out on a date.'

And there it was. The sense of doom settled in her chest. She'd dreaded this moment - not because she didn't want it to happen - but because she wanted it to happen so much and knew that she'd have to give him an answer that would totally suck for both of them.

'I'm sorry. I can't,' she said quietly.

Mike shook his head with a smile that didn't

come quick enough to mask the look of hurt that crossed his face.

'It isn't that I don't want to,' she said hesitantly.

'You don't have to explain,' said Mike.

'I do. I love your company but . . . Mike, I'm just not ready.'

'Is it because of Sarah?' he asked, clearly trying to keep his voice as light as possible.

Kate let out a snort of surprise. 'Are you kidding me? She's been on my case about asking you out for weeks!'

Mike groaned and covered his face with his hands. 'Uhhhh, kiiiiids!' he whined through his fingers, making her laugh.

'It's just this whole mess with Tom,' she sighed.

'You don't think I'm like him, do you?' said Mike, looking even more horrified, if that was at all possible.

'No, of course not. But . . . until that's done and dusted, I just feel like I'm in limbo. I need a clean break from that mistake - and let's not even *mention* "Pierre",' she muttered. 'Maybe I need a bit of time to put that behind me too.'

Mike nodded. 'Okay. I mean, I get where you're coming from. I've felt the same with Sienna - not that it bothered her in the slightest - I think she moved on before we'd even officially split up!'

'God, I'm sorry!' said Kate.

'Don't be. It was over between us long before it was over if you know what I mean.'

Kate nodded. 'Yeah, sadly I do.' She heaved a sigh. Logically she knew that she'd just made the right decision, but that didn't stop her heart from wanting to kick her stupid, logical brain in the nuts for making her miss out on what she knew would have been an amazing first date.

'Kate . . .' said Mike, glancing at her. 'I know now's not the right time, but is there a chance . . . you know, maybe one day, when things are a bit more sorted? Or is this a gentle way of you telling me it's a "never" kind of no?'

Kate looked at him. Mike looked like he was forcing himself to meet her eye, and he was definitely looking quite pink in the face by this point. She had to forcibly stop herself from leaning over and grabbing him.

She took a deep breath. It wasn't fair to lead him on, was it? It wasn't fair to make him wait around for something that might never happen.

'I . . .' she trailed off as her heart gave her head a firm punch and took over. 'It's definitely *not* a never kind of no,' she said quietly.

'So, maybe one day?' he said, his eyes twinkling.

'Maybe.'

CHAPTER 8

Kate yawned widely and dragged the two little tables out onto the pavement in front of The Sardine. It looked like it was going to be yet another beautiful crisp, autumn day. The sea was calm and the early morning mist made everything look magical. She could hear the Chilly Dippers squealing and giggling on their early-morning swim from here, and it made her smile. She hoped Stanley was behaving himself and hadn't decided on a spot of impromptu seal-watching this morning!

Kate let out a huge sigh and smiled. Ever since Mike had asked her out on that date, she'd felt lighter, somehow. Happier. Which was ridiculous, considering that she'd turned him down, but still . . . something about that moment had made her realise that there was a life full of new possibilities and adventures waiting for her beyond this mess with Tom. There were things to look forward to, even if she wasn't quite ready to open up to them yet.

She trundled back indoors and headed into the little galley kitchen. She'd prepared a vat of spiced pumpkin and squash soup the day before using some of the beauties Charlie had brought her from his allotment. It had plenty of cumin in it and was sweet and spicy and very warming - just what the Chilly Dippers would need after a cold dip in the October sea. As soon as it was hot, she'd pop it into the soup kettle and then head down for a quick wander along the beach and watch the girls in action before starting the day.

∽

As soon as she reached the little set of stone steps that lead down onto the beach, Kate spotted the rather unusual sight of Paula, wrapped in a towel, sitting on the beach. From here, it looked like she was watching the others as they either pranced around in the shallows or swam in steady breast-stroke backwards and forwards along the stretch of beach, never venturing too far from the shore.

Kate carefully climbed down the sandy steps and made her way over towards her friend. She'd changed into her swimsuit with the others in the cafe, but Kate could see that she'd pulled a pair of jogging bottoms back onto her legs and had her vast, fluffy towel wrapped tightly around her shoulders.

What was even stranger about this sight was that Stanley was sitting next to her. Kate frowned with worry. His fur was completely dry, so he clearly hadn't been in for a swim either. Paula had her arms wrapped around the big bear, and now Kate was closer she could see that her friend's face was buried in Stanley's neck.

She walked quietly towards them, and it was only when she was about ten paces away that she noticed Paula's entire body was shuddering with wracking sobs.

Stanley glanced up at Kate with worried eyes, but he didn't stir. Clearly, he knew that Paula needed him right now, and there was no way he was going to desert her - not even to greet his best friend.

'Paula love?' said Kate quietly, sitting down next to her, but leaving a space between them. She didn't want to startle her friend, and until she knew what was going on, she didn't want to touch her in case she'd hurt herself.

Paula looked up in surprise at the sound of her voice, and Kate couldn't help but let out a gasp. Paula's eyes were red and puffy - she'd clearly been crying for a while. It broke Kate's heart to think of her here, all on her own, when the other Dippers were having fun so close by. They obviously hadn't noticed that there was something dreadfully amiss with their troublemaker-in-chief.

'Kate!' she said, taking one hand away from Stanley's coat and mopping her eyes with the edge of her towel. 'Sorry! I thought I was on my own. I didn't mean for anyone to see me like this.'

'Don't apologise!' said Kate quickly. She wanted to reach out and hug her friend but something held her back.

'Ignore me,' snuffled Paula.

'Fat chance!' muttered Kate. 'What's wrong?'

'Seriously - ignore me,' said Paula again, with a wobbly attempt at a smile. 'It's probably just insane hormones or something.'

Kate frowned. She knew when she was being fobbed off, but equally, she also knew what it was like when you just weren't quite ready to talk about something.

'Okay,' said Kate. 'But you know I'm right here - if you want to talk?'

Paula let out a huge, shuddering sigh and nodded. 'Thanks. I know. And . . . we will, just not yet - if that's okay?'

'Of course it is,' said Kate. 'Want a human hug?' she asked, smiling across at Stanley.

Paula nodded, and Kate scooted her bum closer so that she could wrap her arm around her friend. Paula snuggled into her, resting her head against Kate's shoulder, but she kept her other arm firmly wrapped around the warm, comforting fluff-mountain that was Stanley.

When Paula's breathing had calmed down and she seemed to have settled a bit, Kate felt like she could talk again. 'Didn't fancy a swim this morning?' she asked lightly.

'I just . . . I thought I did, but then I decided I just wanted to watch the others doing what they love, you know?'

'It's a good sight!' said Kate with a smile. 'I could hear them laughing from inside The Sardine!'

'Yeah. They're like family to me, this bunch.'

Kate swallowed a lump that rose suddenly to her throat. Paula sounded so sad. Completely heartbroken in fact.

'Ignore me,' said Paula again with a little laugh as a couple of fresh tears escaped. 'Like I said - probably hormones.'

'Mm,' mumbled Kate noncommittally.

'I'm really sorry Stanley hasn't had his swim, though! I tried to get him to go down to the sea with the others, but he just glued himself to my side!' She stroked his head gently and Kate saw Stanley lean his weight against her.

'He always knows when someone needs a bit of extra TLC,' said Kate, squeezing her friend's shoulders.

'He really is the best dog,' said Paula.

'He is. And you know where he is whenever you

need an extra floofy hug or a bit of unconditional comfort. Stanley's right here for you.'

Paula nodded gratefully. 'Thanks Kate,' she said, staring ahead at the sea.

'I'm right here for you too,' said Kate quietly.

Paula turned to face her, and even though her lips were still quivering with whatever emotion she was currently struggling with, she gave her a grateful smile. 'Kate - whatever happens, you can always talk to me too, okay? Promise we'll always be friends?' said Paula, her chin quivering.

'Oh love,' sighed Kate, gathering her friend to her with both arms as she broke down into tears again, 'of course I promise.'

⁓

By the time the Dippers had finished steaming up the windows and filling The Sardine with the sound of laughter, Kate felt a bit like a wrung sponge. Lou had cheerfully agreed to head off and take Trixie out on her rounds, leaving Kate to man the cafe alone until it was time for Sarah's shift to start. Stanley had stayed behind too - glued to Paula's side as she picked at her breakfast and joined in with the general banter in a half-hearted way.

'Do you think anyone noticed anything?' she asked as she gave Kate a quick, final hug before heading off to work.

Kate pulled back, gave her a reassuring smile and shook her head. 'You're all good. Hope today gets better - and let's catch up soon, okay?'

Paula nodded gratefully, gave Stanley a final pat and headed off.

For the next ten minutes, every time Kate turned around Stanley was right there, staring at her in concern. The third time she nearly tripped over him as she cleared away the detritus of the Dippers' breakfasts, she gave in. Plonking the plates she was carrying back down onto the tabletop, she knelt down next to him on the floor.

'What's up, boy?' she asked gently.

Stanley wiggled his beautiful eyebrows at her, let out a pitiful whine and then coming as close as he could, he leant his heavy head on her shoulder.

'Oh, my poor bear!' she said in surprise. 'Your turn for a hug, huh?' she asked, gently wrapping her arms around him and holding him close.

They stayed like that in the empty cafe for several long minutes until Kate heard the door open and close.

'Hey - are you okay?' came Sarah's voice from overhead, full of surprise at having found her boss on the floor with her arms wrapped around Stanley.

'*I'm* fine,' said Kate, smiling up at her. 'Stanley needed a hug though, didn't you lad?' she said, pulling back at last and ruffling his ears. 'You better now?'

He wagged his tail, then stood up and turned to greet Sarah.

'Looks like you've worked your magic on him!' laughed Sarah, as he nosed the pocket of her jacket where she usually kept a stash of his favourite treats.

'I think it's just one of those days,' shrugged Kate.

'Sooo, how's project Grumpy Badger going?' said Sarah, peeling off her jacket and throwing a cheeky wink at Kate over her shoulder as she hung it on the pegs.

'Don't start,' sighed Kate. Normally she didn't mind one bit - okay, she *did* mind - but she could deal with it. But after the ridiculously emotional start to the day, and the fact that she knew she wouldn't be able to stop worrying about what was bothering Paula until they had the chance to meet up for a proper chat, Kate just wasn't in the mood.

'Sorry,' said Sarah, looking mildly surprised.

'No,' said Kate, 'I'm sorry. I didn't mean to snap - I'm just getting it from every direction at the moment.'

'Well,' said Sarah, her voice thoughtful, 'if you don't want people talking about you guys and assuming things are . . . erm . . . progressing . . . perhaps sitting in the window of New York Froth and holding hands is a bad idea?'

'Holding hands?!' squeaked Kate. 'We weren't holding hands!'

'Calm down,' laughed Sarah, 'it isn't illegal, you know!'

'But we *weren't . . . oooooh . . .*' That moment when she'd told Mike she no longer had a soft side, and he'd briefly laid his hand on hers.

'Don't try to pretend it didn't happen, because I saw you with my own eyes,' smirked Sarah.

'I was . . . erm . . . upset about something, and your dad was just trying to comfort me, that's all. Just - as a friend,' she added.

Sarah's face fell. 'But you guys would be *so* good together! And I know you like him.'

Kate bit her lip. She didn't want to snap at the girl again, this *was* her father they were talking about after all, but equally, she really *did* need to put an end to this - for her own sanity, if nothing else.

'Look,' she said carefully, 'I *do* like your dad. He's a lovely guy and I'm really enjoying having him as a friend.'

'So-!' Sarah started, her eyes shining in excitement.

Kate quickly held her hand up to stop her in her tracks. 'So - I've just told him that I'm not ready to be anything other than friends.'

'Aw, but-'

'You get it, don't you?' said Kate, looking at her appealingly. 'I had a bad experience with Pierre . . . Ian . . . whatever his name was, and don't even get me started on Tom! Until this mess with getting the divorce sorted out is all over and done with - it's just hanging over me. It's not that I'm not ready for a relationship with your dad - it's more that I'm not ready for one with *anyone*.'

Sarah chewed her lip a moment. 'Okay - I guess I *do* get it,' she sighed.

'Good,' said Kate with a small smile.

'And I'll back off a bit. Sorry - I was just having a bit of fun because I know how much he likes you.'

'That's okay - but thanks.' Kate tried her best to shut up the inner voice that was now jumping up and down like an excited six-year-old shouting *Mike lurves Ka-aaate, Mike lurves Ka-aaaate!*

'Morning ladies!'

'Hey George!' said Sarah brightly, turning to take a wodge of envelopes from their regular postie. 'We've got your cake box if you want to take it now? Or did you want to pop back in when you're done?'

'I'll swing by for a coffee this afternoon when I've finished for the day, thanks Sarah,' he smiled. 'If anyone spots me doing my rounds with my cakes, I'll end up with an empty box again - that's what happened last month - I barely got a look in!' he chuckled.

'Now there's a bit of advertising I would never have dreamed up in a million years,' said Kate. 'And for that - this afternoon's coffee is on the house.'

'Ah, you're an angel. See you both later then!' he

said, raising his hand in a wave as he strolled back out onto the seafront.

'Here,' said Sarah, handing the post to Kate before heading outside to make sure their little yard was all set up to receive the first customers of the day.

Kate flicked through the pile, fully expecting to be able to bung the whole lot into the recycling. There were the usual circulars from the local garden centre and a pamphlet for double glazing. Tucked neatly in between them was a manilla envelope that made her heart plummet. She half wished that she hadn't spotted it at all, but she'd already learned the hard way that envelopes like this shouldn't be ignored.

Kate quickly checked over her shoulder and, seeing that she was alone, tore the envelope open, barely keeping the grimace off her face.

Sure enough, it was yet another letter from Tom's solicitor. Some kind of bill, by the looks of things. As she scanned the list of figures in front of her, her jaw dropped, and when she reached the total at the bottom of the second side of A4, she let out a fluent string of swearwords.

'Pretty fruity for a Wednesday morning!'

Kate spun around, only to find both Lionel and Sarah staring at her.

'So sorry Lionel . . . it's Tom again.'

'What a prat,' said Sarah, wandering past and giving Kate a comforting pat on the shoulder.

'Hand it over,' grunted Lionel.

'I . . .'

'Please, Kate. Let me help you. This has gone on for long enough, don't you think?'

She wasn't sure if it was the memory of Paula sobbing into Stanley's coat, or the massive sense of loss she'd felt when she'd turned Mike down just because she hadn't managed to clear all this mess up yet, but something in Kate finally gave way.

'Here,' she said, handing him the letter. 'He's charging me for all of his solicitor's time - which is bloody massive because he's being such a dumbass - and all his mediation costs. On the second sheet, they've outlined the costs of going to court . . . and I just can't . . . I can't . . .' Kate paused and swallowed. She *would not* burst into tears in the middle of the cafe. Not in front of poor Sarah. Not in front of Lionel. What if a customer came in?

'Come out to the yard with me to take my order a second?' he said to her, glancing quickly over at Sarah.

Kate nodded. 'Back in a sec,' she mumbled and followed Lionel outside.

The minute they reached the empty courtyard, Kate sank into one of the pretty metal chairs and rubbed her face hard with her hands. She *had* to get her act together.

'Sorry - I thought it would be best to speak in private a moment,' said Lionel with a look of concern on his face.

Kate nodded. 'It's not fair on Sarah!'

'No. I'm sure she had enough drama when her parents went through it all.'

Kate nodded.

'Kate, please, *please* let me call in that favour with Philip. This has gone on too long, and I don't know what these fellows are playing at, but it's not cricket!'

'I guess I deserve it!' said Kate.

Lionel shook his head firmly. 'Even if you had misbehaved during your marriage, the law doesn't take it into account in the slightest unless we were talking about extreme violence or something similar. But you didn't - you simply made a mistake and married a man you didn't love.'

Kate nodded miserably, because recently she'd started to realise just how different it *did* feel when you really started to fall for someone.

'Can I pass this on to Philip?' he said, waving the letter. 'Let me help you.'

Kate held her breath for a moment, staring straight past Lionel out at the sea. She'd love nothing more than to get on with her life. It was time.

'Okay - yes. Yes please, Lionel. I would love your help. This has gone on way too long. You're right.'

'Wonderful!' said Lionel, smiling broadly. 'Just you wait, we'll have this all done and dusted before you know it!'

'Thank you.'

'Like I said before - we're family!'

CHAPTER 9

After the morning she'd had, Kate wanted nothing more than to disappear up to the safety of her flat and have a damn good skiving session in front of a film. If it hadn't been for the fact that she knew Paula was at work, she might have even tried to convince her friend to come over and try to get her to open up about whatever was bothering her.

As it was, the little cafe was super-busy all morning, keeping both her and Sarah run off their feet. An entire fleet of cyclists who were working their way along the south coast had arrived. They'd commandeered the little yard and her outdoor tables too - and there still wasn't enough room for them all to perch somewhere.

Kate suggested that perhaps some of them might prefer to make their way along to North Beach and head into New York Froth if they would prefer to sit inside, but every single one of them had stayed put. It had taken a good hour to make sure they all had their drinks and snacks and were happy.

Even the usually indefatigable Sarah was beginning to droop by the time Lou reappeared from the delivery round.

'Why don't you give Ethel a call?' said Lou to Kate as she took over from Sarah behind the coffee machine, giving the poor girl a much-needed break. 'Sarah's got to go in for lectures this afternoon, and I don't mean to be rude, but you look like you could do with a break too, boss!'

Kate paused and raised her eyebrows. Ethel had been in full jam-making flow over the past few weeks. Because they now had Lou, she hadn't been working quite so many shifts in the cafe - preferring to focus on the cake subscription boxes and sneaking off for romantic trysts with Charlie - but she always said that she was more than happy to step in whenever needed. Considering Kate felt like she'd already worked a twelve-hour day, this definitely counted as one of those occasions.

'You know what, I think I will give her a call,' sighed Kate.

'Good. We've all got to look after each other, right?'

Kate nodded. 'Right. And thank you for doing the rounds this morning - I really appreciate that.'

'Happy to do it whenever you need me - I love getting out and meeting everyone!'

'You might not be *quite* so keen when the rain is coming at you sideways,' laughed Kate.

'I'll leave those days to you!' chuckled Lou.

'Any issues at all today?'

'Nope!' said Lou. 'Graphika asked if I could add a couple more cake boxes to their order on Monday because they've got a bunch of interviews lined up - so that'll keep Ethel out of trouble,' she laughed, 'oh, and there was a note on the door of that holiday cottage - you know, the one where the couple for the wedding are staying?'

'Oh?' said Kate.

'Yeah - just asking if we could bring their order back here and they'll pick it up later because they're in town for a last-minute meeting with Veronica. It was very apologetic.'

'Oh, okay,' said Kate, 'well, that's no problem! What are their names again . . . Annabel and . . .? I keep forgetting the groom!'

Lou fiddled in her back pocket, drew out a crumpled note and unfolded it. 'Annabel and Lee,' she said. 'Anyway, I've already popped their order over there ready for them to collect later.'

'Fab. Right, I'll just give Ethel a quick call to see if she can cover me. Even an hour might help!'

Kate grabbed her mobile and within minutes, Ethel had cheerfully agreed to cover a couple of hours so that Kate could take a break. 'Sorry I can't do more than that, but Charlie's taking me to the pictures this afternoon,' she said, and Kate could hear the grin in her voice.

'Oh Ethel, then don't worry about it!' said Kate quickly. 'You'll want to be getting ready for your date, not working!'

'Nonsense!' laughed Ethel. 'I'll just ask Charlie to pick me up from The Sardine.'

Kate did her best to backtrack, but Ethel was having none of it and promised to be there within twenty minutes.

She was just stashing her mobile away again with a mixture of relief at being able to escape the cafe for a couple of hours and guilt for making Ethel change her plans, when Mike appeared in the doorway.

'Well, this is a nice surprise!' she said, unable to keep the smile off her face.

Mike smiled at her, but she couldn't miss the fact that he looked like his morning had been just as bad as hers.

'I've not missed Sarah, have I?' he asked, a worried note in his voice.

'No, she just nipped out the back,' said Lou. 'Would you like a coffee?'

Mike shook his head. 'No - thanks though - I've been pretty much mainlining it all morning!'

'Is everything alright?' said Kate.

'Erm, well . . . yes, but I've had a bit of sad news. My old aunt passed away suddenly last night.'

'Oh Mike, I'm so sorry,' said Kate.

'Thanks,' he said awkwardly. 'I just felt like I should tell Sarah as soon as possible. I know she's meant to have college this afternoon, but she adored Aunty Sally and they were quite close. She was more like her grandmother than an aunt.' He let out a weary sigh and rubbed his face. 'Sorry. I know I probably shouldn't have just turned up when she's still got to finish her shift.'

'Don't apologise,' said Kate gently, moving over to him and giving him an awkward pat on the arm. What she really wanted to do was throw her arms around him and give him a damn good cuddle, but she had a sneaking suspicion that wouldn't be fair.

'Hey dad!' said Sarah with a grin, appearing in the doorway and looking between Mike and Kate, an excited gleam in her eye, 'what's up?'

'I've got a bit of bad news, love,' he said. 'Grab your coat and we'll go for a wander on the beach and over to Nana's for an ice cream.'

Sarah looked at him, and Kate's heart squeezed as she saw the fear cross the young girl's face.

'Is it mum?' she said, her voice trembling, all traces of her smile now completely gone.

Mike's eyebrows shot up in surprise and he quickly shook his head. 'No love, it's not your mum. It's about Aunty Sally.'

Kate grabbed Sarah's coat and bag for her and handed them over to Mike, and both she and Lou watched them leave, Sarah grabbing her dad's hand as they pushed their way out through the door, looking more like a scared little six-year-old rather than the confident sixteen-year-old she was.

'Poor kid,' sighed Lou.

'I know,' said Kate sadly. 'Poor Mike, too. Man, can this day get any worse?'

'Don't!' squeaked Lou. 'You'll jinx it!'

They'd barely had time to turn their back on the door when Ethel bowled in.

'Ah, my hero!' said Kate, smiling at her old friend. 'Thank you so much!' she said.

'Not a problem, deary,' said Ethel quickly, looking slightly distracted.

'Sure?'

'Absolutely - but I'm afraid we might have a bit of an emergency on our hands before you head off.'

'I *told* you that you'd jinx it!' muttered Lou, making Ethel a coffee without bothering to ask if she wanted one.

'If that's my latte,' said Ethel, shooting a grateful smile at Lou, 'you'd better make a triple espresso and a cappuccino with plenty of chocolate while you're at it.'

'Who for?' said Kate.

'Come with me,' said Ethel, nodding at the door. 'I'll pop back in for the coffees in a sec, Lou love!'

Lou gave Ethel a quick thumbs up and loaded up the puck to set the Italian Stallion to work.

Ethel grabbed a pile of napkins on her way out, making Kate raise her eyebrows in question, but her friend just sighed and led her around into the little yard.

'Annabel!' said Kate, spotting the young bride-to-be perched at one of the tables in the corner. She'd been focusing on her phone screen, but as soon as she heard her name, she looked around.

Kate gasped. 'What's the matter!'

Annabel's eyes were red and puffy, and there were still tear tracks on her face. The young man opposite her stood up and held his hand out to Kate.

'Hi - you must be Kate.'

'Lee?' said Kate, assuming that this must be the groom-to-be.

'Yep, that's me.'

'It's lovely to meet you, but what's up?'

'Sorry, Kate,' sighed Annabel. 'I'm being a drama queen, that's all!'

'You are not,' said Ethel stoutly, passing her the napkins. 'She's been Veronica-d,' she added, turning to Kate.

'May I?' said Kate, pointing to the empty chair. Lee nodded, and she sank down into it.

'Veronica-d?' he muttered, as Ethel disappeared back towards the cafe.

'I'm afraid she doesn't have the best . . . erm . . .

reputation. At least, not when it comes to customer service.'

'Oh nooooo,' said Annabel, dropping her face into her hands.

'It'll be fine, Bel!' said Lee, covering her hand with his. 'It's only the cake. I'm sure we can sort it out!'

He widened his eyes pleadingly at Kate.

'Tell me exactly what's going on,' she said. 'Only if you want to, of course!' she added, with a small smile.

'Veronica said that the person supplying the cupcakes that were meant to make up our wedding cake have let her down, and they're refusing to give our money back,' said Annabel, frowning.

Kate did her best to hold back a growl. So *that's* what the cake boxes were for? How much should she tell these two? She didn't want to talk out of turn about Veronica - not when these two still had to deal with her . . . but this was business. She wasn't sure what Veronica was up to, but it didn't exactly sound like she was being upfront with them.

She was about to ask for more details when Ethel appeared carrying a tray with three coffees as well as their order that had been due for delivery up to their cottage earlier.

'Here - coffees - and I thought maybe your lunch might make things look a bit brighter!'

'Thanks so much,' said Lee, beaming at her. 'And for bringing us straight over here.'

'Well, it was clear by the looks on your faces that

you'd just had a run-in with the wicked witch of Pebble Street,' said Ethel, rolling her eyes.

Kate eyeballed her, not wanting to make the pair any more upset than they already were.

'What do you mean?' said Annabel. 'Is she really that bad? I mean, she's always been pretty . . . curt . . . when I've spoken to her, but she's always been adamant that she'd find exactly what we wanted for the big day!'

'Have you . . .' Kate paused. Ah well, they were well and truly spooked by this point anyway, so she may as well just dive in head-first. 'Have you had a proper look around The Pebble Street Hotel yet?' she asked curiously.

Annabel rolled her eyes. 'No, not yet.'

'You booked without seeing it?' said Ethel in surprise, still hovering, clearly intrigued.

'Bel's grandparents got married there,' said Lee. 'We've seen all the beautiful photos. Her grandma, Rose, passed away last year and we thought . . .' he paused and took Annabel's hand across the table. 'We thought we'd like to honour her memory.'

Kate's eyebrows shot up. *That* explained a lot.

'Veronica's having a lot of work done on the place - returning it to its former glory - so it's not safe for us to go in for a look around just yet,' said Annabel.

'We got to have a quick peek into the dining room just now through the double glass doors around the back, and it looks like it's going to be lovely,' said Lee, though Kate noticed that he looked a little bit sceptical.

'And the wedding's in-?'

'Ten days,' said Lee.

'That's why we decided to stay down here,' said Annabel. 'So that we can be on hand as soon as we can get in to see it.'

'Erm . . .' Kate looked up at Ethel in alarm. Should she tell them that she'd been in there just a few days ago, and the place was an abomination and the only work taking place was in the dining room itself?

'Did you explain about the cake?' said Ethel, clearly trying to steer the conversation back to a slightly more manageable problem to begin with.

Annabel nodded. 'Yes.'

'Well, what I'm sure Kate's been too polite to tell you is that Veronica tried to order twenty of our cake subscription boxes for your wedding the other day.'

'Oh!' said Annabel in surprise. 'You're the company? But then . . .'

'It wasn't us that let you down,' sighed Kate. 'Like I said, Veronica has a bit of a reputation . . .'

'What do you mean?' said Lee, frowning.

'She never pays her bills,' said Ethel bluntly. 'So we can't take cheques from her anymore.'

'But she said you'd refused the order and then refused to give her the money back?' said Annabel looking confused.

Kate shook her head and sighed. 'On the contrary.

I would be very happy to do the order - *if* that's what you want, though I'm sure you had something a bit more special in mind for your wedding cake than several takeaway boxes emptied out onto a stand?!'

Annabel nodded then covered her mouth with a gasp. 'Sorry - I didn't mean that in a bad way. You know we're huge fans of yours - but I *did* expect something a bit fancier for three hundred quid!'

Ethel let out a snort. 'That thieving witch!'

'Yes, *thank* you Ethel!' said Kate quickly.

'Sorry. I . . . um, I think I'd better go and help Lou before I say something I shouldn't!'

Kate watched her bustle away, and she could tell from the set of her shoulders that her old friend was decidedly angry.

'Sorry,' said Kate, turning back to the couple, who were looking uncomfortable. 'Ethel's so straight down the line, she hates seeing Veronica pull this stuff. Look, just so you know, I haven't taken any of your money from Veronica - so you're absolutely free to go ahead and find the cake of your dreams and get her to put the order in for you.'

'But why would she say that you've got the money?' said Lee, looking baffled.

'I have no idea,' said Kate. 'Maybe she's just confused. I can assure you, I tore up the cheque in front of her and gave it back to her.'

'I just don't understand why she didn't just give you the cash,' said Annabel, shaking her head. 'Even if it wasn't what we had discussed for our cake, at least it would have been something!'

'Can I ask a personal question?' said Kate carefully.

Annabel nodded.

'Have you also paid Veronica a deposit for the hotel?'

'No,' said Lee. 'It's so important to us that we get to celebrate at The Pebble Street Hotel - and we wanted to be sure that we'd get the whole place. Veronica wasn't happy to close to other guests for the weekend unless we paid the whole fee up front, so we went ahead and did that. She's had the entire booking fee, plus the balance for catering, alcohol and the cake too.'

'And the band,' said Annabel excitedly. 'Don't forget the band!'

Kate could hear alarm bells ringing so loudly it was as though they'd been attached directly to her ears. She did her best to keep her face looking calm. She didn't want the couple to start freaking out as much as she was right now.

'If you want my advice . . .?' she paused and glanced at them, checking. Both Lee and Annabel nodded. 'Okay, I think it might be a good plan to insist that you have a look around the hotel - don't leave it any longer and don't let her weasel out of it. There isn't any work that should stop you going in.'

Lee raised his eyebrows and nodded. 'Yeah, we were just saying that to Ethel on the way over.'

'Then I'd say trust your instincts on that one. Plus - some friendly advice from someone who's had issues dealing with Veronica before - I'd ask to see all the paperwork to prove that your catering and drinks orders are sorted. It might not be a bad idea for you to make a couple of backup phone calls directly to the companies too - just to be absolutely sure it's all in hand.'

'You don't think . . .?' said Lee, looking alarmed now.

Kate tried to give him a reassuring smile, but she was pretty sure she looked just as spooked as they did by this point. 'I'm sure it'll all work out just fine - but it would put your minds at rest, wouldn't it?'

'It's a good idea, actually. Thanks Kate,' said Annabel. 'And we'll talk about the cake while we're at it too - it's getting pretty last minute to find someone now though . . .'

'Well,' said Kate, thinking on her feet, 'if you *do* get stuck, you know where I am. I'll do my best to help in any way I can - I might have a young, talented baker who'd love to work with you.'

CHAPTER 10

'Hey Sarah, how're you doing?'

Kate smiled as she watched Sarah fight to get herself and her umbrella through the door of The Sardine without drenching everything - without much luck. It was one of those days where the rain was lashing horizontally across the seafront. Somehow, she doubted they'd be particularly busy today.

Kate hadn't seen Sarah since Mike had picked her up from her shift a couple of days ago, and as she watched her shake out her long hair and bend down to cuddle Stanley, she couldn't help but notice how pale she was.

'I'm okay,' said Sarah.

Kate waited for her to say more, but she was too focused on fussing with Stanley. That was okay - she'd primed both Lou and Ethel to be a bit gentle with her over the next few days as she came to terms with the sad news about her great aunt.

Mike had texted Kate the previous day to apologise again for turning up at The Sardine and stealing Sarah away a bit early from her shift. He'd also warned her that Sarah seemed to be struggling more than he'd expected with the news.

'How're things at college?' asked Kate, trying to draw her out a bit.

Sarah shrugged. 'Pretty good. All the boring hygiene stuff is done for this term now, so we get to bake more.'

'What are you working on at the moment?' asked Kate, wanting to keep her chatting now that she'd got her going.

'Celebration cakes. That's the next bit. I could really do with a bit more practise. All my experience has been baking practical stuff. You know what I mean?'

'Yep!' said Kate. 'Good food that people want to eat. You're not going to have any problem!' she added cheerfully. 'Lots of people know how to make it look nice but forget to make the cake underneath actually taste of something!'

Sarah nodded and sighed. 'Idiots.'

Kate sniggered. 'Pretty much. But you're coming at it the right way round!'

'But I don't know any of those fancy decorating techniques!' said Sarah frowning. 'Maybe this course isn't going to teach me what I need after all . . . maybe I *should* be looking for something different . . .'

'Erm . . . I'm pretty sure they don't expect you to know everything before they've actually taught it to you,' said Kate, raising an eyebrow. It was the first time she'd heard Sarah say anything remotely negative about her course, and she was surprised. It almost sounded like she was repeating something someone else had said to her.

Sarah just shrugged at her, looking fed up.

'Anyway, don't worry,' said Kate, giving her an encouraging smile, 'if you want to give yourself a head start you could ask Lou to show you some stuff. I know she hasn't done loads of baking for us yet, but I know she's meant to be a dab hand at sugar work. And Ethel's a genius with a piping bag!'

Sarah nodded. 'Thanks Kate.' She let out a huge sigh.

'Sarah, if you ever need to talk - about anything - I'm right here, okay?'

Sarah looked at her with a frown, and for a second Kate wondered if she'd just said entirely the wrong thing. But then Sarah gave her a slightly wobbly smile. 'Thanks.'

'I hope you've got that coffee machine fired up!' boomed Lionel, bounding through the door with a grim expression on his face, water dripping off the edge of his trilby. He yanked it off of his head, gave it a quick shake and hung it from the coat stand near the door. 'It's raining cats and dogs out there!'

'Blimey, you're early!' said Kate.

'I thought you'd still be out on your rounds,' he said. 'I was expecting to have to camp out here until you got back!'

Kate grinned. 'Lou to the rescue. She really fancied the exercise, apparently - little weirdo that she is - and Stanley would have hated it out there this morning!'

'It'll be more like swimming than cycling for her out there today. I hope she's got a change of clothes for when she gets back, she's going to need it!' said Lionel.

'I'll send her up to the flat for a shower. She can borrow some of my clothes and make use of the hairdryer,' said Kate with a smile. 'I owe her that at least for letting me off the hook.'

'Did you want your usual, Lionel?' asked Sarah.

He shook his head. 'Any chance of some scrambled eggs, bacon, a couple of pieces of toast . . .'

'I can do the full works if you'd like?' said Kate trying not to show just how surprised she was.

'You know what, yes please! But can I start with a coffee? I'm gasping!'

'What's going on - Veronica on strike, or has she just not bothered to go to the cash and carry?'

'Neither. I've not seen her since yesterday!' said Lionel.

Kate paused to stare at him. 'What do you mean?'

'I reckon she's done a bunk.'

Kate shook her head. 'No chance. She'd never just disappear without telling anyone. If she was off on holiday she'd have been bragging about it for at least a couple of months by now. Blimey, I've not known her to go away even for a weekend in all the years I've known her,' said Kate. 'She's too tight for that!'

'I know, that's what I thought,' said Lionel. 'Luckily, there aren't any guests in at the moment, and there won't be until after the wedding, otherwise they'd have to fend for themselves.'

'What if she's hurt or something,' said Sarah, quietly. 'Someone should check!'

Kate glanced at Sarah and frowned. 'That's a good point.'

'She's not hurt or ill,' said Lionel. 'Same thing crossed my mind, Sarah. I've already been up to her rooms to make sure. The door was locked and this was pinned to it.'

He drew a piece of paper from his jacket pocket and handed it to Sarah as she made her way over with Lionel's coffee.

'What's it say?' asked Kate, cracking eggs as she went.

"Gone away for a while. Sort out wedding. Veronica."

'Noooo!' gasped Kate.

'What does she mean by "sort out wedding"?' said Sarah, her eyes wide.

'Lionel, I think you're right,' said Kate. 'I think she's done a runner!'

'She wouldn't . . .' said Sarah.

'Looks like she already did,' said Lionel.

'But . . . the wedding!' said Sarah.

'I'm sure we'll be able to reach her somehow and find out exactly what's going on,' said Kate, doing her best to keep her voice calm. What on earth was going *on* this week? Everything seemed to be going haywire.

'You're right,' said Lionel, nodding. 'I knew you'd be the right person to talk to.'

'Question is, what should we do first?' said Kate.

'Why don't you call dad?' said Sarah. 'He told me last night that he'd just quoted for a wedding reception. Maybe he can help?'

'He *what?*' said Kate in surprise.

Sarah nodded. 'Yeah - he said someone was looking for alternative quotes and that he was going to put some stuff together and send it through to them . . . maybe he can help you with this couple too?'

Kate blinked as a lump of hurt hit her in the chest. She couldn't exactly say anything in front of Sarah, but she couldn't believe Mike hadn't even mentioned to her that weddings were a part of his plan too.

'Okay,' she said at last, trying to keep her voice even. 'I'll go over and speak to him as soon as Lou's back and dried off. Lionel, do you mind holding off on contacting Lee and Annabel until I've had the chance to report back?'

'Of course!' he said, sipping his coffee. 'I don't have any details for them anyway. I don't know where they're staying and I've never even met the poor blighters. In actual fact, I'm not exactly sure what Veronica means by "sort out wedding" anyway.'

'You don't think she expects you to run it rather than cancel it, do you?' said Sarah thoughtfully.

Lionel's already worried expression took on a hunted air.

'Okay, wow. Halt. Let's not panic!' said Kate, plating up Lionel's breakfast and bringing it over to him. 'Let me talk to Mike first. At least maybe that'll give us some kind of alternative to offer them when we break the news. In the meantime - do you reckon you could try to find out where Veronica's disappeared to? We really could do with a bit more information on what's going on before we can do anything to help.'

Lionel stared dazedly down at his plate full of food then looked back up at Kate. 'Let me work my way through this and another coffee or two, then I'll go back over to the hotel and rummage through that eyesore she calls a desk. Maybe there'll be something on there that might give us a clue or two.'

Kate found it incredibly difficult to wait patiently for Lou to get back from the delivery round. She wanted to march straight round to New York Froth and demand an explanation from Mike about his sudden interest in catering for weddings, and why he'd not seen fit to fill her in. On the other hand, she also wanted to beg for his help to sort the whole mess out.

With Veronica AWOL, they would soon have a rightly grumpy pair of soon-to-be-weds on their hands, and a disaster like this wasn't just a problem for Veronica - it would impact the whole town if the word got out.

When Lou finally turned up - drenched to the skin and freezing cold - Kate sent her straight upstairs for a hot shower and change of clothes. She told her to take her time and make sure to get her hair properly dry too - the last thing she needed was a member of staff down with the flu!

By the time Lou emerged looking more human than drowned rat, Kate was still desperate to see Mike but she was actually grateful for the delay as it had given her enough time to calm down a bit.

'So - you two okay to man the fort while I try to sort this mess out?' she asked.

'You go, boss!' said Lou. 'But make sure you put your hood up!'

'You want to come, boy?' said Kate, looking at Stanley as she pulled on the heavy yellow mac she kept in the cafe for days like this.

Stanley stared at her from his bed under the radiator, barely bothering to lift an eyebrow in response, let alone his head.

'Okay, I'll take the hint!' laughed Kate. 'Be good, you three!'

Despite her best efforts to keep her hood up as she made the dash over to North Beach, Kate was soaked by the time she pushed her way into New York Froth. She paused on the doormat and grabbed her soggy plait, doing her best to wring out as much water as possible so that she didn't drip all the way over to the counter.

'Hi Kate!' said Robbie, grinning at her. 'Out for a swim? Not your usual morning for a visit, is it?'

'Hey,' said Kate, smiling at the lad. 'Is Mike around?'

'He is - but it's so quiet he's disappeared back upstairs to get some paperwork done.'

Kate nodded. 'Mind if I go up?'

'Be my guest,' said Robbie. 'Want me to call ahead for you?'

Kate shook her head. 'Nah. I don't want to give him the opportunity to pretend to be busy,' she laughed. 'I'm afraid it's a bit urgent.'

'Uh oh,' he said. 'That sounds ominous - you go on up!'

Kate dashed around the counter and through the swing door that led to the internal staircase. Taking two steps at a time, she quickly wound her way up to Mike's flat.

She knew it was silly, but by the time she reached the door, she was feeling ridiculously nervous. She'd only been up here once before, and that had been to help Sarah with a bunch of cake boxes she'd borrowed for a project at college.

Kate paused and did her best to smooth down her hair. She knew it would already be busy springing into ridiculous corkscrews after getting so wet. She quickly gave it up for a bad job and knocked lightly on the door.

'Kate?!'

She jumped as Mike's face appeared just a second later.

'Hi! Sorry to interrupt but we've got ourselves a bit of a situation,' she said, not really knowing quite where to start.

'Is Sarah okay?' he demanded, looking freaked.

'It's not Sarah!' she said quickly. 'Sorry, I didn't mean to scare you.'

'Oh, thank God!' he said, then looked her up and down, taking in her damp clothes. 'Come on in and warm up.' Mike, stepped back inside and indicated for her to follow him. 'So Sarah's okay?' he checked again as he lead her straight into the beautiful open-plan space.

Kate nodded. 'She's okay - a bit quiet, but I guess that's to be expected, given the circumstances,' she said, looking around the flat. It was absolutely massive. Taking up most of the front of the building, it benefitted from floor to ceiling windows that stretched across the room and looked right out over the sea. It was a spectacular sight, even on a stormy day like today.

Mike let out a sigh and ran his fingers distractedly through his hair. 'Sarah was already upset enough about losing Aunty Sally, but we've just discovered that she's left us both money. Sarah's really struggling with that - it's like she feels guilty about it or something . . . I don't know.' He shrugged. 'Has she talked to you about it at all?'

Kate grimaced at him and shook her head. 'No. But I did tell her earlier that she can talk to me any time if she needs to.'

'Thanks Kate,' said Mike with a grateful smile. 'Don't tell her I told you about the inheritance if you don't mind? At least, not unless she brings it up first,' he said, suddenly looking awkward.

'Of course I won't,' said Kate.

'Thanks. Anyway - have a seat!'

Kate peeled off her mac, not wanting to leave a damp patch on Mike's pristine sofa. He dashed forward to take it from her and strode across the room to hang it over the back of one of the chairs in the kitchen area.

'You know, I'd forgotten what a beautiful job your guys did on this place!' said Kate, distracted for a moment by just how lovely it was in here. It was painted a very dark green - but with the light pouring through the windows, it felt calming rather than dark - in spite of the gloomy day outside.

'Thanks!' said Mike, coming back over towards her. 'We love it. Anyway, what's up?'

'Well,' said Kate, perching on the sofa as Mike sank down onto the other end, staring at her intently, 'we need to talk weddings.'

Mike let out a spluttering cough. 'Bit early for all that, isn't it?' he laughed.

Kate raised her eyebrows. Perhaps he was just as nervous about her being here as she was. Something warm bloomed in her chest and she felt her earlier irritation with him soften a bit.

'Look,' she said, giving him a smile, 'there's a bit of a problem at The Pebble Street Hotel.'

CHAPTER 11

'So, we have no idea where she's gone, why she's gone or when she's coming back,' said Kate. She'd just spent the last five minutes filling Mike in on everything that she knew so far. 'Anyway, someone's got to talk to Lee and Annabel and tell them what's happened - and Sarah suggested I talk to you first.'

'Why?' said Mike looking worried.

'Because she said . . .' Kate swallowed down her urge to start getting cross with him for not telling her about his plans. 'She said you've just been asked to quote for a wedding reception, so you might be able to help with an alternative for these two as well.'

'Well,' said Mike, 'this isn't quite how I wanted to tell you about all this.'

'All what?' said Kate.

'The wedding I was approached about. It's actually for the same couple you're talking about.'

'Okay - now I'm completely confused,' said Kate.

'You suggested that they chase up their bookings with Veronica, didn't you - and insist on seeing the hotel?' he asked.

Kate nodded.

'Well - they did both those things. Veronica still wouldn't let them in to look around the hotel - said it would be too dangerous - but they made the phone calls. The caterers were booked but hadn't received their payments. The wine supplier had no record of any order, and the band had already cancelled the date because they hadn't received any money either.'

Kate's hand flew to her mouth, her eyes wide. No cake, no band, no food, no drink.

'What did they do?' she breathed.

'Asked for their money back so that they could find alternatives,' said Mike, 'and then approached me to ask for a quote for catering as well as any suggestions I might have for the rest of it.'

'Oh,' said Kate, her spine stiffening. 'I had no idea you were planning on taking New York Froth in that direction!'

'Kate,' he sighed, 'I didn't. I don't. But these guys are desperate, and I thought . . . I thought that maybe between us, we could do something for them. You were just telling me the other day that you'd like to do that with Trixie . . .'

'I did,' said Kate in surprise, 'but *one day* - in the future. We don't have a venue or enough staff, or . . . well . . . anything!'

'I didn't promise them anything - I just thought I could put some ideas together and run them past you to see what you thought. Then, if we thought we could make it work, we could give them a quote and see whether they wanted to go for it.'

'You wanted us to work together?' said Kate, double-checking she'd understood him properly.

Mike nodded, looking hopeful and excited.

'But we're not *ready*, Mike!' she said, trying her best to stomp on her exasperation. 'They're getting married in less than two weeks!'

'I know,' said Mike, 'but I just really wanted to help!'

'In case you hadn't noticed,' said Kate in a low voice, 'I managed to run my business perfectly well before you arrived in town. I don't need your help!'

'I didn't mean you,' said Mike with a frown. 'As of yesterday Lee and Annabel no longer have the reception of their dreams lined up. It's *them* I wanted to help. And . . . and I thought it would be an adventure for us to work on this together. I thought it would be fun!' He let out a huge sigh. 'Clearly I'm an idiot,' he added as an afterthought.

'You're not an idiot,' muttered Kate, standing up and going over to stare out at the sea, trying to make some kind of sense of the jumble of thoughts that were whizzing around her head. 'Look, let's forget this whole joint-catering thing for just a second while I try to get this straight. Lee and Annabel cancelled their booking at the hotel and got their money back from Veronica?'

'Yes and no,' said Mike. 'They cancelled the booking. Veronica tried to give them a cheque for what she owed them - but after the dire warnings you and Ethel had given them, they knew better than to accept it.'

'Thank goodness for small mercies!' said Kate, turning back to look at Mike. 'But they *did* get their money back?'

'Nope,' said Mike with a heavy sigh. 'Veronica told them she'd need to visit her bank to arrange it for them today.'

'And now she's gone,' said Kate, a sick feeling hitting her in the stomach.

'Now she's gone,' echoed Mike. 'Somehow, I can't imagine Veronica popped into the bank before pulling her disappearing act.'

'Well . . . shit,' sighed Kate.

'Pretty much,' nodded Mike.

'What are we going to do?' said Kate.

'Well,' said Mike, 'for starters, someone's going to have to tell Annabel and Lee.'

Kate nodded. 'Lionel's back at the hotel trying to see if he can find any information on where Veronica's gone. Maybe we should go and find out if he's got anywhere with that - then we can all come up with a plan?'

'Sure,' said Mike with a shrug. There was a slightly mutinous expression on his face. 'But only if you're sure you *want my help?*'

Kate flinched. She *knew* she shouldn't have thrown that at him. It hadn't been fair. 'I'm really sorry,' she said. 'I didn't mean that.'

'Yes, you did,' sighed Mike, 'but it's fine, I get it. I know The Sardine is your baby and I've got so much respect for what you've achieved. I would *never* presume to know better - because I really, *really* don't. It's just . . . I just really like spending time with you, and I thought . . . never mind.'

'What?' said Kate softly, sinking back down on the sofa, not taking her eyes off of him. 'What did you think?'

'I thought it would be fun to make someone's big day special together - and that maybe it would remind us both that not all marriages end up like our two disasters!'

Kate snorted out a laugh. It had been the last thing she'd been expecting him to say - but it was just about perfect.

'Come on,' she chuckled, grabbing his hand and hauling him to his feet. 'Let's go and try to save this shit-show!'

'Should we just go in or knock?' said Mike, awkwardly pushing his damp hair back and staring at the peeling paint of the door to The Pebble Street Hotel.

'Both?' said Kate.

'Good call,' laughed Mike. He knocked loudly then turned the handle and cracked the door open. 'Hellooooo?' he called.

'Come on in!' came Lionel's voice.

Kate followed Mike into the foyer, only to spot the top of Lionel's head behind the reception desk. He was on his hands and knees rifling through the old desk drawers. There were piles of paper strewn all over the foyer floor.

'Try not to step on the paperwork,' he laughed, peeping over at them. 'As I was going through it, I figured I may as well try to set it in some kind of order. Veronica's going to kill me for doing this anyway - if she ever finds out - so I thought if I tidy up a bit for her she might go a bit easier on me!'

'I really wouldn't worry about Veronica right now,' sighed Kate, staring around at the heaps of paperwork. 'Did you manage to find anything useful in all this?'

Lionel grabbed the edge of the desk and hauled himself to his feet with a groan before dropping into the desk chair. 'Useful - not really. Surprising - definitely!'

Kate frowned. That sounded ominous. 'Do you

want to go back over to The Sardine to talk about it?' she said, wrinkling her nose against the cabbage-y smell that still seemed to be lingering in the old building.

'I would say yes, but . . . well, I think it's probably better that we talk about this in private first.'

Kate nodded. 'I guess you're right. Plus, we need to fill you in too - Mike knows more about what's happened with Veronica and the wedding.'

'What *is* that smell,' said Mike distractedly, wrinkling his nose and looking around, clearly taking in just how filthy the place was.

'Sadly,' said Lionel, getting to his feet and gathering a small pile of papers off the desktop, 'that's the kitchen. Why do you think I haven't eaten anything here for months?'

Kate pulled a face. 'It's making me feel a bit sick.'

'Tell me about it,' said Lionel. 'Look, let's go up to my place to talk, shall we?'

'Only if you're sure,' said Mike. 'Or we can go over to mine if you'd prefer?'

'I'm not going back out into that weather unless I have to!' said Lionel. 'Come on, let's go up and I'll put the kettle on!'

They followed him up two flights of stairs and then along the hallway of the third floor. Things weren't any better up here. It looked like these rooms hadn't been used in ages. The bedroom doors stood open, and as they walked past Kate noticed that most of the beds were unmade and the rooms clearly hadn't been cleaned in aeons. The dust lay thick on every surface and even the carpet seemed to have a grey-brown extra layer of the stuff.

'Doesn't Veronica ever come up here?' she asked in surprise.

'I don't think she bothers,' said Lionel. 'She sacked Annie the last cleaner months ago - she dared to ask for her pay on time!'

'Sounds about right,' muttered Mike.

'Yes, well,' said Lionel. 'I'm afraid I've tried to keep out of it as much as possible.'

'It must be so sad for you, having to pass all this on your way in and out all the time,' said Kate, drawing a finger along the edge of a bookshelf and then flicking the thick ball of dust she'd gathered onto the floor.

'Actually, I don't tend to come this way anymore. Like you said - it's depressing! I've been using the fire escape steps to come and go, and basically pretending that my apartment has nothing to do with the rest of the place! Today's the first time I've been down this way in ages, and only because I ran out of coffee!' He paused and let out a long sigh. 'It makes me really sad, you know. It used to be a joy living here. I loved popping down to the bar of an evening for a nightcap, meeting the guests and then sharing breakfast with them the following morning. But it's never been the same since Veronica took over.'

'I'm surprised you've stayed as long as you have!' said Mike.

Lionel shrugged. 'I love my home. But you're right. Maybe it's time to move on. Anyway - looks like I might not have much of a choice in the matter very soon,' he said, tapping the pile of paperwork he was carrying.

Kate's heart squeezed at the sorrow in his voice. She was about to ask him what he meant when they came to a halt in front of a dark wooden double door.

'Here we are!' said Lionel, taking a large key from his pocket. He fitted the key into the old fashioned lock and then beckoned for them to follow him in.

'Wow!' said Mike, wandering into the sitting room and staring around him. 'I thought my place had a good view, but this is . . . amazing!'

Lionel smiled at him over his shoulder as he flicked on a large standard lamp which came to life with a golden glow. 'Now you can see why I fought so hard to stay!'

'Uh - *yes!*' said Kate.

Lionel's suite clearly took up a good portion of this floor, and the sitting room was situated right on the corner of the building. It had huge windows set in both the outside walls - one looking out over towards West Beach and the other looking out over towards North Beach. The place was filled with sea, and clouds, and glimpses of Seabury.

'I've lived here for years but I never get tired of this view,' he sighed. 'Now then, why don't you both grab a seat and I'll pop the kettle on.'

Kate followed Mike over to a petrol-blue, buttoned leather sofa and sank down into its worn embrace. She was desperately trying not to be nosy, but she couldn't keep her eyes from darting around, taking in the details of Lionel's sanctuary. It was a cosy, comfortable gentleman-cave. The inner walls were completely lined floor-to-ceiling with bookshelves that were groaning with what looked to be everything from huge art reference books to small, gold embossed, soft leather classics. Kate longed to get up and have a proper look through them, but she kept her bum firmly in her seat.

'What a beautiful place,' said Mike as their eyes met.

'I know,' said Kate in a low voice. 'It's like we've walked into a different era!'

'Or into an entirely different building at the very least!' laughed Mike.

'Here we go,' said Lionel, reappearing and popping a delicate silver tea tray down onto the table in front of the sofa.

Kate smiled at the three beautiful bone-china cups sitting in their saucers alongside the old brown and white striped teapot.

'What a treat,' she sighed, 'thanks Lionel.'

'My pleasure,' he said, picking up the metal

strainer and pouring for them all. 'Help yourself to milk and sugar,' he said, settling himself into the armchair across from them. 'Now then - tell me what you've discovered about the wedding!'

Mike glanced at Kate and she nodded encouragingly. 'Go on,' she said, taking a sip of her tea, 'you do the honours!'

By the time Mike had filled Lionel in, the old man's eyebrows had practically disappeared into his mop of silver hair.

'Well, well, well,' he said, puffing out a breath. 'I knew old Veronica was a pain in the derrière, but I hadn't thought she'd be capable of this,' he sighed. 'And now she's done a runner with Lee and Annabel's money.'

'I know!' said Kate, shaking her head. 'But - you said you'd found something in all those papers?' she said, pointing at the little pile Lionel had left, face-down on the table.

He nodded. 'Well, for a start . . . it looks like she's gone to Australia!'

'*What?!*' squeaked Mike, choking on a sip of tea.

Lionel shrugged. 'I found booking details for her flight.'

'But why Australia?' said Kate, confused.

'I'm not one hundred per cent sure, but I think she once mentioned having family over there,' said Lionel.

'Well then, she's definitely not going to be back in time for the wedding,' said Mike.

'Actually, I'm not sure she's planning on coming back at all,' said Lionel.

'What makes you say that?' asked Kate.

Instead of answering, Lionel rummaged through the wodge of papers, drew out a few that were stapled together and handed them over.

Kate flicked through them quickly while Mike leaned in to peer over her shoulder. It looked like some kind of contract with the logo of one of the large Plymouth estate agents at the top of each page. Veronica's name jumped out a couple of times as Kate scanned them. When she reached the last page, she let out a gasp. It was a photocopy of the kind of advert displayed in estate agents' windows across the country. There, in all its dilapidated glory, was a photograph of The Pebble Street Hotel.

'Yep,' said Lionel sadly, 'looks like the old girl's up for sale again.'

CHAPTER 12

'Please tell me you're joking?' said Annabel.

Kate swallowed hard, trying to battle the sick, squiggly feeling in her stomach. She'd been building up to this evening all day, driving Lou, Ethel and Sarah slowly mad. She'd been so distracted she'd kept getting orders wrong and generally wreaked havoc on their well-ordered little world.

After speaking to both Mike and Lionel at length the previous day, Kate had returned home and got straight to work calling in favours left, right and centre. By the time she'd finally gone to bed, she'd been cautiously excited that they really might be able to make this wedding happen. But now that it was time to finally explain everything to Lee and Annabel, she suddenly didn't feel quite so sure.

Mike shook his head and smiled sadly at the

couple. 'No, I'm sorry. I wish we *were* joking, but it looks like Veronica really has gone away. And, by the look on your face, I'm assuming you've not had your money back?'

'No,' said Lee, glowering and shaking his head. 'Look, I really appreciate you guys taking the time to let us know, but I think it's best if we head home and try to figure all this out.' He paused and ran his fingers through his hair, leaving the blond strands sticking out at odd angles, making him look a bit like a lost little boy. 'I guess we'd better sort out a lawyer or something.'

Kate's heart gave a sympathetic squeeze as Annabel bit her lip and reached out to grab Lee's hand. She looked so incredibly sad.

'Please stay,' said Kate gently. 'Just for a coffee. We've come up with a plan.'

Lee sighed, looking like he wanted nothing more than to hotfoot it out of Seabury as fast as he could, but Annabel looked at him pleadingly.

'Okay, fine,' he said, 'I guess there's not much we can do tonight anyway, and you guys have been so kind. I just can't see what more you can do though . . .'

'Well,' said Mike, as Ethel got to her feet to make the coffees, 'first, I should introduce everyone.' He peered around at the little group they'd gathered together. 'Lionel here is a permanent tenant of The Pebble Street Hotel - he's got an apartment on the top floor. I guess you know Ethel and Lou, and might have already met my daughter Sarah?'

Lee nodded and smiled weakly. 'In passing while we've been in here stuffing our faces!'

Mike nodded. 'Right, so . . . you asked me for an alternative quote for your reception.'

'Oh,' said Annabel, looking horrified. 'Mike, I'm really sorry, but now that Veronica's disappeared with our money, we're not going to be able to go ahead. In fact,' she stopped and took a deep breath, clearly trying to force down a swell of rising emotion, 'we've actually decided to cancel the reception altogether.'

Lee nodded sadly. 'We'll still get married as planned, but we'll just have to have a celebration when we've either managed to recoup our cash from Veronica . . . or saved up again.'

'We've got an alternative!' said Kate.

'But we can't pay you-'

'Hear us out!' grinned Mike.

Lee shrugged and sat back in his seat, but he looked defeated.

'First of all - the most important thing to you was to hold your event in the hotel, am I right?'

Annabel nodded, looking like she was pretty close to tears. 'That's why we've decided not to have it at all.'

'Well, thanks to Lionel here, we can still make that happen,' said Kate.

'But how?' said Lee. 'I don't want to be arrested for breaking and entering on my wedding night!'

Lionel chuckled. 'Well, here's the note Veronica left me.' He passed over the crumpled bit of paper that he'd found pinned to her door.

"Sort out wedding!" huffed Lee. 'Charming.'

'I know,' said Lionel, frowning. 'But - we can just interpret that as - *make sure it goes ahead*.'

'I'm pretty sure that's not what she meant!' said Annabel, staring at it in disgust.

'No,' said Kate, 'but as Lionel's got access to the entire hotel, and technically you're fully paid up, what's to stop us using the venue?!'

'I don't know . . .' said Lee slowly, glancing at Annabel.

'What about the renovations she was going on about?' she asked.

'I'm pretty sure Ken finished up the dining room floor - but if not, I'm sure we can reach him,' said Kate.

'And the rest of the place?' asked Lee.

'I'm afraid that was another lie she told you. There isn't any work going on in the rest of the place.'

'But why would she-'

'Because it's filthy,' said Kate, her tone matter of fact. They'd all agreed to be completely upfront with the not-so-happy couple, but still - she hated this!

'Veronica clearly didn't want to put you off paying up!'

'That's not good!' said Lee, scrunching up his nose.

'Well, no, it's not,' said Lionel, 'but here's the thing. There's an old pathway that leads around the back of the building that I've been using to reach my own apartment without having to go through the rest of the hotel. There's a lovely area outside the dining room that looks out over the sea that has already been done up, and there's a set of double doors that lead to the dining room itself - which, last time I looked, was actually looking rather beautiful. You and your guests can use that!'

'But . . .'

'We've got a team together who're more than happy to blitz the kitchen, the downstairs bathrooms and the whole of the ground floor,' said Kate.

'Right . . .?' said Lee.

'You weren't intending on staying the night, were you?' asked Kate, suddenly worried. If she'd got the wrong end of the stick and they needed all the bedrooms too, then that would be one step too far for this little plan of theirs.

Annabel shook her head, looking thoughtful. 'No. We weren't planning on staying there. Everyone's got accommodation nearby sorted out already - it's only a small group of us anyway. About thirty. All we needed was a room in the hotel where we could get ready.'

'Well, I think that can be arranged in one of the other downstairs rooms,' said Lionel. 'So, what do you think?'

Lee glanced at Annabel and raised his eyebrows, then shook his head and looked back at them. 'It's really generous of you guys to offer to do this, but even with the venue sorted, that wouldn't solve the issue of a band, or food, or a cake, or decorations or . . .'

'Let us worry about all that,' said Ethel excitedly.

'But how can we!' said Annabel looking mystified. 'There's no way we could ask you to take all that on. Besides, we couldn't afford it.'

'You're after a 1940s themed do, aren't you?' said Mike.

Annabel nodded sadly. 'Yes - my dress is vintage and the men will be in uniform too. In honour of my grandma . . .' her lip quivered and Lee put his arm around her shoulders protectively.

'Well, I don't know if you're aware, but we have a rather lovely town band here in Seabury,' said Lionel. 'And a couple of those fellows have a little swing band. They do all the classics - lots of Glenn Miller and whatnot. They only play for fun, but they said they would be honoured to play at your wedding, as long as they could take some photos?'

'You're kidding?' said Lee, looking amazed.

'Nope - they've been practising in the town hall mostly, but they're excited for the chance to play for an audience!'

'That's amazing,' breathed Annabel.

'And Sarah here has agreed to do the cake,' said Mike proudly. 'She's training to be a professional baker - and as long as you don't mind her writing up an assignment about the whole thing . . .'

'It wouldn't be too big a deal,' said Sarah quietly, clearly a bit nervous at being singled out. 'I'd just need to get you to give me a bit of feedback about how I did and what you thought of the cake.'

'How much would you charge?' asked Lee.

Sarah raised her eyebrows. 'Nothing - you'd be the ones doing me a favour!' she laughed. 'I promise I won't let you down though.'

'I can vouch for Sarah,' said Kate. 'She already designs half the recipes in the cake boxes you love! And both Ethel and Lou will be on hand to help.'

Annabel's mouth was now partially open. She looked like she'd been stunned.

'As for the food,' said Mike, 'Kate and I would very much like to use your wedding as a trial run for an idea we've had for a brand new joint venture. So - if you'd be able to cover the basic costs of the ingredients, our time and services would be completely free.'

Kate glanced nervously at Annabel, only to see tears making their way quietly down her face. 'Of course,' she said quickly, 'don't worry if it's not what you want. We completely understand. We just really wanted to help if we could.'

Annabel shook her head and quickly wiped her eyes with the back of her hand. 'It's not that!' she said.

'It's *definitely* not that!' said Lee, hugging Annabel to his side. 'It's just . . . you're all so . . . *why* would you do all this for us?' he said, looking overwhelmed.

'Because this is Seabury,' said Sarah quietly. 'It's what we do.'

'Couldn't have said it better myself,' said Lionel, patting Sarah on the shoulder.

'And you really think we can pull this off in the time?' said Annabel, staring around at their motley little group.

'I think it's going to take a bit of channelling some wartime spirit,' said Ethel with a glint in her eye. 'But with the hotel empty until the big day, there's plenty of time to get in there and get it sorted out. And we've already mobilised the whole of Seabury's WI to help!'

'Lord help us,' laughed Mike, earning himself a friendly swat around the back of the head.

'What was it old Churchill said?' murmured Lionel. 'Ah yes -*victory at all costs!*'

'Hear hear!' said Mike with a grin.

CHAPTER 13

Kate had been floating around her flat in a daze all afternoon. There were a million things she knew she should be getting on with before Paula came over for the evening, but she couldn't settle to any of them. She just kept grinning to herself like an idiot at how amazing Mike was, and how determined he was to make sure Lee and Annabel had everything they wanted for their big day.

'We really do like him, don't we Stanley boy?' she said, slumping down onto the sofa and grinning over at him in his bed.

Stanley just let out a huge sigh.

'I know,' she laughed. 'No point mooning around when I'm not allowed to do anything about it, is there?'

Stanley closed his eyes.

'You know, you give the best cuddles, but you suck at advice!' she laughed. 'Thank goodness Paula's coming over!'

She'd been over the moon when her friend had called and asked if she was free for the evening. It had been far too long since they'd had a proper catch-up. Kate was desperate to find out what was going on with her friend, but as Paula had headed off for an impromptu visit to see her mother over in Dorset, she'd had to wait longer than she'd hoped to get to the bottom of things. Even if it *was* "just hormones" like Paula had kept insisting, if they were causing her that much distress, she definitely needed some help.

Kate started to fidget again and got to her feet before she managed to pick a hole in the arm of her sofa. Paula should be here any minute.

WUFF!

Stanley lifted his head and let out another booming bark just as her doorbell rang.

'It's aunty Paula, idiot,' laughed Kate, before running downstairs to open the door for her friend.

'Kate!' Paula grinned, throwing her arms around her as if she hadn't seen her for years.

'Yay! I'm so glad you called,' said Kate holding her close. She felt thin. Far too thin.

'Well - we need to talk,' said Paula quietly, giving her a squeeze and then stepping back.

Kate did her best to ignore the knot of fear that

had just formed in her stomach. Something in Paula's tone had just made a shiver go down her spine

'Oh - mum sent you this, by the way,' said Paula, brandishing a monster bottle of Baileys. 'She knows you love it and we can't stand the stuff!'

'Ohhh, thank you!' said Kate, taking the bottle. 'Come on up. Are we on a wine kind of a night or a tea kind of a night?'

'Have you got mint tea?'

'Actually, I do!' said Kate. 'Mike unearthed a jar when he was here.'

'Oh yes?' said Paula wiggling her eyebrows. Then she bit her lip. 'Sorry, I promised I wouldn't tease you about him anymore, didn't I?' she sighed.

Kate shrugged as she reached the kitchen and flicked the kettle on. Instead of the mild annoyance she usually felt when anyone teased her about Mike, she felt a kind of delighted tingle in the knowledge that he really did like her.

'I don't mind,' she said lightly.

'Well,' said Paula, peeling her leather jacket off and unwinding her scarf, 'that's definitely a change of tune!'

'I'm still not going to do anything about it,' sighed Kate, trying not to frown at just how skinny Paula looked now that she'd taken off a layer. 'Anyway - I want to hear about you first. How's your mum? Did you have a good visit?'

Paula shrugged as she watched Kate pour their

drinks. 'It was a . . . *difficult* visit,' she said, following Kate through to the living room and plonking her jacket and scarf onto the arm of the sofa. She bent down to stroke Stanley, who instantly sat up and tried to lick her face, making her laugh.

Kate perched on the sofa and waited until Paula joined her, kicking off her shoes and curling her feet up underneath her like she always did.

'Why was it difficult?' asked Kate, forcing the words out. She had a feeling she didn't really want to know.

Paula took a sip of tea and then wrapped her hands around the scorching mug with a weary sigh, clearly gearing up to say something she didn't really want to.

'Is this something to do with how upset you were the other day - down on the beach?' prompted Kate.

Paula nodded. 'Yes. I'm afraid so. I got some pretty shitty news, and it's . . . it's taken me a few days to wrap my head around it.'

Kate swallowed nervously and placed her mug down on the side table, waiting for her friend to carry on.

'Kate - do you remember back in the summer when I wasn't feeling well? They thought I might have some kind of weird infection and I went for those tests?'

'Of course!' said Kate, nodding. 'But you said they didn't find anything.'

'Well, I went for some follow-ups,' she paused again, placing her mug down and rubbing her face roughly. 'Shit - I've really got to figure out a better way to tell people this,' she said.

Kate watched her, suddenly not wanting to speak - not wanting to interrupt whatever this was. She heard a scuffle and looked down only to find Stanley had abandoned his bed and come over to join them. He sat on the floor in front of Paula and plopped his head down on the sofa cushion next to her leg.

Paula smiled. 'Thanks lad,' she said, resting her hand on his head as if she was drawing courage from him. 'Kate, I'm ill,' she said gently.

'Ill?' croaked Kate.

Paula nodded. 'They were worried about something strange in those first tests. I didn't bother mentioning it because it could have been nothing. A blip. But I've been for a bunch more,' she paused again, stroking Stanley's head gently. 'I've got leukaemia.'

Kate shook her head, staring at her friend in horror. 'But - but...'

She shut her mouth, stopping herself from saying something stupid. She wanted to say *you can't have*, or *there's been a mistake*, or *you can fight this!* - but how would any of that help her lovely friend right now?

She slowly reached over and laid her hand on top of Paula's. 'How long have you known?' said Kate at last, her voice shaking slightly.

'Not long,' sighed Paula. 'I needed a few days to get used to the idea before telling anyone. But then on Wednesday, I'd just found out that it's the type that I can't get better from.'

'No,' said Kate, shaking her head, horrified to feel tears welling up in her eyes. They broke free, rolling hot and fast down her cheek as she fought to hold it together for her friend. She chewed the inside of her cheek, biting hard, hoping that the jolt of pain might stop her from crying and help her to focus on Paula.

She refused to make this about herself. She refused to force Paula to have to comfort her. 'No,' she said again, wishing that by saying it, she could make it true.

Paula squeezed her hand. 'I'm sorry.'

'Don't you dare apologise!' said Kate steadily, roughly wiping her tears away with her hand.

Paula nodded.

'Have they said anything about treatment? I know you said you can't get better from it, but surely-'

'There are things they can try to slow things down,' said Paula.

'When will they start?' asked Kate, feeling like these practical things might anchor her to this weird, screwed-up reality she'd suddenly landed in.

'Pretty soon,' said Paula. 'And when things get bad - towards the end-'

'Don't!' said Kate, swallowing hard.

'Please, Kate,' said Paula, turning to face her properly. 'Please. I need to be able to talk about this - I need to make it as normal as possible. I'm going to explode if I have to keep it all inside!'

Kate nodded, biting her cheek again. She could kick herself. The word had burst out of her in an instinctive reaction, but how could she be so selfish? Of course it hurt - hearing about this, but what must it be like for Paula - living with it - knowing what would eventually happen?

'I'm sorry,' said Kate, taking Paula's other hand. 'I'm sorry. Tell me.'

Paula nodded. 'I was just going to say that when the time comes, they can make me comfortable. I'll have help to manage it.'

Kate felt the tears start up again, but she refused to look away from her friend. She nodded and squeezed her hand.

'I'm here,' she said. 'I'm here for you - for whatever you need, okay?'

Paula nodded. 'There is something I need from you.'

'Tell me,' said Kate, nodding. 'Anything!'

'I need you to help me stay me,' she said. 'All this stuff is going to pile in - hospital visits, consultants, treatment . . . fucking *end of life* plans!' she paused and let out a gasp that was half sob, half incredulous laugh. 'I need you to be my anchor - someone who'll still giggle with me over a glass of wine, watch cheesy romcoms with me, ogle cute guys with me, gossip about Seabury with me, come swimming with me!'

Kate was now crying hard, but she nodded again.

'You've got to promise me, Kate. I don't know how long I've got left. It could be years - or it could be a lot less - but the thing I'm most frightened of is people treating me differently when they find out. I've still got life to live, and I'm buggered if I'm going to waste it. Do you promise?'

Kate nodded, sniffing hard. 'I do. I promise!'

Paula sighed and a huge smile spread over her face. 'Thank you.'

Kate tried to wipe her eyes on her arm without letting go of Paula's hands, making them both giggle. It felt like the weirdest thing to do at that moment, but it felt like the medicine they both needed.

'Now then,' said Paula, sitting back and releasing Kate's hands. She grabbed her mug, gulped her tea and ruffled Stanley's ears.

Kate mopped her face and then picked up her own mug.

'On the phone, you said you had gossip for me!' said Paula.

Kate shook her head. 'That's not important,' she said. *How* could she jabber on about Veronica and the hotel and the wedding? How could she whine about Tom and ask Paula's advice about her feelings for Mike? None of it was important now.

'Oh no you don't!' laughed Paula. 'This is *exactly*

what I'm talking about. Kate! Gimme the gossip! Cough up the goods! Spill! Don't make me torture you for the information.'

Kate bit her lip, fighting down a sob. 'Oh my god, you're right. I failed at the first hurdle!'

Paula shrugged. 'I think you get a bit of a grace period, given the circumstances. But I'm still me!'

Kate nodded and forced a smile onto her face.

'So - tell me everything!' said Paula gently. 'I want normal. I want to laugh. I want to help!'

Kate nodded again, took a deep breath and launched into the whole tale of Annabel and Lee's wedding and how Veronica had done a bunk with their funds. Then, with as much drama as she could inject into the story, she told her about the plan she'd concocted with Mike and the others.

'Wow!' breathed Paula as she came to the end. 'Right - you can count me in.'

'Into what?' said Kate, confused.

'Into sorting things out for this wedding, dumb-ass! I've taken a couple of weeks off of work - just to get my head around things and get a plan in place. I'd *love* to help!'

'Really?' asked Kate, looking doubtful.

'Hell yes! I might not be firing on all cylinders, but I'd love to be involved.'

'Okay then - count yourself well and truly roped in!' said Kate with a smile.

'So . . . erm . . .' said Paula, suddenly looking uneasy.

'What?' asked Kate. 'Talk to me about anything. I mean it.'

Paula snorted. 'Okay - you asked for it. My question is - why haven't you snogged Mike Pendle's face off yet?!'

Kate let out a surprised giggle. 'Well, as this is a night of being completely honest with each other . . . it's getting more and more difficult not to!'

'Yay!'

'No, not *yay*. Seriously. I keep feeling like I'm falling for him, and there's nothing I can do about it.'

'Eh? There's *everything* you can do about it!' said Paula, practically jumping up and down on the sofa in excitement, making Stanley wag his tail.

'No,' said Kate. 'Like I told him, now's not the time. Not with all the nonsense with Tom still up in the air. I can't just dive into something new - it wouldn't be fair to him.'

'Well,' said Paula with a frown, 'I think recent events mean that I'm newly qualified to tell you this - life's too short for all that rubbish!'

Kate felt the smile drop off her face.

'I promise not to keep using this card,' smirked Paula, 'but just this once, let me tell you that you deserve to be happy *right now*. It's what I'm planning to do - and I think you should too.'

'But-'

'No buts Kate! Don't let time just keep passing you by. It's finite. Do the things you want to do, love the people you want to love. Stop waiting for the perfect moment - because no moment is more perfect than right now.'

CHAPTER 14

It had been a couple of days since her evening with Paula, and Kate still felt like her well-ordered little world was inside out and upside down. She'd cried herself to sleep that night after Ryan had picked Paula up - but that was all she was willing to give herself for now. Kate absolutely refused to go into mourning when Paula was still right there - alive, kicking and needing her support.

In a way, it was a godsend that she had so much to do. Planning for the wedding meant that she was dropping into bed late, so exhausted that she was practically passing out instead of falling asleep. Her days were non-stop, working with Mike to get all the details ironed out on top of keeping The Sardine up and running.

She knew, deep down, that it would probably be a good idea for her to take a bit of time to digest what was happening and work through the news that one of her favourite people in the entire world was going to be facing this huge, sad struggle. That her best friend was - at some point - going to disappear from her life forever. But she just couldn't. Not yet.

The worst moments had been the quiet ones when she was able to take a breather and think. For that reason, she was very glad to be handing the delivery round over to Lou for the next few weeks. The long, quiet ride gave her brain way too much time to chase itself down grief-filled rabbit holes.

Sadly, she couldn't escape from *all* the difficult moments. Paula had asked Kate if she'd be willing to share the news with Lou, Ethel and Sarah for her. She wasn't quite ready for her diagnosis to become common knowledge just yet, but as she was planning to help them out with the wedding, she'd decided that it would be best for Kate's little team to know what was going on.

After taking a couple of days to wrap her own head around things, Kate had finally bitten the bullet and gathered the trio together after closing time. Right now, she was feeling like the worst person ever for making three of her favourite people so very sad.

'Well, she's a brave lass - no mistaking that!' said Ethel, letting out a shuddering sigh. 'I really admire her attitude. I do feel for poor Ryan though, I wonder how he's doing?'

'Paula said he's being his usual, sweet self,' said

Kate, with a soft smile. 'He'll be there for her through thick and thin, just like he's always been.'

Where Paula had always been a whirlwind of wild-swimming, wine-drinking, giggly energy, her husband was a gentle, easy-going soul - dedicated to books, reading and pots of tea. They were one of those couples you'd never have put together in a million years, and yet their marriage had been rock solid ever since their "I do" moment just after they'd graduated from uni.

'Well, we'll have to make sure we're there for him too,' said Lou, her face sombre.

Ethel nodded and patted her on the back. Lou might not have lived in Seabury long, but she was one of those people that just seemed to belong there.

'I wish there was something we could do to help her,' said Sarah, wiping under her eyes with a piece of kitchen roll, trying to remove the mascara smudges from the tears she'd been unable to hold back.

Paula and Kate had discussed at length whether they should tell Sarah or not, but in the end, they'd decided that - provided Mike agreed - it would be kinder to let her know and support her, rather than risk her accidentally finding out when Seabury's gossip-mill kicked into gear.

'There is,' said Kate, putting her arm around Sarah's shoulders. 'It's what she asked me to do - and you guys can help too.'

'What. Anything!' said Sarah earnestly.

'Well . . .' Kate wracked her brains for the best way to paraphrase their tear-soaked conversation, 'she's going to be going through a lot - hospital and treatments and all that. She wants my help - *our* help - to still be the Paula we know and love.'

'I don't understand,' said Sarah, frowning.

'She wants *normal*, love,' said Ethel, raising her eyebrows at Kate, checking that she'd got this right.

'Exactly,' said Kate, nodding. 'She wants to giggle and have fun and do things like help us with this wedding. She still wants you to tell her rude jokes and share news about college with her like you always do when she comes in here.'

'But how does that help?' said Sarah, sounding mildly desperate.

'Because the thing she's dreading most is people treating her differently,' said Kate. 'Paula wants to enjoy every second she can. I think having a bunch of people she can rely on to treat her the same - no matter what she's going through, or how much she changes outwardly - is going to give her a boost when things get difficult.'

Sarah nodded. 'It doesn't seem like much though . . .'

Kate smiled at her. 'To Paula, it means everything.'

Sarah nodded again, grabbed Kate's hand and squeezed it. 'The four of us can be here for each other too, *and* for Paula and Ryan.'

'Yeah boss,' said Lou, frowning at Kate across the

table. 'Don't forget that we're all here for you too, okay?'

Ethel and Sarah both nodded vigorously as Kate swallowed hard and smiled at them, trying to push her emotions back into place. She was so grateful, but right now it was time to get her practical head back on before she lost it completely.

'Right!' she said, letting out a long breath, 'it's going to have to be a case of divide and conquer over the next few days to get everything done! Lou - are you certain you're happy to take on Trixie for me?'

Lou nodded eagerly. 'Yup - and the morning prep for the deliveries too.'

'Fab!' said Kate gratefully. 'Sarah - are you still happy to do the cake for Lee and Annabel now you've had a couple of days to think about it?'

Sarah nodded, staring hard at the table.

'Brilliant! You're very welcome to use the kitchen in The Sardine any time after closing if you need to work on ideas or trial runs - though your dad's place has got lots more space and is probably easier for you!'

'I've got some sketches I'm working on,' said Sarah. 'I'd love to bring them in and see what you guys think before I show them to Annabel?'

Ethel and Lou nodded, looking excited.

'Happy to help with anything, if you need me too,' said Ethel.

'Yep, me too,' said Lou.

'Not that you'll need either of us,' laughed Ethel.

'And are you still happy to lead the charge with the WI over at the hotel?' Kate asked Ethel. 'I'll help as much as I can in the evenings, but if you guys can get the place clean, I can man the fort here while you're all out on your missions!'

'Happy with that!' said Ethel. 'Then when we've got the place smelling a bit better, I'll take over from you in here for a few days Kate, and that should free you up to work your magic with Mike!'

Kate smiled, but dropped her head in her hands as all three of them started on their usual round of *nudge, nudge, wink, wink, Kate lurves Mike!*

'For heaven sakes, you three,' she sighed.

'Ah come on,' said Lou, wiggling her eyebrows.

'Yeah - I had to put up with it for years about Charlie!' laughed Ethel.

'No offence Ethel,' said Sarah, 'but you two ended up as the cutest couple ever . . . so . . .'

'Oh hush, you,' giggled Ethel. 'But that does remind me - Charlie told me to pass on that he's available to help in any way you need him for the wedding - or anything else. Even if it's just to look after Stanley or walk him while you're so busy.'

'You've got a good one, there, Ethel!' said Kate with a smile.

'Don't I know it, love!' she beamed. 'Just don't tell him - I'll never live it down!'

This really was the most spectacular view. Veronica might be a conniving, bitter woman, but she'd been quite right to think that people would give a lot to celebrate their wedding day out here.

Kate had arrived early for her meeting with Mike at The Pebble Street Hotel, so she'd decided to sit out on the newly renovated area outside the dining room. The low, autumn sunshine on her face combined with the gentle lapping of the sea below was exquisite. She'd meant to run through her plans while she waited but instead, she'd just been sitting here, gazing dreamily out over The King's Nose, and across the bay to where the lighthouse stood sentry out on the point.

Her picnic up there with Mike felt like months ago, not days, and she wished that they could be up there right now, with the fresh breeze blowing off the sea and Stanley snuffling around them while they tucked into a picnic like last time. And maybe, just maybe - if he asked her on a date again - this time she'd say yes.

Paula's words about living for the moment kept echoing around her head. She knew her friend was right, but on the other hand, she still hadn't heard anything back from Philip about what Tom was up to. It had been a relief just to know that he was on the case, though, and he'd promised her – if nothing else

– that she wouldn't have to wait too long for a resolution.

She hated all this waiting - but if she was being totally honest, ever since Paula's news it had shifted into the background a bit. Still - could she really think of moving on without making sure that The Sardine was safe?

The thing was, every time she saw Mike, she just wanted to run her hands through his hair and cuddle into him. Considering they were now working together to make sure Lee and Annabel's big day was as special as they could make it, it was getting harder and harder to ignore how she felt. And given the number of times she'd caught him gazing at her when he thought she wasn't looking, she was pretty sure he was in the same boat. At least – a little bit.

'Penny for them?' came a quiet voice from behind her.

Kate smiled without turning. 'Hey Mike!' she said gently.

'Hey yourself. Sorry I'm late,' he said, dropping onto the wooden bench next to her and staring out at the sea. 'Where's our boy?'

'Stanley?' she asked. 'Charlie took him up to the allotments for a run around while he went to fetch some tools.'

'That's good. You know he's invited to the wedding, right?'

'He is?' laughed Kate.

Mike nodded. 'Lee and Annabel have issued a general invitation to all of us who're helping - but Lee added a special mention for Stanley - I think he's fallen for him!'

Kate grinned. 'Not the only one, eh?'

Mike smiled. 'My first four-legged love,' he laughed.

'Right,' said Kate, sitting up and trying to stop herself from staring at Mike like a love-sick idiot, 'shall we run through where we're up to with everything so far?

'Erm . . . before we get onto all things wedding . . . can I ask you something a bit awkward?'

Kate raised her eyebrows at him. Holy crap - was he about to save her a job and ask her out again?

'It's about Sarah,' he said with a slight frown.

'Oh,' said Kate, trying to ignore the fact that her heart just sank a little bit. 'Of course, what's up?'

'Well - that's what I was going to ask you,' said Mike, running his hand around the back of his neck and looking decidedly uncomfortable. 'She's been pretty quiet recently - ever since the news about Aunty Sally.'

'Well, that's to be expected, I guess,' said Kate.

'Yeah - but I was wondering what happened at that last staff meeting you had? I know you talked about Paula - and that must have been incredibly difficult for you all,' he paused and took Kate's hand, giving it a squeeze.

Kate simply nodded, but she didn't move her hand away.

'But . . . did anything else happen?'

Kate frowned. 'Not really. We *did* talk about Paula - and although it was really hard, we discussed the ways we could all be there for her. Sarah was upset, but I think she understood.'

'But nothing else?'

Kate shrugged. 'Erm - I just made sure that everyone was happy with what we're all doing to keep things running while we're busy . . . and I double-checked Sarah's still happy to make the wedding cake - which she was. Why?'

'Since she got back, she's gone from quiet to angry and snappy. I know she's a teen and everything, but it's really not like her!'

'Blimey,' said Kate, frowning at him. 'Well . . . I guess it could have been the news about Paula?'

Mike shrugged. 'Maybe . . .'

'Or perhaps stuff around your Aunty . . . or . . . maybe having to do this cake is actually too much for her?'

'I guess it could be,' said Mike, looking uncertain. 'But she was really excited about that. She's been doodling pages of ideas ever since we asked her.' He stopped and let out a huge sigh. 'All I know is that there's something really wrong, and whenever I ask her what's up, she just bites my head off.'

'Hmm . . . I hate to say it, but that can be pretty

standard practise for a teenage girl,' chuckled Kate, her mind wandering back to her own handful of scary hormonal outbursts.

'I get what you're saying, but . . . this is something more. Something different.'

Kate frowned at him and then, realising she was still holding his hand, quickly gave it a squeeze and let go. 'I'll see if I can sound her out a bit if I get the opportunity,' she said, getting to her feet.

'Thanks Kate!' he said, following suit. 'And you?' he asked, suddenly. 'How are you doing with all of this?'

Kate traced the crack in the brand new paving slabs with her toe, wishing she could disappear between them. 'I'm just glad we're busy,' she said, her voice giving her away with a little wobble.

Mike nodded. 'If you need me, I'm here, okay?'

Kate nodded and screwed her hands into tight fists at her side, digging her fingernails in hard – whether it was in a bid to stop herself from crying or from throwing herself at him and kissing his face off – she wasn't quite sure.

'Right,' she said, taking a step towards the double doors into the dining room, 'I think it's time to whip this wedding into shape.'

CHAPTER 15

'I can't believe how much they've already done!' said Kate, her jaw dropping as they stood together in the middle of the newly pristine kitchen. There wasn't any sign of the washing-up mountain, the grimy, fat-stained backsplash or the stinking slops bucket. Everything had been emptied out, scrubbed to within an inch of its life and then left in apple-pie order. This was now a kitchen that Kate could imagine a professional chef hard at work in.

'You know,' said Mike, looking around, 'this country would be in a much better shape if we just let Ethel and Seabury's WI run it!'

'Now there's a terrifying thought!' laughed Kate. 'But this is perfect, isn't it? It will be far easier to prep everything for the wedding in here rather than trying to do it all over at The Sardine or your place. It's enough of a battle keeping the cafes running as well as making sure this bun fight goes off without a hitch!'

'Spot on,' agreed Mike. 'I know Annabel has completely fallen for the idea of everyone helping themselves to food from the back of Trixie - so we might have to look at fitting up some kind of display for the trailer. Any thoughts?'

Kate glanced around her, her mind racing. 'Ken,' she said with a flash of inspiration. 'The guy who did the repairs to the floor in the dining room. I bet he would help or would know someone who could.'

'Think he'd be up for it?'

Kate shrugged. 'He gave me his card when he came in for lunch, so I can always call and find out. He was a really nice chap.'

They wandered out of the kitchen and into the hallway, which now smelled of polish rather than cabbage. 'Huh!' said Kate, 'the carpet's a different colour.'

'Yes - amazing what a spot of hoovering does!' laughed Lionel, striding towards them from upstairs.

'Hi!' said Kate with a grin.

'Tour of inspection?' he asked.

Kate nodded. 'Sort of. We just wanted to see where we're up to - Lee and Annabel are popping down in a bit for a look around.'

'Jolly good,' said Lionel. 'Oh - by the way, I was talking to Ethel when she was here - and we were wondering if the breakfast lounge might make a nice space for the happy couple to have as a kind of dressing room to relax in away from everything?'

'It's so grim in the breakfast lounge though,' sighed Kate, thinking of the dregs of cold coffee and congealed cornflakes awaiting them.

Lionel shook his head. 'Look again!' He led them along to the lounge and threw open the door with a flourish.

'Blimey,' exclaimed Mike wandering in, 'the cleaning fairies have been in here too!'

Kate took one step in and stopped dead. 'Okay - Ethel for president!' she laughed.

'Actually, I should tell you that Paula was most definitely in charge of this bit,' chuckled Lionel.

'That figures,' said Kate, blinking hard as she felt a couple of rogue tears appear in the corners of her eyes. Not wanting the others to notice this sudden swell of emotion, she took several steps into the space, facing away from them in the pretence of taking it all in.

The manky little tables and spindly chairs were gone - along with the echoes of breakfasts long past. The room somehow looked larger and cosier at the same time. The windows had been cleaned and the soft autumn light flooded in.

Kate longed to throw herself onto one of the two squashy sofas that had appeared as if by magic . . . but she just about managed to stop herself. She had a sneaking suspicion that if she lay down right now, the siren-call of a nap might prove to be way too tempting.

'So,' said Lionel, 'Paula got us to roll this massive old carpet back, then a team of them scrubbed the floor and gave it some kind of treatment. When that was dry, they went to work on the carpet too - I never knew it was such a handsome one if I'm honest - it's always been too covered in bits of breakfast before!'

Mike shook his head in wonder. 'You know, I'd be happy to actually get married in here, it's that nice,' he said. 'You could just imagine those lovely windows making the perfect backdrop, and you could have the chairs here, and a stand of flowers over there and . . .' he petered out as Kate turned to him with her eyebrows raised in amusement. 'You know what I mean!' he added, clearing his throat and turning a beautiful berry red.

Lionel chuckled. '*I* do! Now that you can actually see out through the windows, look at that view!' he said, pointing through the great arches of glass. You could see right to the other side of Seabury from here, all the way to where the allotments lay on the slopes of the far hill.

'Where did all this gorgeous furniture come from though?' said Kate. 'It must have cost a fortune - I feel like I've stepped into an Austen adaptation!'

Lionel shook his head. 'Nope - it's all from the

hotel,' he said, patting an ornate wooden bureau. 'Paula, Charlie and I went for a nose around upstairs. Paula chose the bits she wanted for in here, and Charlie and I - with a little bit of help from a couple of the other chaps from the allotments - brought it all down for her.'

'Sounds like Paula,' Kate laughed. The emotion swelled in her chest again, but this time it was pure pride. She'd turned the room into an elegant, cosy place to spend time - and Kate was excited to let Lee and Annabel see it. 'I think they're going to love it!'

'Me too,' said Mike. 'But hearing you mention "upstairs" has just made me think - I reckon we'd better rope the stairs off somehow. It's one thing letting the guests wander around down here where it's all been cleaned, but upstairs is . . .'

'Yucky?' said Lionel.

'Erm . . . yep!' said Mike.

'Well, it's not quite as bad now. A handful of over-enthusiastic WI ladies and a fleet of Henry hoovers have had a good rampage up there since you last saw it.'

'You're joking,' said Kate. 'We didn't mean for them to take on the entire bloomin' hotel!'

Lionel shrugged. 'I overheard Doreen from the Post Office tell Celia Jones that she wouldn't be able to sleep unless she did something about it.'

Mike snorted. 'I might have to tell Doreen that my

place is in a state too - just to see if she'll come around once a week and hoover for me!'

Kate smirked at him. 'So, how far did they get?'

'The whole lot,' grinned Lionel. 'I mean, not like down here, where everything - including the door-knobs - has been polished. But everything's been hoovered and dusted, and the public bathrooms have been scrubbed too. If we just close the bedroom doors and turn a key in the locks, then it won't matter if the guests decide to take a wander around, will it?'

'When this is done,' said Mike, 'we're going to hold a special event at my place and invite everyone for free coffees and cream teas to say thank you.'

'They'd like that,' said Kate with a soft smile. 'Though be prepared for plenty of critique on your jam and the lightness of your scones.'

'Ha - no chance,' he chuckled, 'I'll rope Ethel into making them for me!'

'Poaching my staff now, are we Mr Pendle?' she laughed.

'It's not poaching if we're working together, is it?' he said with his eyes twinkling.

'So what are you going to name this little joint events-venture of yours then?' asked Lionel.

'Frothy Sardine?' said Mike, trying to keep his face straight as Kate gave him a hefty dig in the ribs.

'Um – eeew!' laughed Kate, shaking her head.

'You know what keeps bothering me,' said Lionel.

'What?' asked Kate.

'Well, you're doing all this work – and so many people are getting involved to make it happen - and it's all benefitting Veronica. It just doesn't seem right, somehow.'

'How's it benefitting Veronica?' said Mike. 'I don't know about you guys, but I'm doing this for Lee and Annabel - and us a little bit too,' he shot a sly grin at Kate.

'Well,' said Lionel, 'Pebble Street's going to be in a much better state when all this is over - and that's only going to help her sell it, isn't it?'

'Maybe think about it like this,' said Kate gently, 'hopefully it will bring a new owner who really cares about the old place. Someone who'll love the hotel as much as you do. If that happens - then it's got to be worth it, hasn't it?'

Lionel nodded, though she could see his mind was still working under those frowning, bushy brows. She gently took his arm and smiled up at him. 'It'll work out, Lionel. I know it will.'

∽

'So - what do you think?' asked Mike.

Kate watched Annabel and Lee as they stared around the dining room and then back out through the open double doors towards the sea.

'I think you are my new heroes,' said Annabel,

turning to them with tears in her eyes. 'You have no idea how much this means to me. I know we didn't see it at its worst, but I can see how much work you've already done in here. I just . . . I . . .'

Kate stepped forward and instinctively put her arm around Annabel as her chin quivered. She understood how much a place could mean when it held treasured memories of someone you loved so dearly. It was like the way the old lighthouse made her feel closer to her lovely dad – like he was still there with her.

'I'm so glad you like it,' said Kate. 'And when it's all decorated and Trixie's here with the food, it should look quite special.'

'I love the outdoor space,' said Lee.

'Well,' said Lionel, 'Ethel's chap, Charlie, is coming down later on today. He's got the green fingers, so all those new planters will be filled up. He said he's got just the thing to plant in there to give you some colour for your big day, as well as some huge tubs of autumn crocuses that are about to bloom.'

'Crocuses were nan's favourite!' said Annabel, leaning her head on Kate's shoulder.

Kate smiled over at Mike, and she saw his shoulders relax a little.

'Charlie's also going to clear the outdoor passage like we talked about so your guests can come around the back like you asked,' said Kate, 'but, as the WI ladies have done such a fab job, we can actually open up the whole ground floor for you - and you can use the main entrance too.'

'I still can't believe you've done all this for us,' said Lee. 'Thank you so much!'

Mike grinned. 'It's nothing.'

'Erm - nope!' laughed Lee.

'Okay, it's *something* . . . but we're enjoying it, aren't we?' said Mike.

Kate smiled at him and nodded. Yes, even though her life should feel like it was crumbling at the seams right now, this was definitely something she was enjoying.

'Oh,' she said, 'I forgot to tell you. My friend Paula, who's been helping out, knows Emmy Martin who owns Grandad Jim's Flower Farm over in Little Bamton.'

'Wow,' said Annabel, 'what a wonderful job!'

'I know,' said Kate, 'I thought that too! Anyway - I know Veronica was meant to be sorting out that side of things – and I don't think she even tried to get flowers booked. Emmy does buckets of mixed, cut flowers and we figured - if you still wanted some flowers in here - we could get our crack team of WI flower arrangers to work their magic with a couple of them?'

'Yes,' said Lee, wrapping his arm around Annabel's shoulders as she went to stand next to him. 'Yes please. And if she's got dahlias, it's a triple yes please.'

Kate raised her eyebrows in delight. She'd

expected Annabel to be the one to jump at the flowers.

'Lee's a sucker for flowers,' laughed Annabel.

'And thank goodness I'm marrying a woman who likes buying them for me.'

Kate watched as Lee gathered Annabel into the sweetest kiss, then without meaning to, her eyes drifted over to Mike, only to find that he was staring at her, and the look he was giving her took her breath away.

Lionel let out a huge sigh. 'Young love,' he said. Kate nodded and glanced at him, but instead of watching the canoodling couple, he was looking between her and Mike with misty eyes.

'Don't *you* start!' laughed Kate, making Mike snort with laughter.

CHAPTER 16

Kate stretched and let out a huge yawn, promptly echoed by Stanley in his bed. Ethel and Lou had booted her out of the cafe for the last few hours. The weather was so bad that there was barely anyone around, so she'd taken them up on the offer of a couple of hours to herself. She'd promised them she was going to have a nap and chill out, but in reality, she'd just spent most of the afternoon making sure that everything was ready for Lee and Annabel's big day.

She'd called Emmy at Grandad Jim's Flower Farm, and when she'd told her the story, Emmy had given her a whopping discount. Mike had already ordered several cases of sparkling wine from his contact at the vineyard just outside of Little Bamton, so she called them to ask if they could pop in to collect them on the same trip.

Her last call had been to Ken - who'd greeted her like an old friend, waxed lyrical about how much he'd enjoyed his lunch at The Sardine, and then happily agreed to make her a speedy display for Trixie. The only proviso was that she'd cater his fortieth wedding anniversary the following year.

It was only when she'd ended the call that Kate had realised she might not even be the owner of The Sardine in a year's time. The thought had been enough to puncture the happy bubble she'd managed to surround herself with, and suddenly she needed to get out of the flat.

'Right, Stanley lad!' she said, getting up and wincing as her spine let out a series of snaps, crackles and pops from sitting still for far too long. 'Let's grab a walk and then take Trixie over to the hotel.'

Deep down, she knew that Trixie would be able to navigate the newly-cleared passageway around the back of the hotel with no trouble, but she didn't want to leave such an important element untested. She'd mentioned it to Mike earlier, and he'd suggested that Kate wheel Trixie over there to do a quick walk-through - just to make sure and set her mind at ease.

The minute she grabbed a jacket and Stanley's lead, he hopped straight out of his bed and followed her downstairs, letting out a massive yawn.

As she expected, The Sardine's blinds were down and by the looks of things everyone had headed home for the evening. Making sure that all three of her staff had their own key was the best thing Kate had ever done. It took the pressure off having to be there for opening and closing time every day - even if it was a bit weird not being one hundred per cent sure who was still pottering around downstairs when she was up in her flat.

'Ah bollocks!' she breathed as she turned towards the yard where Trixie was tucked up for the night. There, blocking the entrance, was a posh estate car. 'Hang on a minute, I recognise you,' she said with a frown.

She stared around her but there was no sign of anyone, let alone Mike or Sarah. She sighed and fiddled around in her pocket for her phone.

'Pick up, Mike,' she muttered as it rang. 'Come on, come on, come on. Balls!' she said as it went to voice mail. 'Okay. Change of plan. Come on Stanley, we're off to New York Froth!'

It wasn't quite the chilled, relaxing walk she'd been hoping to have along the seafront. Kate was quietly seething. It always rubbed her up the wrong way when anyone parked across the entrance to the yard. For one thing, it had signs all over it indicating that the gates were in constant use. Yes, she *knew* that it was after closing time - but with that idiot parked there, it meant she wouldn't be able to get Trixie out and over to the hotel as she'd planned.

She blew out a frustrated breath. Of course, this was worse than some random, thoughtless visitor blocking her in - because she was pretty sure that was Sienna's car. Mike's ex. Otherwise known as the evil cow-bag who'd run her and Stanley off the road earlier in the summer. The accident had resulted in Stanley getting injured - and Kate swearing an oath never to let the woman off the hook for hurting her boy.

By the time they reached New York Froth, she was out of breath and in a decided huff. Kate impatiently hit Mike's doorbell.

'Come on,' she muttered. She knew it was totally unfair on him, but if his ex was in town, he was the most likely person to know where she was. Or had she got this very wrong? Perhaps Mike had borrowed the car for some reason, and parked it there because . . . why? For some kind of strange joke? Or because he was in a rush . . . or maybe . . . maybe he was at the hotel?

Stanley let out a massive sigh and sat on Kate's foot, making her laugh. 'I know, boy,' she chuckled. 'I'm an idiot. He's clearly not here. Let's try calling him again!'

She yanked out her mobile and pulled Mike's number up again. This time he answered on the second ring.

'Hey Kate!' he said, and she could hear the smile in his voice.

'Hey yourself! Where are you?'

'Oh, I'm . . . er . . . why? Where are you?' he said.

Kate raised her eyebrows. 'I'm outside your place, looking for you,' she laughed.

'Oh! Sorry, I'm not in town at the moment.'

'Bugger.'

'Sorry?'

'There's a bit of a situation. I didn't realise Sienna's in town?'

'Huh? You've lost me!'

'Your ex-wife . . .?'

'Yes, I know who Sienna is, unfortunately,' laughed Mike.

'Well, her car's currently blocking Trixie's yard. I thought maybe you'd borrowed it or something, but-'

'No, not me,' said Mike quickly. 'But it can't be Sienna - she's miles away. Kate are you *sure* it's not just some other random person with the same car?' he asked.

Kate was suddenly intensely grateful that he couldn't see her as the blush started somewhere in her toes and quickly made its way right the way up to her face.

'I guess it could be,' she muttered.

She heard Mike let out a chuckle.

'Sorry,' she said. 'I just saw it and instantly saw red!'

'Oh trust me - I understand that better than you'd ever imagine!' he laughed.

'It's cocked up my plans for taking Trixie over to the hotel tonight, though,' she sighed.

'Well - maybe just take a night off?' he said lightly. 'I reckon you've earned it.'

'Thanks boss!' she laughed. For a long second, Kate was tempted to ask him if he'd like to meet up for a drink . . . but then, that could lead to-

'Kate, you still there?'

'Oh, uh, yeah - sorry.'

'I've got to head off - I should be back in town in about an hour or so.'

'Okay. Erm. Okay, cool. I'll catch you tomorrow then?'

'Tomorrow,' said Mike.

Stanley stared at her as she slipped her mobile back into her pocket. 'What?' she said, grinning down at him.

Stanley let out another sigh.

'I know. I'm a wuss. I'm nowhere near as brave as Aunty Paula. She'd have just asked him out already. Anyway - looks like it's just you and me, old boy. Come on!'

～

'Huh,' she said, drawing to a halt on the pavement opposite The Sardine. She was sure the lights had been off when she'd passed the cafe on her way out, but now she could see light sneaking around the edges of the blinds. Perhaps one of the others had forgotten something and popped back in. 'Come on lad, let's check it out.'

Casting the shiny estate car a filthy look, Kate let Stanley off his lead but suddenly paused at the cafe door, certain that she could hear raised voices coming from inside. She glanced down at Stanley, and his raised ears and the fact that he was staring at the door in alarm seemed to confirm it. What she wasn't expecting to hear from him was a grumble low down in his throat. It was very rare for her big softy to make that kind of sound!

She listened intently for a moment, but completely unable to make out the words, she pushed her way inside.

'Sarah?' she said. The young girl had her back to the door, and it looked like she was busy with something over on the stove.

'Kate?' Sarah whipped around, and Kate let out a shriek. Sarah's eyes were red and swollen from crying and her face was all puffy.

'What's wrong, sweetheart?

'What's wrong is that she is being a baby,' came a hard, angry voice from behind Kate.

Kate spun back to the little table in the corner. A woman was sitting there, glaring at her. She hadn't spotted her on her way in because she'd been so focused on Sarah. She looked a lot like her young member of staff - but at the same time, nothing like her. She didn't have the warmth dancing behind her eyes, or the wide smile Sarah had clearly inherited from her father.

'You must be Sienna,' said Kate without an ounce of warmth or welcome.

'And who are you? We're having a private conversation.'

'This is Kate's place,' said Sarah quietly.

'Don't interrupt!' snapped Sienna, and Kate saw Sarah flinch. Before she could react, however, Stanley let out a deep growl and came to stand directly in front of Sienna, his hackles raised and his tail completely still.

'It's okay boy,' said Kate, her voice low and gentle. She'd never seen him like this before and the last thing she needed was for him to go for the woman – even though she wouldn't blame him in the slightest.

'Get your dog away from me,' said Sienna coldly.

'I suggest you get yourself away from my dog,' said Kate, gently laying her hand on Stanley's collar and clipping the lead she was still carrying back in place. She trusted Stanley implicitly - but he had a strong protective streak. Given that Sarah was currently a shaking mess, she wasn't surprised that it had gone into overdrive.

'Come on lad,' she said, practically dragging him away so that he was over nearer to the kitchen. 'What's going on, Sarah?' she said, desperately wanting to put an arm around the girl, but unable to get Stanley to budge far enough to do so.

Sarah looked at her, tears still cascading down her face.

'What's going on is that she's finally seeing sense and coming away with me.'

Kate glanced at Sarah as her sobbing seemed to double.

'Have you talked to Mike about this?' Kate asked, doing her best not to sound threatening.

'Huh, so you're the new bit on the side are you?' she spat. 'No. I don't need to talk to your pathetic boyfriend to take my daughter away. She's being wasted here. I've found her a place at a prestigious culinary college in Paris. She will learn from the best.'

'Paris?' said Kate, desperately trying to catch up. 'She's still got almost two years to finish where she is.'

'She dropped out,' said Sienna with a sneer.

'You made me,' sobbed Sarah.

Stanley strained at his lead and Kate braced herself in case he was about to make a dash for Sienna, but then relaxed as he struggled to get to Sarah instead. She let go of his lead so that he could dash around the corner, no doubt to sit on Sarah's feet.

'I did not *make* you,' said Sienna. 'You agreed that Paris would be good.'

'*One day,*' sobbed Sarah. 'I said maybe *one day!*'

'Grow up. You've got the money to do it now. Stop wasting your life here.'

'Okay,' said Kate, 'that's enough. Sarah, love, do you want me to call your dad?'

'He's not home,' said Sarah, turning to her. 'That's why I came to yours. I don't want to go!'

'You're not going anywhere,' said Kate. She turned towards Sienna. 'I'd like you to get out of my cafe now, please. You can talk this through with Mike, but I'm not leaving you alone with Sarah.'

'Oh, be quiet, you sappy bitch!'

'Get out, or I'm calling the police,' growled Kate, moving around the counter and putting an arm around Sarah. She could feel her quivering all over and it made her anger towards this awful woman swell even further. 'And move your car, or I'll have you towed.'

Sienna got to her feet and moved a couple of paces towards them but came to an abrupt halt as Stanley dashed out of the kitchen with a warning growl.

'You're as big a loser as your father,' she spat at Sarah, not taking her eyes off of Stanley. 'I can't believe I wasted so much energy on you. You've got a day to apologise. After that - I'm cancelling Paris – not that you'll ever make anything of yourself anyway.'

Kate watched Sienna turn on her heel and storm out of the cafe. The minute the door closed behind her mother, Sarah dissolved into a sobbing wreck, her arms around Kate's middle as her tears soaked into the shoulder of her jumper.

Kate held her close for what felt like hours, though in reality, it was probably only about five minutes. But there was no way she was letting go until Sarah's breathing calmed down and her tears had eased up.

When Sarah finally stepped back, doing her best to wipe her face while Stanley desperately tried to lick her hands, Kate let out a long breath. She quickly nipped over to the door and turned the key in the lock. It wasn't that she was afraid of Sienna - but she needed Sarah to feel completely safe while they figured out what to do next.

'I'm going to give your dad a call,' she said.

Sarah nodded, sinking down onto the floor and wrapping her arms around Stanley. Kate had a sneaking suspicion that she was crying again. She quickly grabbed her mobile and called Mike.

'I'm feeling very popular right now,' came his booming laugh.

'Where are you?' said Kate. She did her best to keep her voice calm, not wanting to alarm him - or Sarah, for that matter.

'Why?' he said, and she could hear the instant worry in his voice. 'What's wrong.'

'It's Sarah,' she said, not quite sure how to tell him what she'd just walked in on. 'That car *was* Sienna's.'

'Oh God, what's she done?' he said, and she could hear the anger already building in his voice.

'Can you come straight to The Sardine?'

'I'll be there in ten minutes.'

'Great. Give me a call when you're outside - I've got the door locked.'

CHAPTER 17

'Well,' said Mike, handing Kate a glass of brandy and then throwing himself down into the sofa next to her, 'she's stopped crying and Stanley's practically in bed with her!' He gave her a weak smile and took a sip of his drink.

'He can stay with her tonight,' said Kate smiling back.

'Thank you. I swear that dog is the best therapy there is!'

'I don't think your ex would agree,' muttered Kate, 'it's a miracle Stanley didn't go for her. I've never seen him quite so protective.'

'Sarah's basically terrified of Sienna. Stanley was just protecting a scared pup.'

Kate nodded. 'I don't quite get what I walked in on,' she said. She didn't want to interrogate Mike, but equally, she was desperate to know that Sarah was safe and wouldn't be forced into something against her will.

Mike sighed. 'I think Sarah and I have quite a bit of talking to do when she's calmed down, but reading between the lines, Sienna's somehow found out that Sarah's inherited a bunch of money from Aunty Sally. I guarantee she will have already blown through what she got in the divorce, so I'm guessing she figured she'd like to get her hands on it.'

'*What?!*' squeaked Kate.

'Mmm,' growled Mike. 'She's been in far more regular contact with Sarah since the news. I didn't say anything because I know Sarah's been having a hard time and I figured that maybe she needed her mum. I mean - there's a first time for everything, right? As it turns out - Sienna *is* the hard time she's been having.'

'Oh my goodness,' said Kate, absolutely horrified that someone would do that to their own child.

'Yeah. Anyway - Sienna's been in town for several days now - hounding Sarah. Sounds like her and her boyfriend were after an all-expenses-paid year in Paris courtesy of Sarah while they "looked after her".'

'You don't think she would have actually tried to force her to leave, do you?' said Kate, feeling sick at the thought.

Mike frowned. 'Sienna's quite full-on . . .'
'Yeah, I noticed,' muttered Kate.

'Let's just say, I'm really glad you were there. Thank you.'

'I'd do anything for either of you,' said Kate, reaching out and resting her hand on his. Mike turned to her and locked his eyes on hers.

'Same, Kate.'

Kate swallowed. This wasn't the moment.

'What is it?' he asked quietly, not taking his eyes off her.

Kate could feel herself growing red, but she couldn't look away. 'It's not the moment,' she said out loud, shaking her head slightly. Right now, she wanted nothing more than to lean in and kiss him - but she'd waited for so long, she didn't want it to happen under the shadow of what Sienna had done.

'Okay,' said Mike giving her a small nod and taking another swig of brandy. 'Anyway, it looks like I'm going to have to call Sarah's college in the morning and make sure they know what's what. It sounds like this plan got way further than it should have. There's no way I'm letting her miss out on something she's loving so much and is so good at just because her mother's a lunatic.'

'Good,' said Kate. 'Erm - do you think it might be a good idea to talk to the police . . . or maybe a solicitor?'

Mike frowned. 'I think I need to find out exactly what's happened - but yes, it might be time to put a few more barriers in place to stop this kind of thing from happening again.'

～

Kate was so tired, she almost felt drunk with it. It had taken her some serious convincing before Mike had agreed to her walking back to The Sardine alone the previous night. He was torn between wanting to make sure she got safely home and staying with Sarah. In the end, after Kate pointed out that it wasn't late and that she didn't have anything to fear from Sienna, he agreed to let her go provided that she called him the second she was back in her flat.

It had ended up being a restless night, and her dreams had been full of Sienna's angry face, and Mike's lips, and finally leaning in for the kiss that she now knew was about far more than simple, physical attraction.

She fired up the Italian Stallion for the second time in half an hour and poured herself a treacly triple espresso - it was the only way she was going to keep her eyes open today - and there was a lot to do.

Ethel and Charlie were driving over to the large theatre in Plymouth to pick up costumes for them all for the big day. They'd decided that there was no way they were going to let the side down - if Lee and Annabel wanted a wartime-themed wedding, that was what they were going to get - right down to the last victory roll.

Sarah was due in any minute - not to work a shift, but to get ready to meet with Annabel and Lee. It was time for her to show off her designs so that they could choose their final cake. In her heart, Kate knew that it wouldn't be the end of the world if Sarah decided that she simply wasn't up to it after yesterday - after all, both Lou and Ethel would no doubt be more than happy to step in if they needed to.

That wasn't the point though. Kate knew just how much this project meant to Sarah. She'd poured so much energy and passion into it. Plus, Kate had a sneaking suspicion that it was just what she needed to regain her confidence - as well as giving that bitch of a mother the middle finger.

Kate took a sip of her coffee and grimaced. Espresso was *so* not her drink - but it was definitely giving her the kind of jolt she needed to keep her on her feet. It really hadn't been late when she'd got back from Mike's, but the flat had been so quiet without Stanley there. She'd spent most of the night wishing she'd taken Mike up on his offer of sleeping in his spare room . . . but she hadn't dared to say yes.

From that moment their eyes had met on the sofa, Kate had been seconds away from crawling onto his lap and telling him that she'd fallen in love with him.

One more sip of brandy and disaster would most definitely have struck! Okay - not disaster, but-

'Hey!'

The tinkle of the doorbell made her look up, only to find Paula grinning at her.

'Paula!' she said, rushing over and opening her arms for a hug. 'What brings you here so bright and early?'

'Well - two things,' she said, taking a step back. 'But first - why do you look like shit?'

'Gee thanks!' chuckled Kate, rolling her eyes. 'Just a rough night, that's all. Stanley had a sleepover with Sarah and I'm not used to him being away.'

'Aww!' said Paula. 'I can imagine. Okay - as long as you're not as ill as you look.'

'That might have something to do with the triple brandy I had with Mike,' sighed Kate.

'Oooh, Miss Hardy - is there gossip to share?'

'Nope,' said Kate. 'But almost. I nearly jumped on the poor guy!'

'Come on, Kate, what did we say about all this the other day?'

'I promise I'm working on it,' sighed Kate. 'But it's getting more complicated. Paula - I think I'm in love with him.'

'Holy shizzle sticks - the words I never thought I'd hear you say!' Paula grinned at her and jiggled excitedly on the spot. 'So . . . why not last night?'

'Bit of a long story,' muttered Kate, spotting a

couple of people approaching the door, 'and not my story to tell,' she added in a whisper.

'Fairy snuff,' said Paula with a wink, sinking down into a chair and patting the table with her hands. 'Right, my hungover little turtle-dove. Back to *my* two things! Number one - scrambled eggs on toast and a latte pretty please!'

'You've got it!' said Kate with a smile.

'Number two - is Sarah here yet? She told me about her cake designs and I was hoping she might give me a sneaky peak.'

'She isn't, not yet. If I'm honest I'm not one hundred per cent sure that - oh!'

She'd just been about to tell Paula that she wasn't certain that they were going to see Sarah at all today when the teen in question bounced through the door and bounded right up to Kate.

'You are seriously the best and I love you,' she said, thrusting a bunch of flowers at Kate and then grabbing her in a massive cuddle.

Kate let out a delighted laugh and squeezed Sarah back with one arm, holding the flowers out to the side with the other to stop them from getting crushed. 'You okay, lovely?' she said quietly in her ear.

'Yes, thanks to you,' said Sarah. 'Sorry Paula,' she added, grinning over in her direction. 'Major drama with my bitch mother yesterday - she basically tried to kidnap me but Kate and Stanley saved me from a lifetime of servitude in Paris!'

The look of complete confusion on Paula's face made Kate giggle. 'Looks like I'll be able to share that story with you after all,' she said.

'Forget that - I'll tell it way better than you!' said Sarah, beaming at Paula.

'Erm, first - where's my dog?' said Kate.

'He's here,' said Mike, struggling into the cafe with a giant art portfolio under one arm, Stanley's lead looped over the other and a cardboard box precariously balanced in front of him. He plonked the box straight down on one of the tables and dropped Stanley's lead.

Stanley trotted up to Kate and she squatted down to bury her face in his fur. She'd really missed him - but that wasn't the only reason for the cuddle - he was the perfect way to distract herself from just how gorgeous Mike looked this morning - all pink-cheeked and flustered. Man, this was getting hard!

She could practically feel Paula's eyes boring into her back as she snuggled into Stanley, and she wasn't ready to meet her eyes until she'd got this blush under control!

'Careful with the box, dad!' squeaked Sarah, 'Jeez!'

Kate heard Mike laugh and peeped up at him. He was looking at his daughter with adoration, and suddenly she thought her heart was going to explode.

She quickly got up and turned her back to make Paula's coffee.

'What *is* in the box?' asked Paula.

'It's one of the ideas I want to show Lee and Annabel!' said Sarah.

'Can I see?'

'Of course!' said Sarah. 'Kate - did you want to look too - I'd . . . erm . . . I'd really like to check you're happy with them before I take them over to the hotel and set them up for the others to look at. Dad says he likes them - but he *would* say that!'

'Sure,' said Kate over her shoulder. 'Give me two secs.' She quickly poured the foamy milk into Paula's cup, then took it over to her as Sarah unzipped the massive portfolio and flipped the cover open.

'I've done three different ideas,' said Sarah. 'Only two of them are any good.'

Mike moved back so that Kate and Paula could see better, and as he did so, Kate's hand brushed the back of his. The tiny contact made all the hairs on the back of her neck stand on end.

Get a grip woman!

She stared down at the intricate drawings on the first page of the portfolio, doing her best to ignore Mike standing just behind her. If she leaned back just a little, she'd probably touch him.

'So!' said Sarah, sounding a bit nervous. 'This one's quite simple, but I wanted to go for that slightly "make-do-and-mend - everyone in it together" vibe where everyone might have given their rations to make it happen.'

The drawing showed a quirky take on the classic victoria sponge. There were the usual thick layers of jam and cream in the centre - but six layers made up three different cakes, all stacked on top of each other, angled slightly to give it a topsy-turvy look. The whole thing was finished off and decorated with piped cream and fresh strawberries.

'I know it's not exactly historically accurate - but I thought it had that quirky vintagy-vibe,' said Sarah, now sounding decidedly nervous as all of them stared at the drawing in complete silence.

'Um - Sarah,' said Kate slowly, 'how come you never mentioned you could draw like this?!'

Sarah grinned at her and shrugged.

'Isn't it beautiful?' said Mike with a proud smile.

'I'd put that on my wall!' said Paula.

'Don't be silly,' said Sarah turning pink.

'I'm serious!' laughed Paula.

'But what about the cake?' whined Sarah.

'Perfect,' said Kate simply. 'It is beautiful. We've got a winner!'

'Hey - don't say that - you'll upset the other two!' laughed Sarah.

'Why do I get the feeling Lee and Annabel are going to end up with three wedding cakes, whether they want them or not?' chuckled Mike.

'Okay, next,' said Sarah flipping the page.

'Wow!' breathed Paula.

'I'm not sure about this one for the wedding, to be honest,' said Sarah, 'but I kinda needed to do this drawing for college so thought I might as well show them.'

This cake had the full VE day vibe - covered in little union jacks, poppies and Khaki piping details.

'It's so bold!' said Kate.

Sarah nodded. 'I had to show one with the theme - it's got vanilla and chocolate tiers too because I know they both love those flavours - but I don't think it's really *weddingy,* you know?'

'Okay, show us number three!' said Kate excitedly.

Sarah flipped the page to reveal drawings of ten different, exquisite cupcakes. 'These should work individually *and* give you a feel for the theme together,' she said.

Union Jack bunting, tiny fields of piped poppies, Vera Lyn lyrics, delicate creamy lace designs and many more all came together to create the perfect wartime vibe.

'You've just made this impossible to choose!' said Kate, shaking her head in wonder.

'They aren't the best bit!' said Sarah, her eyes sparkling. 'Pass me the box, dad!'

Mike grabbed the cardboard box and handed it over. Paula and Kate both leaned in, but Sarah kept her hand on the closed lid for a moment.

'Did you know that during the war and just after,

because of rationing, the cake would often be just a small, simple fruitcake that friends and family would club together and pool their rations to make?'

'Not sure the happy couple want a tiny fruitcake though, love,' chuckled Mike.

'Not the point dad!' said Sarah, rolling her eyes. 'They used to make them look like fancy wedding cakes by creating a fake one out of cardboard and plaster that fitted over the top!'

She opened the box and drew out one of the most beautiful cakes Kate had ever set eyes on. It was all creams and whites, with lace and pearls. The quintessential wedding cake - finished with little blue and white cameos on each tier.

'Wow!' said Paula.

'Yes, but . . .' Sarah flicked the edge of the cake with her finger and it made a hollow, thudding sound.

'Erm . . . what?!' said Kate.

'It's a wartime cake cover!' said Sarah with a grin. She quickly flipped to the next page in her portfolio. 'Instead of covering a tiny fruit cake, it's going to cover the cupcakes on a stand - and then they get revealed when Lee and Annabel come to "cut the cake!"' She grinned at them triumphantly. 'Do you think they'll like the ideas?' she suddenly added, her smile dropping.

Kate nodded. 'Definitely. These are absolutely beautiful - and seriously professional.'

'Thanks,' she said, breathing a sigh of relief. 'Erm . . . would it be okay if I go over to Pebble Street and set the pages out on the tables - just so it's easier to show them?'

Kate nodded. 'Of course, here . . .' she quickly rummaged in her handbag and drew out the front door key Lionel had given her.

'I'll help!' said Paula. 'You grab the portfolio, I'll bring the box. I'll grab my breakfast when we get back!' she grinned at Kate.

Mike and Kate watched the pair of them as they trooped back outside.

'Sarah seems to have bounced back well,' said Kate in wonder.

Mike nodded, giving her a weary smile. 'I've spoken to her tutors already. She was never unenrolled in the first place. Sienna's not down on their paperwork as Sarah's guardian - but the head of her course was going to contact me directly to find out what was going on. Apparently, they'd noticed that she was struggling with something.'

'So everything's okay?'

'It *will* be,' Mike nodded. 'We've had a good talk - and we will talk some more. Sienna's not coming anywhere near her for a very long time!' He paused and ruffled his hair awkwardly. 'Kate - I can't thank you . . . I don't know what would have happened if . . .'

He took a step towards her, and Kate swallowed as he reached out and took her hand.

'Kate, there's something we really need to talk about. I-'

The door of the cafe bashed open making Kate jump and quickly whip her hand away from Mike.

'What a to-do!' boomed Lionel, then he stopped dead, staring at them. 'Oh my, I'm terribly sorry!' he said with an awkward grin.

Kate shook her head and forced a smile at him.

'I'm just going to nip over and help Sarah,' said Mike, giving Kate a quick glance. 'We'll talk later?' he said and then quickly made a dash for the door.

As soon as it closed, Lionel looked back at her sheepishly. 'I'm so sorry Kate - seems I interrupted at a bad moment?'

'Not at all,' said Kate briskly, doing her best to squash down the temptation to dash after Mike. 'You look rather worked up about something - everything okay?'

Lionel nodded and sighed. 'Only those duffers at the council up to their usual tricks,' he said.

'Uh oh, what ridiculous scheme have they come up with this time?'

Lionel grabbed the newspaper he had clamped under his arm and spread it out on the table, doing his best to iron out the creases.

Kate gasped as her eyes landed on the headline.

Seabury For Sale

'What do they mean, Seabury for Sale?' she demanded.

'They've gone and picked up on the story of Pebble Street being on the market,' said Lionel.

'But what were you saying about the council?' said Kate, trying to scan the article as fast as she could.

'In their wisdom, they've decided to sell off The King's Nose and-'

'Who'd want The King's Nose?' she huffed.

Lionel shrugged. 'Some developer or other, I guess. If they put a house on there, that'll more than ruin my view,' he sighed.

'Oh Lionel, they *wouldn't!*' she squeaked.

'Maybe,' he said. 'That's not all. They've put the old lighthouse on the market too.'

Kate felt like someone had just punched her in the gut, and she sank into the chair opposite him.

'I know. More change,' said Lionel sadly, but then he shook his head with a naughty grin. 'Typical of this rag to be behind the times as usual, though.'

'What do you mean?' said Kate weakly, not sure if she could take another ounce of bad news.

'The hotel's already sold!'

'Eh? Already?' said Kate, her surprise puncturing the fog of gloom that seemed to have suddenly descended.

'Yup,' said Lionel. 'I bought it.'

CHAPTER 18

Kate yanked the rack of costumes into place and looked around the breakfast lounge with her hands on her hips. She couldn't believe that the big day was finally here. She knew that she should be both excited about the afternoon to come, and proud of everything they'd achieved here at The Pebble Street Hotel - but all she felt right now was slightly sad and hollow.

Her whole life felt like it was up in the air. She knew that, in comparison to what Paula was going through, her problems were nothing. But with the future of The Sardine so uncertain, her best friend facing such a dark time and now, the lighthouse up for sale - well, putting a smile on her face to celebrate a wedding was proving to be far more difficult than she could have ever imagined.

Kate reached up to stroke a stray hair back into

one of her victory rolls and sighed. It was time for her to channel some of the bravery of the world war two wrens. She couldn't let the side down considering she was wearing their uniform. Today, she would put on the performance of a lifetime. She'd work the stiff upper lip and plaster a smile on her face. Starting now.

'Hello, beautiful - all ready?'

Paula's smiling face appeared at the doorway. 'Ooh look at it in here - it's perfect!' She beamed around, taking in the various dressing tables that had been added, complete with 1940s accessories, bobby pins, hair spray and anything else the wedding guests might require to fix their outfits throughout the day. 'I can't wait to see everyone in costume,' she sighed. 'Thank you so much for letting me be involved.'

'Are you kidding me?!' laughed Kate, going to stand beside her friend. 'We honestly couldn't have done this without you. And by the way - you look incredible!'

Paula was in costume too, her red lippy bringing some colour to her pale face.

'Hey - have you heard?' said Paula. 'Doreen and another one of WI girls have prepared a surprise for the happy couple.'

Kate raised her eyebrows. 'Uh oh,' she chuckled. 'I just hope Lee and Annabel won't regret inviting half of Seabury to their big day!'

'No chance,' said Paula, 'without half of Seabury, the day wouldn't be happening at all, would it?'

'Good point!' said Kate, and this time the smile that spread across her face was genuine. 'So, is Ryan dressing up too?'

'You'd better believe it,' said Paula wiggling her eyebrows. 'Bet you can't wait to see Mike in uniform?'

Kate pulled a face. 'Actually, I . . . oh! Sorry!' her mobile had just started trilling. 'Better get this!' she muttered, not wanting to miss any kind of wedding related, last minute emergency.

'See you later!' whispered Paula, retreating out of the room.

'Kate speaking!' said Kate.

'Kate - it's Philip.'

A drop of ice-cold fear quickly dowsed her newly-found good mood. Her new solicitor calling her . . . on a Saturday?

'What's happened?' she gasped.

'Don't worry, it's good news,' said Philip quickly. 'I'm sorry to call, I know you're busy today - Lionel told me about the wedding - but I knew you wouldn't want to wait a second longer than necessary.'

Good news? He'd just said good news, right?

'Kate - it's all over. The Sardine's safe. Tom is dropping all further claims.'

'Wait,' she breathed, her heart hammering, 'what?!'

'No court case. No having to sell the cafe. Oh, and

you're to stop paying your spousal payments immediately.'

Kate grasped the back of the chair in front of her with her free hand for support.

'But - how?! I don't understand?!'

'We'll go through all the nitty-gritty next week. I've got some paperwork for you to sign as long as you're happy with everything. But it'll mean a clean break and your divorce will be finalised without delay.'

'I think I love you!' said Kate, barely able to contain herself.

She heard Philip chuckle.

'Sorry, sorry!' said Kate quickly. 'This is just . . . I . . . *thank you!*'

'It's very much my pleasure,' he said earnestly. 'It turns out that Tom is engaged to be married. Plus, his new partner is pregnant. I'm afraid he had some rather outlandish ideas about you funding his new life.'

'*What?!*' gasped Kate.

'Yes. As Lionel said to me the other day - despicable. But you're free, Miss Hardy, and - most importantly - The Sardine is safe.'

'I don't know how to thank you,' breathed Kate, barely daring to believe what he was telling her.

'Well, Lionel tells me you do the most exquisite cakes?' he chuckled.

'You're on free cake boxes for life!' laughed Kate.

'All the best with the wedding, Miss Hardy. And I look forward to meeting with you next week to finalise everything.'

Kate slipped her mobile back into her pocket, then grasped the chair with both hands and squeezed hard, watching her knuckles turn white. She wasn't asleep. This wasn't a dream. The Sardine was safe.

Taking in a deep breath, she squeezed her eyes closed and let out a loud squeal.

'Kate?!'

She whirled around to find a soldier standing framed in the doorway.

Kate went completely still. She couldn't say a word, but she let out a breathy little gasp as she took in the cap sitting on his perfectly swept-back hair, then her eyes travelled down to his neat khaki shirt and perfectly polished boots. She opened her mouth to speak but she still couldn't make a sound.

'What's the matter?' said Mike, not taking his eyes off of her as he took a step into the room.

'I . . . you . . .'

'Are you okay? I thought I heard you scream or something?'

She nodded quickly, watching as Mike fiddled awkwardly with his cuffs.

'I . . .'

The Sardine was safe and Mike was here. This wonderful man she'd completely fallen for. What on earth was she waiting for?

Something inside her snapped. Letting go of the chair, she flew towards him and jumped. Mike's arms wrapped around her instinctively, lifting her against him as her lips found his, even as their combined weight made him stumble backwards, out into the hallway.

'Get a room, you two!' came Sarah's delighted squeal.

Kate could feel Mike chuckle even before her lips left his. Without letting go of him, she turned her head only to find Paula, Lou, Sarah and Ethel watching them with matching Cheshire-cat grins on their faces.

Stanley trotted up to the pair of them and wound around Mike's legs, excitedly wagging his tail. Mike still had his arms wrapped around Kate, holding her entire weight up off the floor as she clung to him.

'So romantic!' sighed Lou.

'Eew!' laughed Sarah, though it was clear by the look on her face she was thrilled. 'What got into you crazy kids?!'

'The Sardine's safe!' said Kate quickly, unable to keep the huge grin off of her face.

'What?!' said Mike.

'Oh my goodness! This is the most wonderful news,' said Ethel, grabbing Sarah's hand and jumping up and down on the spot.

Mike turned back to Kate with a smile and Kate stared at him, losing herself in his beautiful eyes, and for a moment it was as if everything else faded into the background.

'Erm . . . we've got a wedding to run here, guys!' laughed Paula.

'It'll wait a moment,' said Mike not taking his eyes off of Kate, and then, totally ignoring the fact that they now had an audience, he leaned in and kissed her again.

～

Kate leaned back against the makeshift bar in the corner of the dining room and watched as Lee led Annabel out into the middle of the floor for their first dance. The band struck up an old Glenn Miller favourite, and the handsome soldier drew his beautiful bride into the slowest of slow dances.

Kate turned to watch the band with tears in her eyes. Who'd have thought they'd be so amazing?

'Just about perfect,' said Paula, snagging a glass of bubbly from behind the bar as she joined her. Kate nodded and leaned her head on Paula's shoulder.

The room really was just about perfect. There were flowers everywhere - the old-fashioned kind that looked like they came from a cottage garden - and bunting and union jacks looped across the ceiling. Trixie had started proceedings in pride of place in the centre of the room - but now that everyone had eaten their fill, she'd been moved off to the side to make room for the dancing. Kate would need to move her out to the kitchen shortly to load up Sarah's stunning cake - ready for its grand entrance. The pair had opted for the monumental Victoria sponge, and Ethel had sourced a whole load of vintage side-plates and cake forks so that the guests would be able to help themselves in style.

'Ladies!' said Lionel, coming over to them, taking his cap off and giving them a little bow. He looked every inch the proud soldier in his uniform.

'Not a bad house-warming party, eh Lionel?' chuckled Paula.

He smiled warmly at her. 'Watch this space, my dear. I've got a feeling this is just the first of many.'

Kate let out a happy sigh, watching as other couples started to join Lee and Annabel on the dance floor. She could just about make out Stanley over the other side of the room. He was wearing his own miniature soldier's cap that Doreen had made for him, and he looked like he was in his element. Guests had been taking it in turns to feed him titbits and take selfies with him all night.

'May I have this dance?' said Ryan, coming up and holding his hand out to Paula.

'You've got it!' said Paula, giving Kate a quick peck on the cheek before disappearing out onto the dance floor.

'Aw, look at old Charlie,' said Kate, as she watched him lead Ethel proudly into position.

'I wouldn't be surprised if theirs is the next shindig we hold here,' chuckled Lionel.

Kate beamed. 'Imagine that!' she said. 'I'm so happy that this place is in your safe hands.'

'I've got big plans,' said Lionel, 'but there's plenty of time to fill you in on all that. Looks like you've got more important things coming your way,' he wiggled his eyebrows at her as Mike drew near.

'Slacking, are we?' grinned Mike.

Kate blushed. 'Just for a moment, yes!'

'Well, time to put that drink down, Miss Hardy.'

Kate groaned. 'Why, what's up?'

'Absolutely nothing! But if Lionel can spare you for a moment, may I have this dance?' he asked, holding out his hand.

Kate smiled shyly at him and then let him lead her onto the floor, only for the song to come to an end the minute they started to dance.

'Awkward,' chuckled Mike and they turned towards the band to clap with everyone else. 'Erm - what's Sarah up to?'

She was carrying an old fashioned silver microphone on a stand and set it down right next to the trumpet player.

'We've got a surprise for Lee and Annabel,' she said shyly, her voice coming through loud and clear. 'I'd like to welcome to the stage . . . Doreen and Celia!'

There was a scattering of confused clapping as the

pair of them, their matching victory rolls and red lippy still perfectly in place, took up position behind the microphone.

Kate let out a gasp as, without another word, the band struck up a slow number and Doreen launched into the Vera Lynn wartime classic, *We'll Meet Again*.

'Oh my goodness,' breathed Kate, as Celia's voice joined her friend's in perfect harmony. She glanced over at Annabel and watched as Lee drew out his handkerchief and dabbed at the happy tears that were now trickling down her face.

'Just about perfect,' whispered Mike.

Kate nodded with a sigh and turned back to him, only to find his eyes on hers.

~

The cool evening breeze felt wonderful against her hot face, and Kate sucked in a long breath of sea air.

'Here,' said Mike, handing her a fresh glass of bubbly.

'Thank you,' said Kate gratefully. 'And here's to it all going without a hitch,' she added, clinking her glass against his and smiling as the music drifted out of the dining room behind them.

'Not too bad for a first attempt,' said Mike with a smile, then shyly reaching down, he stroked a stray hair back from her cheek. 'Almost perfect.'

'Almost,' she said, unable to stop her eyes from straying over towards the lighthouse.

'Kate?'

'Hm?'

'Remember the other day I said there was something we needed to talk about?'

'Erm . . . not really!' said Kate with a sheepish smile as she turned back to him. 'Sorry - there's been so much going on.'

'Yeah,' said Mike. 'There has . . .'

Kate raised her eyebrows. It was strange to see Mike looking so nervous. 'What's up, soldier?' she said, giving him a cheeky wink.

Mike took her hand and Kate's heart did a summersault as he kissed the back of it.

'I . . . well . . . the lighthouse . . .'

'Oh!' said Kate in surprise.

'I know how you must be feeling, but-'

'DAD!'

They both turned to find Sarah standing in the doorway of the dining room.

'What's up?' called Mike, a slightly dazed look on his face.

'Can you help? One of the strings of bunting just came down and nearly garrotted everyone,' she laughed.

Mike rolled his eyes and glanced at Kate. 'I'll be right back!'

Kate smiled and nodded, watching as he disappeared inside to help Sarah.

'Hi!'

Kate jumped as one of the wedding guests appeared next to her.

'Oops, sorry, I didn't think you'd spotted me!' she laughed, patting her hair and taking a swig from her glass. 'I just wanted to say thank you for making this such a special night.'

'Oh,' said Kate, beaming at her, 'it's been our pleasure.'

'Well, I hope you're ready for lots more events!' she laughed. 'I work for one of the estate agents over in Plymouth, and trust me - you're getting *all* the corporate events from now on!'

'Well, erm . . . gosh!' said Kate, slightly taken aback. 'This was our first one, just to test things out - you know?'

'Yes,' she said, raising her eyebrows. 'But I assumed that, as you're purchasing a premises, you'll be going great guns!'

'Premises?' said Kate, shaking her head in confusion.

'Yes!' laughed the woman. 'You *are* the other half of Frothy Sardine, right?'

'Well, I . . . erm . . .'

Kate's mind was racing. What the hell was going on here?'

'I mean, you guys have bought the old lighthouse . . . so?'

'Lighthouse? The lighthouse? I . . . I'm sorry, I . . .'

'Mike!' said the woman, turning to greet him as he strode back outside. 'I think your partner might have had enough bubbly,' she giggled. 'Congratulations again on buying the old place. I *know* you're going to love it.'

'Mike?' breathed Kate. Her heart was hammering, and the hairs on the back of her neck were prickling. 'Frothy Sardine? The Lighthouse? What's she talking about.'

'I've been trying to talk to you for days,' said Mike, looking freaked.

Kate raised her eyebrows, unable to say a word. He came to stand right in front of her and took both of her hands in his.

'Look - there's no other way to put this. I'm in love with you.'

Kate's mouth dropped open. She wanted to tell him that she was in love with him too. That she really and truly had *never* felt like this before. But she couldn't get the words out.

'Kate,' said Mike, squeezing her hands lightly. 'I bought the lighthouse.'

THE END

CHRISTMAS IN SEABURY

SEABURY - PART 3

CHAPTER 1

'*And finally, we've got a warning for residents on the south coast of Devon and Cornwall.*'

The serious note in the newsreader's voice stopped Kate in her Christmas crafting tracks. She paused with her scissors suspended in mid-air, holding the sheet of gold paper still in their jaws as she pricked her ears to catch more.

Kate had woken early with the mad idea of making the longest paper chain known to mankind. So, she'd made herself a large pot of tea, emptied half the biscuit barrel onto a plate and had been merrily snipping up colourful strips of paper for the last hour or so with the radio burbling away in the background. It seemed like the perfect way to start Christmas Eve.

Until this point, the presenter had been busy

rambling on about local Christmassy good news stories, and Kate had been enjoying zoning in and out of it as she worked - sipping tea and munching biscuits while Stanley snoozed on his bed in front of the still-warm wood burner.

'The Met Office has issued an amber warning that's due to come into force from midday Christmas Eve-'

'Uh oh,' she murmured, 'that'll be today then!'

Stanley shuffled up to a sitting position on his bed and cocked his head at her in concern.

'...and extends all the way through Christmas day, with possible disruption for several days afterwards. Strong winds will herald the arrival of Storm Bernard. Residents should be prepared for possible damage from flying debris, localised flooding and a high possibility of travel disruption.'

'Batten down the hatches, eh boy?' sighed Kate as Stanley flopped back down onto his bed. Clearly, he wasn't in the least bit worried by the news because he was asleep again in seconds. Kate smiled at him and rolled her eyes. She plonked her scissors and paper down onto the table and swept the brightly coloured strips she'd already chopped up into one huge pile for later.

Getting to her feet, Kate stretched out her back then grabbed the teapot and topped up her mug. It was still just about warm enough to drink. Wrapping her hands around it, she wandered over to the living room window.

Staring down across sandy West Beach towards the sea, it was pretty difficult to believe that Storm Bernard was just over the horizon, somewhere out in the Atlantic, waiting to hit Seabury. Sure - this was the coast, and the weather could change incredibly quickly - but the early-morning sky was a clear blue, there wasn't a cloud in sight. The sea looked to be just about as calm as it got at this time of year. It was the most beautiful December morning that you could wish for.

Still, even if Bernard did turn up, they'd be okay here at The Sardine. She'd just have to bring in some extra logs from the yard and get old Bertha going if she needed to.

Bertha was the great big wood-burning stove down in the kitchen of the café. Kate didn't have enough fingers to count the number of times she'd been advised to rip it out over the years – but she'd never agree to that. Maybe she was ridiculous - it *would* make a lot more space in the tiny kitchen - but she'd always been adamant about keeping Bertha.

The old stove kept the café nice and toasty on chilly days when the electric heaters simply didn't cut the mustard. Besides that, the larger of Betha's two ovens was amazing for baking bread. In fact, it always surprised Kate just how much she could fit into them. The smaller one was great for keeping things warm, and the hotplate on top could keep an old-fashioned kettle and pan of soup on the go for hours.

Add to all that the fact that Bertha was a Godsend when the power went out - which was a sure bet at least once every winter here in Seabury - and Kate simply couldn't imagine life without her. It meant that no matter what was going on outside, Kate had a way to keep the café beautifully warm as well as filling people's bellies with all manner of tasty treats.

Of course, there was the added bonus that Stanley loved nothing better than curling up in front of Bertha when she was stoked up. Sure, that tended to make working in the tiny kitchen even more of a squeeze than usual - but Kate had always been clear - Bertha stayed. She was part of the family, just like Stanley and just like Trixie, her beloved delivery tricycle – and you didn't give up on family!

Kate took a great gulp of lukewarm tea and turned back to her little living room. It might be Christmas Eve, but she hadn't hung any decorations in here - there simply wasn't the room because of all the Christmas cards. There were hundreds of them. They'd started arriving back in early November - bearing lovely notes and Christmas wishes from happy customers all over the world. Every single Christmas greeting delivered by her postman had made Kate's heart sing. There was something magical about knowing just how many people loved The Sardine as much as she did.

CHRISTMAS IN SEABURY

The cards were tucked into every little nook and cranny - she'd balanced them along the tops of all her paintings, hung great long strings of them across the walls and the top of the doorway, and even her books had disappeared behind rows of them precariously placed along the front of every single shelf.

Kate already knew that she'd feel sad packing them all away after the festivities were over - but she'd never get rid of them. These love letters to The Sardine were something she'd pack up carefully and treasure forever. Just like she did every year.

Kate stared around the room, taking in the cards one by one. She couldn't believe it was Christmas Eve already. What a year it had been! So much had happened - and a lot of it made her even more grateful than ever to be standing here, in her cosy living room above The Sardine. She felt so lucky to be getting ready to celebrate Christmas in her favourite place in the entire world.

Honestly, what a year! She'd come so close to losing The Sardine to her idiot ex-husband. Thank goodness for Lionel swooping in to save the day! And, of course, it was impossible to think about Lionel these days without her mind wandering to The Pebble Street Hotel. He'd bought it on a whim after Veronica had done a disappearing act with a bunch of her guests' money. Bless him - he was doing his best, but Kate had a feeling that Lionel might have bitten off a bit more than he could chew!

Then, of course, there was Mike… probably the biggest surprise the year had thrown at her. It had felt a bit like a disaster when the surly stranger had bowled into town and opened his rival coffee shop, New York Froth. But Mike's arrival in Seabury had actually turned out to be the beginning of something really special for her. Something she still didn't quite dare believe was happening.

Kate took a deep breath and shook her head as her eyes came to rest on the card that Mike had given her. A simple lino-printed blackbird sitting on a snowy gatepost. It had pride of place, right at the centre of her bookshelf. Inside it just said *Merry Christmas, Love Mike*. She blushed as she thought about the number of times her thumb had traced the word "love". Her toes seemed to tingle just thinking about him. If only they'd had the chance to spend a bit more time together, but the last few weeks had been full-on for both of them. Never mind – hopefully they'd get the chance to put that right now that it was nearly Christmas.

Kate let out a long sigh. Yes, it certainly had been an interesting year - and it wasn't over yet. But Seabury? Well, Seabury just seemed to carry on regardless. Sure, there were changes, but at its heart, the town was exactly the same as it had been when her old dad was alive.

Popping her cup down on the side and wrapping

CHRISTMAS IN SEABURY

her arms around herself, Kate let out a huge yawn. She really wasn't used to being up and about this early in the day, and she couldn't believe that it was an urgent desire to make a paper chain that had dragged her from underneath her warm duvet. But then - it was something she'd always done with her dad when she was little. Every Christmas she'd begged him to help her, and every single year their little house had ended up full of them - looping across the doorways and ceilings - even in the bathroom.

She smiled sadly, wishing that her dad could be there to help her finish this year's paper chain. What was it about this time of year that made her look for as many ways as possible to feel as close to him? If only they could have one more Christmas together. She'd love nothing more than to sit here with him in companionable silence, drinking tea, listening to the radio and getting Pritt Stick and glitter all over the furniture.

As Nat King Cole's voice came crooning out of the radio, Kate glanced at her watch and realised that there was a good chance that her paper chain might not make it beyond the pile of colourful strips on the table - at least, not until later. She had an errand to run before joining Sarah and Lou in The Sardine for their traditional Christmas Eve opening hours - and she didn't want to miss too much of it. She loved being in the café on Christmas Eve - after all, the residents of Seabury were basically family - and what better way to spend the day than surrounded by their cheerful, chattering brand of love?

It was time to get going. She'd enjoyed her early-morning crafting session, and daydreaming about her dad had been the perfect way to start the day. Christmas always managed to turn her into a pile of sentimental mush, but she was pretty sure that a good dose of fresh sea air would blow the cobwebs away and get her feet back on the ground. In fact, she'd better hurry up and get her coat on before Storm Bernard decided to put in an appearance - that's if the Met Office had got things right for a change!

Kate glanced at Stanley who was still flat out and snoozing soundly in front of the wood burner. Maybe she should just leave him behind this morning, especially if the weather really was about to turn nasty. It had been so mild and dry for the last few weeks that she'd had the chance to wash, dry, and put away all his doggy towels. It would be a shame for him to come back soaking wet and have to start the process all over again.

But then, how bad could it get out there? They wouldn't be out for too long, and the sky was such a beautiful blue that it seemed mean to make him miss out on a trip in Trixie. He always loved coming with her when she was out on her rounds.

Still undecided, Kate took a couple of steps towards the living room door. The moment Stanley heard the creak of the floorboards, he opened an expectant eye and lifted his head to stare at her.

Kate laughed. 'What was I thinking? There's no way you'd ever miss out on the chance of a W.A.L.K!'

Stanley continued to stare at her, his tail wagging slowly. The one thing her big bear loved even more than walks on the beach was the feeling of the fresh air blowing his fluffy ears around as they whizzed along the seafront on Trixie.

Making up her mind at last, Kate grabbed Stanley's lead. The simple action caused the massive dog to leap up, his tail going into overdrive as his tongue flopped out. He panted, grinning at her.

'You coming then?' she laughed. 'I could do with the company this morning!'

Stanley bounded over to her, and she ruffled his ears before grabbing a rich tea biscuit from her early-morning stash on the table and offering it to him. Stanley inhaled the treat in a couple of bites and then matched her strides step for step out into the hallway.

'Go careful now lad,' laughed Kate, holding onto the bannisters a little tighter than usual as she picked her way past the bundle of wires that ran down from her flat, through The Sardine, and out onto the street to power the lights of the town Christmas tree. It was something she was more than happy to agree to every year, but the last thing she needed was a stray wire causing a festive tumble down the stairs!

She giggled as Stanley pushed past her in a big bundle of fluff and paws - eager now to get outside to where Trixie and her trailer were waiting to take them both on their morning's adventure.

CHAPTER 2

*R*eaching the downstairs hallway in one piece, Kate couldn't help but laugh at the sight of Stanley with his nose pressed up against the door, waiting not-so-patiently to be let outside.

'Come on, idiot,' she laughed, giving him a quick pat on his silky head, 'we're not going that way today.'

Rather than opening her front door, Kate made her way around the side of the staircase to the wooden door that led to the under-stairs cupboard. It stood ajar and the wires that snaked their way down the stairs trailed through the gap into the pitch-dark space beyond.

After a brief pause and an eyebrow waggle of confusion, Stanley followed her and was soon close enough that he was practically stepping on her heels she felt around the dark, cobwebby space. Kate knew there was a light switch here somewhere - she just didn't use it often enough to put her hand straight on it.

'Got ya!' she said as she found it at last. Flipping the switch, a dim light flickered to life, and Kate squinted around the cramped space until her eyes adjusted. It was just about bright enough for her to navigate her way between the boxes piled high on either side without breaking her neck as she went.

Doing her best to keep her feet under her as Stanley barged past, sticking his nose into everything as he went, Kate kept her head bowed in an attempt to avoid getting a face full of cobwebs. Reaching a heavy curtain, she pushed it aside and was surprised to be met by a glimmer of light on the other side. She must have left a light on in the café by mistake.

Carefully stepping through the narrow gap in front of her, Kate followed Stanley's feathery tail and soon found herself standing in the tiny storage space at the back of The Sardine.

'Morning Kate!'

Kate jumped, catching her foot on a large, stainless steel preserving pan with a loud clang.

'Oops, sorry!' Sarah's laughing face appeared around the corner. 'Didn't mean to make you jump! Merry Christmas Eve!'

'You too,' laughed Kate, 'but what on earth are you doing here this early?' Kate clutched one hand to her pounding heart as she nudged the pan aside with her foot so that no one went flying over it later.

'I wanted to try out that Christmas cinnamon cookie recipe Ethel mentioned the other day. Thought they might be a nice addition for anyone who stops by this morning for a coffee!' she said, stooping to scratch Stanley's fluffy ears in greeting.

'Sounds like a wonderful idea,' said Kate, following the pair of them out into the café.

'Thanks! I bet you wish you could keep that passageway open all the time?' said Sarah, heading over to the sink to wash her hands.

Kate shrugged and glanced around at the café with a sigh. 'I wish! I can't deny that it's lovely to be able to trundle down here without having to go outside. Just one problem though…'

'Storage?' said Sarah, picking up her rolling pin and starting to roll out her batch of cookie dough.

'Storage,' Kate agreed with a nod.

She stared around at the random selection of boxes, Tupperware and pans that she'd had to oust from the cubby hole so that she could keep the passageway open for the wires to come through the café and out to power the Christmas tree lights at the front. No matter how hard she tried to keep things organised, The Sardine always ended up in a bit of a mess at this time of year.

Of course, she didn't mind one little bit - it meant that Seabury's Christmas tree was always really close to the café - which she absolutely loved. She always managed to make it work for a couple of weeks - even if it meant that there were boxes and random bits and pieces piled high in every nook and cranny.

Kate watched as Stanley stuck his nose into a stack of giant cake tins that she'd left on the floor near the end of the counter. They'd been hidden away at the very back of the cupboard, and currently she didn't really have a clue where else to put them. Maybe she should get rid of some of them - that would probably be the sensible option considering that she barely ever used them… but if she did that, she knew she'd regret it.

'Oh,' said Sarah, 'I meant to ask – what's in Bertha's oven? I was looking for the baking sheets that you usually keep in there.'

'Ah,' said Kate. 'Sorry, I moved them. Here…' she wandered over and, reaching into the smaller of the two ovens, pulled out a baking sheet for Sarah to use. 'The big oven's got a bunch of candles and old oil lamps in it.'

'Of *course* it has,' said Sarah, rolling her eyes. 'Why don't you just get rid of them if they're in the way?'

'I can't do that!' said Kate looking scandalised. 'They've been here longer than I have. They're part of the place. Anyway, I'll find a use for them someday.'

Until that day came, and while the storage space was out of action, Kate had made the executive decision to stash them inside Bertha. The weather had been so mild recently that she hadn't had to light the old stove in ages. But - if the weather really was about to change - it looked like she'd have to move them again. The only problem was... *where?!*

'Well,' said Sarah, with a good-natured laugh, 'I guess it won't be too long before you can hide everything back in the cubby hole again until next year. Though – if there's any chance you could shift that box of spare Christmas decorations before we open, that'd be amazing,' she said nodding to the large box that was standing right in the way. 'I've tripped over it about three times already this morning.'

Kate nodded. 'Yeah, sorry. They're left over from when me and your dad trimmed the town tree.'

She headed over to the box, picked it up and then paused. 'Okay – these are going to have to live upstairs somewhere,' she said, 'there just isn't any room left in here.'

'Pop them out in the passageway. I'll take them up to the flat for you later when Lou turns up if you'd like?' said Sarah, now busy laying holly-leaf shaped biscuits onto the freshly oiled baking sheet.

'Perfect, thank you! Right, I'll just take these through and then Stanley and I had better get a wiggle on. Charlie's expecting us!'

After fighting her way back through the narrow passageway with the cumbersome box, Kate decided that she'd better make a break for it before the weather did anything untoward.

She looked around for Stanley, and then laughed as she spotted him over by the front door of the café, standing staring hopefully at the handle, clearly wondering what the hold-up was.

Kate shook her head. 'One second boy, I need a hat if we're going to be blown down the seafront by the beginnings of Storm Bernard!'

'Have a look under the counter at the end there,' said Sarah, nodding to the shelf under the till where the odds and ends of café life always ended up being shoved out of sight. 'I'm sure I spotted a hat under there the other day.'

Rummaging around, Kate pulled out a ball of string followed by what looked like a pair of thick, woolly socks, a penknife, several miniature birthday candles, a pack of blu-tack… and not one, but four different hats.

'Bingo!' she said, triumphantly grabbing her favourite pea-green, handknitted beanie. She'd been wondering where it had got to and was over the moon to be reunited with it.

Kate was about to pull the slouchy old thing over her hair when she paused. Actually… perhaps this one wasn't the best choice. If they really were going to be treated to the high winds and driving rain the weather forecasters seemed to be promising, she'd need something a little bit tighter so that it didn't get

CHRISTMAS IN SEABURY

blown off her noggin as she pedalled Trixie up the hill.

Reaching back under the counter, she pulled out a stripy number. It was a bit too small, so she didn't tend to wear it that often - but today, that particular feature might actually be a bonus.

'I've never seen that one before,' said Sarah.

'Ethel made it for me,' said Kate, running her fingers over it with a smile. It was quite a knobbly affair. 'You know, I've always wondered if she might have made it from a pair of unravelled old socks.'

'Knowing Ethel, I wouldn't be surprised!' said Sarah with a laugh.

Pulling it firmly over her hair, Kate wandered over to join Stanley who was still waiting - rather impatiently - at the door. She quickly tucked in her long, curly locks as best as she could in the hope that it would stop her from transforming into a scarecrow the moment they stepped outside.

'Ready to face the weather, Stanley lad?' she asked, patting him on the head.

Stanley let out a low, excited *woof,* and started to wag his tail so hard that his entire fluffy backside got in on the action too.

'Come on then! Catch you later, Sarah – I'll try not to be too long!'

Sarah gave her a quick wave before picking up the tray of cookies and turning to place them carefully in the oven.

Kate flipped the lock and turned the door handle. Half expecting to be confronted by a gale, she braced herself and bowed her head as she stepped outside.

She stopped.

Nothing. Nada. It was dead calm.

Kate quickly straightened up and shrugged, hoping that no one had noticed her rather peculiar exit from the café. It seemed that, once again, the Met Office was getting all worked up over nothing. Not only was it not in the least bit stormy out here - it was actually rather lovely. She grinned to herself and took in a deep lungful of fresh air.

'Oi - Stanley, don't you dare,' she said quickly, catching sight of him just in time. Stanley had wandered over to the town Christmas tree and was eyeing it up with great interest. Not for the first time either.

Kate laughed as she watched him reluctantly turn back to her. She'd already had to tell him several times that the tree was off-limits. He gave her a baleful look.

'I know boy,' she chuckled. 'It's just not fair, is it? A blooming great big tree appears right outside your house, and you're not even allowed to have a sniff, let alone a morning piddle on it!'

Stanley waggled his eyebrows and swished his tail gently from side to side.

'Come on then, boy,' she patted her thigh and

turned to lead the way around to the gates of the café's courtyard.

The space had been incredible as extra seating during the summer and late into the ridiculously mild autumn - but come November, Kate had had to admit defeat. It was officially either too cold or too windy most days for customers to even consider enjoying their morning coffees outside. Besides, she still had her two little tables right outside the doorway on the pavement for the few brave souls who did want to face the elements whilst munching on their breakfast baps.

So, Kate had packed everything up - stacking the chairs and tables and making enough space to give Trixie full use of the courtyard for the winter. It had also meant that there was plenty of room out here for the generous stack of firewood she'd had delivered to see her through.

Pausing, Kate unlocked the gates and drew them open.

'Morning Trix!' she said, heading straight over to her and peeling a heavy tarpaulin back off her beloved tricycle, revealing the beautiful red handlebars and bright pink body. She was careful as she lifted the sheet away from the trailer, not wanting to dislodge the swathes of twinkling blue tinsel she'd decorated it with weeks ago.

The festive touches had survived remarkably well considering the number of miles she'd covered on her delivery rounds. The lead up to this Christmas had been the busiest she'd ever had at The Sardine, what with orders for their festive cake boxes going through the roof. Not that she was complaining, of course!

With the news of the impending storm - even if she didn't *quite* believe it was really going to arrive - Kate was glad she'd taken the time a few weeks ago to swap out Trixie's road tyres for her winter ones. They were much bigger and chunkier. Sure, they made pedalling up the hills around Seabury a bit harder than usual - but Kate knew from long experience that the fiddly job and extra effort was more than worth it. The roads around here could get seriously slippery when they were wet.

Kate pushed Trixie out of the yard and parked her on the pavement, ready to take them both up to see Charlie at the allotments. Thankfully, she didn't have any deliveries to do today.

All the businesses who bought her sandwiches were already closed for Christmas. Paula had told her that the owner of Graffika - the large graphic design company she worked for and one of Kate's largest customers - had headed off on a skiing trip and had decided to close the entire office until the New Year.

Kate couldn't imagine wanting to go somewhere even colder for a winter break. She liked the sun - but nothing too warm either. She loved somewhere she could cool off easily by dipping her toes into the sea whenever she fancied it. Maybe even her ankles too. Total bliss! Yes - that was her perfect holiday - and it had to be somewhere she was surrounded by good food, lovely people and a friendly atmosphere too.

Kate laughed out loud, realising she'd basically just described Seabury as her perfect holiday spot. You could take the girl out of Seabury but... actually, scratch that - you *couldn't* take the girl out of Seabury!

Before setting off, Kate carefully weighted the tarp back down with an old brick - just in case the wind *did* decide to make an appearance while they were gone. She didn't fancy having to fish it back out of the sea!

'Up you get then lad!' she said to Stanley, holding the back of the little trailer open for him. He promptly clambered up and settled down on his pillow. For a brief moment, Kate wondered if she should nip back inside for Stanley's weatherproof coat - but decided against it. He seemed to like it best when all his fur was standing on end in the wind. The last time she'd made the colossal effort of wrestling him into the coat, he'd somehow managed to wiggle out of it and was already using it as an extra cushion by the time they'd reached their first stop.

'Okay, no coat,' she said, stroking his ears. Then, as an afterthought, she grabbed the Santa hat that was sitting in Trixie's basket and popped it on his head.

Stanley looked at her in bemusement.

'You look sooooo cute!' she squealed, kissing his nose. She quickly grabbed her phone from her pocket, snapped a photo and sent it to Sarah. She knew the hat would probably be long-gone in seconds, but that didn't matter – it was worth it just for the picture!

'Right, Stanley lad - let's go! It's time to go up to the allotments to see Charlie. He said he might have some veggies for us to pick up. I know you're not that bothered about sprouts - but I bet you he'll have a treat for you in one of his pockets if you ask nicely!'

CHAPTER 3

Kate hadn't got very far along the seafront when she caught sight of Lionel just up ahead of her. As if sensing Trixie behind him, Lionel came to a halt. Turning, he raised a hand in greeting.

Kate had to bite the inside of her cheeks to stop herself from laughing out loud. Lionel - usually so immaculately dressed in a waistcoat, shirt and a jacket with elbow patches - appeared to be wearing an apron. A very fetching, white, frilly apron.

'Morning Lionel!' she called. Her voice came out more than a little bit high pitched as she tried to swallow the laugh that was bubbling away, determined to find its way out. Doing her best to keep her face straight, Kate drew to a halt and waited for him to reach her.

'Hi Kate,' Lionel called back, running a hand

through his already decidedly scruffy hair as he bustled along the pavement towards her. He looked more than a little bit distracted.

Kate's smile dropped slightly as a wave of concern hit her. It wasn't the first time she'd caught Lionel looking a bit like he was at his wits end over the last couple of weeks. She was used to him being so suave - so calm and in control... if a little eccentric. But after buying The Pebble Street Hotel back in the autumn, Lionel had made the courageous (though a lot of people were using the word *idiotic*) decision to look after the hotel on his own. Ever since then, he'd been steadily growing more and more scatty. By the looks of him right now, he'd managed to reach a whole new level!

'Morning!' he said, slightly out of puff as he came up alongside them. 'Hello, Stanley old boy, I like your hat!'

Kate watched as Lionel tickled Stanley's nose so as not to interfere with her big bear's festive headgear which was - miraculously - still in place.

'You're out and about early!' she said, raising her eyebrows slightly and doing her best not to stare at his frilly pinny.

Lionel nodded, looking rather wide-eyed and worried. 'I've got to get everything ready for my guests!' he said.

'But Lionel... I thought you'd managed to dissuade all the Christmas bookings Veronica had in the diary from turning up? Didn't you say most of them had already cancelled and you were going to work on the last few stragglers?'

Lionel nodded morosely. 'That's right. I used the old "change in management and disruptive renovations" line. That did the trick for most of them - and then the news about old Storm Bernard has been really handy – that put the rest of them off. No one seems to want to travel for Christmas with that on its way!'

'So, what's the problem?' asked Kate curiously.

'There's one couple who just wouldn't take the hint. No matter what I said. I tried everything I could think of, but they're stubborn blighters and dead set on spending Christmas in Seabury. It got to the point that I just didn't have the heart to tell them "no". So now - the Davies's are on their way and…' he glanced at his watch, 'due to arrive sometime this morning.'

'Take a deep breath,' said Kate with a small smile, 'it's just one couple, and it sounds like they're pretty determined to enjoy a holiday in Seabury! You've given them fair warning that the hotel isn't in tip-top condition, and it doesn't sound like they're going to let that bother them in the slightest. Anyway, I'm sure you'll make Christmas really magical for them - I've heard you've got an amazing turkey!'

The gossip about the size of the bird Lionel had ordered from the local butcher had been all over town the previous week.

'I know everyone's laughing at me,' said Lionel, with a good-natured twitch of his bushy eyebrows. 'And I know that turkey I ordered is probably big enough to feed half of Seabury and still have some left over. But all I could think about when I was in the butcher's was Veronica's paltry Christmas dinners. Remember last year? She cooked one chicken breast, hacked it up into tiny chunks and gave everyone a single piece on a side plate, along with a lonely carrot and one sprout!'

Kate snorted and shook her head. 'Yep. That sounds like classic Veronica!'

'Well,' said Lionel, rolling his eyes, 'there's no way I want to be anything like her. I don't want that to be my guests' memory of Christmas at The Pebble Street Hotel. I want to spoil them – even if there *are* only two of them!'

'Well, it sounds like you're doing everything in your power to make that happen,' said Kate stoutly. 'Just don't worry yourself to distraction while you're doing it, okay? Remember to actually enjoy Christmas yourself too! Anyway, I know that you'll make sure your guests have a Christmas they'll remember forever.'

Lionel nodded vigorously, though Kate could see that his eyes had glazed over a bit. She knew that look – he was clearly running through some kind of urgent festive "to-do" list in his head.

'I've given them the nicest room on the first floor,'

he muttered distractedly, starting to tick a list off on his fingers, 'I mean, the place really *does* need a lot of work – and I *had* hoped to get it all done before any guests came to stay. Never mind. I searched all the other rooms and managed to find a bath plug that fits their tub. I've given the whole room a really good scrub and I've hoovered the curtains in there and put down some rugs over the holes in the carpet. Oh - and Charlie helped me to bring down the best mattress for their bed. I just... I really want their stay to be perfect.'

Kate reached out a hand and patted him on the arm, making him jump. She was pretty sure he'd forgotten that she was still there.

'It sounds like you're going to make them feel really welcome,' she said, hoping to reassure him at the same time as maybe drawing their little chat to a close for the moment. She really did need to head off up to the allotments. The wind was starting to get up a bit, blowing the frills on Lionel's pinny hither and thither.

'Thanks Kate, I hope so,' he said, coming back down to earth a bit. 'Actually – while I've got you, I need to ask you a favour.'

'Anything!' said Kate. After all, she owed Lionel everything - he was the one that had stepped in and helped her save The Sardine. He was the reason she was still here in Seabury, looking forward to spending Christmas with the people she loved best.

'Well,' said Lionel, 'I was wondering if you happened to have any spare Christmas decorations that you're not using? There are still a few spots at the hotel that just feel a little bit bare and unwelcoming.'

Kate smiled at him. 'Now that's something I can definitely help with. I've got an entire box of really nice bits left over from decorating the town Christmas tree – and everything I usually use in my living room is going spare too. I've had that many cards arrive this year, there just isn't room in there for much else. You're welcome to use anything you fancy.'

'Oh, that's brilliant. Thanks a million, Kate!' said Lionel, beaming at her.

Kate waved his thanks away. 'It's nothing – I'm glad to help! Look, I'm sorry to dash off, but I'd better head up to the allotments. I promised Charlie I'd meet him up there to collect some bits and pieces – but Sarah's already in the café and Lou's going to be there in time to open up for me. Just pop in and they'll point you in the right direction! And make sure they treat you to breakfast and a coffee while you're in there too. It sounds like you deserve a treat!'

'Will do - thanks so much!' said Lionel.

Kate smiled at him, relieved to see that he seemed to have calmed down a bit. She didn't say it out loud, but he would actually be doing her a huge favour by taking that massive box of decorations off her hands over Christmas. It would certainly solve a tiny fraction of her storage problem. Two whole extra feet of floor space? Bliss!

'Right,' said Kate, placing her feet determinedly back on the pedals. She adored chatting to Lionel, but she knew from many years of friendship that they could be here for at least an hour if she didn't make the first move. Besides, she needed to warm up a bit. That breeze coming up off the beach really was a bit chilly.

Unfortunately, no matter how much of a panic Lionel was in about getting the hotel ready for his guests – he clearly hadn't finished with her quite yet.

'I know it's none of my business,' he said, sticking a hand out to tickle Stanley again while not quite meeting Kate's eye, 'but I don't suppose you know what Mike's plans are for the old lighthouse, do you? I mean – I know it's taking some time for the sale to go through, but... any idea what he's going to do with it when the council do finally hand over the keys?'

Kate felt herself stiffen on Trixie's saddle. It wasn't the fact that he was asking that bothered her – after all, it was a fair assumption that she might know what her own boyfriend was planning to do with the *lighthouse* he'd just bought. Nope – the problem was... she had quite literally no idea.

'Sorry Lionel,' she said, shaking her head and doing her best to keep her voice light, 'I'm not sure. We haven't really talked about it much.'

Or ... at all, she added inside her own head.

To begin with, every time Mike had gone anywhere near the subject, she'd done her best to change it. She just couldn't face talking about any changes he had planned for the old place. After all, he was a businessman, and he was bound to be looking for ways to make his investment pay.

Of course, Kate knew in her heart of hearts that the old place was probably better off in Mike's hands than some random, unknown developer – but that didn't mean it was any easier for her to stomach the idea of it changing. She couldn't help it – she'd always seen the lighthouse as *her* special sanctuary. There were so many memories of her dad wrapped up in it that she was having a really hard time unpicking how she felt about the whole thing.

She'd become so successful at avoiding the subject that Mike had eventually given up trying to talk to her about it. Then, December had brought the same busy rush to New York Froth as it had to The Sardine. They'd both had their hands full and had barely managed to spend any time together at all. They were like two ships passing in the night, and Kate was starting to worry that maybe… perhaps… what if he'd changed his mind about her?

The whole issue of the lighthouse was now like a great big elephant between them. She knew they'd have to talk about it eventually, but-

'So - no idea at all?' prompted Lionel, interrupting

her train of thought and looking at her expectantly. 'Nothing to do with *Frothy Sardine?*'

Kate shook her head. *Frothy Sardine* had been an idea Mike had thrown into the mix back in the autumn. They'd teamed up to plan a wedding that had taken place at The Pebble Street Hotel. It had gone so well that Mike had suggested they join forces and run an event catering company together - but she'd firmly vetoed the whole thing. At least for now.

'No,' she said smiling, 'that was a bit of a joke really - maybe something we might consider in the future… but waaaaaay down the line.'

'Oh,' said Lionel, pushing his salt and pepper hair back out of his eyes and looking troubled. 'Oh,' he said again. 'So… no idea if he plans to turn it into a… *hotel* or something then?'

Ah! There was the crux of the matter. Lionel was worried that he was going to have a rival hotel in town before he'd even got on his feet at Pebble Street.

'I don't think so,' said Kate. 'I'm pretty certain he isn't going to do that. Fairly certain. I mean, I've not seen him for a while, and…'

'Speak of the devil!' laughed Lionel, pointing to the road.

Kate turned her head just in time to see Mike trundling along the road towards them in his old car. She grinned at him and returned his wave, her heart doing a little summersault just at the sight of him –

but then it sank again as he drove on by without stopping.

It wasn't that she blamed him - not if he was busy. A short chat with Lionel could easily turn into half the morning. But still… it was a *bit* strange that he didn't just pause to say hello properly, wasn't it?

Kate gave herself a little shake. It was Christmas Eve. Poor old Mike was run off his feet. Fingers crossed she'd manage to catch up with him later… preferably alone. She was sure that after a good chat, a mince pie or ten and a festive snuggle on the sofa, everything would be just fine.

'Right Lionel,' she said in a determined voice, 'Stanley and I had better get up to the allotments before grumpy old Bernard decides to put in an appearance… that's if he's going to.'

'Right you are,' said Lionel, stepping away from Trixie at last and giving her a little salute as she pulled away from the curb. 'Pedal safely.'

Kate breathed a sigh of relief as she pumped her legs, pedalling hard. Right. Next stop – the allotments!

CHAPTER 4

The hill that led to the allotments used to be Kate's nemesis. She'd always dreaded the slog of cycling Trixie up to the top. It was narrow and wiggly and incredibly steep, and she'd always ended up a sweaty mess – and that was before she'd even reached halfway. Now, however, it was no longer the daily torture that it had been when she'd first started her delivery rounds.

In fact, as Kate threw a quick glance over her shoulder to check that Stanley was doing okay in the back, she realised that she was actually enjoying the ride. Seeing her big old bear grinning back at her, the little white pompom of his Santa hat dancing in the breeze as they went, she laughed out loud. The fact that she still had enough puff to do such a thing took her by surprise.

One thing was for sure – she was a hell of a lot

fitter these days than she'd been when she'd started riding Trixie around Seabury. Today, the steep hill almost seemed easy, even though towing Stanley around in the trailer was a little bit like weight training – something her muscly calves and strong thighs could thoroughly attest to! In fact, if all her customers kept feeding him treats left, right and centre, she'd have to watch she didn't end up looking a bit like a gladiator. She was already developing legs of steel!

'Vain idiot!' laughed Kate, shaking her head at her own silliness. After all, here she was riding a tricycle in the middle of nowhere, wearing a hat made out of wool that very likely came from a pair of old, repurposed socks. Who cared what she looked like? She was strong and healthy, warm and happy. Surely that's all that mattered?

As she pedalled, Kate's mind wandered, as it often did these days, back to Mike. She guessed that by now his car would be heading up the hill on the other side of Seabury towards the lighthouse. She was pretty sure that's where he'd been off to. For a moment, she wished that she was on her way up there too. She really hadn't seen enough of him recently and she was starting to regret that she hadn't been more supportive and listened to his plans.

She might not have given *Mike* the chance to tell her what was happening with the lighthouse, but she hadn't been able to avoid the gossip that had been around going around the town. Apparently, it had taken Mike several meetings with the council just to get this far with the sale. It seemed that the local council were proving to be a nightmare to deal with and as far as she knew, it still hadn't been sorted out yet.

The lighthouse needed a new power supply and from what she'd heard, the council weren't keen on footing the bill – and neither was Mike. According to Doris in the Post Office, they were working towards an agreement, but Kate honestly didn't have a clue if that had happened yet. Maybe she should pay Doris another visit and ask her what the outcome was - she was sure to know if there had been one. After all, Doris knew everything.

One thing was for sure – no matter what Mike's plans were, he'd need a decent power supply up there. Mind you, the same thing could be said for the whole of Seabury. The entire town could do with an upgrade. The power was notoriously flaky – there simply wasn't the grunt to keep the supply stable, and the slightest wobble would cause an outage that could last for hours.

Unfortunately, there were other towns further along the coast that seemed to get all the investment for that sort of thing. After all, they *did* get more visitors... not that Kate was about to start complaining about that. She liked Seabury just as it was, dodgy power supply and all.

Kate took in a long, deep breath of fresh sea air before standing up on the pedals and pumping her legs as hard as she could to tackle the steepest bit of the climb. She really did need to make some time and go and find Mike later. The last time she'd seen him properly was when they'd spent that lovely afternoon decorating the town Christmas tree together.

Seabury's Christmas tree was a tradition going back years – and always seemed to cause some kind of ructions. The town council usually footed the bill, but this year they'd announced that there wouldn't be a tree due to budgetary cuts. Of course, the news had been met with a general outcry.

Mike had earned himself an awful lot of brownie points from the locals when he'd paid for it himself as a gift to the town from New York Froth. The general consensus was that the new kid in town was a jolly good egg – and that Kate was one lucky lady to have snared him. Or at least, that's what her customers liked to tell her every single day over their hazelnut lattes!

Mike had chosen a beautiful tree. It was a bit smaller than last year's but an awful lot bushier too. Everyone seemed to have an opinion about it. It wasn't unusual for Kate to head out of The Sardine only to find a small crowd standing around the tree, debating its merits in loud voices. Some, it seemed, preferred larger trees. Others preferred smaller. Then there was the debate between the old-fashioned type that dropped their needles but had the lovely smell, and the modern, bushy type that didn't drop their needles and stayed looking beautiful for weeks - but didn't give you that delicious pine-scented waft. The only thing that everyone seemed to agree on was that it made the place feel more Christmassy - and that she and Mike had done a lovely job of decorating it.

There had been something so cosy about spending an afternoon together – layering on tinsel and unknotting what felt like miles of lights in companionable silence. The baubles had been tricky to place *just so* given how bushy the bugger was, but Mike had held the bottom of the ladder steady for her, and he'd barely complained at all as she'd taken her time to place them on the dense branches, dropping the occasional glittering icicle down onto his head.

In fact – things had become incredibly quiet between them, and Kate had had the nagging feeling that Mike had something on his mind. She'd done her best to draw it out of him, but even with a bit of light prompting he'd stayed quiet.

They'd ended up turning the lights on together up in her flat, and the minute they'd hit the switch they'd heard a great cheer go up from outside. Rushing over to her living room window, they'd discovered that half the town seemed to have appeared from nowhere and had thoroughly enjoyed catching the impromptu switch-on.

It did look lovely. In fact – as Mike had wound his arms around her and pulled her back against his cosy, cashmere jumper – just for a moment, all her niggling fears had disappeared, and she'd known that there wasn't anywhere in the world she'd rather be. If only that sense of calm comfort had lasted.

Kate let out a sigh. She wished they were together again right now. There were so many things they needed to talk about – so many things that should be said out loud rather than just written in a Christmas card.

At last, the hill started to ease off a bit. Kate sat back down in the saddle, pedalling at a slightly more sedate speed as she finally neared the entrance to the allotments. She stared for a moment out across the sea, now a long way below them. Blimey, this hill brought you a long way up in a very short space of time! The waves below were already looking choppier than they had when she'd first got out of bed. Some of them were now wearing frothy white caps.

For a moment, Kate couldn't help but wonder how the Christmas tree would fare if Storm Bernard did blow in to make a nuisance of himself. They'd made sure that it was fairly well strapped down, but there was only so much you could do, wasn't there? It wasn't as though you could superglue every bauble and strip of tinsel to the branches, was it?! Ah well, time would tell. Worst-case scenario, they'd all be gathering baubles from the four-corners of Seabury for weeks to come.

Anyway, she still thought there was a good chance that the whole thing had been rather exaggerated. They did like to do that, didn't they? Better safe than sorry sometimes. Of course, there was always the chance that, even if Bernard did decide to grace their shores after all, he might make landfall further along the coast. Then, all they'd get in Seabury would be a few drops of rain and just enough wind to set the frills on Lionel's pinny dancing!

Oh, the thought of Lionel in that apron! Kate started to giggle again. It wasn't an image that she was going to be forgetting any time soon.

CHAPTER 5

Leaving Trixie parked on the rough, grassy path that led to the vegetable patches, Kate let Stanley out of the trailer. He dashed on ahead of her, keen to find Charlie. He'd spent plenty of time up here with Charlie and Ethel, and probably knew his way around the place blindfolded.

Kate watched as he hurtled around the corner, fluffy tail and pompom flying. She couldn't believe that the Santa hat was still in place after the blowy trip up here. As Charlie's deep, booming laugh greeted her through the hedgerow, she suspected Stanley's headgear might have something to do with it.

'Ah – there you are!' he chuckled, wiping at his eyes with the corner of a red and white spotted handkerchief as Kate rounded the corner.

Stanley was sitting on Charlie's feet, leaning his

head back against the old man's earth-covered trousers and staring lovingly up at him.

'Sorry I'm so late!' said Kate, wandering over towards him. 'Lionel caught me on my way out of town and wanted a chat.'

'That explains it,' laughed Charlie, fiddling with a piece of twine that he was busily tying a loop in. 'Has the old fella calmed down at all? Last time I saw him, he was having kittens about the couple who're coming to stay for Christmas.'

Kate shook her head. 'Afraid not,' she chuckled.

'Just imagine what he'll be like when the whole place is full to bursting with guests!' said Charlie, bending low over a collection of watering cans at his feet and doing his best to feed the piece of twine through the handles while Stanley proceeded to lick his cheeks. 'Get away with you, you monkey,' he tutted, trying to push Stanley back a little bit before he got a full-on dog snog.

'Well,' said Kate, taking pity on Charlie and putting a hand on Stanley's collar, tugging her errant hound away from him a bit, 'if Lionel's white, frilly apron was anything to go by, I dread to think what fashion faux pas even more guests might cause!'

Charlie grinned as he proceeded to tie the watering cans to the leg of his shed that stood nearby.

'Erm… what are you up to, by the way?' said Kate, cocking her head as she watched him.

'Bain't no room left inside the shed – all me tools are in there and put away for the winter, and I don't want to have to go down and retrieve this lot from the beaches if this 'ere storm does arrive!'

Kate nodded. If there was one thing she understood well, it was a lack of storage space!

'So, you think it might actually get a bit rough here?' she asked, watching as Charlie started to gather loose bamboo poles that were scattered around the plot. When he had them all bundled together, he tied them tightly with more twine from the seemingly endless supply from his pocket.

'Aye. I reckon it's a dead cert. Don't you believe that 'ere blue sky!' he said, casting a suspicious look upwards. 'I remember that there storm back in the late seventies… or it could have been the eighties… either way – old Arthur Crouchley's wooden greenhouse ended up in bits all the way down on West Beach!'

'You're joking?' said Kate, peering down across the gently sloping allotments, back towards where West Beach and The Sardine lay.

'Nope – weren't no joke. And there was no putting it back up neither, it was that damaged. It was a long time ago, but I remember all the broad beans got flattened and the cauliflowers were washed away. I remember I was right sad about that 'cause they were doing so well that year.'

'Blimey,' said Kate, 'that sounds like a right doozy!'

'Oh aye, it was,' said Charlie, coming to a standstill and peering around, clearly looking for what needed to be done next. However, before he had a chance to move, Stanley was back sitting on his feet and leaning into him – just like he always did when his old friend was around. Stanley thought that Charlie gave the best tickles and Charlie didn't seem to mind – even though there was currently enough dog leaning against him to push him off his feet if he wasn't careful.

Charlie's hand went to Stanley's ears – the Santa hat now lay in a heap at their feet. Charlie clearly hadn't noticed - or didn't mind - that he was being used for tickles. He was far too intent on regaling Kate with all sorts of weather-related disasters that had befallen the allotments over the years. There was a tale about everything from ruined rhubarb to smashed cold frames.

'Anyhow,' he said at long last, 'you don't want to be standing around, listening to me jabber on right now.' He looked at her in concern. Kate had just wrapped her arms around herself in an attempt to stop the wind from working its way under her jacket. It was definitely stronger up here on higher ground. 'I've got a lovely bag of sprouts for you,' he said. 'I reckon this storm will have the plants over and I want 'em used up, not wasted!'

Turfing Stanley off his feet again, Charlie ambled

back over to the little shed, opened the door and took out a large, orange net of sprouts.

'Blimey Charlie, they can't all be for me?' said Kate, incredulously.

'Aye, all for you. You can make use of 'em in The Sardine. I mean, normally I'd be giving some to Ethel too, but she can't exactly make a cake out of 'em, can she?! Or jam, come to that.'

Kate grinned. 'Actually, let's face it – I wouldn't put it past her. And if Sarah got in on the act with one of her more… um… *experimental* ideas…'

Charlie wrinkled his nose up. 'Aye, you might have a point there.'

'I can just imagine Sarah trying to sell "chocolate glazed sweet sprouts",' chuckled Kate.

Charlie pulled a face. 'I think Ethel would be more likely put them in a Victoria sponge!'

'How would that work?' laughed Kate.

'Victoria sponge with a sprout and buttercream filling?' said Charlie with a shrug.

'Oh don't!' said Kate, horrified.

'Well, don't you mention it and I'll keep my mouth shut too. I'm not sure any of us would ever be the same again after being force-fed that particular experiment!'

'Okay, you've got a deal!' said Kate, grinning.

'Now then,' said Charlie, plonking the large net of sprouts on the ground and then heading back to the shed. He pulled out a cardboard box full of newly dug parsnips and a few potatoes. 'I've been overwintering these beauties up here too, but it's time they're used up. I don't want them ending up like those poor caulis did - getting washed away like that!'

'Well… that makes sense,' said Kate, wondering where he was heading with this. It was clear Charlie was gearing up for something.

'Aye. Well, they're yours as well as the sprouts, but I've got a favour to ask in return,' said Charlie, digging the heel of his boot into the ground and looking more like a young lad than an old gardener somewhere in his late seventies.

'Of course,' said Kate, raising her eyebrows in surprise. It was usually Charlie dishing out the favours left, right and centre and it was so unusual to hear him ask for anything, she felt a bit befuddled. 'As long as you're not asking for any Christmas decorations – because I've just promised all my spares to Lionel! Mind you, I bet he's got way more than he needs in that box and I'm sure he'd share…'

Charlie shook his head. 'Not decorations!' he said with a laugh. 'I was wondering if you'd be willing to transport some sandbags I've got back there behind the shed down to Ethel's cottage for me? I've only got my sack truck up here and I'm not even sure that would be possible – it'd take me hours!'

'Of course I will!' said Kate. 'Not a problem.'

Charlie's face broke into a wide smile, and she

saw his shoulders relax. Clearly, he'd been worrying about this more than he was letting on.

'Thank you, Kate. I'm just that worried she might get flooded again. You know how badly her cottage gets hit when the weather gets bad, what with it being right by the sea and all!'

Kate nodded. Poor old Ethel had had the heartbreak of seeing the ground floor of her cottage under a foot of water more than once. In fact, last time it had happened, she seemed to remember her old friend swearing that it would be the last time. One more flood and she'd move out.

'It's good thinking,' said Kate.

She peeped at Charlie. She knew that he absolutely adored Ethel. The pair of them had been gadding about like a couple of teenagers for weeks now – heading off on dates and spending as much time together as they could. She also knew that Charlie wanted to ask Ethel to marry him. He'd confessed as much to her in a moment of weakness when she'd delivered a slice of carrot cake that Ethel and made especially for him.

'Erm, Charlie?' she said, as she followed him around to start moving the sandbags.

'Aye?'

'How's it coming with you and Ethel?' she asked carefully.

'What do you mean?' said Charlie, giving her a stern look.

'With the whole… proposing thing?' she ventured.

Charlie shook his head and ran his fingers through his hair. 'Ethel is a wonderful woman,' he said slowly.

Kate nodded but kept her mouth shut, not wanting to stop him in his tracks.

'And I'm just a muddy gardener,' he continued. 'That's the thing – I *would* ask her, but what would she want with a silly old man like me?'

Charlie's eyes met hers, and Kate felt her heart melt. Without thinking about it she stepped forward and pulled him into a hug. He smelled of earth and sunshine and freshly picked sprouts.

'Now what on earth was that for?' he laughed, clearly delighted, as she stepped back.

'You're a lovely man, Charlie Endicott, and you'd make Ethel very happy.'

'I don't know, Kate,' he mumbled, shaking his head. 'I'm not so sure.'

Kate smiled. 'Charlie – what's the worst that could happen? It's Christmas after all – what better time is there?'

Kate left Charlie seemingly deep in thought as she headed back over to where she'd left Trixie and steered her over towards the shed.

'Shall we get these loaded?' she asked eventually when he didn't stir from gazing out across the sea, a distant expression on his face.

'Oh, yes... right you are!' he said, giving his head a little shake.

Kate shifted Stanley's giant cushion out of the way and between them they hoisted the heavy bags into Trixie's trailer.

'Ah,' said Kate. 'I wasn't expecting them to take up quite so much space! There's no room left for Stanley in there with that lot - and I don't want him perching right up on top – he's way too big!'

Charlie shrugged. 'Why don't you leave the old lad up here with me while you cycle these down to Ethel's cottage. I've only got a few more bits and bobs that I need to do here before the storm comes. I promised Frank I'd make sure everything over on his plot is secure too. As soon as I'm done, I'll walk the lad down and we'll meet you at Ethel's, and I'll unload Trixie.'

'Are you sure?' said Kate, looking around to see what Stanley was up to.

'Of course,' laughed Charlie. 'Look at him – he's having a whale of a time!'

Kate finally laid eyes on Stanley and let out a loud laugh. He'd clearly had more than enough of his Santa hat and had concocted a plan to stop her from subjecting him to wearing it ever again.

Stanley was standing in the middle of the veggie patch where Charlie had just finished digging up the old sprout plants. His nose was muddy, his paws were muddy, and there was a newly filled-in hole just in front of him. All that was left visible of the Santa hat was one decidedly grubby pompom and a tiny flash of red. Stanley had buried the offending festive accessory and was now looking thoroughly pleased with himself.

'You horror!' she chuckled. 'I'm sorry Charlie!'

'Blimey, no harm done,' said Charlie with a genuine smile. 'Clever lad!'

Stanley simply grinned at them both and wagged his tail proudly. He gave the pompom one last nose before making his way over and snaffling the doggy treat that appeared, as if by magic, from Charlie's trouser pocket.

'Right,' said Kate, bending to stroke Stanley's head, 'if you're sure this little Grinch won't be too much trouble...?'

'Not at all!' said Charlie, patting Stanley on the head and giving him another biscuit.

'In that case I'll see you both down at Ethel's place in a little while.'

'Right you are!' said Charlie cheerfully.

'Thanks again for my veggies – I promise I'll make good use of them!'

'You're very welcome... as long as there's no sprout cake on your menu!' he laughed.

'Promise!' she said, giving him a salute. 'And Charlie?'

'Aye?'

'Promise me you'll think about what I said? Ethel adores you, you know.'

Charlie didn't say anything but instead gave her a vague nod.

Kate pushed off and had to press down even harder on Trixie's pedals just to get her moving over the rough grass now that she had such a heavy load on board. When she came to the allotment gate, she glanced worriedly back over at Charlie. Perhaps she'd said too much? He hadn't budged but was staring dreamily out across the sea – with Stanley sitting on his feet, leaning against his legs and looking up at him adoringly.

CHAPTER 6

Kate thanked her lucky stars that Trixie's brakes were pretty good and that she kept them well maintained. It turned out that keeping control of the wayward tricycle whilst whizzing down a steep hill with half a dozen extremely heavy sandbags in the trailer was quite a challenge.

To begin with, Kate did her best to keep control of her speed as much as she could while keeping her fingers crossed that she wasn't stripping her brakes down to the bare metal. Eventually, she realised that she was fighting a losing battle and decided to give in. Hoping that she didn't meet anyone doing anything ridiculous coming the other way, Kate gave Trixie free reign and freewheeled down the rest of the hill, squealing at the top of her lungs and hoping against hope that she didn't end up in the hedge right at the bottom.

It wouldn't have been the first time she'd crash-landed with Trix into that particular patch of greenery. There weren't too many hawthorns in it and the last time she'd used it as a crashmat, it had been so lush and leafy that it had provided a landing that was almost comfortable. Almost. She didn't much fancy repeating the exercise today, however. After all – it was now the middle of winter, and there were far fewer leaves to cushion the blow.

In the end, Kate found herself safely – minus any mishaps or crash-landings – cycling along the stretch of seafront at the far end of North Beach towards Ethel's cottage. Frankly, she could have been airlifted here while blindfolded and she'd still know that she was close to Ethel's house. The smell of freshly baked cake had been tormenting her all the way down the lane. It was absolutely delicious and had set her stomach rumbling - especially after the morning's thorough workout.

Kate pulled Trixie in as close to the front door as she could. She didn't want to block the narrow lane while she waited for Charlie to turn up. Hopping gratefully down from the saddle, Kate willed her aching legs not to give in on her as she straightened up. She raised her hand to knock on the front door, but before she could even make contact, Ethel's smiling face appeared in front of her.

'Kate! I wasn't expecting you – what a lovely surprise!' she said, leaning forward to kiss her on the cheek.

Kate grinned and returned her hug, breathing in Ethel's unique scent of cinnamon, fresh baking and talc.

'I come bearing gifts, she laughed. 'Not gold, myrrh or frankincense I'm afraid - just boring old sandbags!' Kate pointed at Trixie and her laden trailer. 'Just doing Charlie a favour. He's still up at the allotments battening down the hatches in case Storm Bernard is as bad as everyone seems to think he's going to be. He's worried about you getting flooded again so asked me to drop these down for him as I was coming back this way!'

'He shouldn't be getting you to do his hard work for him!' chided Ethel with a gentle, good-natured tut. 'Even if he is being sweet and lovely by thinking of me. I would have thought he'd have got someone else to drop them down - or gone back for his own truck!'

Kate smiled at Ethel. The way she talked about Charlie would make anyone think they'd been married for decades. 'It's no problem at all.'

'Well, I can't leave you out there in the cold. Come on in and have a piece of cake!'

'Ah, you know how to tempt a girl!' said Kate, her stomach giving another loud grumble in anticipation as she yanked the tight, woolly hat off her head.

Shaking out her curls, she ducked through the low doorway, following Ethel into her tiny cottage.

'Where's Stanley?' asked Ethel in concern, turning to peer back out into the lane as Kate stood in the warmth of her living room.

'Oh – there wasn't room in Trixie with all the sandbags, so Charlie's going to walk him down when he's finished up at the allotments.'

'Ah good. I've baked some Christmas biscuits especially for him!' beamed Ethel, pushing the front door closed and leading Kate through to her kitchen.

'You spoil that dog!' laughed Kate. 'Goodness Ethel, it smells incredible in here... how many cakes are you baking?!'

Kate peered around. There were three large mixing bowls full of different kinds of batter, at least fifty mince pies that were currently set out on cooling racks, six Victoria sponge halves lined up ready for their fillings... and a tray full of bone-shaped delicacies that she guessed were Stanley's special Christmas treats.

'Oh – it's nothing much,' said Ethel, 'I just like to have some spares for Christmas – you never know how many people you're going to run into, and they always make for perfect last-minute gifts!'

'Well, yes... that's true,' said Kate, grinning.

'Don't worry – I've already finished up a giant walnut and coffee cake, there are plenty of cool mince pies in that old Quality Street tin, and there's an iced carrot cake too. What do you fancy?'

'Erm… carrot cake? If it's not too much trouble?' said Kate, quite overwhelmed at the sheer array of goodies. This much baking on the go would stress her out thoroughly, but Ethel was as serene and cheery as ever as she bustled about, popping a full kettle of water to heat on her gas stove then taking the largest, scariest cake knife she'd ever seen and cutting into a beautifully decorated carrot cake.

'Blimey, you didn't need to make a start on that beauty just for me!' said Kate, mildly horrified.

'Don't be silly,' laughed Ethel, waving her worries away as she plopped the huge slice onto a little plate edged with painted holly berries and robins.

'Well, I'm happy to repay you by lending a hand to get this lot finished up if you'd like?' said Kate. She looked again at the overwhelming line up of cakey jobs that were dotted around the kitchen, awaiting Ethel's attention. 'Or I can send Sarah over when I get back to The Sardine?'

'Don't be daft,' laughed Ethel, 'this is nothing. You sit yourself down, tuck into that cake and have a rest after your ride. And thank you for offering to lend me Sarah – but as much as I adore that girl and her experimental cooking… I rather like to work alone. Always have done!'

Kate nodded, unable to say anything as she'd just

taken an almighty bite of sweet, moist carrot cake and was doing her best to surreptitiously lick off the blob of cream-cheese icing that she'd almost managed to get up her nose.

'Though,' continued Ethel more quietly, as she whipped the buttercream for the Victoria sponges while she was waiting for the kettle to come to the boil, 'I do like the company. I wouldn't mind a bit more company around here now and then.'

Kate paused, watching her old friend closely. Somehow, she didn't think Ethel meant Sarah.

'Company of the… erm… male persuasion, you mean?' Kate asked lightly.

Ethel let out a little huff. 'I don't mean someone that would just sit around on the sofa all day watching the telly – I mean someone that might be… useful. I've got a few things around this place that need doing… and…' she trailed off, staring hard at her icing.

Kate raised her eyebrows. She knew that Ethel was talking about Charlie, but she decided not to name the elephant in the room. 'What jobs do you need doing?' she asked, trying to tactfully lead the conversation onto slightly less sticky ground.

'I've actually written a little list,' said Ethel, plonking the heavy mixing bowl back down onto the table, striding over to the bread bin in the corner and taking a sheaf of papers from beside it. 'Here,' she said, handing them to Kate.

Kate did her best to stifle a giggle. Ethel's "little list" was actually several pages long. She glanced down the long list of jobs that needed seeing to – mostly things like "unstick all windows" and "wallpaper is lifting". She'd put good money on the fact that most of the problems on here were probably down to the vast amounts of steam that emanated from Ethel's kitchen on a daily basis as she worked her baking magic.

'Erm... do you reckon the wallpaper might be from all the baking?' asked Kate carefully.

Ethel shrugged. 'I wouldn't be surprised,' she agreed, somewhat reluctantly. 'But I love baking. Always have. And anyway – it's not like I'm going to stop now!' she laughed.

'You'd better not,' grinned Kate, placing the list carefully down on the table and taking another great big bite of cake.

Just as Ethel turned to lift the now-whistling kettle off the hob to make one of her famously strong pots of thick, ten-bag tea, there came a knock at the door.

'Well, there's timing for you!' said Ethel, placing the kettle back down and bustling over to open the door.

Assuming that it was probably Charlie come to help unload the sandbags, Kate followed hot on Ethel's heels. There was no way she was going to let him struggle with those alone, no matter what Ethel thought!

However, when Ethel opened the door only to reveal that it was indeed Charlie standing there with Stanley at his feet, something stopped her in her tracks. She wasn't sure what was about to happen, but there was something different about Charlie that she couldn't quite put her finger on. Perhaps it was the fact that he was grasping a bunch of onions in his hands – but then that wasn't a particularly strange thing for Charlie. Then she realised that he'd straightened his collar and even taken the time wash his hands – probably in the rain butt up at the allotments if she had to guess.

Kate glanced quickly down at Stanley and noticed that even her big bear had gone unusually still. He was sitting, staring at Ethel with his big, soulful eyes – probably wondering when he'd get a piece of cake.

'Are you coming in, then?' asked Ethel, her voice quavering in the strange silence.

'Well,' said Charlie in a low voice, 'that depends.'

'On what?' said Ethel, raising her eyebrows.

Charlie held out the bunch of onions towards Ethel. 'Ethel Iris Watts,' he said, his usually steady voice sounding husky with nerves, 'will you be my lawfully wedded wife?'

Kate's eyes grew wide as she held her breath.

Ethel was staring back at Charlie, not saying anything.

'I'm sorry about the onions,' he added, clearing his throat. 'I wanted to bring you flowers, but I don't have any right now – tis just not the season – but I wanted to bring you something. I promise I'll make it up to you when the weather warms up, though.'

Kate glanced at Ethel again. Her old friend was never one to make a snap decision, and it didn't look like she was about to change now - even with Charlie poised nervously in front of her, holding out the great big bunch of onions.

But then... Ethel started to smile. It was the same warm smile that Kate had seen so many times before when a cake turned out perfectly – well risen and golden on top.

'Well then,' said Ethel, at last, not taking her eyes off Charlie. 'You'd better come in then.'

Charlie hesitated. 'Does that mean...'

'Yes,' said Ethel, the wide smile now filling her whole face as she took the onions from him. 'I'll marry you. But what on earth took you so long to ask, eh?'

Kate clamped her hand quickly over her mouth in an attempt to muffle the giggle of delight that had just escaped her. It didn't matter though – neither of them had noticed. Charlie had just bundled Ethel up into a warm hug as he bent to kiss her tenderly on the cheek.

'Come on then,' said Ethel at last, pulling away from him, her face now pink and rosy and still smiling away, 'you'd better come in – the kettle's just boiled.'

Ethel led her new fiancé into the little cottage, leaving Stanley sitting by the door, probably wondering where on earth his piece of cake was.

CHAPTER 7

Kate didn't stay at Ethel's cottage for very long after Charlie had popped the question. She downed her thick, scalding tea in record time, and helped Charlie to remove the sandbags from Trixie's trailer. Then she re-loaded it with a massive Tupperware tub full of mince pies and balanced the tin with the rest of the huge carrot cake on top of the net of sprouts and box of veggies. She *certainly* wouldn't be going hungry this Christmas!

After Stanley had demanded – and been treated to – yet another one of his special biscuits to eat on the ride home, the pair of them had beat a hasty retreat, leaving the newly-engaged love birds alone at last. After all, they had an awful lot to talk about – mostly concerning how to unstick the window in the living room and stop Ethel's toilet cistern from dripping. How romantic!

Kate couldn't help but grin to herself as she cycled her way back through Seabury towards The Sardine. She slowed right down, following a car at snail's pace along the seafront. She didn't mind though. She wasn't in any rush – it was still a rather beautiful morning out here and Kate was happy to potter along, digesting everything that had just happened.

She couldn't be happier for Charlie and Ethel, and as she re-lived Charlie's proposal, she blinked back a couple of happy tears. What a romantic moment. Perhaps there was more to a bunch of onions than she'd ever given them credit for before. If only Mike was one for grand, sweeping, romantic gestures like that! Okay, maybe *not* with onions – she had a feeling that had only worked because it was Charlie holding them – but she was sure Mike could come up with something else. Something more... him. Though, for the life of her, she couldn't imagine what that might be! It would be nice though, wouldn't it?

Kate cleared her throat and blinked hard. Goodness, she was getting ahead of herself! Hadn't she sworn after the disaster that had been her first marriage that she'd never, ever consider tying the knot again? And here she was, just a couple of months after it was all over, daydreaming about bended knees and white dresses.

'Bloomin' Christmas is making me all soppy again, Stanley lad!' she called over her shoulder with a rueful smile. Because sure, her and Mike had had a lot of fun together so far... but they'd not exactly talked about the future very much. Especially not with everything that had been going on recently.

Kate let out a sigh. Yup – it was just that strange Christmas magic getting to her again and making her feel all... *fizzy*. But seeing Charlie and Ethel agree to spend the rest of their lives together... well... it had made her realise that perhaps she *wasn't* completely closed off to the idea of her very own "onion moment" with someone. As long as that someone was the *right* someone this time. Maybe someone... like Mike?

Kate came back to reality just in time to realise that the car in front of her was indicating to pull over, even though there wasn't really anywhere for them to go. Huh, maybe they were lost? It wasn't unusual to find holidaymakers who'd stumbled into town by mistake while they were looking for one of the larger resort towns further along the coast.

Rather than pedalling past, Kate pulled in behind them.

'Stay there, boy,' she said to Stanley before heading over to the passenger side of the car. The woman was already rolling down her window with an apologetic expression on her face.

'Hi!' said the stranger, 'sorry for holding you up!'

'Don't worry about that!' said Kate, smiling at her and then the elderly gent behind the wheel. 'Everything okay?'

'Actually, I don't suppose you could help us out with some directions?' he said, looking a little bit sheepish.

'Of course!' said Kate. 'Where are you headed?'

'Well, we're meant to be staying at somewhere called The Pebble Street Hotel,' said the woman, 'do you know it? We're just about ready to give up. We've been driving for ages, and the Satnav brought us down some of the tiniest lanes I've ever seen!'

'Yes,' huffed the man. 'I'd have already done a U-turn - if only I could find somewhere wide enough. I'm sure there are still rooms available somewhere that's a bit easier to find!'

'Oh no,' said Kate, 'don't do that – you'd break Lionel's heart! He's so looking forward to having you both stay for Christmas. Besides, you're nearly there!'

'Oh, how wonderful!' beamed the woman. 'It's bad enough that the weather almost put us off coming at the last minute – but it doesn't look that bad, does it?' she said, peering up at the sky.

Kate shook her head. 'Not yet, but my old friend who's a gardener reckons it might get quite rough. Either way – you'll be safely tucked up at Pebble Street long before that happens – it's only just along the road!'

Kate gave the couple directions on exactly how to get to the hotel and then wished them a Merry Christmas before patting the roof and waving them off. No doubt she'd run into them again later when she was out giving Stanley his evening walk. After all, Seabury was only small, and everyone knew everyone – even if they were only passing through!

She wandered back to Trixie and stopped to give Stanley a quick kiss on the head before hopping back on the saddle. Before setting off again, Kate glanced up at the sky and then over at the sea. She wasn't so sure about the weather after all. It was definitely getting windier by the minute, and in the time she'd spent stuffing her face with cake at Ethel's, thin, high streaks of cloud had appeared, and the waves were now white-topped, and definitely quite a lot more forceful than they'd been earlier on. Never a good sign.

It was time for her to get back to The Sardine, tuck Trixie up under her tarpaulin and get her Christmas Eve properly started.

As she trundled around the corner and pedalled along West Beach towards the café, Kate could swear that she could hear singing. It seemed to be drifting towards her on every gust of wind, making the hairs on the back of her neck stand on end. The closer she got to The Sardine the louder it became, and she couldn't wait to get inside and find out what was going on.

Kate parked Trixie out in the yard, let Stanley out of the trailer and hastily grabbed the sweet treats Ethel had sent home with her. She made her way into the café with Stanley at her heels, and the minute she stepped through the door, it became clear what the singing had been about. The Chilly Dippers had descended on The Sardine.

'Kate!' cheered Paula from her perch at one of the tables. 'Just in time – we're practising our carol singing for this evening!'

Kate headed over to her best friend and gave her a huge hug. Even though she was very ill and in the middle of treatment, today Paula looked really happy and pretty rosy. Though maybe that wasn't surprising given that she was all bundled up in a warm scarf and soft hat. That said, Kate had the feeling that it was most likely the company she was in that was making her smile quite so much.

Paula was surrounded by every single member of the Chilly Dippers – Seabury's wild swimming group - and by the looks of the piles of empty plates and mugs littering the tables in front of them, they'd been here for some time.

'Hi Kate!' said Sarah, giving her a one-armed squeeze as she made her way behind the counter to make herself a coffee. 'You've been a while!'

Kate grinned at her, desperately wanting to share the amazing news about Charlie and Ethel. She quickly bit her tongue, deciding against it. It wasn't her news to share, and no doubt the lovebirds would tell everyone when they were good and ready.

'Yeah, sorry about that!' she said instead. 'I had to

drop a bunch of sandbags from the allotments over to Ethel's.'

'Good thinking!' said Lou, who was busy buttering a large round of teacakes.

'Thank you both for helping me out today, by the way,' said Kate, beaming gratefully at them. 'I know it's a lot to ask on Christmas Eve.

'Are you kidding me, boss?' said Lou, shooting her a grin. 'I wouldn't have missed this for the world.' She nodded at the Dippers as they debated which song to practise next.

'How long have they been at it?' asked Kate with an amused smile.

'Well,' said Sarah, 'quite a while, actually. They keep talking about whether to have a quick swim or not. But then one coffee turned into three… and they've gobbled a decent amount of Ethel's cake already… so I'm guessing they *might* have given up on the idea?'

'You *can't* be seriously thinking about going for a swim today!' Kate called loudly across the counter to Paula.

Paula grinned at her and shrugged, but another one of the ladies nodded. 'The sea looked gorgeous,' she said.

'Not everyone fancied it though,' said Doris from beside her.

'So, we thought, instead of arguing about it outside…'

'We'd come and grab a coffee…'

'Sing a few songs…'

'And see what happened,' finished Paula, her eyes twinkling.

'My goodness,' whispered Kate, stifling a giggle, 'this lot are better than watching a panto!'

'And,' added Lou in an undertone, a huge smile on her face, 'what happened was that they drank and drank, ate and ate … and then ate some more, sang lots of songs and created an awful lot of washing up!'

Sarah giggled and nodded. Taking the hint, she grabbed a tray and dashed over to start clearing some of the empties off the tables so that there would be room for the large platter of teacakes.

'Okay, ladies,' said Paula, 'what's next?'

'O Come, All Ye Faithful?'

'Perfect! One, two, three…'

Kate listened as a dozen voices of the Chilly Dippers rose together, filling The Sardine with one of her favourite Christmas hymns. But then another voice – clear, high and pure - soared above the others. Once again, the hairs on the back of her neck prickled. Kate peered around only to find that this voice of an angel was coming from Lou.

By the looks of shocked delight on everyone else's faces, this was just as much a surprise to them as it was to her – but they didn't stop singing. Sarah came to a standstill, holding her tray full of empty mugs and plates while staring at Lou until they all reached the end of the song.

'Okay,' laughed Sarah, 'where on earth did *that* come from?!' She was joined by an excited chorus of whoops and cheers.

Lou shrugged, looking unusually bashful.

'Sarah's right!' said Kate. 'You dark horse, hiding a voice like that. And you knew all the words too!'

Lou shrugged again, going red. 'Sorry, I couldn't help it – I love that song! We used to sing it at school every year – that's why I know the words.'

'Don't apologise!' laughed Paula. 'I don't think I've ever heard all those high bits before. So beautiful.'

'It's nothing,' said Lou, looking both embarrassed and pleased as punch.

'Erm,' said Sarah, 'it's definitely *not* nothing.'

Lou looked to Kate for backup.

'Don't look at me,' she laughed. 'I'm with Sarah. You've got a lovely voice.'

'You know,' said Paula, 'I think that might just call for another round of coffees and we'll carry on singing for a bit – that's if you don't mind, Kate?'

Kate shook her head with a delighted smile. 'Stay as long as you like – and please keep singing,' she paused and turned to Lou. 'You too!'

'Yes boss!' Lou grinned.

'I need to go and grab a couple of things from Trixie's trailer,' she said, peering around for a spot she could stash the massive bag of sprouts when she brought them in.

'Oh, I meant to tell you,' said Sarah, 'Lionel popped in and we gave him that box of decorations you put in the passageway. Luckily, I hadn't taken them upstairs yet! I hope that was the one you meant for us to give him?'

Kate beamed at her, nodding. 'That was the one.' And hurrah! That meant the perfect space had opened up back there just in time to be filled by the huge net of sprouts.

CHAPTER 8

At last, the morning rush was over. The Dippers had sung every song they knew multiple times over while sampling as much cake as they could hold. Then they'd moved on to a round of cheese toasties "to fill in the gaps" before eventually admitting defeat. There wouldn't be so much as a paddle happening today, let alone a swim!

With many a hug and a Christmas kiss, they'd eventually said their goodbyes and headed off.

'What a morning!' laughed Lou, as the last stragglers waved on their way out through the door. 'I can't imagine a better way to spend Christmas Eve, can you?'

Sarah grinned and shook her head. 'I loved all the singing.'

'Me too!' said Lou. 'I'd forgotten how much I enjoyed it.'

'Maybe that can be one of your New Year's resolutions?' said Kate, loading a tray of crockery into the dishwasher. 'To make sure you sing more often?'

'Don't think I'll have to wait until New Year,' said Lou. 'Did you know the Dippers are off out carolling later? They've invited me to go with them.'

'Oh, that'll be so much fun!' said Sarah.

'And I'm not surprised,' laughed Kate. 'With a voice like yours, how could they not ask you along.'

'They told me to invite you two as well if you fancied it?' said Lou.

Kate smiled and shook her head. 'I can't sing for toffee – I much prefer listening, so make sure you all come to my door on your rounds!'

Sarah laughed. 'It's a no from me too. I'm looking forward to hanging out with dad for a bit later. It's like I haven't seen him properly for ages. He said he'll collect me after my shift, on his way back down from the lighthouse. Oh!' Sarah quickly covered her mouth and shot an awkward look at Kate. 'Sorry, I didn't mean to bring that up…'

Kate just winked at her and gave her a friendly nudge. She hated the idea of Sarah feeling caught between the two of them in any way, but it had been practically impossible to hide the fact that she was finding the whole lighthouse purchase a bit hard to handle. It was interesting that Sarah felt like Mike had been a bit awol recently too, though. Maybe she'd been taking everything a bit too personally after all.

'Right, you two – if you don't mind, I'll leave you both to get this place back together after the Dipper whirlwind and I'll nip out and make sure that everything is safe and secure in the courtyard. I guess I may as well leave that lump where he is for now,' she added, pointing at Stanley. He'd flopped down on his side under one of the electric radiators and was busy snoring loudly.

Lou gave her the thumbs up, and Kate left the pair of them to rearrange all the chairs and get the little tables back into their usual places.

She wasn't really expecting many more customers today anyway. It was always the way on Christmas Eve. She'd get a flurry of activity over breakfast and into mid-morning, but by the time lunch was over everyone started to head home to begin their celebrations with their own families. They still might get the odd straggler turn up, but she was planning on closing up a bit earlier than usual. After all, she had a paper chain she'd quite like to finish off, and another slice of Ethel's carrot cake was calling her name.

Kate made her way around to the courtyard. Now that The Sardine wasn't bursting at the seams with a bunch of singing swimmers, she needed to make sure that Trixie was tucked up safe and sound under her tarpaulin. Plus, she wanted to check there wasn't anything out there that might come to any harm if the storm did arrive.

Pulling the old gates open wide, Kate wandered in and had a good look around. The chairs and tables were already securely stacked and tied back against the wall – so they'd be okay. She quickly grabbed a large armful of dry logs from the pile she'd had delivered, took them out of the yard and dumped them on the pavement ready to take back through to the café when she was finished. Better safe than sorry, and she didn't want to be venturing back out here in the piddling rain to bring in armfuls of soggy logs if she could help it. She'd add them to the pile she already had stacked up in the kitchen against the side of Bertha. That way, she could take them up to her flat when she was ready without having to set foot outside. Sure, it would make it feel even more cramped in the kitchen – but that didn't really matter as long as she could keep the place nice and toasty!

'Alright, Trixie my girl, time to get you all cosy under your duvet!' she murmured, grabbing the end of the tarp. Kate dragged it right over the tricycle and trailer, making sure that every inch was covered. Then, with her mind on the dire warnings about Storm Bernard, she carefully tucked the edges in and weighted them down with a few extra logs she pilfered from the stack of firewood.

Standing back to admire her work for a moment, Kate scratched her head. Hmm, maybe that wasn't going to be enough. She scouted around and found the four old bricks they'd been using to keep the space heaters steady during the cooler autumn afternoons. Perfect! She grabbed them one at a time and weighted down the corners of the tarp. Just in case. After all, she really didn't want poor old Trixie coming to any harm!

Looking around her once more, Kate gave a little nod of satisfaction. There. Even if it rained and the wind decided to whip in here, there wasn't really much damage it could do now.

Pulling the gates closed behind her as she headed back out onto the pavement, Kate carefully lowered the two metal pegs into the holes in the paving stones. She didn't want them swinging open and breaking the hinges. They'd probably need replacing soon anyway – they were getting old and starting to rust badly. The wooden sections were beginning to rot too. That's what came of too much sunshine and salty sea spray - nothing lasted very long this close to the sea.

'But some things do,' Kate murmured to herself as she unhooked the ancient padlock and held it in her hands, running her fingers over its familiar shape. It was yet another thing that reminded her of her dad. After all – it had once belonged to him. It was still oiled to perfection and always trustworthy. Something she could always rely on – just like him, really.

She threaded it gently back through the latch that

held the gates together and listened to it close with a reassuring *snap*. There. All safe and sound, no matter how stormy things got out here.

Kate took a deep breath and tried to swallow the random bubble of emotion that had risen to her throat. How ridiculous - getting emotional over a padlock! But of course, it wasn't about the padlock at all. It was about her dad. She wished with all her heart that he was still here with her. She'd give anything to visit the lighthouse together one more time. It had always been their special place.

Kate turned and stared down across West Beach. As her gaze drifted out to sea, it naturally wandered up to where the old lighthouse stood sentry on the point. Was Mike still up there? What was he planning? Maybe she should have listened when he wanted to talk. What if he wanted to turn it into a hotel like Lionel was worried about… or worse still, some kind of awful tourist attraction! She couldn't bear the idea that she might lose the place forever.

For one mad moment, Kate considered opening the courtyard gates back up, grabbing Trixie and riding up to the point to confront him. Maybe it was time to finally find out what was going on! She owed it to her dad's memory to make sure that Mike understood how special it was before he turned it into… whatever he was going to turn it into!

Kate turned back to the gates, fished the padlock key out of her pocket and was on the verge of opening it back up when she felt all the fight go out of her. Her shoulders slumped and she let out a long, slow breath.

What was she thinking? It was Christmas Eve and Storm Bernard was meant to be arriving in town any moment now! She'd already pushed her luck once today by taking Trixie up to the allotments. She'd been lucky - but she really didn't want to get caught out by the weather up on the point. Not on a tricycle. That would be asking for it, wouldn't it?!

Besides, Trixie was nice and snug and tucked up for Christmas now. Plus, she could just imagine the look on Mike's face if she turned up out of the blue after she'd been avoiding talking about the place for weeks on end. He'd know something was wrong straight away.

No. She wouldn't do it. This was business and she couldn't let her over-emotional, personal fears get in the way of his business. It just wouldn't be fair. She'd managed to stay out of it until now. She needed to stick to her guns... even if it was starting to eat her up inside.

Kate let out another long, slow breath and turned back to stare out at the sea. Again, her eyes wandered straight up to the lighthouse. She cracked a rueful smile. As *if* she could manage to cycle all the way up there right now anyway. Her calves were already screaming from cycling the heavy sandbags down to Ethel's house earlier. She doubted she'd manage to get even halfway up there before she'd be forced to give in.

'Come on Kate,' she muttered, 'cheer up – it's nearly Christmas!'

With that, she tore her eyes away from the lighthouse and stooped down to gather the logs up from the pavement. Everything out here was all safely tucked up – now it was her turn!

CHAPTER 9

'Come on, boy!' laughed Kate, giving Stanley's lead a hefty tug in an attempt to pull him away from the Christmas tree yet again. 'It's still not for you!'

The time had come for Stanley's final, long walk of the day. Kate had hung on for as long as she could, hoping to catch Mike when he turned up to collect Sarah, but poor old Stanley hadn't been able to keep his legs crossed any longer. She'd left Sarah waiting for her dad in the doorway of the café and headed out with Stanley into the decidedly grumpy looking afternoon.

Although they'd only just started out, Kate was already planning to turn the walk into a quick stomp down the seafront and back. Then they could hotfoot it back inside where it was warm. She didn't think Stanley would mind too much given the fact that he'd spent most of the day so far practically glued to the little heater in the café.

The wind was definitely a lot stronger than it had been earlier on in the day and the branches of the town Christmas tree looked a bit like they were shivering. As she watched, the tinsel and baubles danced up and down, and the glinting swathes of lights trembled with every gust. It was all rather pretty – but that didn't stop Stanley from wanting to pee on the trunk.

'Nope,' laughed Kate. 'Come on, let's head over the road and see what's going on down on the beach!'

The pair of them trotted across the quiet seafront road, and as Stanley stopped for a good, long sniff along the bottom of the railings, Kate stared out at the sea. The waves were choppy and insistent – and quite a lot bigger than they had been earlier on - and the sky above looked sort of lumpy and rather ominous.

Stanley let out a little whine and Kate looked down at him in concern. He eyed her and then pulled on his lead, clearly wanting to head back to The Sardine.

'You're not sure this walk is such a good idea either, are you boy?' she laughed. Stanley pulled on the lead again. He was clearly keen to turn around and resume his place by the radiator or, even better, next to the wood burner upstairs instead.

'Not yet,' she said, patting his head. He promptly

gave up pulling and leaned against her leg, a look of pure adoration on his face. 'Silly boy,' she grinned. 'You need to stretch your legs, and I need a bit of fresh air too - before I hit that bottle of Baileys!'

They carried on walking in the direction of The King's Nose and The Pebble Street Hotel. Over the crashing of the waves and grumpy gusts of wind, Kate was sure that she could just about make out the sound of singing, far off in the distance. The Chilli Dippers must have started their round of door-to-door carolling.

As she strained her ears, trying to make out what they were singing, she thought she could just make out Lou's high, clear voice rising above all the others. She gave a little shiver of pure joy. What could be more Christmassy than the twinkling lights looping between the streetlamps above and the sound of carols drifting on the winter air?

Kate peered ahead as they approached The Pebble Street Hotel. Her eyes combed along the cottages opposite, hoping to catch a glimpse of the carollers, but there was no sign of them. It looked like their voices must be drifting on the wind all the way over from somewhere near North Beach.

Her attention was caught by a movement at the door to The Pebble Street Hotel, and she spotted Lionel standing there, still wearing his frilly white apron. She hoped that he was getting on okay with his guests. She wasn't close enough to speak to him yet, but as if Lionel could read her mind, he gave her a quick wave followed by a double thumbs up. She took that as a good sign and returned the gesture with a huge grin, raising her hand to give him a wave back.

Just as she did, everything went strangely still. Kate paused, and Stanley glanced up at her in confusion. It was like someone had just switched off a giant fan. The wind had dropped away to nothing. In the same split-second, everything went oddly dark – like someone had decided to dim the lights on the day. Uh oh. Maybe it was time to turn tail and head back home even sooner than expected!

Too late.

The thought had barely formed in her head when the heavens opened. Kate caught sight of Lionel scuttling back into the hotel, and far off, the sounds of singing stopped abruptly.

'Come on, Stanley boy!' she yelled. It was time to run for cover.

He didn't need to be told twice. Stanley led the way at full gallop back towards The Sardine and Kate followed as fast as her burning legs would let her.

The pair of them reached the door to the café just in time. It was like some invisible hand had just turned a dial, making the rain ratchet up another notch. It started pelting down around them, and at the same time, the wind kicked back in with almost indecent ferocity.

It hit Kate in the back so hard that she was practically blown through the door into The Sardine, landing right in Sarah's outstretched arms.

'Oof!' Kate grunted into Sarah's shoulder. She scrambled, doing her best to stand up straight, wrestle with Stanley's lead and force the door of the café closed all at the same time. It was a lot harder than it should have been as she wrestled against the mad gusts of wind now buffeting the door.

'Sorry Sarah!' she gasped. 'You okay?'

Sarah nodded, taking Stanley's lead and unclipping it while Kate latched the door, breathing a sigh of relief and relishing the relative calm inside the café after their mad dash.

'I wasn't expecting you to still be here. I thought your dad would have collected you by now,' she said, striding over to the counter and grabbing one of Stanley's clean doggy towels from underneath.

'He's not turned up yet,' said Sarah, pointing out the obvious but looking unusually worried as she turned to stare out at the rain that was now lashing against the windows. 'He's not responding to my messages, and he didn't pick up when I tried calling either!'

'Don't worry too much,' said Kate, giving her own hair a quick once over with the tatty old towel in an attempt to stop icy drips from making their way down her back. 'I'm sure your dad's absolutely fine. He's probably still caught up at the lighthouse – and you know how bad the signal can be up there. I bet he'll be here soon.'

She turned to deal with a very soggy Stanley, but before she could set to work again with the towel, he beat her to it with a full body shake that covered the café floor with a thousand tiny droplets.

Sarah nodded. She came over and took the towel from Kate before kneeling next to Stanley and giving his head a thorough rub.

'I can't believe the council have got him up there on Christmas Eve. It's ridiculous,' she muttered, moving on to dry Stanley's back. The big dog closed his eyes and stuck his nose in the air in total bliss. 'After they've been digging their heels in for so long about all the little details of this stupid sale… it's stressing him out way too much.' Sarah paused and glanced up at Kate. 'Sorry,' she muttered, 'I know you don't want to hear it.'

Kate shrugged and waved her apology away just as she had earlier. 'I know what you mean. He works so hard - he should have his feet up in front of the fire with a glass of mulled wine in his hands by now!'

'Exactly,' sighed Sarah. 'He's been missing you like crazy, you know. He's hated being so busy that you guys haven't had the chance to hang out much.'

Kate raised her eyebrows.

'Sorry,' said Sarah again. 'He'd kill me for saying something like that.'

'It's fine,' said Kate. 'I've been feeling exactly the

same. Hopefully, things will calm down again soon. It'll be nice to spend a bit more time together again.'

Sarah nodded and watched as Stanley wandered off to make good on his promise of setting up camp by one of the radiators. Kate offered Sarah a hand up, which she took gratefully, then the pair of them turned to stare out of the café windows again.

Kate shook her head, her eyes wide in awe. 'Blimey,' she breathed. It was almost as though the town had completely disappeared behind the thick curtain of driving rain. The noise of it pummelling the pavements and windows and gushing down the drainpipes was almost deafening. 'I'm going to turn the radio on – see if there's any update on the news about how long Bernard's going to be hanging around for.'

Sarah nodded, not taking her eyes off the downpour as Kate made her way over to the faux-vintage digital radio that sat on the counter at the back of the kitchen. It was always tuned to the local station, and as she switched it on the voices that filled The Sardine weren't exactly cheerful. In fact – they were positively doom-laden.

After listening for all of about thirty seconds, Kate promptly switched it back off again in the fear that it might send Sarah into a renewed panic about Mike's whereabouts. In fact, if she wasn't careful, she'd be going the same way!

'Well,' said Kate, 'sounds like they haven't changed

their tune. Old Bernard's going to be around for a good few days. Apparently, it's going to get even worse this evening and into the night. So much for any chance of a white Christmas, eh? It's going to be a stormy, wet and windy one instead.'

'Erm, Kate?' said Sarah, a note of mild hysteria in her voice, 'get back over here!'

Kate rushed to her side just in time to see the large star from the top of the town Christmas tree go whizzing at speed past the window.

'Uh oh!' said Kate.

But in this case, *uh oh* was a bit of an understatement. The star was promptly followed by strand after strand of tinsel. It went glittering past the windows, twisting and twirling in mid-air.

'Holy F...ather Christmas!' squealed Sarah as an array of colourful baubles pelted past, one after the other like festive cannonballs. But it wasn't over yet. The pair of them watched in horror as the cables that snaked through the café to power the lights on the tree pulled tight.

Kate quickly grabbed Sarah's arm and they both shifted as far away from them as they could get. Turning quickly back to the window, they were met with the sight of the entire Christmas tree being dragged down the middle of the road by the wind.

'Wooooow!' gasped Sarah as a violent gust threw it up into a summersault before finally pushing it across to the other pavement and pinning it against the railings. It seemed to pause for a moment as if deciding what to do next, before toppling right over the highest bar. The tree tumbled out of sight, down onto the sand of West Beach.

'At least it's out of the way down there!' said Kate in shock. 'I wouldn't fancy having to heave it out of the middle of the road in this!'

'Me neither,' gasped Sarah. 'You know, I hate to say this, but I think this Bernard dude might be as bad as everyone's been saying.'

Kate nodded. 'As bad as… or maybe even worse.'

CHAPTER 10

'Well,' said Sarah, blowing a strand of hair out of her face and turning back to Kate, 'it's not like it can get much worse, is it?'

The moment she said the word "worse" out loud, the lights in the café started to flicker. The pair of them glanced at each other.

'Now you've done it,' chuckled Kate as they gave another almighty dip.

'I didn't mean... I...' stuttered Sarah, looking horrified. Another flicker caused them both to look up at the lightbulb overhead just in time to be plunged into darkness.

'Oh no!' gasped Sarah.

Kate heard the young girl's quickening breath in the thick darkness that had descended on the café. It might not be that late in the afternoon, but the storm had put paid to any daylight that might have been bravely lingering outside.

'Don't panic,' said Kate, keeping her voice low and calm. She could sense that Sarah was on the cusp of losing the plot.

'Is it just us?' asked Sarah.

Kate shook her head, then realised that there was no way Sarah would be able to see her. 'Nope,' she said, glancing towards the window where there was absolutely nothing to be seen now that all the Christmas lights, streetlamps and friendly warmth spilling from Seabury's cottage windows had been extinguished. 'It'll be the whole town. It's just Seabury's classic flaky power grid failing yet again!'

'Does it do this a lot?' asked Sarah, her voice quavering.

'Only when it's most inconvenient for everyone involved,' laughed Kate, 'like Christmas Eve with an amber weather warning in place! Now, don't move a sec. I've got a torch behind the till somewhere.'

Kate slowly and carefully made her way towards the counter, praying that Stanley wouldn't choose this moment to appear at her feet and trip her up. With her hands outstretched in front of her, she found the smooth wooden edge and used it to navigate her way slowly around into the kitchen. She swore as she caught her foot on the towering pile of cake tins that she'd left stacked in the way. They toppled to the floor with a deafening crash.

'You okay?' asked Sarah from the darkness.

'Yeah - just a bunch of tins going flying,' said Kate, raising her voice a little bit as the wind started to howl outside, causing the rain to clatter against the windowpanes. 'Ah ha! Got it,' she said, triumphantly wrapping her hand around the handle of the huge barn torch she always kept in the café – just in case. She'd learned from years of experience never to be too far from a battery-powered torch here in Seabury.

Flicking the switch, the beam of yellow light that sprung to life was just about strong enough to reach all four corners of the café. It showed Sarah, now kneeling in the middle of The Sardine with her arms wrapped around Stanley.

'He was frightened,' she said sheepishly.

'Uh-huh,' grinned Kate, taking in just how pale Sarah looked – though that might just be down to the torchlight. 'Are *you* okay?'

Sarah nodded. 'Of course,' she said. 'Will it come back on again soon, do you think?'

Kate would love to tell her that - yes, of course, give it just a couple of minutes and everything would be back to normal. But long experience of power cuts in Seabury had taught her that they were likely to be in this for the long haul.

'Honestly? I doubt it,' she said. 'They'll probably need to get some engineers out to fix it… and that's a hard enough job at the best of times given how antiquated the town's grid is. But…'

'It's Christmas Eve,' said Sarah, kissing Stanley's head, 'and it's totally mental out there.'

'Exactly,' agreed Kate. 'It might take them a while to round up a couple of poor souls and get them into their wet weather gear.'

'What are we going to do?' said Sarah, sounding a lot younger than she actually was.

Kate smiled at her. 'Well, we've got a decision to make. Either we can head upstairs, settle down in front of the wood burner and wait for your dad to appear.'

'Sounds good,' said Sarah, nodding. 'What's the other option?'

'We could stay down here and do our best to help,' said Kate.

'What do you mean, help?' said Sarah, getting to her feet.

'Well, no one in Seabury has any power. They're all in total darkness and it's going to get pretty cold.'

Sarah nodded. 'Actually yeah - with that wind coming through the windows, it already is!'

'The temperature hasn't even started dropping yet,' sighed Kate, 'and a lot of people will be relying on electricity to keep them warm.'

'What can we do?' asked Sarah, her expression changing from fear to determination.

'Well… we've got Bertha, and plenty of logs,' Kate

said, thinking fast and peering around. 'If we get her going, that'll keep it nice and warm in here.'

Sarah nodded quickly. 'Maybe we could cook something too? I mean, we're both going to need to eat anyway, aren't we?'

'Good plan,' said Kate. 'Look, let's get some light going on in here, then if anyone does need a bit of shelter or is looking for help – it'll be obvious we're in here. Flip the sign back to *open* for me and I'll grab the candles.'

Kate turned to Bertha and, opening her large oven door, started to pull out the candles and oil lamps she'd stashed in there for safekeeping, piling them on the counter as she went.

'Right, what else can I do?' said Sarah, watching Kate over the counter.

'Why don't you put this lot out on the tables and windowsills and get them lit so that we can see what we're doing a bit better,' said Kate. She rummaged around next to the pile of logs until she located the box of matches and tossed them up to Sarah. 'While you're doing that, I'm going to get Bertha lit. At least that way it'll be nice and cosy in here!'

She turned back to the old stove and eyed her warily. She just said that as if it was the easiest thing in the world to accomplish, but in reality, the old girl could be an absolute beast to get going. Like a lot of things at The Sardine, it took time and a bit of know-how to get her to play ball. Sometimes you had to talk to her nicely, and other times, only the choicest swear words had the desired effect.

Either way, there was no time to waste. Kate began scrunching up sheets of newspaper and quickly laid the fire in the old stove, adding a generous amount of kindling and a chunk of firelighter. It felt a bit like cheating – but given the circumstances, Kate wasn't about to take any chances.

Thankfully, it seemed that Bertha was feeling charitable. It took just one match, and within moments she started to roar – the comforting sound doing its best to rival the wind outside.

Kate closed the door on the crackling flames, straightened up and turned to see how Sarah was getting on. While she'd been busy with Bertha, the rest of the café had been transformed from a mostly dark and slightly ominous space into a cosy refuge filled with magical light that flickered from the candles and lamps that Sarah had dotted all over the place. With no other lights as far as the eye could see, the little café seemed to shine.

'Not bad, eh?' said Sarah, grinning at her.

'Not bad at all,' replied Kate, relieved to see that the shadow of fear seemed to have lifted from the young girl's face - only to be placed with a hint of excitement.

'What else can I do?' asked Sarah eagerly.

'Well, if you could dig out the old kettle for the

top of Bertha? I think it's in one of those boxes over near Stanley.'

At the sound of his name, Stanley stood up and decided to "help" Sarah while she searched, sticking his nose into each box as she opened the top, and making her laugh as she did her best to shove him gently out of the way as she hunted for the kettle.

Kate watched the mini wrestling match, doing her best not to giggle. Right. She needed to focus. What else did she need to do? The windows started to rattle again, distracting her for a moment.

Think, Kate. Think!

She could do with taking the torch and nipping up to the flat to unplug the cable for the tree lights. She dreaded to think what kind of state they were in. After seeing the tree disappear over the edge onto West Beach one thing was for certain – they were no longer doing anything useful out there.

'It's getting really rough again,' said Sarah, staring out of the window for a moment.

Kate glanced at her. Maybe now wasn't the time to leave her alone – even if it was just for a few minutes. After all, the power was already off so it wasn't like the cable was going to cause too much mayhem.

'Come on,' said Kate. 'Let's get that kettle filled up and on top of Bertha. Then, if anyone does turn up in need of a cup of tea or coffee, we'll at least be able to give them one. And you're right, we'd better have a think about some food too. We've got plenty of cake and mince pies thanks to Ethel. Plus, there's still some bread and cheese, ham and milk in the fridge that'll need using up.'

Sarah nodded and handed over the old metal kettle she'd just unearthed from one of the boxes.

'You okay?' Kate asked lightly, turning to fill it before sliding it onto Bertha's hotplate.

Sarah shrugged. 'I'm worried about dad,' she said in a quiet voice.

Kate nodded. 'I get it - but I'm sure he's probably sheltering up at the lighthouse, waiting for it to calm down a bit. There's bound to be a lull.' She paused. She wasn't sure how true that was if she was being honest, but Sarah didn't need to know that. 'Anyway, if he's up there he'll be completely safe – that old place has seen centuries of storms, and it's still standing.'

Sarah nodded, letting out a long, slow breath. 'I hope you're right.'

'Your dad's sensible – he won't do anything stupid. That's why I love him.'

Sarah stared at her, gaping slightly.

Oh. Oops.

Typical. The first time she'd ever admitted it to herself, let alone said it out loud, and she'd just gone and told Mike's *daughter* that she loved him rather than Mike himself. Classic.

'I mean - just you wait,' blustered Kate deciding

that the best option right now was to pretend that she'd not just gone and dropped the L-bomb, 'he'll come wandering through that door as if nothing's even happened.'

Kate turned to Bertha and opened the door to the fire, giving it an unnecessary poke. At least the heat from the flames would give her an excuse for the fact that her cheeks were probably bright red.

'Soooo…' said Sarah, and Kate braced herself for the interrogation. 'What now?'

Kate spun back to face her and smiled awkwardly, grateful that Sarah seemed to be happy to take her lead and not ask her a million questions. 'I guess, now we wait!' she said. 'It might end up being just the two of us… I'm kinda hoping everyone else is safely indoors and battening down the hatches!'

Sarah nodded. Pulling her mobile out of her pocket she checked the screen. 'Out of service,' she sighed.

'I bet it is!' muttered Kate.

CHAPTER 11

The pair of them had just about managed to convince themselves that no one would be mad enough to venture out into the storm - and that they'd likely be spending the evening together in an empty café - when Sarah stared hard at the door.

'Kate? I think there's someone out there!'

'Eh?' said Kate, straightening up after feeding another log into Bertha. She had to do her best not to step on Stanley who – predictably – was now spread, full length, in front of the lovely warm stove. She glanced over at the door and spotted a couple of shadowy figures moving around outside. 'Quick,' she said, 'run over and invite whoever it is inside before they get blown away!'

Sarah dashed across the café. Gripping hold of the handle so that the wind didn't get the chance to snatch it away from her, she opened the door.

In stepped three bedraggled figures – the first two were carrying a crate of bottles each, and the third was carrying something huge and heavy, wrapped in silver foil.

'Lionel?!' said Sarah, staring at the third figure with a yellow rain hat tied tightly on his head. 'Is that you under there? Are you okay?'

'Hi Sarah!' spluttered Lionel. Rain was dripping off the wilted brim of his ridiculous hat into his eyebrows and then running down his face. Clearly, he was having a hard time seeing very much around him.

'Here,' said Kate hurrying over and taking pity on him, 'shall I take that from you?'

Without waiting for any kind of answer, she hefted the tray carrying the massive turkey out of his hands and plonked it down on a table.

'Thank you!' said Lionel, shaking out his arms, untying his hat and then rubbing his face in an attempt to wipe away some of the water. 'Kate, Sarah – this is Mr and Mrs Davies – my guests at the hotel.'

Kate turned to them and smiled. 'We've met before!' she said, taking in the soggy newcomers. 'Welcome to The Sardine. Here – let's grab your coats and hang them up to dry!'

Kate bustled over to them both and, after they'd placed their boxes down on the tables, she helped them remove their sodden outer layers.

'Thank you so much,' said Mrs Davies as she tried to pat a couple of dripping ringlets back into place. 'Looks like you've come to our rescue for the second time today, Kate!'

'Ah!' said Mr Davies, wringing out his handkerchief and doing his best to wipe away the steam that had just obscured his glasses, 'I thought I recognised you. And it's Stuart and Margie – none of this Mr and Mrs-ing – it's Christmas Eve after all!'

'Well, it's lovely to meet you both properly,' said Kate, indicating for them to make themselves comfy at one of the tables, 'though I'm sorry about the circumstances!'

'Don't go apologising,' laughed Lionel. 'I was *that* relieved to see the light shining in your windows!'

'Erm... Lionel,' said Sarah, staring at the tray with the turkey, 'what's with the half-baked pterodactyl?'

'Ah... well...' said Lionel, looking a little bit embarrassed as he stripped off his long mac and threw a sheepish look at his guests before answering. 'Well,' he said again. 'See... it's my first time cooking a big Christmas roast and I have to admit I didn't really have the foggiest what to do with it.'

'O-kay?' said Sarah, with a bemused glance at Kate.

'Well, see – it's already half-cooked,' muttered Lionel. 'I had a little mix-up with the cooking time calculations. I mean, what does *"and twenty minutes over"* actually mean? Then there's that great big oven in the hotel – that's a bit confusing too. Worst of all it's electric, so…'

'You've got a half-cooked turkey!' Kate finished for him.

'Exactly,' sighed Lionel with a nod. 'I'm not really sure why I brought it with us, to be honest, but it would be a shame to waste it.'

'Well,' said Kate, lifting the layer of damp silver foil and peering underneath it, 'you might just be in luck. We've lit Bertha and I might be able to save it.'

Kate hefted the tray over to the kitchen and set about repositioning the mammoth bird in one of the trays that she knew for sure would fit into Bertha.

'Moment of truth,' she muttered, opening the door to the largest oven. It fitted – but only just. 'Okay – we're officially going to be eating turkey for the next month once that beast's cooked!' she laughed.

'Wonderful!' said Lionel. 'Thank you so much!'

She grinned at him, pleased to see that he was already starting to look a bit less chilly and bedraggled now that he was out of his wet gear and had managed to sweep his hair back away from his face.

'Don't forget the wine!' said Margie, giving the box she'd been carrying a little rattle.

'Wine?' said Kate, her ears pricking up.

'Oh yes!' said Lionel, with a twinkle in his eye that

definitely wasn't just down to the soft candlelight that surrounded them. 'It's the good stuff that I managed to hide away from old misery guts Veronica!' He reached into a box and drew out a bottle. 'I've been saving it for a special occasion, and this seems to be it!'

As if agreeing with him, the wind outside gave a particularly loud growl, setting the windowpanes rattling and the candle flames stuttering.

'What do you say, Kate? Shall I get one of these on the go?' he asked, waggling the bottle at her. 'We've got a crate of red and one of white.'

'Why not?' said Kate with a wide smile. 'It's Christmas Eve after all! Give me two seconds and I'll find a corkscrew. I know I've got one here somewhere from the launch event we had for the cake boxes.'

'I'll go and dig out the wine glasses,' said Sarah. 'I'm sure I spotted some in one of those boxes in your under-stairs cupboard, didn't I?'

Kate nodded. 'That sounds about right.'

'I'll help!' said Stuart, getting to his feet and following Sarah into the narrow passageway.

'What do you fancy, Margie?' asked Lionel. 'Red or white?'

'Ooh, red for me,' she said with a wide smile.

'Woman after my own heart!' said Kate.

'Great – well, we'll open one of each then!' said

Lionel as Kate handed him the corkscrew. He'd just removed the second cork with a decidedly merry *pop* when Sarah and Stuart returned.

'We weren't sure how many we'd need,' said Sarah, nodding to Stuart who was carrying an entire box of dusty wine glasses.

'We'll wash enough for us lot,' he said, carefully placing the heavy box up on the counter before starting to roll his sleeves up, 'then we can always clean some extras if anyone else turns up.'

'Sounds like a good plan to me!' grinned Kate.

'Mind if I commandeer your sink?' he asked.

'Be my guest!' said Kate. She was more than happy to sit down across from Margie for a moment – and she couldn't help but think how lovely it was that Lionel's guests seemed to be happy to join in and get their hands dirty.

'Oh my goodness,' gasped Stuart, pausing at the end of the counter.

'What?' said Kate in concern, half rising to her feet and expecting some mini-disaster from the look on his face.

'Who does the bear belong to?' he said, not taking his eyes off the patch of floor in front of Bertha.

'Oh! Stanley?' laughed Kate. 'He's mine. Well… he's kind of *everybody's* in a way… or at least, he thinks he is given the number of treats he gets given every day. But he lives here with me.'

'Is he... erm... friendly?' asked Stuart, taking a tentative step backwards.

Clearly, Stanley had woken up and was now approaching this stranger who'd unexpectedly appeared near his snoozing spot.

'Seriously, Stu,' Sarah laughed, 'the worst that dog will do is love you to death!' Nevertheless, she hurried over and edged past Stuart, bending down to give Stanley a big hug to demonstrate just how friendly he really was.

Kate watched Sarah with a gentle smile. Sarah knew all about people who were wary of dogs – after all, Mike had had a terrible fear of them when he'd first arrived in Seabury. He was still afraid of them – but not Stanley. The pair of them were best friends by this point.

'See!' said Sarah. 'Here – give him one of these and he'll love you forever.' She rummaged around for the pack of rich teas that always sat under the counter and handed one to a bemused looking Stuart. Within seconds, Stanley was sitting at his feet, staring up at him with his huge, soulful eyes.

Stuart broke the biscuit in half and very slowly held a piece out towards him. Seeming to sense the newcomer's nervousness, Stanley took it from him so gently that it made Kate's heart melt.

'What a good boy,' said Stuart, a smile spreading over his face.

'Well I never,' Margie said in an undertone to Kate, 'I never thought I'd see the day!'

Kate smiled at her. 'Stanley has a habit of converting people.'

'Alright lad,' said Sarah once he'd finished his second piece of biscuit and let Stuart give him a nervous tickle on the head, 'come out of the way a minute so we can get these glasses washed!' She grabbed him by the collar and led him out of the kitchen and over to where Kate was sitting with Lionel and Margie.

'Oh, you handsome boy!' crooned Margie.

Clearly sensing a new friend in the making, Stanley promptly sat on Margie's feet and dropped his head into her lap with a sigh.

∽

Lionel had only just finished pouring them all a glass of wine each when Stuart pointed to the door. 'I think you've got more visitors!' he said.

Kate whipped around and, recognising the faces of some very soggy Chilly Dippers, dashed over to let them in.

They bundled inside, dripping all over the floor as they went.

'Don't tell me you've been out there singing all this time?!' demanded Kate, pulling a drenched Lou through the door before peering outside to check for any stragglers. Quickly retreating back inside, she closed the door firmly against the wind.

Lou shook her head. 'Nope. We ran for cover pretty sharpish, but it doesn't look like it's planning on easing up any time soon!'

'Where's Paula?' asked Kate, a spike of worry running through her as she scanned soggy, cold faces in front of her.

'Don't worry, love,' said Doris quickly, giving her arm a pat. 'That lovely hubby of hers arrived after we'd been singing for about twenty minutes and whisked her home for a rest. I expect that she's already tucked up and toasty with that handsome fella and a hot water bottle!'

Kate nodded, relieved that her friend would at least be safe and dry. She knew they had a gas cooker too, so they'd be okay for drinks and food, even if they had to spend Christmas Eve by candlelight while wrapped up under a blanket together.

She turned her attention back to the Dippers. They were busy stripping off their outer layers, but she could see that most of them had got soaked to the skin.

'Sarah?' she said, 'would you and Lionel mind taking the torch and nipping upstairs to my flat. I need to check that turkey, but this lot need some dry jumpers if they're not going to catch their death of colds just in time for Christmas! Ransack the big cupboard in the corner of my living room – that's got all my woollies in it that won't fit in my bedroom!'

'On it!' said Sarah, giving her a nod. Lionel quickly got to his feet and grabbed the torch from the counter where Kate had left it.

Suddenly, the little café felt like it might burst at the seams, but the Chilly Dippers were so grateful to find somewhere warm and dry after their drenching, they seemed more than happy to perch - two to a chair - as they all introduced themselves to Stuart and Margie.

Kate quickly headed over to the kitchen to check on the turkey before washing up a dozen more wine glasses.

'What smells so good?' asked Doris as she accepted a glass of white from Margie with a grateful smile.

'It's Lionel's turkey,' laughed Kate from the kitchen, 'he brought it with him!'

'Oh yum!' said Lou. 'Hey – should we get those sprouts on to go with it?'

'Now that's a genius idea,' said Kate, nodding.

By the time Lionel and Sarah returned - bearing a washing basket piled high with assorted dry woollies for the Dippers to change into - Kate had set them all to work peeling the mammoth net of sprouts.

Soon, they had all pulled on a nice dry jumper and were working their way through their first glass of wine each. As they moved on to a second glass, the Christmas carolling returned with gusto. The sprouts were eventually ready to head over to Bertha as they reached the last verse of Good King Wenceslas.

'Well,' said Stuart, beaming at Kate with a glass of red wine in one hand and one of Ethel's mince pies in the other, 'this wasn't exactly the Christmas Eve we were expecting – but I wouldn't have it any other way!'

'Hear hear!' cried Margie, taking another bite of the slice of carrot cake Kate had just brought over to her.

'I'm so glad,' said Kate, giving them both a warm smile before glancing at Sarah. She paused and frowned.

Sarah was perched with half a butt-cheek on the chair she was sharing with Lou, but she was clearly not listening to half of what was going on around her. Every few minutes, she pulled her phone out and flipped open the case before shoving it back in her pocket and throwing a worried look at the door.

Kate couldn't blame her. By this point, she was starting to get worried about Mike too. If anything, it seemed to be getting wilder outside, as if the storm was building up to do something drastic.

The whistle of the kettle coming to the boil interrupted her train of thought, and she headed over to shove it off the hot plate.

'Anyone fancy a hot drink?' she called. 'Tea? Coffee?'

'More wine!' cheered Doris. This was greeted by a storm of laughter and cheering that filled the little café and drowned out the sound of the Bernard raging around outside.

CHAPTER 12

Kate's second glass of wine had done away with her dislike of singing in front of people. She launched into the long *Glooooooooooria* runs in Hosanna in Excelsis with gusto. So what if she sounded a bit like a drunken goose? She was sitting next to Lou – which had the added bonus that her honking was mostly being drowned out by her friend's glorious, rich voice. Their arms were linked, and they swayed merrily on their shared chair.

'Hey!' shouted Sarah, whose constant watch of the café door hadn't yet managed to make Mike appear out of thin air, no matter how hard she tried. 'Hey!' she shouted again, struggling to make herself heard over the hooting and singing, 'someone's on their way in!'

The song abruptly came to an end as the door

crashed open, and Kate looked around, her heart full of hope that it might be Mike at last. But it wasn't.

'Well!' said Ethel, stepping into the café, 'sounds like you lot are in fine fettle!'

She was closely followed by Charlie who dumped a huge armful of drenched tree lights on the floor in the corner then shook himself like a dog.

'Thought I'd better bring those in,' he said casually. 'They were all over the place. No idea what happened to the tree!'

'It's somewhere down on West Beach,' laughed Kate, 'probably in the sea by now, I should imagine! Anyway, what on earth are you two doing here?'

'I wanted ter check everyone was okay!' said Charlie stoutly.

'And I didn't want my brand-new fiancé going out and getting lost in the storm,' said Ethel with a grin. 'At least, not without me!'

'Wait...' gasped Sarah.

'Now hang on a minute...' said Lionel.

'Your - *what now?!*' demanded Doris.

'Her fiancé!' repeated Charlie proudly.

'You got engaged?!' squealed Sarah, leaping to her feet.

'Aye,' said Charlie with a grin. 'That we did.'

'About time too!' hooted Lionel, getting to his feet as well and bustling over to clap his best friend on the back, while Sarah rushed over to Ethel and threw her arms around her, before recoiling at just how wet she was.

The Sardine erupted into a wave of congratulations and cheering. Kate took both their coats and did her best to find somewhere to hang them with all the others to dry. Margie quickly poured a glass of wine apiece for the newcomers while the others begged Ethel to recount every detail of the proposal.

There was so much commotion that, until she heard Sarah's cry of relief, Kate hadn't noticed that the door to the café had opened again. She turned to see Mike's bedraggled figure edging his way in out of the storm.

'Dad! You're okay!'

'Course I am,' he said, sounding slightly winded as Sarah threw herself at him before quickly drawing away again.

'Eew! You're soaked.'

'Well… I don't know if you'd noticed, but it's raining out there a little bit!'

Sarah giggled, grinning at her dad like he was the best thing she'd seen all evening. Kate quickly nipped back behind the counter and grabbed one of Stanley's clean doggy towels from the stash underneath.

'What on earth happened to you?' asked Kate, making her way through the cheerful, chattering crowd and handing the towel over.

'The road back into town's blocked by a fallen tree,' said Mike, taking the towel gratefully and drying his face and neck before giving his hair a rough rub, leaving it sticking up in tufts. 'I'm so sorry if you were worried. I would have called, but my mobile's dead!'

'Ours too,' said Sarah, nodding. 'But how come you're so wet – where's the car?'

'I had to leave it on the other side of the tree and walk the rest of the way,' he said. 'There was so much water, I didn't want to risk going back up to the main road and trying the other way. Glad I did too – apparently, it's been washed out. The little stream's burst its banks.'

'Oh my goodness!' said Kate, staring at him. No wonder he looked like he'd just gone for a swim.

'Dad – that's really dangerous!' said Sarah, her lip quivering slightly as she stared at him. 'You shouldn't have been wandering around out there. What if you'd got hit by something?!'

Mike reached out and patted her gently on the arm. 'I'm fine. I couldn't stay in the car all night, could I – I'd have frozen!'

Sarah nodded and then, ignoring just how wet he was, threw her arms around him again.

Kate smiled at Mike over Sarah's head, and he winked at her.

'Thanks for keeping Sarah company,' he said in a low voice. 'At least I knew she was safe.'

'Are you kidding?' said Kate with a little laugh,

reaching out and patting Sarah's back. 'She's been brilliant company – and loads of help too.'

Sarah turned her head and smiled gratefully at Kate before extricating herself from her damp dad and going to find Stanley for a hug now that she knew he was safe.

'Oh,' said Mike, still doing his best to soak up as much of the rainwater as he could with the towel, 'I almost forgot - I bumped into a couple of engineers from the power company on the way down. Poor buggers – they were drenched and filthy. Horrible conditions out there for them to have to work in.'

'What did they say?' asked Charlie from his perch on one of the windowsills.

'They seemed to reckon that it might take all night before they get the power back on,' replied Mike.

These words were a bit like a bucket of cold water as they doused the festive mood in the café. Everyone fell silent, looking more than a little bit worried.

'Blimey,' said Doris. 'That means we're going to be stuck in town all night, doesn't it?'

Mike nodded. 'With the river blocking one way, a tree down on the other and no light… I'm afraid so. I wouldn't advise that any of you drove anyway…' He trailed off, glanced around at the empty wine bottles littering the surfaces. 'Even if you lot hadn't worked your way through most of Upper Bamton's finest –

there's that much water on the roads, they're more like rivers.'

There was a beat of complete silence in the cramped little café, but then Lionel clapped his hands together. 'Not to worry,' he said, his voice warm and cheerful, 'there's a free bed for anyone who needs one over at The Pebble Street Hotel. I mean, it might not be that comfy with the power off – but you'll all be safe and dry until it comes back on, and I'm sure we'll be able to rustle something up for Christmas breakfast!'

'Thank you, Lionel,' said Doris, patting the back of his hand as he sat down next to her. 'Our very own Christmas angel!'

'Hardly,' he chuckled modestly, 'but I do have enough duvets over there to keep everyone warm and snuggled up until the morning.'

The news that they'd all have a comfortable bed for the night seemed to cheer everyone up immensely. The Sardine was warm and cosy, and thanks to old Bertha, the sprouts were on the go and a mini version of Christmas dinner wouldn't be too far off. There was still plenty of wine to go around, and now that the one or two designated drivers knew that there was no chance they'd have to get back behind the wheel, they decided to start making up for lost time. More glasses were washed, and fresh bottles were opened and passed around.

Ethel had brought an entire freshly baked walnut

cake over with her, and even though its little run-in with Storm Bernard had left it a bit soggy around the edges, it was nothing a quick trim with a knife wouldn't solve. Besides, it wasn't as though anyone would notice anyway.

Somewhere in the midst of the merry chaos, Kate glanced over at Mike only to find that he was shivering. Edging her way over to him, she laced her fingers through his.

'You're freezing!' she gasped.

'I'm a bit damp,' he said, his voice deadpan.

'Come on,' she said, giving his arm a tug, 'let's go upstairs a sec. I'm sure I've got something you can change into. You need to get dry. I don't want you catching a cold – and I'm guessing you don't much fancy stripping naked in front of half the town?'

Mike did his best to grin at her, but his lips seemed to be stiff - slightly tinged with blue and trembling from the cold.

Grabbing the torch, Kate bustled Mike past everyone, through the little passageway and up the stairs to her flat.

'Straight into the bathroom and out of those wet clothes,' she ordered, handing him the torch.

'Yes miss!' said Mike, giving her a little salute and a peck on the lips.

'There's a towel hanging on the back of the door,' she called after him, trying to ignore the fact that the tiny contact had set her skin tingling. 'I'm going to grab something for you to wear.'

She pulled her phone out of her back pocket and used it to light her way through to her bedroom. It was weirdly quiet up here after the mad, happy chaos going on downstairs and she hugged herself for a moment. Whatever strange distance she'd been imagining between herself and Mike... well... it had gone. It had melted away into nothingness the moment he had appeared, dripping, in the doorway of The Sardine. Kate grinned to herself and opened her wardrobe door. There must be something in here that would fit him.

She needed to focus, but her head was full of images of Mike, just the other side of the landing, stripping off his wet clothes.

'Pull yourself together!' she muttered, pushing clothes aside as she searched.

Maybe she should join him in the bathroom. After all – he could probably do with a hand getting warmed up.

It took Mike's cough from over by the doorway to interrupt Kate's rather ex-rated daydream. She tried to pull herself together. Taking a deep breath, she turned to face him - but the sight of him standing there wearing nothing more than her bath towel wrapped around his hips really didn't help matters.

'You okay?' he asked.

Even in the torchlight, it was obvious that there was a naughty smile tugging at Mike's lips.

'I... erm... here!' said Kate, doing her best to hide her flaming cheeks by reaching into the wardrobe. She grabbed a pair of floppy tartan pyjama bottoms and an oversized Christmas jumper and turned to lob them at him.

Bad plan. Very. Mike nearly dropped his towel as he stretched to catch the flying clothes.

Kate closed her eyes for a split second. She *really* needed to keep it together. There was no way she could give in and jump on him – no matter how tempting it was right now – not when the café downstairs was packed to the gunnels with half the town... including Mike's own *daughter!*

'I'll... erm... I'll leave you to change,' she said in a ridiculously squeaky voice before pushing past him. 'See you back downstairs?'

Mike winked at her and nodded. Kate turned tail and practically ran back down the stairs to re-join her unexpected guests. With any luck, the fact that she was probably a fetching shade of puce by now wouldn't be too obvious in the candlelit café.

CHAPTER 13

It was almost midnight on Christmas Eve. The weather outside The Sardine hadn't calmed down at all. In fact, if anything, it was getting even worse. But inside the little café, no one seemed to care in the slightest. The space was filled with the scent of roasting turkey, the clinking of wine glasses and the chatter of happy voices.

Although it was a squeeze, between them they'd managed to line up the tiny tables and lay them with cloths, candles and cutlery, ready for their Christmas midnight feast.

Every single chair was occupied – some of them even more so than usual given that several people were having to share – but no one minded. There was a lot of laughter as they all huddled up together and attempted to balance – one butt cheek apiece.

Mike was helping Kate to refill everyone's glasses,

and she kept having to bite her lip to stop herself from laughing at his outfit. The jumper with the comedy Christmas pudding combined with the pair of tartan PJ bottoms that were at least a couple of inches too short made for a comical sight.

Mike didn't seem to care in the slightest. Now that he was warm and dry and had a glass of wine on the go, nothing seemed to be able to wipe the huge smile off his face. Kate was finding it most distracting, and it was only Sarah's mischievous grin that made her realise that she was just standing there, staring. She quickly left Mike to his wine pouring duties and made her way around into the kitchen. It was time to get the beast out of Bertha and start carving.

'Alright lad, you can stop guarding it now!' she laughed. Stanley had been standing sentry in front of the old stove ever since the delicious turkey smells had started wafting from it. Right now though, his fluffy brand of enthusiastic, slobbery help wasn't exactly what she needed. Kate didn't want to end up giving the humungous bird an impromptu festive flying lesson by tripping over Stanley's fuzzy butt.

'Sarah?' she called, 'can you grab Stanley for me a second? He's like a walking, dribbling trip-hazard over here!'

Sarah came to the rescue and tempted Stanley out of the kitchen with one of the delicious doggy treats that Ethel had baked for him. He shot a baleful parting look at Kate over his shoulder as he went – clearly unable to believe her treachery.

Even after Kate had carved an enormous mountain of succulent turkey slices – the bird looked like it had barely been touched. By the looks of things, the entire town really would be surviving on turkey curry long into the New Year.

Mike wandered over to help her, and between them they ferried the turkey and several huge dishes of sprouts over to the tables. There was even a tray of roasted parsnips and a few golden, crispy potatoes to share out between everyone.

'You even made gravy?' said Lionel with a delighted look at the china jug in Mike's hands.

'From the juices!' grinned Kate with a nod. 'There isn't much – but it's the thought that counts, right?'

It seemed that no one was about to complain – they were too busy filling their plates with delicious, piping-hot food and getting ready to enjoy their unexpected feast while Bernard rattled the windows and stomped around outside like a grumpy toddler who was late to bed. Not that anyone was paying him any attention anymore.

They were all just about ready to tuck into their very late... or very early (depending on how you looked at it) Christmas meal, when there was a loud knock at the door.

'Crikey!' said Mike, looking around in surprise.

'It's the poor old engineers I met up on the road earlier!'

'Someone let them in!' said Kate, standing up but realising that she was completely hemmed in.

Margie got to her feet and, with a little difficulty, managed to manoeuvre her way to the door.

'Come on in!' she said, beaming at the rather stunned faces of the three guys in their dripping high-viz jackets.

'We shouldn't,' said the one at the front. 'We're soaked – we'll get the floor all wet!'

This caused a round of laughter and there was a chorus of cheers encouraging the men to get inside (and close the door pronto!) At Kate's bidding, everyone got to their feet and with much screeching of table legs and shuffling of chairs, they managed to make enough room for the three extra bodies to squeeze into the cramped café.

'Sardine by name, Sardine by nature, eh?' chuckled Charlie, as the three men shuffled in, blinking as if the golden candlelight hurt their eyes after so long out in the pitch-dark storm.

'Sorry to gate-crash,' said the second man, a guilty look on his face. 'We're wiped, and we just thought that if we came down into town, we might manage to find somewhere to get a warm drink and something to eat.'

'Stupid, I know,' said the third man, with an

embarrassed little shrug, 'what with it being this close to midnight on Christmas Eve.'

'But... we were a bit desperate!' said the first guy, his eyes trained on the food on the table with something that looked a bit like longing.

'Well,' said Kate from across the table, 'you came to the right place! Budge up everyone and make room!'

All three of the engineers opened their mouths, clearly in an attempt to politely decline, but their protestations were drowned out by the round of renewed giggling as everyone scooched up even closer to make enough room around the table.

Kate ended up perched on Mike's lap, Margie was in Stuart's, and with much wolf-whistling and giggling from the Chilly Dippers, Ethel hopped into Charlie's. He looked delighted with the new arrangement and wrapped his arms around his newly-betrothed, only to earn himself a back-handed swat from his lady-love.

'Take your coats off lads, and make yourself comfortable!' called Mike, lobbing the towel he'd used earlier over to them so that they could wipe their hands and faces dry.

Kate started to load up three extra plates, piling on the sprouts and doling out the last few parsnips and potatoes. She was just about to add giant helpings of turkey to each one too when one of the engineers spoke up.

'Erm, sorry to be a pain, but I'm a vegetarian.'

Kate shrugged. 'No problem.' She added even more sprouts and then added a large slice of Ethel's walnut cake to the side of the plate before handing it over.

The engineer looked down at it in surprise, and then, without further ado, started to devour it as if it might be his last meal.

'By the way, I'm Tim – and this is Bruce and Kev,' said the largest of the three, pushing his still-sodden sandy hair back out of his face and grinning around at everyone. 'Thanks so much – you're all lifesavers. We really didn't mean to ruin your party!'

'Ruin it?!' said Lionel, 'you've just made it even better!'

There were cheers from all around the table, and Kate couldn't help but notice that Lou had her eyes glued on Tim's face as if he was some kind of Christmas miracle in the making.

'A toast!' said Lionel. 'Has everyone got a drink?'

The newcomers all shook their heads, but this was quickly rectified. Two glasses of red and one of white were quickly passed around the table to them.

'We shouldn't really,' said Bruce, glancing at Kev.

Kev shrugged. 'It's what... two minutes until Christmas?'

Mike checked his watch and nodded.

'Then I think we can let ourselves off the hook,'

said Kev. 'It's not like we can go back out there again until it's light anyway!'

'In that case – a toast!' said Lionel again, shuffling with some difficulty to his feet. 'To old friends-' he raised his glass in the vague direction of Charlie and Ethel, 'and new ones-' he raised his glass towards the three newcomers and then over to Margie and Stuart. 'Here's to full bellies and plenty of laughter – and candlelight on a very dark night. A very merry Christmas to you all.'

Just as he stopped speaking and everyone raised their glasses, they heard the clock on the town hall begin to strike midnight in the distance.

'It's Christmas day!' squealed Sarah.

As Kate joined in the cheers and yells of *merry Christmas*, her eyes travelled around the table, taking in the happy faces that were all packed into The Sardine together. She couldn't help but think that this was a Christmas that she would remember forever.

CHAPTER 14

Kate yawned widely and tried to force her drooping eyelids to stay open. It felt a bit like a herculean task. Bertha was still kicking out a beautiful, cosy warmth that got right into her bones. With all the golden, flickering candlelight and her ridiculously full belly, all Kate wanted to do at that moment was curl up and go to sleep. Maybe she could join Stanley down on the kitchen floor. He looked comfy enough!

'Come on, sleepyhead,' chuckled Mike. Clearly noticing that she was about to drop where she was standing, he wrapped an arm around her waist and pulled her close.

Kate smiled and rested her head against his shoulder. No. This wouldn't do. There was some serious tidying up to be done in here before she could curl up for the night… or, to be more accurate, for the morning!

'What time is it?' she yawned, straightening up again and looking around The Sardine. It looked a bit like Storm Bernard had had enough of mooching around outside and had whipped through the café instead - such was the aftermath of their impromptu Christmas party. Kate smiled. It really didn't matter. A bit of tidying up was totally worth the amazing time they'd all had.

'It's just gone three in the morning,' said Mike, rubbing his own eyes and watching as Sarah finished rinsing the dinner plates and stacking them in the dishwasher.

'There,' said Sarah, 'at least it'll be ready to run as soon as the power comes back on tomorrow.'

'You're my hero,' yawned Kate. 'You know, I reckon it might be time to call it a night.'

'Or a morning!' Mike nodded in agreement.

Their guests had made the most of a very slight lull in the strength of the storm about twenty minutes ago. Donning their coats and hunching their shoulders, they'd all shouted their farewells and made their way back through the town towards The Pebble Street Hotel with Lionel. Even Charlie and Ethel had agreed to stay there for the night to give him some moral support.

Before heading out, they'd all promised to be back

in the morning for breakfast – a thought that made Kate long for her bed more than ever!

'Do you guys mind if I go upstairs now?' asked Sarah, yawning widely.

'Of course not!' said Kate. 'Here – you take the big torch up. Me and your dad can use our phones. We won't be too long – I just need to make sure everything's locked up safely and then we'll blow all the candles out and come up.'

'Thanks for tonight,' said Sarah, turning to give Kate a sleepy grin. 'It was amazing.'

'Thank *you* for all your help,' said Kate, going over to Sarah and giving her a huge hug before she turned and made her way through the passageway and up the stairs to Kate's flat.

They'd decided earlier that it would be best for Mike and Sarah to stay the night rather than venturing back out into the storm. Besides – their own flat would be dark and freezing cold by now, but the little flat upstairs should be nice and toasty.

Kate and Sarah had nipped upstairs a couple of hours ago to make Sarah a bed up on Kate's couch. Since they were already up there, they'd decided to get the wood burner going while they were at it, and they'd taken it in turns to keep it plied with logs ever since.

Kate had warned Sarah that she'd probably end up spending the entire night fighting with Stanley for snoozing rights to the sofa. Luckily, she didn't seem to mind the idea of sharing it with the big, fluffy, snoring hot-water bottle.

Turning back to the café, Kate realised that she was alone with Mike again, and this time, half of Seabury wasn't busy partying in the same building. For the first time in what felt like ages, it was just the pair of them. Even though she was fighting the waves of snooziness that kept threatening to force her eyes closed, Kate suddenly felt a little bit nervous.

'So,' he said. 'Do you want to do more tidying or…'

'Or…' She shook her head. 'No, I think it's time to lock up and go to bed, don't you? This lot will wait for the morning. I definitely need at least a couple of hours of sleep before facing Christmas morning with the Chilly Dippers,' she laughed. 'If there's tidying up still to be done when they arrive – they can help!'

Mike nodded, but he didn't smile. Suddenly his face looked so serious in the golden, flickering candlelight that Kate felt her heart leap in her chest.

'I'm so sorry, Kate,' he said, his voice low.

She felt the smile slip off her face. She went to open her mouth to say something, but he shook his head and carried on.

'I mean – I'm sorry that we've not really seen much of each other lately. I don't want you to think…' he paused and swallowed.

Mike was clearly nervous, and suddenly Kate's

exhaustion seemed to leave her. She wasn't sure what he was about to say, but she *was* sure that her knees had just turned to jelly as a sudden rush of adrenalin coursed through her.

'I don't want you thinking that I didn't want to spend time together.'

'I didn't think that,' she whispered, as he took her hands.

'I'm sorry,' he said again. 'Buying the lighthouse just kept dragging on, and it took so much more time than I thought it would, and the council made me jump through so many hoops to get the change of use approved...'

He paused again and just stared at her for a long moment. Kate swallowed hard. Should she say something? She wasn't really sure what, though. The words *change of use* just kept echoing through her head. There it was. It looked like he was about to tell her what his plans were. The thing she'd been dreading for so long.

'It's mine now, though,' said Mike at last. 'I can't believe they left it until Christmas Eve to close the deal. But it's finally mine.'

Now she *definitely* didn't know what to say. She knew that they needed to talk about it at long last – she knew that she needed to listen to his plans – but right now, she wasn't sure she could handle it.

'Kate?' said Mike.

Kate realised that she'd dropped his hands and

was staring intently at the patch of floor between them. Slowly she looked up, only to find that he was holding a tiny box out towards her.

'It's not what you're thinking!' he said quickly, his eyes twinkling.

Kate blinked. The box was a bit too big for a ring anyway. She shot a tight smile at him, suddenly unsure what was going on.

'Go on, open it,' he urged.

With shaking fingers, Kate took the little box. It was surprisingly heavy. Slowly, she took off the lid. Inside, sitting on a bed of black velvet and glinting in the candlelight, was a large old key. It was the key to the lighthouse.

'Kate Hardy – will you come and live with me in our new house?'

'Live with you?' she echoed, stroking the key with the tip of her finger.

'Yes. You, me, Sarah and Stanley.'

'In the lighthouse?'

Mike nodded, smiling. 'In the lighthouse. Our lighthouse. Our home. I've wanted to tell you about it for ages, but I've had to fight the council every step of the way for the change of use. It could have all fallen through at any moment.'

Kate stared at him. She knew she should answer him, but she couldn't seem to form a sentence.

'I didn't want to get your hopes up if there was any chance it could all collapse on us. And now it's all done… well… I know you might not say yes… I know you might not want to leave The Sardine for me, but-'

'Of course I will,' said Kate, feeling tears spring to her eyes. 'I'll come and live with you at the lighthouse,' she said again, barely able to believe that this was happening.

'You will?' said Mike, his face splitting into a wide smile, the golden light reflecting in his eyes as he stared back at her.

Kate nodded. 'This is the most wonderful Christmas present,' she said, having to force the words out around the lump in her throat. 'The best present ever.'

Mike stepped forward and pulled her into his arms, kissing her forehead.

Kate giggled and swiped at the couple of rogue tears that were making their way down her cheeks. 'You know that I'll only move in if you take this box and cover it properly in wrapping paper, right? Bow and all, Mike – I'm not even joking,' she laughed.

'It's a deal,' said Mike. Taking the box from her, he slipped it into his pocket. 'I love you, Kate Hardy,' he said quietly, before gently pulling her in for a soft Christmas kiss.

Over by the counter, Stanley let out a long sigh. He'd been watching the entire thing unfold. Now that he was sure that everything was well in his world again, it was time for bed. He turned tail, wiggled his way through the passageway and slowly climbed the stairs up to the flat. It was time to fight with Sarah about who was going to get to sleep on the bigger half of the sofa.

THE END

ALSO BY BETH RAIN

Little Bamton Series:

Little Bamton: The Complete Series Collection: Books 1 - 5

Individual titles:

Christmas Lights and Snowball Fights (Little Bamton Book 1)

Spring Flowers and April Showers (Little Bamton Book 2)

Summer Nights and Pillow Fights (Little Bamton Book 3)

Autumn Cuddles and Muddy Puddles (Little Bamton Book 4)

Christmas Flings and Wedding Rings (Little Bamton Book 5)

Upper Bamton Series:

A New Arrival in Upper Bamton (Upper Bamton Book 1)

Rainy Days in Upper Bamton (Upper Bamton Book 2)

Hidden Treasures in Upper Bamton (Upper Bamton Book 3)

Time Flies By in Upper Bamton (Upper Bamton Book 4)

Standalone Books:

Christmas on Crumcarey

Seabury Series:

Welcome to Seabury (Seabury Book 1)

Trouble in Seabury (Seabury Book 2)

Christmas in Seabury (Seabury Book 3)

Sandwiches in Seabury (Seabury Book 4)

Secrets in Seabury (Seabury Book 5)

Surprises in Seabury (Seabury Book 6)

Dreams and Ice Creams in Seabury (Seabury Book 7)

Mistakes and Heartbreaks in Seabury (Seabury Book 8)

Laughter and Happy Ever After in Seabury (Seabury Book 9)

Seabury Series Collections:

Kate's Story: Books 1 - 3

Hattie's Story: Books 4 - 6

Writing as Bea Fox:

What's a Girl To Do? The Complete Series

Individual titles:

The Holiday: What's a Girl To Do? (Book 1)

The Wedding: What's a Girl To Do? (Book 2)

The Lookalike: What's a Girl To Do? (Book 3)

The Reunion: What's a Girl To Do? (Book 4)

At Christmas: What's a Girl To Do? (Book 5)

ABOUT THE AUTHOR

Beth Rain has always wanted to be a writer and has been penning adventures for characters ever since she learned to stare into the middle-distance and daydream.

She currently lives in the (sometimes) sunny South West, and it is a dream come true to spend her days hanging out with Bob – her trusty laptop – scoffing crisps and chocolate while dreaming up swoony love stories for all her imaginary friends.

Beth's writing will always deliver on the happy-ever-afters, so if you need cosy… you're in safe hands!

Visit www.bethrain.com for all the bookish goodness and keep up with all Beth's news by joining her monthly newsletter!

facebook.com/BethRainBooks
twitter.com/bethrainauthor
instagram.com/bethrainauthor

Printed in Great Britain
by Amazon